A white line fluttered across the screen, then cleared. Riitha gasped as the image of an alien being appeared in the phosphor light.

Golden brown hair shagged around his ears and over his forehead, and a thick brush of hair grew over his upper lip. Brilliant blue eyes gazed solemnly at Riitha from a face covered with milky white skin that was lined around the eyes and mouth. Not with age, she thought, but with worry and fatigue.

"I'm Michael Jamieson, reporting—"

Riitha's hand went to her throat in thrilled shock as his melodious voice, a voice from an ancient, alien past, drifted through the small terminal speaker. The human paused to wipe a hand across his eyes. There was a tremor in his voice when he began again.

"—reporting to you from the moon on, uh—let's call it Luna Base plus nineteen months." He made a coughing sound into his hand. The skin around his startling blue eyes was moist. "I've, uh—just been told that all data not related to the care and feeding of humankind will be erased from the databanks. I think that's a mistake . . . a big mistake, but—" He stopped talking and lowered his head.

Riitha sat mesmerized, too stunned to do anything but watch and listen.

The human raised his head and stared from the screen. "The biggest story in the history of the world, and no one to tell it to. . . ." The reporter shook his head, sadly it seemed, then turned to look directly out of the screen. "Except you. Whoever you are."

Other ~~TSR~~ Books

THE
ALIEN
DARK

Diana G. Gallagher

Cover Art
DOUG CHAFFEE

TSR
B·O·O·K·S

THE ALIEN DARK

Distributed to the book trade in the United States by Random House, Inc., and in Canada by Random House of Canada, Ltd.

Distributed in the United Kingdom by TSR Ltd.

Distributed to the toy and hobby trade by regional distributors.

DRAGONLANCE, FORGOTTEN REALMS, TSR, and the TSR logo are trademarks owned by TSR, Inc.

First Printing: December, 1990
Printed in the United States of America.
Library of Congress Catalog Card Number: 89-52096

9 8 7 6 5 4 3 2 1

ISBN: 0-88038-928-1

TSR, Inc.
P.O. Box 756
Lake Geneva, WI 53147
U.S.A.

TSR Ltd.
120 Church End, Cherry Hinton
Cambridge CB1 3LB
United Kingdom

For my mother, Beryl M. Turner, who is always there when I need her—no matter what.

Acknowledgements

For their continuing support and friendship I would like to thank Cherry Weiner, Ruth Ricks McKee, and Mac McKee.

Special thanks to: Susie Robertson for reading this manuscript over and over again; Betsey Wilcox for her creative input and enthusiasm; Sharon Stanton for her concern and expertise in juggling schedules; Teri Lee of Firebird Arts and Music, Inc., for keeping Tahl d'jehn alive in song; Rob Chilson for his technical advice; and William F. Wu for his unfailing faith in me.

I am especially grateful to Mary Kirchoff and Jim Lowder of TSR, Inc., for recognizing the potential in the original manuscript of this book; to Ricia Mainhardt for taking a chance on an unpublished writer and being persistent; and most particularly to Chelsea A. Gallagher for taking care of things around the house so I could meet my deadline and Jay R. Gallagher for support under fire in the early days.

PROLOGUE

For years the satellite had been spiraling inward, losing momentum to the solar wind. Now, its orbit around the trojan point of the third planet's large moon nearly trimmed, *Hawk-eye* began to retract its magnetic sail. A methodical scan of inner-system space, constant for uncounted millennia, continued uninterrupted.

The first indication of an anomaly within range of *Hawk-eye*'s sensors almost went undetected because only two of the satellite's six receivers remained operational. Locking onto the trace emission trail, the ancient device monitored and analyzed for several seconds.

The source was technological.

Another seconds-long delay ensued when the transmitter, unused since *Hawk-eye* had been placed in orbit, failed to activate. The satellite switched to a backup system. Secondary relays connecting the transmitter to the compact U-238 nuclear power plant responded instantly, and *Hawk-eye* began to orient the transmitter toward the haze-covered planet as directed by its original programming. An override aborted the command and replaced it.

After adjusting the position of the transmitter again, the satellite initiated the sequence which sent an "attack-alert" warning signal outward through the solar system into interstellar space.

PART ONE

THE LIGHT IN THE ALIEN DARK

CHAPTER ONE

Tahl d'jehn had no choice but to abandon the missing scientists on the planet below.

Angrily, he peered through the forward port as the shuttle flew high above the surface. The flat terrain was bleak, but not barren. There was life on the second world of the target star system, but there were no signs of intelligence. His three renegade crew members had sacrificed their scientific reputations, endangered the *Dan tahlni*'s mission, and forfeited their lives for nothing.

"I think I've found them, Tahl."

The dull ache throbbing at the base of Tahl's silver-tipped, pointed ears intensified suddenly. He turned to Chiun s'wah with a frown. "So soon?"

"They set down almost exactly where you thought they would." The short hairs on Chiun's light brown muzzle bristled with expectation as he piloted the shuttle toward the stolen craft's landing site.

Tahl studied Chiun closely for a moment. The pilot did not

seem surprised that he had pinpointed the unauthorized expedition's destination on the uncharted world, but then, Chiun did not know what Tahl knew. Chiun accepted, without question, Tahl's *shtahn* ability to analyze the facts of any given situation and draw accurate conclusions accordingly. Under ordinary circumstances, a precise determination would not bother Tahl, either. However, the present circumstances were anything but ordinary, and the accuracy of this prediction was more than a little disquieting.

Tahl shifted his gaze back to the forward port, but his mind was not on the shuttle's descent. He was certain Riitha f'ath had instigated the plan to investigate the surface of Chai-te Two. She was *venja-ahn*, born with the aberrant mental mode that disrupted logical thought processes and compelled her to equate supposition and assumption with fact. Only a deviant *venja-ahn* mentality had the cunning to conceive of such an audacious scheme and the temerity to openly defy the orders of a mission leader. That Riitha had also convinced two sane, analytic scientists to participate in her misguided folly was troublesome, but not nearly as much as Tahl's correct anticipation of her actions.

"Tighten in, Tahl," the pilot said.

Tahl adjusted the webbed straps holding him in his seat and braced himself. The precaution was wise, but unnecessary. Chiun set down the craft without ruffling a tuft of Tahl's silver-streaked black mane.

While Tahl waited for Chiun to secure the ship, he continued to mull over the twisted paths of reasoning that had brought him to the exact location of the runaway expedition's shuttle. Surely, Tahl thought, Riitha must realize that the most likely place for me to begin my search is the spot on Chai-te Two's surface most advantageous to all three scientists' objectives. Logically, she should have chosen a more inconvenient site to avoid him, even if it meant jeopardizing one of their excursions. Expecting him to be logical, Riitha had chosen the most probable site instead, confident he would scan far afield of it first.

She had been wrong, but Tahl was not reassured by his sudden understanding of intuitive deduction and manipulation. The unfathomable mental processes of the *venja-ahn* minority usually eluded his analytic perception.

"The skimmer hatch is open." Chiun spoke softly, the sound of his words almost lost in the low growl rumbling deep in his throat. The pilot's gaze remained fastened on the stolen shuttle for several seconds. Then Chiun turned to Tahl, his large, liquid brown eyes narrowing with uncertainty, his square, black nose twitching nervously. "They're gone."

Tahl flinched as the strong stench of Chiun's fear assaulted his nostrils. The ominous scent had become pervasive aboard the ship after Riitha, Stocha, and Verda had proposed the theories that had finally led to their insane flight. The whole situation was unprecedented, illogical, and potentially dangerous. Chiun, like everyone else aboard the *Dan tahlni*, was acutely aware that the three scientists' speculations, combined with their unsanctioned foray to the planet's surface, not only put the lives of those on the mission at risk, but also the future of the species as well.

Chiun continued to stare at the *shtahn*, his nostrils flaring. It was obvious to Tahl that the pilot had hoped that the scientists, having suddenly come to their senses and recognizing their mistake in judgment, would be waiting for them.

But they were not waiting. Driven by a mysterious urgency Tahl couldn't begin to understand, let alone explain, the three were stubbornly pursuing their quest for evidence to substantiate their impossible theories.

A quiet growl of distress escaped Chiun as he looked to Tahl for reassurance.

Grunting with apparent unconcern, the *shtahn* slipped out of the webbing. "I didn't think we'd find them here," Tahl said calmly. "Once they had come this far, there was no reason not to go on."

Chiun nodded as his gaze flicked back to the other shuttle.

Although his immediate apprehension seemed to lessen, Tahl sensed that the pilot was still very tense and agitated.

"Scan for their locations," Tahl said, deciding that the performance of simple tasks might help Chiun to stabilize.

The pilot's slim, down-covered fingers deftly swept over the control panel before him. "They're not in range."

"Good. We're going to need some time to check out that shuttle. Let's suit up."

Chiun shivered slightly, then silently followed Tahl to the storage area at the rear of their own shuttle.

A short time later, Tahl cautiously stepped through the shuttle's open field-barrier onto the surface of an alien world. He felt heavy and weak in the unaccustomed gravity, in spite of the isometric maintenance reflex that had kept his muscles toned during periodic hibernations. He had not slept enough to counter the effects of twenty-five years in the zero-gravity environment maintained aboard the *Dan tahlni*.

After walking a couple of steps, Tahl turned and waited for Chiun. The pilot hesitated on the far side of the hatch, then catching Tahl's nod, slipped through and bounded down the ramp in two easy strides. Chiun seemed sufficiently fit, Tahl noticed. The pilot, who served as a systems technician aboard the *Dan tahlni*, had obviously taken full advantage of his winter-sleep cycles.

As Chiun approached, Tahl pressed a button on his belt. The hatch field-barrier grayed, and Tahl entered a personal code to prevent anyone but him from unlocking it again. Then, nodding for Chiun to follow, he started across the barren landscape.

Tahl moved sluggishly, hindered by his imperfect physical condition and the suit encasing his body. The atmosphere of Chai-te Two was breathable, and although contamination from alien biological forms was not probable, it was not impossible, either. The suits were a necessary nuisance.

Opening the suit-to-suit com-channel, Tahl listened to the irregular rhythm of Chiun's breathing and sensed the pilot's struggle to control a rising panic. Once they were inside the familiar interior of the other shuttle, Chiun would probably settle down. Tahl just had to get him there without incident. He spoke to Chiun softly, hoping to alleviate some of the pilot's fright.

"Chiun." The pilot did not respond, and Tahl sharpened his tone. "Chiun!"

"Yes?" he answered hoarsely.

"The gravity. Are you experiencing any ill effects?"

"No." The pilot took a deep breath, then another as he focused his attention on the movement of his feet and the performance of his body. "I'm fine. The gravity here is very much like that on Hasu-din."

"Slightly less," Tahl said. To his relief, the stress factors in Chiun's voice dropped as he spoke.

"Nothing else is like Hasu-din, though," Chiun went on. "This world is so . . . different."

So alien, Tahl thought as he studied the desert that stretched before them. Where Hasu-din was green in the warm times and white during the long cold, this world was only brown. The hard, brown terrain was dotted with nothing but sparse patches of short, brown, needle-sharp grasses as far as he could see. At a glance, the area did not seem a very likely spot for an expedition seeking evidence of intelligent life, except that the shore of the planet's ocean, the edge of a major forest, and the base of a ragged mountain range were all equidistant from that location.

Riitha had planned well. Not even a *shtahn* could know which direction they had taken first.

When he reached the stolen shuttle, Tahl stood aside to let Chiun enter first. The hatch field-barrier was closed, but not locked. Chiun pointed to a panel as Tahl came to stand beside him at the controls.

"They left a message." A hint of anger broke through the anxiety that had been dominating Chiun's tone. "Why would they leave a message, Tahl? To plead for their lives?"

"Let's find out." The *shtahn* eased into the pilot's web and keyed his communication code into the board. He was aware of Chiun's mounting anger as he pressed his thumbs against the identification plate. Light and shadow suddenly shimmered across the console.

Riitha's message was simple and direct. Fuel and time expenditures for her survey expedition had been carefully computed. The *Dan tahlni*'s main mission would not be threatened by the unauthorized trip.

Unless something else goes wrong, Tahl thought. A low, guttural growl sounded in his own throat as he read the rest. The runaway scientists had temporarily disabled the shuttle and expected to return to the orbiting *Dan tahlni* within fifty hours.

Behind Tahl, Chiun snarled. "They endanger the mission and then dare to think they might escape punishment. They are fools."

Tahl only grunted. Chiun, like everyone else aboard the orbiting ship, expected him to leave the renegades to whatever fate this world held for them. They had ignored his orders and taken a shuttle. They had wasted valuable time and fuel. They had damaged the mental stability of the crew. He had no choice but to bring down a judgment of exile.

Or did he?

"I can probably repair the shuttle," Chiun said softly. "None of them are engineers. The damage won't be too serious. They had to be sure they could fix it themselves."

Tahl grunted again. He was glad Chiun was regaining his mental equilibrium, but that was just going to make the next phase of the operation harder. The pilot would probably not understand his sudden decision to use the bio-analytic power of the *shtahn* trance to make a final determination concerning Riitha's expedition.

"I've got the tools and spare parts," Chiun noted. "I'll have the shuttle ready to launch in an hour or two."

Tahl nodded. The original plan had been for him to pilot

the stolen shuttle back to the *Dan tahlni*. "I'll consider that. Right now, I need you to keep a trance vigil."

Chiun blinked and flicked his ears back and forth in confused agitation. "Trance vigil? Now? For them?"

Tahl scowled. He, too, was alarmed by his own sudden and inexplicable uncertainty, but he could not ignore it. He was missing some important facet of the situation that could only be discovered through the precise processes of trance analysis. In this, he definitely had no choice.

"I can't just leave them." Tahl rose quickly and motioned Chiun into the pilot's web, then edged toward the cargo bay hatch.

"You can't go into a trance now—here," Chiun gasped, his throat constricting with a new and different fear. "It's too soon after your last! If anything happens to you—"

"I'll be all right," Tahl said evenly. Chiun's terror was more powerful than he had suspected though, and it was causing the pilot to forget his station. No one questioned a *shtahn* decision. Chiun had to be brought back into control before Tahl dared enter the deep-sleep state of the trance. "Everything will be all right."

Chiun shook his head and grabbed Tahl's arm. "If the mission fails—"

"Sani won't let it fail."

"Sani's a mediator, not the *shtahn jii*." Chiun's eyes widened with desperation as he used Tahl's full title. "You've got to wait until we're back aboard ship. When you're rested—"

"No," Tahl said tightly, sensing that he was in danger of losing his patience. "We don't have any more fuel reserves. If we take their shuttle and strand them, there's no coming back for them later."

Chiun's brow furrowed with puzzlement. "Coming back for them? You're not thinking—"

"Enough!" Tahl pulled his arm free and fixed the pilot with a steady stare. "I am a *shtahn*. I am going into trance now— here, on this shuttle. And you—" Tahl placed his hands on

Chiun's shoulders and squeezed, trying to focus the pilot's mind "—you must watch me. You must protect me from any disturbances. Do you understand?"

Chiun nodded, but his expression remained anxious.

"Very well. My life is in your hands."

Tahl waited until Chiun had settled into the pilot's web, then ducked through the hatch to the cargo bay of the ship. He knew the pilot's concern was not unfounded. There was a risk. Sleep-analysis required enormous energies, and Tahl's reserves were drained. Yet, he could not abandon his people without giving them the benefit of total consideration as afforded by the trance. Death or exile or exoneration—the decision could not be made casually.

Exile and death were irrevocably bound together in the cases of Stocha d'vi and Verda l'shi. They were analytics, *du-ahn*, and, isolated on an alien world with no hope of rescue, they would succumb to death-wish sleep and die painlessly within days. Riitha's fate would be worse. She was *venja-ahn*. Submission and the tranquil transition from life to death were beyond her. She would slowly starve to death—awake and aware.

Exile and death. One and the same.

A dull ache below Tahl's ears became a sharper pain as he sank into a passenger webbing and fastened the straps. Slowly, methodically, the corded muscles in his neck and under the thick mangle of long fur that ran across his shoulders and chest began to loosen. The relaxation radiated through his body, flowing smoothly into torso, arms, and legs. The steady rhythm of his breathing slowed further. His mind began to drift into a pre-hibernation state of detachment. Checking his decline into winter-sleep, Tahl locked onto the thought trance.

CHAPTER TWO

Riitha gently placed the small plant in a vile, capped it, then tucked it into the collection unit. She breathed a sigh of relief. Although the gloves that were part of the contamination suit were form-fitted, they did not give her complete freedom of movement. The biologist felt awkward and clumsy, but in spite of the suit's restrictions, she had still managed to gather a respectable assortment of specimens. She glanced at the environment-controlled biological device that contained bits and pieces of Chai-te Two and smiled with joy and a measure of grim satisfaction.

Alien life.

Riitha's intense feelings of excitement and awe were dampened only by the frustrating events that had brought her to the edge of this strange forest so many light years from home. It was hard for her to accept that only two others in the thirty-member crew of the *Dan tahlni* seemed to appreciate the extraordinary discovery.

Alien life.

A shudder passed through Riitha with the realization of just how startling, grave, and important this moment was, and how uniquely fortunate she was to be part of it. Although she, along with the Council of Mediators and everyone associated with the six scouting missions sent from Hasu-din, had considered the possibility of encountering life in their respective target star systems, actually finding it, touching it, and experiencing it was something Riitha had not dared hope to achieve.

The *Dan tahlni*'s target star, Chai-te, was only one of billions of stars in the galaxy, and it was situated a mere twelve light years distant from the *bey*'s home star, Chai-din. One of Chai-te's planets teemed with life, life that was lower on the evolutionary scale than that on Hasu-din, but life nonetheless. If two stars in such proximity had brought forth life on their worlds independently of each other, how many other wombs of potential life circled countless other stars? In how many different stages of development? And most important, how many of these worlds had given birth to intelligence?

The possibilities were staggering.

And lost on most of the *ahsin bey*.

Riitha's sense of euphoria and wonder faded into the shadows of sobering reality. The questions that had sprung so quickly to her mind were those only a *venja-ahn* would ask. Exploring the possibilities the questions raised was an endeavor only a *venja-ahn* would want to pursue for the sheer joy of the pursuit and a chance to find the answers. The hunger to know, the ability to speculate, the power to dream about things unknown and irrelevant in the immediate arena of one's existence—these traits were lacking in the *du-ahn* mind-set that dominated the *ahsin bey* species.

Rubbing a muscle cramp in her thigh, Riitha scanned the horizon, unable to shake a rising feeling of sadness and great loss. The wonder of this strange, new world, with its scientific treasures and undiscovered secrets, was of no concern to the *du-ahn* majority on the mission. Except for Stocha and Verda, the *du-ahn* aboard the *Dan tahlni* were interested in one question and one question only: Did this planet or this star system harbor an intelligence that would prevent the *ahsin bey* from colonizing and using Chai-te's resources for themselves?

With a despondent sigh, Riitha looked at the biological collection unit again. The few specimens she had managed to gather, in addition to those Stocha and Verda had promised to collect for her, might be all the pieces of Chai-te Two she would ever have.

Unless, of course, she had guessed wrong about Tahl's final decision concerning their fate.

Weariness, depression, and gravity tugged at her, and Riitha sank into a pile of dry leaves for a moment's rest and reflection. She had been surprised when Stocha and Verda had agreed to explore their respective sites alone. Separating was the most efficient way to proceed with their individual studies, affording each of them the maximum amount of time available to prove or disprove their various scientific theories. And Tahl would not expect them to split up.

What is Tahl doing now? she wondered. What is he doing at this very instant in time?

Reclining, Riitha stared at the cloudless, blue, alien sky and pondered the possible consequences of her actions. She knew it might have been a mistake to trust her instincts about Tahl's reaction and ultimate disposition in the matter of her unauthorized and apparently impulsive expedition to the planet's surface. At the time she was considering the excursion, Riitha had felt strongly that he would somehow see the logic of their arguments and reconsider his stand. There was no doubt in her mind that he would not have sanctioned her expedition before the fact, but—would he let them come back?

Riitha realized that she was not worried for herself. Death was not too high a price to pay for the privilege of exploring this fascinating world. Stocha and Verda, however, were another matter. In retrospect, the biologist was afraid that the *du-ahn* scientists had agreed to come with her because she had been so certain Tahl would not strand them.

Closing her eyes, Riitha tried to recall the details of the discussion that had prompted her to take such desperate action. She had been sitting opposite Tahl at the conference table, her expression deliberately more serious than usual.

*   *   *   *   *

Tahl glanced at Riitha with a perplexed frown. The attention of the others seated around the oval table shifted from screens, to Tahl, to her. The scent of distress and tension hung so heavily in the room, it was almost overpowering. Tahl's matter-of-fact tone and calm demeanor did little to diminish it.

"An expedition to the surface of Chai-te Two is out of the question."

Ignoring the finality of Tahl's words and forcing herself to remain equally calm, Riitha pressed the issue. "We can't possibly tell whether an intelligent species inhabits this world unless we descend."

Tahl held the biologist's unwavering gaze for a moment, then looked down to scan her recommendation again.

The problems her proposal presented for the eventual success or failure of the mission were not lost on Riitha. The expedition was intended to explore the Chai-te system, declare it uninhabited, and transmit a signal back to Hasu-din so a colony ship could be sent. That signal, however, had to be transmitted within a specific, very rigid time frame.

The *Dan tahlni* was very close to failure by default because of lack of time and fuel. The alien sun, Chai-te, was not only brighter and hotter than Chai-din, its planetary system was more expansive. Extra fuel had been allotted for this contingency, but not enough. Because of this, the crew had not been able to explore the inner planets as thoroughly as they had those in the outer system. In addition, several large equipment pods, including the interstellar transmitter that was their only link to Hasu-din, had been left in orbit around Chai-te Five to conserve what fuel remained.

The energy reserve was decreasing daily, and Tahl had to be certain that they had enough fuel to power the *Dan tahlni* back to Chai-te Five, to power the transmitter that would send the signal back to Hasu-din telling of the mission's success or failure, and then to provide maintenance power aboard the ship until the hydrogen energy plants were set up and operational in the atmosphere of Chai-te Five. All these things were necessary for the crew's survival. Riitha knew Tahl would not waste fuel on a survey he considered to be an intuitive whim. She had to convince him her reasoning was sound.

"My report is not based on unaccepted speculation."

Tahl glanced at the biologist curiously.

Unable to keep the strain out of her voice, Riitha continued. "I've applied theories concerning possible alien cultures as outlined by the Analytic Board of the Worlds University." Her delicate silver-tipped ears twitched nervously, and she silently cursed herself. Tahl would sense her agitation and that alone might undermine his confidence in her evaluations. Riitha was not usually bothered by the disdain and skepticism with which *du-ahn* viewed a *venja-ahn*'s theoretical assumption, but the present situation was more important than any she had dealt with in the past. She concentrated on maintaining control.

Tahl ran his hand over the luxurious, long, silver-black fur on his head, then leaned forward with a soft, tolerant sigh. "Our orbital scans show no signs of civilization, Riitha, no indications of an existing order of intelligence."

The short hairs covering Riitha's face, lower arms, belly, and lower legs bristled at Tahl's patronizing tone. She stiffened slightly, then hesitated, all too aware that Tahl's gaze had shifted to the small mounds of her four, milkless breasts. His admiring scrutiny in conjunction with his refusal to listen with an open mind strengthened her resolve to pursue her arguments concerning the proposed survey. Sadly, it also reminded Riitha that she must continue to abstain from choosing Tahl as a mate during her bonding cycles, even though she desired him more than any other male aboard the *Dan tahlni*. Riitha chose the others to satisfy her inescapable sexual needs. She wanted more from Tahl, an emotional pairing that he, being locked into his *du-ahn* insensitivities, would never understand or be able to give.

Hardening her heart and her voice, Riitha countered Tahl's statement about the orbital scans. "The activities of a primitive culture would not register, nor would those of an advanced non-technological society. You're assuming intelligence will progress as we have. An alien mentality will be . . . alien. We have no way of knowing how it would respond to its environment."

"Tahl." All eyes turned to Sani s'oha, the ship's mediator.

Tahl acknowledged the mediator with a respectful nod. "Yes?"

"We know that life forms on this world are carbon-based like us—" Sani cast a disparaging glance at Riitha, then looked back at the *shtahn*. "Those forms are sustained by an oxygen-carbon dioxide photosynthesis cycle, as on Hasu-din. Given these basic similarities, I see no need for further, wild speculation."

Riitha's black eyes narrowed, and her nostrils flared. "Organic similarities have nothing to do with how an alien being might think."

"Additional robotic landers could be deployed," Tahl said.

Every muscle in Riitha's petite body tightened as she turned back to Tahl. "They would not be effective without proper programming, and we don't have the necessary data. A direct-contact survey is essential. Without it—" The biologist held Tahl's gaze, lowering her voice and slowing her speech to insure that every word was firmly impressed on the *shtahn jii*'s mind. "Without it, you'll be forced to consider assumptions rather than facts during the decision trance. First-hand observation is the only way to determine if our position in this system is secure under the Law."

Tahl frowned thoughtfully.

*   *   *   *   *

Riitha started, then shook her head vigorously. She had almost nodded off while remembering that fateful conversation. She rose quickly to her feet and picked up the collection unit. Her time downworld was precious. Sleep would have to wait until she returned to the *Dan tahlni*. If she returned.

The weariness was difficult to shake. Gravity was taking its toll on Riitha, as was the constant necessity of having always to consider the response of the inflexible *du-ahn* in every aspect of her life. Too often, simple abstract thoughts and concepts that were perfectly obvious to Riitha's *venja-ahn* awareness were totally beyond *du-ahn* understanding. On more occasions than she cared to remember, she had been forced to explain why she had said this or why she had done that, in matters ranging from her preference for a swift and compassionate kill of the animals that fed her, to her scientific speculations on the infinite wonders the universe might hold. Her explanations about these things usually evoked blank, uncomprehending *du-ahn* stares or, worse, tolerant nods and condescending shakes of the head.

As she walked deeper into the forest, alone and away from the ever-present *du-ahn* surveillance and reproach she faced aboard the *Dan tahlni*, Riitha had to admit to herself that she was tired of having to cope with the problem. It was, she knew, a strange quirk of the *bey*'s evolution that had brought about *du-ahn* dominance. And even stranger, without the intuitive, questioning functions of the *venja-ahn* mind, the *ahsin bey* would eventually stagnate, wither, and fade from existence.

Pausing to take in the glory of a brilliant green fern whose six-foot fronds formed a canopy above her, Riitha wished for an escape, a haven from the mental restrictions and prejudicial torment she had endured since she was born. Even her parents had rejected her, preferring to send their tainted, *venja-ahn* offspring to a nursery at birth rather than subject themselves and Riitha's two normal, *du-ahn* litter-brothers to her dangerous and disruptive influences. In the end their decision had worked to Riitha's advantage, since she had been raised and trained by various schools as a potential candidate for the star-scouting missions being planned at the time. She would not have traded the opportunity for anything, but the pain inherent in the events that had brought her across twelve light years of space to another star and an alien world was always with her.

Riitha reached up and touched a delicate leaf with her gloved hand, drawing peace and a renewed sense of purpose from its virgin, unblemished existence. As always when she momentarily gave in to her feelings of frustration and persecution, Riitha found more of the inner strength that helped her endure. Even though she continued to hope, she knew that nothing, no amount of reason or evidence, would alter the prevailing social structure. Throughout *bey* history, *shtahn* trances had repeatedly proven that *venja-ahn* theories were accurate and sound, and still the *venja-ahn* segment of the population remained a powerless, despised minority.

Leaving the soothing sanctuary of the fern, Riitha moved into the thickening tangle of foliage that had probably remained undisturbed by the passage of any creature bigger than the large tortoise-type animal she had seen fleeing from the skimmer she had ridden as she crossed the grassy plain. A movement overhead caught her eye, and Riitha watched in amazement as a small lizard sprang from the upper branches of a tall tree. A thin sheet of skin attached to its front and back legs unfolded and buoyed the creature as it gently floated down to the leaves of a lower branch. The biologist studied it, noting every detail as it paused to bask in a spot of sunlight that filtered through the overhanging growth.

It was a vertebrate, covered in blue scales that shimmered with flecks of red and green, earless, with independently tracking eyes, a long, tapering tail, and clawed, separated toes. Definitely a reptile, she thought with an astonished gasp. Her studies of the data collected by the robotic scans had indicated the presence of amphibious life, which of itself would have been remarkable considering the planet's short evolutionary time frame. The discovery of a reptile was a stunning revelation.

Slowly, so as not to frighten the lizard, Riitha pulled a smaller recorder from the pocket of her suit and made a visual entry of the creature. Hoping to prod it into another flight, she wiggled the base of the branch, but the creature only scampered away into the safety of the sheltering leaves. Riitha was disappointed, but at least she had managed to secure the evidence she needed to prove that her theories, in part, were correct. Not that it would matter much to her *du-ahn* associates, who were only interested in whether or not she found concrete evidence of an indigenous intelligence.

Changing her course to circle back toward the skimmer, Riitha kept an eye overhead in the hope of recording one of the lizards in flight. Her thoughts turned back to the possibly fatal situation she had created.

Riitha had long ago given up trying to monitor the routine conversations and actions of her everyday life that sometimes offended and often confounded the *du-ahn* around her. Still, she had been unwaveringly cautious and methodical about her scientific endeavors. By employing systematic logic and making precise presentations of any proposed project, she was always given the time and the facilities she needed to pursue her different fields of study. Producing positive results most of the time had earned her a measure of credibility, respect, and trust from Tahl d'jehn during the course of their long journey. As *shtahn jii* aboard the *Dan tahlni*, Tahl was the final authority and the only one she had to convince in any given situation. Her methods usually worked—but not this time.

This time Tahl had not been swayed to her way of thinking. No one had. Except Stocha and Verda, Riitha reminded herself.

Frowning suddenly, the biologist paused. She had been surprised when the two scientists had agreed to go with her to the planet's surface, and surprised again when they had agreed, although reluctantly, to go their separate ways in order to use their limited time to the best advantage. However, Riitha had been so involved in planning and executing the expedition, she had not stopped to examine in depth Stocha's and Verda's unusual behavior. Now it suddenly occurred to her that their actions were even stranger and more bizarre than the alien world that had captured their attention.

Two *du-ahn* scientists had risked their lives to prove or disprove theories based mostly on conjecture. Why?

Spying a bright red, fungus-type growth, Riitha hurried toward it, but the question continued to plague her. She could only hope that the same question would occur to Tahl, and that he would realize there seemed to be a motive driving the two *du-ahn* scientists that went far beyond the gathering of evidence to support their individual theories. Riitha knew that there was at least one reason other than scientific curiosity that pushed her on: someone had to prove, beyond a doubt, that no intelligent species inhabited the planet. If the decision was made to colonize the system before this was settled, the *Dan tahlni*'s mission would be in danger of violating the Law, the one and only rule that had successfully and peacefully guided the *bey* for thousands of years.

CHAPTER THREE

To take that which belongs to another without mutual consent is forbidden.

Tahl used the familiarity of the Law to focus his trance-state.

Before the time of Aru f'dihn five thousand years before, the primitive tribes of the *ahsin bey* had been confined to a small, island continent in the southern part of the eastern hemisphere of Hasu-din. War had been the only known means of balancing limited resources and overpopulation. *Du-ahn* warriors had fought and died in combat or succumbed to death-wish when faced with certain defeat. Surviving *du-ahn* on the losing side became submissive to their conquerors and were incorporated into the victorious tribes. Conquered *venja-ahn* were exiled or killed.

This constant life and death struggle, which limited the development of intellect and invention as well as the population, had persisted until Aru f'dihn, the greatest *shtahn* in history, determined that there were other, larger land masses on the planet, and that they were easily accessible through connecting chains of islands. He also proposed that the *bey* begin to negotiate their differences rather than fight over them. The abundance of resources made available by the exploration of the other continents in conjunction with a *du-ahn* predisposition to cooperation and mediation provided the *bey* with the ideal circumstances for the initial and successful implementation of the Law.

Acceptance and adherence to the Law strengthened trade relations among the early territorial groups as the *bey* began to migrate to all the continents of Hasu-din. Industrial development followed in the wake of continued peace, and eventually the first Council of Mediators was formed to ensure the efficient use and distribution of the planet's resources for the benefit of all. Ultimately, respect for the Law had accelerated the *bey*'s expansion throughout the Chai-din star system and finally brought them to the stars.

The delegation of mediators managing the interstellar expansion project had interpreted the Law to include any and all sentient, intelligent beings. No one aboard the *Dan tahlni* wanted to abandon the Chai-te star system and its wealth of resources, but to take resources from another was a violation of the Law and the amendment that forbade contact with any intelligent species they found.

By amending the Law to forbid contact with intelligent life forms, the mediators were protecting the billions of *bey* in the home star system, as well as the members of the scouting expeditions.

Should one of the *bey* missions contact an alien species that was stronger, more advanced, or more aggressive than the *bey*, the results would be disastrous. Conflict with such a species would mean certain defeat for the *bey*, whose ships carried no weapons. Once defeated, *du-ahn* crews would either surrender, or, more likely, submit to death-wish. Then the scouting ships would fall into hostile, alien hands and possibly lead aggressors to Hasu-din.

Tahl's thought mode shifted abruptly.

Huge colony ships were being prepared to follow the scouts to target star systems found to be rich in minerals and void of intelligent life. Yet, what if Riitha's theories proved correct? Could he transmit an abort message, preventing the launch of a colony ship toward Chai-te, simply because some creature on the system's second planet exhibited primitive tool use or showed a tendency to social order like some animal species on Hasu-din? An intelligence with no concept of technology would never consider expansion beyond the planetary sphere. The *ahsin bey* wished only to exploit the asteroids and gas giants, not the inner planets. To abandon the *bey*'s hopes of colonization on the basis of a species that might never go into space to use those resources and now showed no technological inclinations at all seemed illogical.

But the Law made no distinctions. There could be no exceptions.

Tahl felt himself being dragged down into a deeper sleep by a dark and heavy sense of desperation. He struggled to maintain trance stability. Distressed by the intrusion of an emotional flutter in his analytic patterns, he quickly forced his mind back to the problem at hand.

Riitha had not gone to Chai-te Two alone. Verda l'shi, a *du-ahn* mineralogist, and Stocha d'vi, also *du-ahn* and the *Dan tahlni*'s primary geologist, had gone with her.

* * * * *

Stocha's hand shook slightly as he powered-up the filament probe and watched it bore into the hard earth. The geologist sat, staring at the probe for several minutes, as though he could will the equipment to find the proof he so desperately wanted. Then Sani s'oha would have to retract her outrageous accusations and insults.

The steady whir of the geological surveying device was comforting, a stabilizing, familiar sound in the midst of the silent and eerie desolation that surrounded Stocha. He stretched, trying to loosen the knotted muscles in his shoulders and back, but he could not relax. The tension that gripped his short, sturdy body would not go away until he was safely off the alien planet and back aboard the ship.

A wave of nausea twisted Stocha's stomach. Doubling over, he was suddenly stricken with a weakening dizziness. He collapsed onto the ground and forced himself to take a long, deep breath, then another and another. Stocha had never been alone before—not like this—completely cut off from everything secure and familiar. He didn't like it, but the only way he could reinstate himself with Tahl and Sani was to get solid, physical confirmation that his hypothesis was correct.

The nausea passed, and Stocha pulled himself up into an unsteady sitting position on shaky haunches. Taking another deep breath, the geologist brushed off a layer of fine, brown dirt from his shaggy, gray fur and scanned the mountain ridge across the valley before him.

The rough peaks and sheer face of the distant cliffs were identical to the rock formations that towered above and behind him. The ancient depression that separated the twin ridges had been filled in and leveled over the passage of time by wind and drifting sand, but the origin of the huge rift in the planet's surface could not be mistaken. The filament probe exploring the deep strata under the valley floor would only confirm what Stocha already knew: the rift had been formed by an impacting asteroid of tremendous size and velocity. Stocha needed material proof to convince Tahl and Sani of that fact.

With the fear-induced nausea under control and his confidence bolstered by the visual evidence surrounding him, Stocha tried to stand. Another wave of dizziness forced him down again. He closed his eyes, surrendering to an overpowering urge to sleep. Rest did not come easily, though. His mind seemed intent on recounting events he would rather forget. The geologist remembered clearly, too clearly, every detail of the confrontation that had eroded his scientific reputation and threatened his sanity.

* * * * *

"If I might add something, Tahl." Stocha's grim expression intensified as his forehead creased and the shaggy hair above his smoke-gray eyes drove together in thought. He spoke hesitantly, uncertain, yet somehow compelled to support Riitha's request for a surface landing. "I believe a geological survey is warranted."

Tahl's eyes narrowed. "What possible bearing could a geological investigation have on this issue? Either there is an indigenous intelligence with a claim on this system, or there isn't. If there isn't, you'll have many opportunities to study the planet after we've established operations at Chai-te Five."

"There, uh—" Stocha coughed to quell his nervous stammer. "There are, uh, indications this planet has undergone dramatic change in its recent geological past. I can't say whether these changes have any, uh—any bearing on the existence of a past or present intelligence unless I have more information."

"Past?" Startled, Tahl pressed for an explanation.

A sharp pain arrowed through Stocha's head. He winced, then frowned, his train of thought lost in a tingling fog. The sensation and resulting confusion passed suddenly. He blinked.

"Make your point, Stocha."

The geologist met Tahl's intimidating gaze without flinching. "Chai-te Two has a distinct equatorial bulge on one side, the result of gravitational tidal effects. The planet once had a rotation period slow enough to keep this one side facing the third planet at all times. The constant pull of Chai-te Three over billions of years is the only explanation for the bulge."

"That would mean—" Dar m'ote stared into space for a moment before punching a series of figures into his terminal.

"Something important?" Tahl asked.

Dar shrugged and continued his computations.

Curious and tense, Stocha used the ensuing silence to study

his associates. Tahl's expression was calm, but worry creased the
faces of the others and the scent of apprehension hung in the
air. Sani sat with her eyes closed. Riitha's attention was fast on
her terminal screen. The others glanced back and forth between Tahl, Dar, and Stocha.

"Interesting," Dar said. The physicist stroked the wispy
long-fur on his chin, his gaze lingering on his terminal.

"What?" Tahl prodded.

"If Stocha's theory is correct, at one time the planet took
longer to spin on its axis than to orbit the star."

"That correlates with my findings," Stocha said.

Tahl looked perplexed. "Then how do you account for its
present rotation period of only sixty hours?"

Stocha activated the console before him. A hologram of the
planetary sphere appeared in the open space in the middle of
the oval table. "As the image turns, you will notice a large, cir-
cular area in the equatorial zone between the smaller elevated
continent and the volcano chain."

"An impact crater?"

Stocha smiled at the secondary biologist, Siva s'hur. "Yes,
but not typical. Watch."

The image of the crater region enlarged, revealing not a cir-
cular configuration, but an elongated scar with defined ridges
along the sides and at one end.

Stocha explained. "This is the result of a large body striking
the planet in just such a way as to increase its spin rate substan-
tially. This system does have a group of asteroids whose orbits
bring them into the region of the inner planets."

"That's all very well," Tahl said, "but I don't see the connection between the impact of an asteroid and the existence of an
intelligent species."

"If you'll just bear with me a moment—"

Tahl nodded, but Stocha sensed the *shtahn jii*'s mounting
impatience. He chose his words carefully, knowing that it was
crucial for Tahl to have every piece of available information so
he could make his decision concerning the launch of the colony

ship from Hasu-din. Stocha also realized that the theory he was
about to present might seem far-fetched and irrelevant. Still,
because he had formulated the hypothesis based on his geological knowledge and observations, he was duty-bound to bring
it to Tahl's attention.

"It's possible that this impact was simply a natural occurrence. However—" Stocha paused for effect, augmenting the
intensity of everyone's interest, especially Tahl's. As he resumed speaking, he looked only at the *shtahn jii*. "The
chances of an asteroid of this immense size being pulled out of
orbit by the gravitational field of Chai-te Two and hurled inward are almost non-existent. The gravitational forces holding
the asteroid belt together have been stable for a long time."

A thoughtful frown wrinkled the black velvet smoothness of
Tahl's forehead, but he said nothing. Stocha plunged ahead,
interpreting the *shtahn jii*'s silence as an indication that Tahl
was giving his words serious consideration.

"Also, the chances of an inner-system asteroid randomly
hitting the second planet with the precision necessary to produce the life-sustaining effects of a faster rotation period are
several billion to one. That may be a conservative estimate."

Tahl hesitated, rubbing the back of his neck, then turned to
the physicist. "Do you agree, Dar?"

After studying his terminal intently, Dar sighed then answered. "An impact as Stocha describes it would not be impossible, but it's highly unlikely."

"I see." The sleek, black and silver hairs that fell in long
strands from Tahl's muzzle fluttered slightly as he snorted in irritation. The look he gave Stocha was chilling. "But I still
don't see what any of this has to do with the existence of intelligence."

Lowering his eyes, his confidence wavering, Stocha tried to
explain. "It's, uh—also possible that the, uh—asteroid was
deliberately sent crashing into the planet for the express purpose of transforming it. Not only would the increased spin rate
create a suitable day-night cycle, but it would also produce the

dynamo effect essential for the generation of a magnetic field. This is exactly what the impact did accomplish."

"*Shtahn jii!*" the mediator, Sani s'oha, gasped. "I must protest. I will not sit here and listen to this *venja-ahn* nonsense any longer!" She glowered at Stocha, her chest heaving with anger. "Analytic groups should not be subjected to meaningless *venja-ahn* ravings during serious discussions. At least Riitha and Bier can be counted on to restrain themselves—usually." The mediator glanced at Riitha with a look of unguarded scorn.

Stunned by the insulting implication of Sani's words, Stocha froze.

After pausing a moment to assimilate what Sani had said, Tahl rose to the geologist's defense. "Stocha is not *venja-ahn.*"

A startled look crossed the mediator's face. Her gaze quickly shifted to Bier t'ahi, the ship's psychologist. His eyes narrowed warningly.

Stocha noticed all this without comprehending. His troubled mind was focused on the *shtahn jii*'s reassuring words.

"Stocha's brain functions are not in question here," Tahl continued. "As a scientist, he must explore all possible logical explanations for his discoveries. When we decided to inhabit Merje, we dismantled Chol's second moon and hurled ice chunks at the planet to increase the water supply. The possibility Stocha proposes is not much different."

Sani quickly grew indignant. "There's a great deal of difference between dropping ice chunks on a world and proposing that some past, alien species attempted to speed up a planet's rotation period by hitting it with an asteroid."

The *shtahn* cut her short. "Leave it alone for now."

Sighing with relief, Stocha was thankful that Tahl, not Sani, was in charge. On the planets and space installations in the home star system, a Council of Mediators would consult the *shtahns* on crucial matters. The sleep-analytics advised them. The mediators then considered the advice and made the final decisions. Aboard ship, the *shtahn jii* had the last word.

* * * * *

Stocha woke suddenly, feeling refreshed and stronger. The dizziness, tension, and weakness that had afflicted him since landing on Chai-te Two were gone. Cautiously, he stood. There was no sickening recurrence of the nausea to send him falling in a helpless heap on the ground, no wooziness in his head to muddle his thinking. Relieved, the geologist stepped gingerly to the filament probe to make sure it was still operating properly.

As he checked the readings and tested the monitors, Stocha could not help but recall Tahl's explanation for his unusual theories. The geologist had to convince himself as certainly and as definitely as Tahl had been forced to convince Sani that he had employed logical, scientific reasoning concerning the data available, and more important—that he was still *du-ahn*. To admit otherwise was to contemplate the terrible possibility that he had been inaccurately tested as a child and the status of his mental mode had been misdiagnosed. Stocha shuddered at the very thought of finding out this late in his life that he was *venja-ahn*. Being cast out of the *du-ahn* community that was his solace and security would be an unbearable hardship and difficult to accept, but to not be able to trust the functions of his own thought processes would be worse.

He did not have to worry about that, though. Stocha had never heard of anyone whose mental identity had been wrongly defined. Whether or not an individual was *du-ahn* or *venja-ahn* was too critical to the smooth function of society to be diagnosed lightly. *Du-ahn* had to know if they were dealing with *venja-ahn* in order to take the sometimes muddled and often incomprehensible results of their intuition-laden thinking into consideration, especially in scientific matters.

Besides, Stocha reassured himself, Tahl, the *shtahn jii*, had defended him and his deductive methods. His *du-ahn* integrity was intact.

Unless, of course, the geological specimens brought up by

the probe drill did not verify his theory. There's nothing to worry about in that respect, either, Stocha thought with another glance at the probe's monitors. The planet had been hit by an asteroid, and the hit had not only created the rift valley, it had dramatically altered the rotation period. Whether or not the hit was a natural phenomenon or a calculated feat of engineering was a question that might never be answered. Surface scans from the shuttle had not picked up any signs of technology or intelligence, and any evidence of an ancient industrial capability might have been obliterated long ago. Without proof, Stocha would have to relinquish his theories concerning technological interference. Still, the remote possibility continued to tease and stimulate his thoughts.

Unaware of the nuances in his thinking and satisfied that the probe was properly calibrated, Stocha turned his attention to the valley and the closest mountain ridge, suddenly remembering that he had promised to collect biological specimens for Riitha. There was no plant life in the immediate vicinity, but he had noticed patches of green back toward the shuttle as he had sped over the terrain on the skimmer. Rather than sitting by the probe doing nothing, Stocha decided to take the skimmer to look for more fertile ground.

The geologist grinned sheepishly, remembering how the vast emptiness of the alien world had terrified and overwhelmed him at first. Though raised on space stations and ships, Stocha had never actually been on a alien planetary surface before. Now that he had recovered from his initial fears, he realized that he was eagerly anticipating further exploration. If he chose his next site carefully, he might even uncover some useful fossil evidence.

After placing a homing device on the probe, Stocha hurried to the skimmer. He walked with a sure step and renewed energy, anxious to see as much of the fascinating new world as possible during his short sojourn.

* * * * *

In the cargo bay of the stolen shuttle, Tahl continued to review the conference through his trance. For a brief moment after Sani had verbally attacked Stocha, Tahl had feared the geologist would go into shock. Stocha had looked bewildered, and the odor of fear emanating from him had been strong. Tahl's responsibilities as *shtahn jii* hadn't allowed him to salvage Stocha's pride at the expense of the mission; he had realized, however, that he couldn't risk having the geologist become dysfunctional. As in all matters, Tahl had proceeded cautiously.

* * * * *

In deference to Stocha's discomfort, Tahl maintained a calm demeanor. He was afraid that any hint of annoyance or concern would completely unbalance the geologist. "Since hurling an asteroid toward a planet would require a highly developed technology, we must negate the possibility of an engineered hit. There's no evidence of space-faring technology—past or present—in this system."

Stocha hesitated. His gray eyes clouded slightly, and his shoulders sagged. The tainted scent of uncertainty enveloped him, then disappeared almost instantly. Squaring his shoulders, his eyes bright and clear, the geologist persisted in trying to persuade Tahl that a survey was necessary.

"I mentioned earlier that the rotation rate had been changed recently," Stocha said with a steadiness that emphasized the firmness of his convictions. "This observation is based on the fact that the crater ridge has not eroded to a great extent and that the planetary bulge has not flattened perceptibly. It will eventually."

Worried, but not sure why, Tahl pursued the discussion. "Define recently."

"A few hundred million years—maybe less. Not long by geological standards."

"And the point?"

"The point," Stocha said evenly, "is that an impact of such magnitude would cause planetwide catastrophe, disrupting, if not destroying, all but the simplest and hardiest of life forms. We know for a fact that life on this world has evolved far beyond what should have been possible in a few hundred million years. A recent impact would mean one of two things: either the planet has an accelerated rate of evolution, or . . . someone planted it with advanced life forms after the dust had settled out of the atmosphere."

Everyone stared at Stocha.

"May I speak, *shtahn jii*?" Verda l'shi asked quietly.

"If it's pertinent," Tahl responded.

The mineralogist nodded grimly. "I think Stocha should be allowed to investigate the strata at the impact site, and I'd like to go along. I have independently arrived at a similar conclusion concerning the possibility of accelerated evolution on Chai-te Two."

Tahl sighed, no longer able to mask his impatience. He resented the theoretical implications, but as *shtahn jii* he had to listen. "Would you elaborate, please?"

The mineralogist looked him in the eye, her small mouth stubbornly set. "The ocean is red."

*   *   *   *   *

Ocean, Tahl thought with contempt as another emotional flux disrupted the smooth course of the trance. Tiring, he focused his mind on more familiar oceans as he willed his suddenly erratic pulse back to normal.

The body of water on Chai-te Two was a mere puddle compared to the deep waters that covered three-fourths of Tahl's homeworld, Hasu-din. The northern sea on the alien world covered but one-sixth of the planet's surface—and it was red. Tahl did not see the significance, and Verda had been adamant in her refusal to explain.

Her reluctance was understandable considering the humiliation Stocha had endured when he had voiced his theories.

More disturbed now than at the time of the discussion, Tahl began to consider what seemed to be a shift in Stocha and Verda's thought processes.

Regardless of what Tahl had said at the time of the meeting, Stocha's thinking had definitely gone awry of *du-ahn* parameters. Although the geologist's theory about the asteroid impact was based on acceptable scientific information, his ramblings about the possibility of intentional, technological intervention on the part of an ancient alien species was nothing but irrelevant speculation. There was no evidence whatsoever that supported, or even implied, the existence of an industrialized intelligence in the system. Yet these *venja-ahn* fabrications had emerged from the depths of Stocha's mind.

The geologist was a proven *du-ahn* who had suddenly, and without warning, displayed *venja-ahn* tendencies. The implications inherent in this phenomenon were staggering and even frightening. The testing procedures conducted on all *bey* children to determine their thought mode identity never failed. At least, they never have before, Tahl mused.

Less than five percent of the *bey* population were handicapped by the *venja-ahn* inclination to abstract thought. Throughout the course of their history, defeated *du-ahn* who had not succumbed to death-wish had submitted and been incorporated into the victorious society. *Venja-ahn*, without exception, had fought to the death or been exiled. The *venja-ahn* gene was recessive, and over the generations backbrain dominance was slowly being bred out of the species. Still, the medical examiners were diligent in identifying every *venja-ahn* individual. How could Stocha's back-brain dominance have been overlooked?

Troubled, Tahl drove deeper into his contemplation. The synaptic connections linking the front and back hemispheres of the brain were vestigial in *du-ahn*. The connection was active in *venja-ahn*, and the flow of impulses along the pathway was easily detectable. Was it possible that the linking synapses in some individuals were merely dormant and capable of being activated? And if so, what would cause activation and the subsequent emergence of irrational, conjectural thought processes?

A great weariness began to infect the *shtahn*, but he could not ignore the seriousness of the questions being raised in his mind. Verda, too, seemed to be affected.

Neither the implications nor the severity of Stocha's and Verda's mode deviations had been apparent to Tahl when they had first presented their unlikely theories at the conference. Now, however, he was forming his own startling and alarming hypothesis. It was not at all probable that two *venja-ahn* children had been overlooked by the medical examiners. The manner of testing was too accurate, and mode identification was too important to the *du-ahn* to tolerate mistakes. The only possible explanation was that somehow something had activated the impulse flow to their back-brain. Tahl had to know if *venja-ahn* dormancy was possible, and if so, what circumstances were necessary to activate the synapses in the back-brain pathway. In order to find out, he needed more information, and Stocha and Verda were the only examples of possible *venja-ahn* latency available.

Tahl had no choice but to allow them to return to the ship. Riitha would return by default.

She would live.

The surge of joy Tahl suddenly felt sent his pulse racing again. With effort, he fought the strong emotional tide. When it had dissipated, fatigue threatened to pull him down from the delicately balanced trance into the near-death abyss of hibernation. The rare biological process that enabled a *bey* such as Tahl to analyze a problem completely without prejudice or extraneous data was physically taxing. The emotional fluxes, unknown to him before, were draining his strength and reducing his energy reserves to a dangerously low level. Few *shtahn* were born. Of those, many died victims of mental burn-out, and Tahl did not intend to be one of them.

Recognizing the limits of his endurance, the *shtahn* slowly drew himself up from the trance and prepared for normal sleep. His senses probed his surroundings for disturbances, a primordial alarm reflex that was automatically triggered by the release of a hormone into the bloodstream during the sleep-state. His pulse and respiration rate increased slightly as he rose into night-sleep.

Tahl relaxed. His mind opened to a replay of recent events, a lesser manifestation of the *shtahn* trance that was used by all *bey* to sift and sort information, preventing mental overload.

He saw the *Dan tahlni* speeding toward the alien planet. Suddenly, a tongue of red-gold flame leaped from the world's surface and consumed the ship.

Waking instantly, Tahl tried to remember the frightening image, but his subconscious blocked it. Shaken and dizzy, he could not calm the frantic beating of his heart. A shrill scream from the forward cabin only made the wild palpitations worse. Tearing free of the restraining web, he stumbled into the cockpit.

Chiun was staring wide-eyed at the flashing console.

"What is it?" Tahl demanded.

The pilot's words were barely audible through his choking gasps. "There's something out there! Hane picked it up on scan—"

Tahl glanced at the board, then grabbed the pilot's arm and hauled him to his feet. "Come on. We've got to get back to the *Dan tahlni.*"

Chiun needed no further urging. He ran alongside Tahl to the other shuttle.

CHAPTER FOUR

Tahl deftly maneuvered the shuttle into a berth in the *Dan tahlni's* spacious docking bay, then cast a worried glance at Chiun as he shut down the power. The pilot had sat without moving or speaking during the entire flight back from Chai-te Two. He had been stunned into a dazed silence and unable to function because of Hane d'eta's message.

Another crew member acting strangely, Tahl thought as he keyed into docking bay control and initiated the sequence that would install a life-support field envelope around the shuttle. Chiun's fearful reaction was extreme considering the ambiguity of the engineer's communication. Hane's report had not stated that the *Dan tahlni's* scans had definitely found an artifact in the ship's orbital vicinity, but that they had merely encountered an anomaly of an undetermined nature. Although this was disturbing, it was not uncommon. Gases, micrometeors, electro-magnetic fluxes in the ship's systems, and many other ordinary factors had been known to cause just such anomalies in the readings. Yet, Chiun had latched onto the

idea that there was "something" out there, and that idea had
become as solid as fact in his mind, sending him to the brink of
trauma-sleep. No healthy *du-ahn* mind would turn a possible
glitch in the scans into a definite "something," and no *venja-
ahn* mind would retreat into the catatonic state that held
Chiun. It was almost as though the pilot was stuck in between
the two modes.

Tired and troubled, Tahl noted that the life-support envelope was in place. He spoke sharply to the pilot as he stood and
stripped off the pressure suit.

"Chiun!"

The pilot blinked, then resumed his vacant stare.

"We're back on the *Dan tahlni*." Kicking the suit aside, Tahl
put his hand on the pilot's shoulder and squeezed. "You have
duties, Chiun!"

Blinking again, Chiun turned his head and looked at Tahl
blankly. Encouraged, the *shtahn* shook him. He stopped when
Chiun's dark, brown eyes widened with fear and awareness.

"Tahl," he said hoarsely. The strong odor of fear filled the
small shuttle compartment as Chiun jumped to his feet in
panic.

Tahl pushed the pilot back into the seat and looked at him
steadily. "We're back aboard the *Dan tahlni*. There's nothing
to be afraid of. Nothing."

"There's something out there." Nostrils flaring, Chiun
grabbed Tahl's arm and dug into the *shtahn jii*'s flesh with his
claws.

Ignoring the sting, Tahl continued to look into the pilot's
frantic eyes. "We don't know that, Chiun. We don't know
what the scans picked up. It's probably nothing—nothing at
all."

Chiun's grip relaxed. "Nothing." A visible shudder passed
through his neck and shoulders as his panic subsided. Releasing Tahl's arm, the pilot slumped in the webbing and rubbed
the sides of his face. "What happened to me? I feel so . . .
strange."

Anxious to stabilize the pilot, Tahl offered what he hoped would be a logical explanation. "You just walked on an alien world, Chiun. Too many new and different sights, sounds, and sensations have caused some kind of temporary overload. It's nothing to worry about, I'm sure."

Tahl briefly considered sending Chiun to see the medical staff, but changed his mind. Until he had more evidence to support his suspicions, he did not want to alarm anyone else on the ship. The possibility that any one of them might suddenly find himself catapulted into the terrifying and incomprehensible vortex of *venja-ahn* thinking had a potential for disaster that Tahl did not care to contemplate. Although a medical scan of Chiun's brain might provide conclusive proof, Tahl could not risk ship-wide panic.

"Have you fed recently?" Tahl asked.

Chiun paused thoughtfully, then shook his head. "No. I'm overdue."

"There's the answer, then," Tahl said with a reassuring nod. "I want you to eat and rest immediately."

Chiun brightened, accepting Tahl's explanation with a tight smile and a sigh of relief. "As soon as I secure the shuttle and stow the gear."

Feeling certain that Chiun's mental aberration was under control, at least for the moment, Tahl rushed from the docking bay and headed for the flight deck. Weakened by exhaustion and stress, he found himself hoping that the engineer, Hane d'eta, had already solved the riddle of the anomaly on the scans. The journey to the planet's surface combined with the strain of piloting the shuttle back, then having to deal with Chiun, had depleted Tahl's patience as well as his energies. He did not want another inexplicable problem to handle just now. He wanted to eat and sleep, but the demands of his position came first.

Tahl burst through the unlocked field-barrier onto the flight deck with unintentional force, startling the control crew. Two technicians seated before a long bank of consoles

that followed the sweeping curve of the wall on the far side of
the control center glanced at him to acknowledge his presence, then turned back to the flickering lights on the monitors. Above them, the huge holographic screen covering most
of the forward wall projected a partial image of the planet,
Chai-te Two.

At a large console in the middle of the deck, Hane d'eta
stood, an arm looped around one of the many anchor cables secured from ceiling to floor at strategic points throughout the
room. These cables, along with the thick, stabilizing foam attached to the walls, ceilings, and floors throughout the *Dan
tahlni*, allowed the *bey* to anchor themselves in the ship's null-
gravity.

"Tahl! I wasn't expecting you so soon." Hane said.

"Why not?" the *shtahn jii* asked sharply, fatigue negating
his normally soft-spoken manner. He squinted for a moment,
his eyes adjusting to the orange light emanating from insert
panels on the walls. "You sent a report stating that the scans
picked up something you can't identify."

"Uh—" Hane glanced at the technician monitoring the
consoles on the perimeter of the oval-shaped deck, then back
at Tahl. "Uh, yes . . . we—"

"What?" Tahl dug his foot-claws into the foam floor and
grabbed a handhold suspended from the low ceiling to steady
himself against a momentary dizziness.

"A point of light—reflected light, I think. I'm uh—not
sure it actually registered."

"Not sure it registered?" The *shtahn*'s eyes narrowed angrily. "Are you saying there may not be an anomaly?"

"The contact only lasted three seconds," Hane said nervously. "Tena is reviewing all the sensor scans trying to find
it."

"If it exists!" Tahl growled, then checked his mounting
anger. Hane, a *du-ahn* engineer, had decided to burden him
with unsubstantiated, and therefore useless, information.
Hiding his concern, Tahl pressed Hane for an explanation.

"Why bring this to my attention before you've confirmed the problem?"

The engineer hesitated, his wide brow wrinkling with confusion. "I just wanted to be sure you had all the facts."

Nodding, Tahl decided not to mention that a point of light the scans may or may not have seen and had not relocated was not a fact. The engineer did not seem to be aware of the fluctuation in his analytic mode, for which Tahl was grateful. Keeping Hane functioning normally would be easier than Chiun, who had noticed something odd in his own behavior. To reinforce Hane's confidence, Tahl's acceptance of the report on the elusive point of light was imperative.

"When you find the source of the anomaly," Tahl said calmly, "let me know immediately."

"Immediately." Hane glanced at the large holographic viewscreen showing the planetary curve of Chai-te Two. He seemed more agitated than before when he turned back to Tahl. "We are dangerously close to a point of no return in our fuel consumption. If anything unusual happens during our trip back to Chai-te Five or before the separation plant is operational, the mission will fail."

"Yes, I know." Frowning, Tahl stepped up beside Hane. The tension and uneasiness he still sensed in the engineer was unsettling.

Hane's expression and stance displayed a mixture of menace and worry; the engineer's piercing gaze and accusing tone openly challenged Tahl as he dared to voice his thoughts. "Then why did you leave the shuttle for Verda, Stocha, and Riitha? Why aren't we heading back to Chai-te Five now, while there's still some margin of fuel left?"

Alarmed by Hane's hostility, Tahl spoke cautiously. "I must have a full report on whatever the three of them find on Chai-te Two in order to be absolutely certain that no intelligent species inhabit the planet or this system."

Hane's lip curled back in a snarl, exposing sharp fangs. "What did they find?"

"I don't know," Tahl replied patiently. "That's why I've decided to let them return. I don't expect that they found anything, but I must know for sure before a trance decision is possible."

"But you told them not to go!"

"That's irrelevant now. They went, and as *shtahn jii*, I need whatever information they bring back." Hane relaxed as he absorbed Tahl's words, and the *shtahn* seized the opportunity to allay his other fears. "They'll be docking within the next twenty-five hours. Be ready to leave orbit the moment their shuttle is berthed."

The engineer looked at Tahl steadily for a moment, then nodded and, taking advantage of the null-gravity, pushed himself through the air to the central terminal array. Wordlessly Hane began his preparations for the *Dan tahlni*'s impending departure.

Retracting his claws from the foam flooring, Tahl pushed off toward the hatch. He could only hope that the business of navigating the ship out of orbit would help Hane maintain some semblance of stability. Tahl realized he had greatly misjudged the extent of the engineer's mode deviation, probably because of his own extreme fatigue. He had to sleep. The longer he went without it, the less chance he had of figuring out what was happening to his crew.

Tahl moved slowly through the passageways toward his quarters, pausing only when Lish t'wan and Vuthe f'stiida passed him. They were obviously on their way to quarters, too. Neither seemed to notice the *shtahn jii*'s presence.

Lish's sparse brown fur bristled with the urgency of her mating cycle. Vuthe's nostrils were distended and his facial skin slightly flushed beneath the gray fuzz of short hair. Bonded again, Tahl noted, this time with more than mild interest.

Recurring scent-bonds between the same male and female were uncommon, except in *venja-ahn*. Lish, a *du-ahn* powercom tech, had never varied in her choice of mate, however. Since conception was impossible, all the females having been sterilized before the mission launched from Hasu-din, Tahl had never interfered. Now, though, every mode inconsistency seemed somehow related and important.

The *shtahn jii* frowned slightly as the couple disappeared around a bend, then put his concern aside. Lish's pattern had been established twenty-five years ago, long before the other anomalies had shown up. Sighing, he tucked that bit of information away in his weary mind and continued on.

*   *   *   *   *

Back in his quarters, Tahl finally slipped out of the sleeping webs and began to pace in frustration. More than an hour had passed since his return, and still he could not sleep. His mind seemed intent on settling matters now.

His claws dug into the textured floor surface with practiced ease. The muscles of both legs, although weakened by insufficient winter-sleep, still flexed in graceful curves. An advantage of youth, he thought as he relaxed his hold and floated free. That thought disappeared as his concerns returned to plague him.

First Stocha and Verda, then Chiun, and now Hane, were displaying thought tendencies known only in *venja-ahn*. Proven *du-ahn*, all of them were suddenly compelled to voice improbably theories and unsubstantiated opinions. His key people, rather than trying to prove there couldn't possibly be an intelligence in the system, seemed determined to prove there was, had been, or would be. It didn't make sense. It was also dangerous.

The sudden emergence of *venja-ahn* characteristics in analytic minds was disconcerting in itself. However, the phenomenon posed a more immediate and specific threat to the *Dan tahlni*'s mission than the mere inconvenience and annoyance of having to deal with additional intuitive personalities. It could cripple Tahl's effectiveness as *shtahn jii*.

The deluge of assumptions and unconfirmed data would

cloud his mental focus during the trance that would decide the *bey*'s future in the Chai-te system. Exhaustion and the pressure imposed by his critical role as sleep analytic were already making Tahl physically weak. These new complications greatly increased the risk of burn-out.

Sabotage? The idea of a deliberate attempt to kill or incapacitate him bored through his mind for a moment before he dismissed it. The crew had spent more than half their lives aboard the *Dan tahlni*. If Tahl decided against colonization, a complete mission report would be sent home, and acceptance of their theories and discoveries by the scientific community was all any of them would have to show for their sacrifices. The crew needed his support, the validation of their efforts by a *shtahn*, for their work to be recognized on Hasu-din.

Still, Riitha had always been hostile toward him. Tahl did not know why, only that she seemed to delight in tormenting him. Although he was a *shtahn*, Tahl's biological sleep-analysis ability was simply an extension of his basic *du-ahn* mind. Riitha viewed his *du-ahn* status with a contempt that was not evident in her associations with the rest of the crew. During her mating cycles, Riitha flaunted her sexuality before Tahl. Yet, she never chose him.

A shudder rippled along Tahl's shoulders as an image of the enigmatic Riitha f'ath rose in his mind. A sheen of soft, silver down covered her four petite breasts, belly, arms, and lower legs. The black long-fur streaming from her head, muzzle, and shoulders and shagging from her hips and thighs gleamed with the rich luster of meticulous grooming. Like most of the crew, Riitha usually wore only a vest and fringed loin cloth in the climate-controlled confines of the ship. Thick, silver-tipped black lashes ringed large amber eyes that always shone with a mysterious light when she seduced and then rejected the *shtahn*.

Since Tahl faithfully used the desensitizing drug *muath*, he was immune to Riitha's bonding scent, but still subject to arousal. He had always ignored the discomfort brought on by her subtle, erotic displays and regarded her cruel withdrawals with *du-ahn* indifference. She was *venja-ahn*; her motives were beyond rational comprehension. Now, remembering, Tahl was filled with anger and an elusive desire.

Suddenly too tired to keep his eyes open, Tahl quickly eliminated malicious intent on Riitha's part. She enjoyed taunting him too much to want him dead.

Strapping back into the webs, Tahl closed his eyes and tried to divert his thoughts. He let his mind drift and found himself thinking about his childhood.

He did not remember his family well, having left them while only half-grown. When his *shtahn* capability had been confirmed during testing at age five, he had immediately been enrolled in a special school in the faraway capital of Cheyre-dan. Tahl's only clear memory of leaving home was the deep sadness he had felt and the disquieting knowledge that his family did not share the feeling. His parents had been proud and well-rewarded for having borne a *shtahn*, but he had known they would not miss him. Nor would his sister and two brothers. Young *shtahn* tended to be disruptive and difficult to handle because of their mental gifts. A great sense of loneliness had overcome him as he had stepped into the school's skimmer. That sense of being apart and alone had never left him.

Tahl stirred uneasily as he began to doze, suddenly troubled by the solitude imposed by his *shtahn* nature and position. It was something he had never questioned before. Yet, now, he desperately wished for someone to talk to. . . .

As Tahl settled into a deeper sleep, another image of Riitha's face filled his mind. Through the fog of the dream-state, he was dimly aware of a driving desire to talk to Riitha, to try to understand her, to make her understand him. As though in response to his desperate, subconscious needs, the dream image of Riitha smiled, but sadly. Tahl's mind reached out to the image, then recoiled as a point of light in one of her eyes abruptly burst into flame.

Surprise and confusion jolted Tahl in his sleep, bringing him close to awakening. Exhaustion pulled him back, however, and he was drawn down into a sleep level where he would not dream.

CHAPTER FIVE

Bier t'ahi paused before the hatch leading into the livestock containment sector, his upper lip twitching in nervous anticipation. Since the *Dan tahlni* had launched from Hasu-din, Sani had rarely asked to speak to him privately. Those few occasions had not been pleasant, but then, as now, he could not refuse.

The psychologist entered the animal hold warily, calling softly. "Sani?"

"Here." The mediator's harsh, whispered reply came from the adjacent corridor.

Sighing with resignation, Bier swung hand-over-hand down the pen-lined center aisle. The yapping of caged *reikii* mothers and their litters marked his progress. The noise aggravated his already frayed nerves, and he paused again before rounding the corner to confront the ship's mediator.

Bier glanced at the cage beside him as he mentally prepared to meet Sani. A weaned litter of six *reikii* peered back at him through large, dark eyes. The creatures looked like round balls covered in various shades of long brown and gray fur. Tiny ear flaps, almost lost in the folds of fat that obscured the creatures' necks, rested on their small heads. In fact, their stubby tails and legs were only barely discernible against the bulk of their bodies. As the weanlings suddenly started to bark in their shrill voices, the psychologist turned away in annoyance.

Bier waited at the end of the aisle, watching quietly for a moment as Sani walked slowly from one cage to the next and stared at each *bita* intently. The *bita*, smaller, more ferocious, and with sweeter meat than the *reikii*, snarled and snapped at her from behind steel bars. Sani smiled, her tongue hungrily flicking across her lips. Her predator's grin hardened into a scowl as she came alongside Bier.

"You wanted to see me?" the psychologist asked, flinching as Sani turned to regard him, the glint of the hunt shining in her golden eyes.

"Yes." Sani turned to peer into the nearest cage as a large *bita* pushed off the foam-lined walls to attack. When its long, short-furred body struck the bars, it lashed out with teeth and claws. Sani laughed deep in her throat. "He's a good one, don't you think?" Her tone mocked him.

"It's your dinner." Bier tried to watch the frenzied animal with casual unconcern, but after a moment, he had to look away. Fresh kill was necessary to maintain health, but Sani's sadistic delight in snaring and tormenting her prey made him squeamish.

The mediator snorted with disgust. "You would not last long in the wilds, Bier. It's a wonder any of your kind survived in exile." Shaking her head, she continued down the corridor at a leisurely pace.

Bier followed in seething silence, knowing that if for some unforeseen reason he had to live in the wilderness, he would do whatever he had to do to survive. He was *venja-ahn*. Argument, however, was pointless. Sani's opinions concerning *venja-ahn* abilities was steadfastly negative. The only reason she had sponsored him before the Council of Mediators that

formed the stellar scouting expeditions was to further her own
ambitions. For him, their alliance had been his sole hope of
testing his theories concerning latent *venja-ahn* behavior.

"Tahl has decided to let Riitha and the others return," Sani
said. "Do you know why?"

"No." Bier answered honestly, glad to have the discussion
finally underway. "Chiun wasn't much help, I'm afraid. He's
been in deep sleep since shortly after he and Tahl docked. I do
know that Tahl made the decision in trance. He has a good
reason."

"I don't like it." Sani paused, scowling. "Tahl d'jehn is a
potential threat to this entire mission." The mediator stopped
to watch a *bita* that was scrambling wildly around the foam
walls of its cage. "He will demand retribution from them,
won't he?"

Bier shrugged. "I don't see why not. He's reacting normally
for—"

"Nothing about this situation is normal," Sani snapped.
"In any event, he will want explanations, and I intend to be
there." The mediator's lip curled slightly as she stepped closer
to the barred pen. "Besides, I don't think there's anything to
worry about."

Bier blinked. "Meaning?"

"Meaning that they won't find anything important . . .
nothing that can keep us from settling this system."

Bier nodded, but he did not share Sani's confidence. He had
been bothered by a vague sense of disquiet ever since Riitha
and Stocha had advanced their unusual theories. He recognized a soundness in their thinking Sani could not.

Without warning, Sani pulled open the cage door, grabbed
a squealing *bita* by the throat, and lifted it out of the pen. Panicked, the dangling creature thrashed and clawed at Sani's
hand, its long, sleek body curling and uncurling as it struggled
to free itself. As the mediator's fingers tightened around the
bristling gray fur of the *bita*'s neck, the animal's silver-tipped,
tapered ears flattened against the sides of its head. Slanted yel-

low eyes narrowed, the *bita* snapped viciously with its spiked teeth, drawing blood from Sani's hand.

A low, menacing rumble rose in the mediator's throat, and her nostrils distended as the tantalizing scent of fresh blood fed her urge to kill and feed. She turned to Bier, her golden eyes glazed with the primitive drive to satiate her hunger. "Out!"

Startled, Bier hesitated.

"Now!" Sani snarled, nostrils flaring and fangs bared.

Bier turned and left quickly.

He went directly to the agricultural sector. As usual after meeting with Sani, he needed peace and quiet to calm down and organize his thoughts. She always managed to upset the psychologist, and he cursed himself soundly as he sought the solace of his experimental garden in the high tiers.

Bier paused before pressing into the thick foliage of the carefully pruned *chutei* nut trees lining both sides of the narrow, central walkway. He inhaled deeply, and his finely tuned senses picked out the scents of moist soil, fertilizer, flower, and fern. A soothing calm settled over him as he scanned the immensity of the agricultural pod.

A fine mist hung over the open expanse above the floor, obscuring the ceiling and vine-covered walls, creating the illusion of endless spaciousness. Large overhead lamps dimmed from bright yellow to muted orange, making the transition from daylight to twilight. This lighting, like the pod's seemingly haphazard, natural arrangement, was meant to simulate conditions on Hasu-din as much as possible—despite the absence of gravity in the pod.

Bier smiled as he stooped to pull a mature *tohan* through the plastic that secured the nutrient mix and the plant to the floor. Shaking off loose particles of soil on the *tohan*, he rinsed it under a nearby sprayer. Then, munching the tangy root, the psychologist pushed through the tangle of branches toward the stepped pathway leading to the upper tiers. His private experimental garden, an indulgence allowed with a minimum of tol-

erance and total lack of understanding by Sani and Tahl, was
nestled among the thick, berry-producing *fahtiita* vines growing on the higher levels.

The bright blossoms and sweet fragrances of his private garden's flowers were comforting to Bier, but they could not completely soothe the wounds inflicted by Sani's biting tongue or
his own inability to acquire the immunity of indifference, especially since, without him, the mediator would still be a
lower-level administrator on an asteroid mining outpost. Sani
had arranged his meeting with the mediators in charge of the
scouting expeditions in exchange for his recommendation that
she be assigned to his ship if they agreed to the study.

Bier lay down on the soft, pungent soil under broad, green
leaves and took a deep breath. The council's approval of his
proposal had gained him some respect, yet, he realized, he
could not set aside the habits of a lifetime easily. He had chosen to adjust to the existing social order of *du-ahn* control for
the purpose of advancing his work long ago, convinced there
was no other alternative. Now, the inclination to acquiesce was
too ingrained to change. In the end, however, he would have
satisfaction. Latent *venja-ahn* were the key.

The existence of latents had only been discovered the previous century. Two members of a *du-ahn*-staffed fringe expedition had been found alive after five years of isolation in their
disabled ship. The other seven had succumbed to death-wish.
The survivors had experienced activation of the back-to-front
brain connection, allowing them to override the *du-ahn*'s tendency to die when faced with isolation or any analytically hopeless situation.

Conditions in normal society did not generate the pres-
sures necessary to force the flow of impulses in sensitive latents. When Bier had learned of the interstellar missions, he
had seized the opportunity to present his theories on the subject. A controlled experiment was the only way to accurately
test the reactions of latents under ambiguous and unprecedented circumstances. The dispatch of six scout ships to dif-

ferent stars had provided the Bier with the perfect laboratory. The latent *venja-ahn* aboard the *Dan tahlni* were the experiment. The other five scout ships, staffed only with *du-ahn*, were the control.

The council had quickly recognized that a sudden and significant increase of *venja-ahn* in the population would be troublesome, if not dangerous. Knowing what conditions might cause latent emergence could help avoid that potential problem. The Council of Mediators had readily agreed to conduct the study—so long as it in no way interfered with the real purpose of the scouting missions—and Bier had faced no trouble convincing them that Sani was the mediator best qualified for the *Dan tahlni* assignment. She had technical and administrative experience gained from running an asteroid mining colony, and she was prepared for a long-term association with *venja-ahn*.

At least, Bier thought, that's how she had felt about dealing with latents twenty-five years ago. Her enthusiasm for the project had waned over the years, and now that the latents seemed to be threatening the mission, she was afraid.

Bier smiled and closed his eyes.

CHAPTER SIX

Tahl awoke feeling as though he had not slept at all. His body was stiff and sore, and his thoughts were muddled by the deluge of usual data he had recently assimilated. He needed some solid information before he would be able to make any sense out of the data and ease his mind.

Glancing at the screen on the far wall, Tahl keyed the console by the webbing for the time. He had slept for ten hours. It was not enough, but it would have to do. Still watching the screen, he punched another sequence and scanned for Bier t'ahi.

The psychologist was the other *venja-ahn* aboard the ship. Unlike Riitha, who made the reckless decision to visit Chai-te Two without permission, Bier still demonstrated a high degree of reliability. He was more than willing to disregard intuition in deference to established fact.

The remote scan found Bier in one of the agricultural sections of the ship. Unstrapping from the sleeping net, Tahl slipped a short, cloth wrap around his waist and reached for his belt. He fastened the leather strap at his waist, then drew the underpiece between his legs and secured it to the same buckle in front. He glanced at the long, gold-furred robe that marked him as a *shtahn* and rejected it. He wanted Bier to be at ease when they spoke.

*   *   *   *   *

Tahl found Bier huddled among the rows of crop troughs that filled most of the agricultural sector. The psychologist was tinkering with a nutrient line feed-valve and muttering to himself. Tahl called out instead of trying to squeeze his bulk between the narrow rows.

"Tahl?" Bier looked up with surprise. "What brings you here?"

"I need some advice. Can we talk in the control lab?"

"Sure." Bier's nostrils flared slightly as he clipped his tools to his wide belt and inched toward the *shtahn jii.*

No words passed between them as Tahl led the way to the sector's computer control station.

With a weary sigh, the *shtahn* strapped himself into a chair and motioned for Bier to do the same. His concern for the renegade scientists was put aside for the moment as he pondered the apathetic listlessness he had sensed in several members of the crew he had encountered in the corridors.

"You don't look well, Tahl."

"I'm worried. Something's happening to the crew that I don't understand."

Bier's nose twitched. "Could you be more specific?"

"I just passed Bohn, Miche, Wehr . . . a few others on my way here. They all seem sluggish—withdrawn. Why?" Tahl shook his head as he glanced up. "What's wrong with them?"

The claws on Bier's hands extended and retracted repeatedly. He lowered his eyes for a moment, then boldly met Tahl's troubled gaze. "They're afraid."

"Of what?"

"Isolation. *Du-ahn* can't survive isolation."

"But we're not isolated," Tahl stated flatly.

"Not yet. We may be if Riitha's expedition discovers evidence of intelligence on that planet."

Tahl bristled at the note of accusation in Bier's tone but he chose not to challenge it. "*Du-ahn* would not project failure on the basis of unsupported theories. There's got to be more to it than that."

"There is." Bier hesitated, then spoke haltingly. "When you decided to let Riitha, Stocha, and Verda return to the ship, you sanctioned the expedition . . . which indicates a belief that there may be some validity to their theories."

"I don't believe they'll find anything proving there's an intelligence in this system," Tahl snarled. His ears flattened against the sides of his head.

"Then why didn't you abandon them?"

The *shtahn* paused. He wanted more information about the thought modes and the possibility that some *du-ahn* might actually be latent *venja-ahn*, but he was not prepared to reveal the nature of his suspicions, not even to a *venja-ahn* psychologist. Although Bier was the only *bey* aboard the *Dan tahlni* who would probably be able to cope with this startling revelation should it prove to be true, telling him might alter Bier's educated and unclouded perceptions on the matter. He evaded.

"I have decided to let them return, Bier, because I feel certain they will disprove their theories, removing all doubt. Given the present condition of the crew's mental and emotional state, disproving those theories is even more important now than it was before they left."

Bier's eyes narrowed. "Why is that?"

Tahl paused, then decided to edge closer to his true concerns. "The *du-ahn* aboard this ship are reacting as though those theories are fact. They should not be considering failure at this point. Everything we know about this system indicates that there is no intelligent species. Therefore, there is no reason to think the mission will fail."

"That's not entirely true," Bier said cautiously. "There are other facts—established facts that would evoke a *du-ahn's* sense of despair."

Tahl frowned slightly. Something about Bier's guarded manner made him uneasy. He studied the psychologist as he spoke. "Such as?"

"Riitha's little jaunt cost us valuable time and fuel that may be vital to the successful completion of this mission. The signal to Hasu-din must be dispatched on schedule." Bier's eyes flashed.

"We'll transmit within the designated time frame."

"But it will be close." Tensing, the psychologist leaned forward slightly. "If we don't send the message concerning the suitability of this star system for colonization within the established time limit, the message may not be received by the Hasu-din station. In that event, none of this—the wealth of this system's natural resources, the existence or non-existence of an indigenous intelligence—will matter at all. The council will assume we met with disaster, and they won't launch a colony ship toward an unknown situation. We could conceivably succeed, yet still fail. Concern among the *du-ahn* crew is not unfounded."

Tahl blinked. "Then . . . what I sense in the crew is the beginnings of death-wish?" He had never experienced the syndrome that caused a *du-ahn* to quietly and peacefully die when faced with a hopeless situation, nor had he been in close contact with anyone afflicted by it.

"Without hope, the *du-ahn* die." Bier sat back. "If there could be children—"

Cursing, Tahl unstrapped and drifted free. He dug his claws into the wall by the hatch, then turned and regarded Bier pointedly. "Have *venja-ahn* ever been missed by the early evaluation tests?"

Bier exhaled with a startled grunt. "No—never. Why?"

Tahl ignored the question. "The returning survey team will

be reporting to me after docking in a few hours. It'll be a private session, but I want you and Sani to attend."

"A private indictment? But they've endangered the future of the entire species—"

"No indictment," Tahl said sharply. "When I granted their return to the ship, I assumed full responsibility for their actions."

Bier scowled, but said nothing.

Tahl left abruptly. Until he knew what was causing *venja-ahn* behavior in proven *du-ahn*, he could not defend his decision concerning Riitha's unauthorized landing. No one else, including the psychologist, seemed aware of the deviations, and the crew had enough to worry about.

As the *shtahn* drifted through the ship's corridors, he reviewed the discussion with Bier. He could not argue with the psychologist's reasoning about *du-ahn* concern with the signal. They were far into the time frame and pushing the limit. A go-signal would be meaningless if it wasn't received. The Council of Mediators had no other way of knowing that the *Dan tahlni* scout ship had found a system richer in natural resources than the home star system, Chai-din.

The outermost planet in the new system was a mass of frozen gases and of no appreciable value, but the four giant gaseous planets between the asteroid belt and the ninth planet contained twice the original hydrogen-helium fuel potential of Chol and Winah, the two large gaseous planets in the farthest reaches of the Chai-din system. Chai-te's asteroid belt was rich in heavy metals and the light, life-support elements. If the Chai-te system was not inhabited by an indigenous intelligence, it was perfect for *bey* colonization.

Tahl truly did not believe the survey team would find any evidence of intelligent life on Chai-te Two, but the *Dan tahlni* was short on time and fuel. There was little margin for error.

Time and energy, the *shtahn* thought. Both commodities had been a problem since the ship had first entered the realm of the inner planets. He had elected not to close-scan the first

and third worlds. The first was too near the sun and too hot;
the third, though orbiting in the solar temperate zone, was
shrouded in a heat-insulating atmosphere of carbon dioxide
and water vapor. Not even the third planet's large satellite had
warranted a fuel expenditure. With a gravitational mass too
small to hold an atmosphere, the moon was arid and lifeless.

They had gone into orbit around the fourth world, but had
quickly dismissed the planet as a possible home for intelligent
life. Its thin atmosphere and barren surface showed no signs of
organic activity. Life did not exist there.

Digging his hand and foot claws into the foamed corridor
walls, Tahl stopped short. Riitha had accused him of assuming
all intelligences would respond and progress as the *ahsin bey*
had. He was also assuming life would be found in an organic,
chemical structure like the *bey's* own. Could alien life exist in a
state beyond their comprehension? Would such strangeness be
detectable or need the resources of the system? The Council of
Mediators had not addressed this contingency when they had
outlined the six scout missions' directives.

The council had not considered this, Tahl realized with a
jolt, because the possibility had never occurred to them.

A sudden chill sent tremors shooting through the *shtahn's*
limbs, weakening his grip. Panic rose like bile in his throat. He
closed his eyes and forced himself to relax as he struggled to anchor his thoughts.

A species that could not be detected did not exist—not for
his purposes. They were not protected by the intent of the Law.

With the unsettling question concerning a life form that
might exist beyond the mental and physical reach of the *bey*
answered to his satisfaction, Tahl turned his mind to other
matters.

Death-wish, the final submission, was already festering in
the minds of his people. The colony ship was their only hope of
survival. Without it, they had no purpose, no reason to continue. Sterilized, they could not even perpetuate social conti-
nuity themselves.

Sterilization had been necessary. The crew numbered only thirty, and each *bey* had to be free to function in any capacity at any location as required. Pregnancy resulted in a ten-year scent bond that bound a parenting couple together, irrevocably committing both male and female to the responsibility of raising their children, their *jehni*, to maturity. Separating a bonded pair was dangerous to their emotional and physical health. Experiments had proven that when a bonded couple was forced to be apart, their ability to function was severely hampered by their overwhelming need to reunite at any cost. The crews of the scout ships had been sterilized to prevent any interference with an individual's mobility.

The egg cells had been removed from every female. False ovulation and the hormonal intensification of sex-scent still caused imprint of the chosen male's olfactory receptors, provided he was not taking *muath*. The bonds, however, were temporary, lasting only twenty days of every five months.

When the *Dan tahlni* had left Hasu-din, only Sani and Bier had been older than twenty-five. The eighty year duration of the mission had made the choice of young personnel essential for success. Bier had already decided against children, and Sani had been sterilized according to custom after her appointment as a mediator. As far as Tahl knew, Riitha was the only one who had voiced any serious objections to the decision at the time. She had exhibited an unusual fondness toward children in general at an early age, a fondness that often surpassed that of the *jehni*'s natural parents. This quirk in her personality was viewed as a minor flaw and attributed to her *venja-ahn* status. The council had overlooked it and had chosen her for the mission anyway because of her extremely high ratings as a biologist and her enthusiasm for the project. Riitha had agreed to the operation because it was the only way the Council of Mediators would allow her to join the mission.

At twenty-two, Tahl suddenly realized, the honor and excitement of setting forth on an interstellar mission had negated the prospect of genetic death and a childless existence in his own mind. He had simply accepted the reasoning behind the decision. Now it made him angry. An alternative solution might have been found.

But it hadn't. They were sterile, and although sterility provided for the efficient running of the mission, it might also mean their doom.

Tahl's eyes snapped open, and he clutched for a grip on the wall. The mission had not failed yet. Death-wish born of desperation was premature. He knew that, but then he had more information than the rest of the crew. He could not explain to them why he had let Riitha return from her investigation of the planet's surface, but he could reassure them that the *Dan tahlni* had enough fuel to return to Chai-te Five, retrieve the interstellar transmitter they had left there, and send the signal to Hasu-din on schedule. A detailed report from Hane would quickly dispel the essence of death plaguing the mission.

Tahl kicked off the wall toward the flight deck with an almost savage determination as another question raised itself in the back of his mind.

Why had a time frame for the transmission even been necessary?

CHAPTER SEVEN

Tahl studied the three scientists seated opposite him on the conference oval. They all looked tired and unkempt after their ordeal, and Stocha and Verda reeked of apprehension. Even Riitha seemed unnaturally subdued.

"Does an intelligent species inhabit Chai-te Two, Riitha?" Tahl asked abruptly. He sensed Sani and Bier tense on either side of him.

A hint of defiance gleamed in Riitha's amber eyes as she met his gaze. "No." She paused, her shoulders sagging slightly. "There is no creature on the planet capable of reason, no animal that reacts by anything other than instinct."

Sani snorted, and Bier relaxed with a deep intake of breath.

Tahl checked his own relief as he looked at Stocha and Verda. They exchanged guarded glances, their expressions grim. He addressed Stocha.

"Is there any evidence that the asteroid impact may have been caused by artificial means?"

The geologist glanced again at Verda and Riitha, then shook

his head. "No."

Tahl nodded, feeling the tension ease out of his body.

"My examination of the overlying strata," Stocha continued, "dates the impact at approximately one hundred million years ago and coincides within a century or so of the abrupt appearance of life."

"Abrupt?" Tahl's nostrils distended with alarm. "What do you mean 'abrupt'?"

Stocha answered with sober calm, stating the facts simply and briefly and without undue embellishment. "A hundred million years ago this world was extremely hot. The surface temperature might have been as high as four hundred and fifty degrees, and the atmospheric pressure was perhaps a hundred times what it is now. There was no free oxygen. The conditions I've described could have been caused by the presence of a dense carbon dioxide atmosphere similar to that of the third planet. It also contained substantial amounts of sulfuric acid."

Bewildered, Tahl stared at the geologist.

"All this is geologically recorded in the strata." Stocha frowned uncertainly as his gaze shifted between Tahl, Sani, and Bier. "I'm stating fact."

"I'm not disputing that." Tahl studied the geologist closely, as perplexed by Stocha's reversion to the typical and uncomplicated reporting methods of a *du-ahn* as he was by the inexplicable emergence of *venja-ahn* theorizing a few days before. "I just don't understand how all this relates to the abrupt appearance of life."

With an acquiescing nod, Stocha elaborated. "There is a total absence of sedimentary deposits dating before the asteroid impact. There was no water on the planet for hundreds of millions of years. Then suddenly—there was. The first evidence of the presence of water corresponds with the abrupt appearance of an advanced, single-celled organism that was photosynthesizing and reproducing sexually."

"Can you prove this?" Tahl asked.

"I have fossil proof." As the geologist offered his undisputable evidence, his voice and demeanor became more relaxed. "The organism combined with a second cell rather than simply dividing into two identical cells. The combined cells exchanged and recombined genetic material, then split into four cells—none of which was identical to the parent cells. I believe the genetic diversity of this primitive creature made rapid diversification into various classes of life possible. Accelerated evolution was the ultimate result."

Tactfully, Tahl did not point out that Stocha's findings possibly disproved his theory that someone had planted the world with advanced life forms. "But that doesn't explain how life suddenly appeared on the surface of a planet with very hostile conditions and no water."

Stocha hesitated, his calm certainty wavering. "The, uh—point I'm trying to make is that life couldn't have started on the surface—not in the form it's taken."

"Then how did it get there?" Sani's voice held a hint of menace. "Are you deliberately trying to confuse the *shtahn jii*? If life couldn't evolve there, where did it come from?"

Intimidated by the mediator, Stocha began haltingly. "The, uh—atmosphere."

"Explain," Tahl said quietly, hoping to put Stocha at ease once again. No matter how unlikely or preposterous the geologist's thoughts on the subject turned out to be, Tahl had to be aware of them. An analysis of the question concerning the possible existence of latent *venja-ahn* required any and all information, even if that information seemed irrelevant. It was imperative to the *shtahn's* purposes that Stocha remain lucid and free to express himself.

Composing himself, the geologist went on. "On Hasu-din, millions of years passed after primitive organisms first started photosynthesizing and giving off oxygen as a by-product before oxygen began to accumulate in the atmosphere. Verda and I have reason to believe the early atmosphere of this planet was converted to oxygen before oxygen began to affect certain chemical processes on the surface."

"What reasons?" Tahl prompted.

The aura of anxiety surrounding Stocha dissipated slightly as the focus of the discussion returned to scientific fact. "For one thing, there are large deposits of uraninite below the strata dating back to the sudden change. Uraninite can't accumulate in an oxygen atmosphere. It would be oxidized and dissolved first."

"And the ocean is rusting," Verda interjected.

"Rusting?" Tahl frowned as he looked at the mineralogist, then quickly changed his expression to one of open interest. He did not want to upset her, either.

However, unlike Stocha, Verda showed no signs of distress. She expanded on her statement succinctly and with the conviction of knowledge. "The ocean is red because the iron deposits are in the process of oxidizing. On ancient Hasu-din, the oxygen supplied by the first photosynthesizing organisms caused the iron beds in the oceans to oxidize—to rust. It was not until after the oxidation of those iron beds was complete that oxygen began to collect in the atmosphere."

"Which means?"

"Life must have originated in the atmosphere, not on the surface," Verda stated dispassionately.

The mineralogist remained unruffled as Tahl leaned forward, his total attention upon her. Everything about her—the steady rhythm of her breathing, her clear, unblinking gaze, her casual but respectful posture—exuded confidence and control. She was acting like a true *du-ahn* in every way. But then, Tahl remembered, Verda had never shown any outward signs of *venja-ahn* deviation. During the discussion preceding the three scientists' unauthorized journey to Chai-te Two, the mineralogist had refused to expound on her theories about the red ocean. Her decision to join Riitha and Stocha on their irresponsible mission was the only thing she had done that was out of character given her *du-ahn* status. The question about latent *venja-ahn* grew more complex in Tahl's mind.

Verda did not need to be prodded to explain. "Conversion

of carbon dioxide into oxygen and carbon by a photosynthesizing creature would eventually break down the original atmosphere, releasing the small measure of water vapor contained in it. The water vapor would then condense and fall to the surface, cooling the planet as a consequence. In time, the atmospheric organisms would adapt into species equipped to survive on the surface. Evolution would proceed from there—accelerated, but normal in every other respect by Hasu-dinian standards."

"But there are certain implications inherent in that which must not be overlooked." Riitha's ears flicked forward expectantly as her piercing gaze challenged Tahl to respond.

The *shtahn* watched her thoughtfully for a moment, his gaze shifting from her fiery eyes to the stubborn set of her delicate jaw. "Such as the possibility of the accelerated development of an intelligent species?"

"Yes!" Riitha gasped and clutched the webs encasing her, her eyes widening with surprise.

Tahl sat back slightly, confused by her strong reaction to his simple extrapolation of the facts presented by Stocha and Verda. He frowned, feeling suddenly uneasy as Sani and Bier both turned to stare at him. They were obviously alarmed, but before Tahl could determine the cause, he was overpowered by the pungent fragrances from Riitha. Although it was not sex-scent, the elusive odor had a distinctly provocative effect.

Shaking his head to still the blood pounding in his ears, Tahl forced his attention back to the matter at hand. Riitha, he decided on reflection, had obviously taken his observation of the possibility of a future intelligence as a sanction of her actions and support of her theories. He steeled himself to disappoint her.

Taking a deep breath, Tahl finished the thought Riitha's outburst had interrupted. "The development of intelligence is not a foregone conclusion."

The sparkle of excitement that had briefly brightened Riitha's countenance vanished as quickly as it had appeared. She tensed defensively. "Nor is it impossible. We don't know that it won't evolve."

"We don't know that it will, either."

A puzzled frown passed over Riitha's face. She cocked her head and looked at Tahl quizzically. "What if an intelligent species did evolve in fifty million years?"

Tahl shrugged.

"This discussion is not relevant," Sani snapped.

"But it is, Mediator!" Riitha glared at Sani. "What if some alien species had come into the Chai-din system with the intent to colonize fifty million years ago when our ancestors were eating insects and living in trees?"

Sani scowled.

Tahl stared at Riitha.

Wild-eyed, the biologist scanned the room. "Are you all blind? Don't you understand what would have happened to us if someone had exploited our outer planets and asteroids millennia before we achieved intelligence? We would not have been able to expand throughout our star system without those resources. We would not be trying to colonize other star systems now!"

"It didn't happen," Sani countered.

"That's not the point. It could have!" Riitha hissed with frustration.

Tahl was only vaguely aware of the uneasy silence that suddenly prevailed as all eyes turned toward him. A hand touched him with tentative gentleness. Bier spoke his name softly, but Tahl did not answer. Riitha's argument with Sani had plunged him into a daze of chaotic disorientation. Exhausted and burdened with worry, he could not stabilize.

"Tahl?"

The *shtahn* listened to the sound of Bier's voice, but his gaze focused on Riitha's face. She was staring at him, her large eyes narrowed with shock and worry. His mind reached for her.

Bier's claws bit into his arm. "Tahl—"

"Yes . . ." Tahl's voice was barely audible. He could not

move yet.

"None of this talk of future intelligence is relevant under the Law. You must erase it from your mind. It need not concern you," the psychologist insisted softly.

Tahl winced as a sharp, fleeting pain knifed through his head. "Can't—erase."

"Listen, Tahl!" Bier sounded frantic. "Listen. If an intelligence should evolve on this world, it will never leave it—not even if it gains a high level of technology."

The *shtahn* turned his head slowly to look at the psychologist. "Why not?"

"There are no moons."

Tahl nodded as his mind latched onto Bier's words for support. The presence of the asteroid moons in close orbit around Hasu-din had made moving into space a natural extension of the *ahsin-bey*'s expansion across the entire surface of the planet. From bases built on Chol-motte and Ni-motte, the *bey* had gained easy access to their planetoid satellite, Ni-hasu. Utilization of the large moon's mineral wealth had provided the industrial foundation necessary for their subsequent colonization of the whole Chai-din star system.

Speaking quietly and calmly in spite of the urgency that tightened the muscles of his face, Bier pressed the issue. "The absence of a close target would hinder development of a space-oriented society. Anything beyond a communication and observation satellite system in planetary orbit would not be feasible. With no large moon to mine, space industry would never begin. Expansion would be out of the question."

Blinking, Tahl drew another deep breath and looked at Riitha. He had not imagined the concern etched on her face. Her rigid body went limp with relief when he spoke.

"The life forms on Chai-te Two—are they at all similar to those on Hasu-din?"

Riitha hesitated. "Yes."

"How similar?"

"Except for the differing amino acids that form the protein

chains in the organisms on Chai-te Two, life there is remarkably similar to life on Hasu-din."

Bier's hand was still around Tahl's arm. His grip tightened. "You need rest, Tahl. None of this information is necessary—"

The *shtahn* wrenched his arm free with a warning snarl. He would not tolerate any interference with his efforts to gather data. A momentary lapse due to physical stress had not impaired his judgment, and he resented Bier's presumptuous counsel.

"I'll decide what information is necessary." Tahl saw the helpless glance the psychologist cast toward Sani, but dismissed it as he turned back to Riitha, who was watching him with unmasked curiosity and a hint of apprehension. "Why 'remarkably'?"

Again Riitha paused as though afraid to speak.

"Given similar conditions, wouldn't you expect life to evolve along similar lines?" Tahl asked.

"Not necessarily." Sniffing uncertainly, Riitha spoke slowly and methodically in a determined effort to impress Tahl with the importance of her evaluations. "Conditions on the two worlds were not at all similar. Life on Hasu-din began in the oceans, on a planet with an atmosphere of methane, ammonia, nitrogen, and traces of carbon dioxide. Life on Chai-te Two seems to have started in a carbon dioxide atmosphere containing water vapor and sulfuric acid."

Tahl winced as another sharp pain flared inside his skull, then subsided to a dull throb. Concerned but confident that the pain was just another symptom of the physical punishment he had been inflicting on himself, Tahl ignored it. Riitha's comments had raised questions that could not wait to be answered.

"*Seems* to have started?" Tahl asked the biologist cautiously. "Do you doubt that life could begin under those circumstances?"

"No." Riitha did not take her eyes off the *shtahn* as she explained. "Organic molecules similar to those in Hasu-din's primordial oceans are carried through space on stony meteors. With Chai-te Two's original atmosphere, life might have been generated, but—"

"Go on." Expecting the familiar stubbornness and defiance Riitha was prone to exhibit whenever he questioned her, Tahl was surprised when she answered quietly and simply.

"I think the final results would be dramatically different than what we've found here."

A new uneasiness affected Tahl as he found himself forced to prod the biologist for more information. "Is there something else that might account for the similarities between these life forms and ours, then?"

Riitha shook her head. "No." Sighing, she lowered her gaze. The soft curve of her mouth tightened.

Snorting with irritation and impatience, Tahl paused to consider her sudden reticence. Never before had Riitha refused to disclose a theory or opinion. She offered them whether he wanted them or not.

As Tahl was about to insist that she qualify her curt answer, he felt a tingling sensation at the base of his skull. Almost simultaneously, the remote locator about his neck flashed in emergency blue. Tahl quickly donned an audio module and placed his thumbs on the remote-connect plate on the terminal before him. The console verified his identity and completed the connection.

"This is Tahl d'jehn."

"I think you'd better get up to the flight deck, Tahl," Hane said in a strained voice. "We've established contact with what appears to be an alien spacecraft."

CHAPTER EIGHT

Riitha watched Tahl with mounting fascination and fear as he listened to the audio message only he could hear. His body tensed suddenly, and she felt her heartbeat quicken. She did not need a medical degree to see that fatigue and the extreme stress of their present circumstances were affecting Tahl physically. The sheen of his silver-black long-fur had dulled, and his face was lined with tension. My fault, she thought, then quickly checked herself. She had only been doing her job. The limitations of *du-ahn* understanding were to blame.

A weary sigh escaped Riitha as once again she resigned herself to the immutable fact that Tahl was *du-ahn*. For a brief moment during her interrogation, Riitha had thought she had seen the spark of something more. Now, she realized, it was only so much wishful thinking on her part. Tahl would never share the feeling she had for him, would never know that bonding could mean more than mating for the purpose of procreation and the raising of *jehni*. A great sadness settled over Riitha. She was a prisoner of her own understanding and desires, and she wondered why she could not stop hoping for the impossible.

Because nothing is impossible, the biologist thought ruefully. Almost nothing. . . .

Her reflection was interrupted as Tahl tore the audio-module from his head and freed himself from his web. As he drifted away from the oval conference table, he evasively addressed the unspoken question on the faces of those seated around it. A slight tremor infected his voice, and his gaze, faraway and troubled, denied their presence.

Riitha frowned, feeling a mixture of curiosity and anxiety as she studied this shift in Tahl's normally calm and unshakable demeanor.

"This meeting is adjourned," Tahl said. "I'll . . . reconvene the discussion later." He turned and pushed off toward the hatch, dismissing them without another word or thought.

"What's going on, Tahl?" Sani demanded as she, too, began to unstrap.

Bier placed a restraining hand on the mediator's arm, provoking a snarl and a warning glance from her, but Sani gave up her efforts to pursue Tahl. Settling back in her web, she stared at the hatch and growled between clenched teeth.

Disturbed, Riitha glanced at Stocha and Verda. Verda's eyes were glazed, her stare vacant, and her body was shaking. Stocha returned the biologist's worried look.

"I'm going after him," Riitha said.

Stocha nodded. Unstrapping, he grabbed Riitha's hand and pulled her to the hatch and into the corridor. Tahl was already halfway to the lift leading to the flight deck, moving on all fours at a furious pace along the foamed wall. Riitha opened her mouth to call out to him, but Stocha silenced her with a gentle hand over her muzzle and a warning shake of his head.

Riitha's ears flicked back and forth uncertainly as she regarded Stocha's solemn face, suddenly understanding the need for caution. Something unusual was happening to Tahl, something dangerous and perhaps even fatal. During the past hour, his concentration had slipped twice, he had lost his temper, and now he was running through the ship like a crazed animal. They dared not risk disrupting the tenuous balance of his mind. They followed silently, at a distance.

When Tahl reached the lift shaft, he righted himself and grabbed a mechanized handhold. Riitha caught a glimpse of his face as he pressed a release button and shot upward, out of sight. His furrowed brow and disheveled fur exaggerated the wild image instilled by his flight. His eyes were clear, though, and his expression grim, but sane. Riitha breathed easier as she moved into the shaft behind Stocha, almost colliding with the med-prime, Norii f'ach, as she sped past them upward through the lift shaft. Pulses racing, Stocha and Riitha held on and followed.

Reaching the upper level an instant after Norii, Stocha and Riitha fell into step beside her as she headed for the flight deck.

"Do you have any idea what's going on up here?" Stocha asked.

The med-prime, wide-eyed and breathless, clutched her med-kit against her breast. "No. Hane called a few minutes ago and told me to bring some tranquilizers right away."

Digging into the foam, Stocha urged the two females to move faster.

Suddenly the loud shriek of an alarm siren reverberated through the corridor. Blue lights flashed brilliantly, flooding the passageway with an eerie, pulsating glow. Exchanging frantic glances, Riitha, Stocha, and Norii ran.

Chaos had taken control of the flight deck.

As they stepped through the hatch, all their senses were attacked by the bizarre scene before them. Hysterical cries and angry shouts pounded in their ears. Wrestling bodies seemed to move in slow motion in the blue, strobing glare of the emergency lights. The stench of fear and rage was thick and ominous.

Stunned, Riitha paused to stare. Hane was grappling with

the computer technician, Nian d'char, at the central console, desperately trying to reach the controls. Nian's yellow fangs were bared as she fought to keep Hane away. Bohn n'til, pilot and equipment trouble-shooter, was seated before the large view-screen set into the far wall, apparently talking to himself. Tahl was trying to hold onto Tena s'uch, the computer tech who had been searching the recorded scans for Hane's elusive point of light. The gold-colored female clawed at the *shtahn's* confining arms, then screamed as her body contorted with violent convulsions.

The sound of the alarm ended abruptly, and the lights immediately returned to normal as Hane finally managed to evade Nian and hit the right key on the console. Nian screeched and began raking Hane's back with her claws. The engineer turned suddenly, striking her with his fist and throwing her off-balance. Nian reeled backward toward Stocha. Reacting instantly, the geologist wrapped his powerful arms around her and glanced at Norii.

"I think we could use a shot of that tranquilizer here," Stocha said breathlessly.

Norii, like Riitha, had been watching the strange drama in shocked, open-mouthed astonishment. She hesitated, collecting her wits, then drew the injection gun from her bag and touched it to Nian's arm. The computer tech's struggling gray body went limp.

Tahl called out from the far side of the room, shouting to be heard above Tena's screams. "Norii! Over here!" Still struggling to keep Tena's twisting body pressed against him, the *shtahn* was unable to control his drift in the null-gravity. The entwined pair hovered in midair a meter above the foam flooring.

Riitha and Norii rushed to help Tahl. While the med-prime armed the injection gun for another dosage of tranquilizer, Riitha dug into the floor with her claws, then grabbed Tahl's leg with her hands to pull him and his captive downward. As soon as Tena's arm was within reach, Norii injected the tranquilizer. The computer tech's shrieks ceased the moment the

drug hit her bloodstream. Tahl released the incapacitated female with a heavy sigh and leaned against Riitha for support.
His shoulder was bleeding where Tena had bitten him.

"Tahl!" Riitha placed her hand near the wound. "You're
hurt."

The *shtahn* glanced with mild surprise at the trickle of blood
staining his fur. "Nothing to worry about." He squeezed Riitha's hand as he moved past her toward the central console.
"Put me on ship-wide call, Hane."

"Right." The engineer keyed the sequence and moved back
as Tahl hastened to still the panic he knew must be infecting
the ship. "The alarm was triggered accidentally." His voice was
even and calm, its tone of authority soothing. Even Riitha felt
herself relax as he spoke. "There is no emergency. The ship is
in no danger."

Next, Tahl allowed incoming calls through. Several minutes
passed as he spoke to everyone aboard, calming their fears and
assuring them the incident was nothing more than a minor and
unintentional inconvenience. Although Riitha sensed that the
callers were not all completely convinced—Sani especially—
total panic was averted. She was impressed. To her knowledge,
nothing even remotely similar to the chaotic scene she had just
witnessed had ever happened aboard a ship before. Or anywhere else for that matter, she thought. Faced with an unprecedented and dangerous crisis, Tahl d'jehn had acted swiftly
and surely, with an inner strength Riitha had not known existed. Or perhaps she had, at least intuitively.

Even now that the immediate problem was under control,
Tahl did not relent, but turned his attention back to the still
conscious, but dazed members of the crew. "What exactly
happened here, Hane?"

The engineer shrugged. "They just went berserk. I don't
think they realized what we were tracking until just after I
talked to you."

"Maybe you should get Bier up here, Tahl," Norii suggested.

"No." The *shtahn jii* shook his head adamantly.

"But why not?" Norii asked, genuinely puzzled. "He's a psychologist. He might know—"

"No!" Tahl snapped.

Riitha looked at the *shtahn* sharply, catching his eye.

Tahl quickly averted his gaze and drew a deep breath as he glanced back at Norii. "I just . . ." He paused. When he spoke again his voice had taken on a definitive tone of command. "Bier is not to know anything about this right now. Nothing. Do you understand?"

Norii shrank back, but nodded.

Tahl's gaze swept over the rest of them. "No one outside this room is to know what happened here."

Riitha smiled as the *shtahn jii* looked at her pointedly, as though he expected an argument. "Of course, Tahl, but you must have a reason." She could not resist an opportunity to prod him. Habit, she supposed.

Tahl remained steadfast and unruffled. "None that I can disclose." He held the biologist's gaze a moment longer, until she raised a questioning eyebrow, then turned away with a thoughtful frown.

Riitha's heart fluttered at his discomfort. Did he have a good reason or not? The many questions being raised in her mind about Tahl's odd behavior were shuffled aside as he turned back to Hane.

"What are we tracking?" Tahl asked.

Everyone gave the engineer their undivided attention. Everyone except Bohn. As he had through the entire crisis, the equipment expert, unmoving and muttering soundlessly, continued to stare at the growing image in the view-screen.

CHAPTER NINE

Bier moved slowly through the corridors toward Sani's quarters, his heart still palpitating with the remnants of the adrenaline rush caused by the "danger" lights and alarms. Events of the past hour had left him feeling tired and worn.

The expedition report session had adjourned in confusion after Tahl's hasty and unexplained departure. Sani had assaulted him with questions he could not answer. Then, when the alarms went off, Verda had become hysterical. Bier had not been able to calm her until after Tahl's voice over the intercom assured everyone that the ship was in no danger. The mineralogist had lapsed into a walking state of shock. Hoping to put Sani off for a while, Bier had insisted on taking Verda back to her own quarters. The mediator, however, was not easily dissuaded. She had ordered him to join her immediately after Verda was settled. Now, the psychologist approached the mediator's cubicle with a distinct sense of trepidation.

The field-barrier into Sani's quarters disengaged to let Bier pass through. Sani was strapped into a web by her wall terminal with an audio-module on her head. Her grim and angry expression sent a shiver of cold fear down the psychologist's spine. The mediator would be quick to blame him if the unpredictability of the latent *venja-ahn* on board caused something to go wrong with the mission.

Removing the audio-module and putting it aside, Sani looked at Bier with cold, hostile eyes. "Two com-techs from the flight deck are in the infirmary under sedation."

Bier frowned thoughtfully, but said nothing.

"And yet, Tahl d'jehn still insists that the alarms were triggered by accident." Sani keyed the field-barrier to lock and motioned for Bier to use the recliner on the far wall. "Do you believe him?"

"I have no reason not to believe him," the psychologist said cautiously as he strapped himself into the chair. His muscles ached with tension. "Why would Tahl say it was an accident if it wasn't?"

"Why, indeed." Sani leaned forward and fixed Bier with a calculating stare, a look that accused, challenged, and warned the psychologist that she would tolerate nothing short of total cooperation. "Why did Tahl leave so suddenly? What was that message about? Don't you think it's strange that the alarm went off just a few minutes later?"

"All right." Bier sighed and gave in to the inescapable confrontation. "It is strange, but I don't think it's too serious. Whatever happened on the flight deck, Tahl handled it. He's not incompetent."

"No, but he's not himself, either." Sani paused in agitation and distress. "What happened to him during Riitha's outburst?"

"I'm not sure," Bier answered honestly. "He's tired—weaker than normal."

"What happened to Tahl was more than a response to physical weakness. Riitha's words—" The mediator's facial features twisted in thought. "Tahl was stricken by what she was saying . . . as though what she said made sense to him. Is he emerging, too?"

Bier nodded wearily. "I think so."

Sani hissed through her teeth. "I sponsored your experiment to study latent *venja-ahn*, Bier. If this mission fails because of it, I'll—"

"You'll die—just like the rest of the *du-ahn* analytics aboard this ship. You knew the risks when you agreed to help me present my proposal to the council's Interstellar Expansion Board, Sani. At the time, you thought the risk was worth the chance to become high mediator of an entire star system."

"But to lose it because of *venja-ahn* speculation when I'm so close—" A low growl sounded deep in Sani's throat.

"We haven't failed, yet."

Sani began to knead her claws nervously. She spoke in the clipped, rapid monotone indicative of a *du-ahn* under stress, her eyes downcast and glazed with bitterness. "Latent *venja-ahn* do emerge under extreme duress, and when they emerge, they are subject to some kind of uncontrolled compulsion to theorize. Emergence drives them insane." She looked up suddenly. "They will destroy us!"

"Without them, you wouldn't be here!" Bier stiffened, then sighed again. He understood Sani's fear. Failure of the mission meant death. If they succeeded in colonizing the new system, Sani would govern a star.

The mediator calmed herself by closing her eyes. "No, I wouldn't be here—and the *ahsin bey* wouldn't be faced with the loss of this system, either. The latents aren't reacting the way you said they would."

"Yes, they are. The mission is under pressure, and their modes are beginning to shift."

"But you assured me that emerging latents tempered by years of analytic patterns and training would be able to discern the facts in obscure circumstances. You did not indicate that they would manipulate facts against us."

"They haven't drawn any conclusions outside the parameters of established fact. Only Riitha's mind is develop—" Bier

decided against discussing the biologist any further, and
quickly diverted the conversation. "The crew simply supplies
data. Tahl makes the decisions."

"Tahl." Sani's upper lip curled into a snarl. "How can we
trust the decisions of an intuitive *shtahn*?"

Bier paused, then repeated the theory the mediator had
refused to believe for the past twenty-five years. "When the
expansive *shtahn* studies are finished, I'm sure the council will
find that all sleep-analytics are *venja-ahn* latents."

"I'm not convinced. The mode-tests were modified for
latent-scan long ago. If all *shtahn* are intuitive, some would
have been detected. None have—except Tahl d'jhen."

"Tahl is highly sensitive," Bier explained patiently. "As for
the others, the intricate biological properties in the brain that
give them *shtahn* abilities probably also conceal the evidence
of their *venja-ahn* tendencies. The main thing is that the
Council of Mediators has always trusted the sleep-analytics,
and the *shtahn* have never given faulty advice. Nothing will
change if they are found to be latent *venja-ahn* instead of absolute *du-ahn*."

Sani eyed him skeptically. "Let's assume you're right.
There's one factor you've overlooked."

"What's that?"

"The *shtahn* the council has always consulted had *dormant*
venja-ahn modes. We've never relied on the advice of a *shtahn*
whose intuitive tendencies have emerged."

Bier frowned.

"Worse," Sani continued, "these other *shtahn* are not subjected to an overdose of abstract speculation. We have a situation aboard the *Dan tahlni* in which a *venja-ahn*-sensitive
shtahn jii may be forced to function in the midst of a population that is half *venja-ahn*. Even if all the latents aboard
don't emerge, the percentage of *venja-ahn* will still be much
higher than normal. How do you think that will effect Tahl's
reasoning?"

Bier's frown deepened as he considered the potential ramifications posed by Sani's question.

A shrill note of anxiety slipped into the mediator's tone as she continued to voice the doubts being raised in her mind. "He had a distinct reaction to Riitha's suggestion that an intelligent species might evolve on this world some day. What if Tahl considers that during the decision trance and decides to abort the launch of the colony ship because of it?"

"He can't." Bier spoke with absolute certainty.

"Why not?"

The psychologist looked Sani hard in the eye. "During the trance, Tahl's mind automatically eliminates anything that's not proven fact. He has no conscious control over it."

"Are you certain activation of the back-to-front brain connection won't affect the trance process, Bier?"

"No, I'm not." Ripping open the straps of the recliner, the psychologist drifted to the wall. Clawing in, he began to pace.

Tahl was the first of his kind. There was no previous data on the effects of back-brain activation in a *shtahn*. Tahl might give serious thought to the evolution of a future intelligence on Chai-te Two and the effects of *bey* colonization on its development. The theory Bier had used to draw Tahl out of his shocked daze during the survey session might off-set Riitha's extrapolation, but he couldn't be sure.

The psychologist anchored, momentarily immobilized by a great despair settling within him. The *Dan tahlni* mission had to succeed. More was at stake than Sani's mediator status or the acceptance of his thesis and his personal rise in society. Beyond adding territory and natural resources to the expanding realm of the *ahsin bey*, the Chai-te star system was the *bey*'s only chance to continue evolving.

Ahsin bey evolution had been disrupted ages past by chance environmental and social conditions that favored the *du-ahn* mentality and delayed transition to the higher plane of *venja-ahn*. After thousands of years, complete transition of the entire species was impossible. Most of the population was trapped in the *du-ahn* mode, which imprisoned the reasoning process in the arena of known fact. Only five percent of the *bey* were born aware of their intuitive ability. Another thirty percent were latent. They were the foundation upon which a higher order of *ahsin bey* could be built, but they had to escape *du-ahn* restraints. Such a development couldn't be fostered on the *bey*'s home world, however. They needed the freedom of the stars to establish a viable *venja-ahn* population.

If, Bier thought as he turned back to Sani, Tahl showed any inclination of losing control of his *shtahn* thought processes, the psychologist would have to eliminate the *shtahn jii* himself. The future of the *ahsin bey* was more important than the life of one rogue *shtahn*, more important than his own personal pride or the ambitions of a single mediator. Still, Sani was a necessary nuisance in the plan Bier had set in motion twenty-five years before, and she had to be appeased.

"Stocha doesn't seem to suspect that he's been shifting into *venja-ahn* thought patterns," Bier said calmly. "I don't think Verda does, either. They're just having different subconscious reactions."

Sani looked at him curiously. "And when they do? How will people who have lived as *du-ahn* all their lives accept a sudden lowering of their status?"

Bier bristled slightly at the insult. *Venja-ahn* had ceased to threaten social stability as their numbers had decreased and civilization had matured. Yet the stigma of being a disruptive element had survived, making *venja-ahn* social exiles who were, at best, tolerated by the *du-ahn* majority.

Ignoring the slur, Bier continued his efforts to placate the worried mediator. "I think it will depend on the individual, Sani. We can expect anything from immediate acceptance to shock and trauma-induced death-wish."

"Death-wish? *Venja-ahn* are not capable of death-wish."

"Until the transition is total, latents would still be subject to *du-ahn* traits. Shock could cause death-wish."

Sani nodded. "Yes, that makes sense. However, I do not think any of them will embrace their new status gladly. Immediate acceptance is quite unlikely."

Bier did not bother to argue. Being *du-ahn*, Sani did not have the smallest inkling of how confined she was by her limited thought processes. The psychologist felt confident that at least a few of the latents would quickly come to terms with their new, enlightened status once they recognized it, especially if the transition was gradual and unhampered by an excessive amount of *du-ahn* interference or persecution. Since only he and Sani knew about the existence of latent *venja-ahn*, those conditions were entirely possible. At the moment, Stocha was the most likely candidate for total emergence without any debilitating effects. The geologist was exhibiting pronounced symptoms of *venja-ahn* thought, yet he was still functioning normally.

"Tahl is the main problem," Sani noted coldly. "Do you think he knows what's happening to him?"

"I don't think so, although he may suspect emergence in the others."

"And if he finds out that he's *venja-ahn*? What then?"

Bier's gaze was direct, his tone matter-of-fact as he answered. "His physical condition seems to be deteriorating steadily, and he's under extreme pressure because of the impending decision concerning the colony ship. I think in his case, we can expect the worst—burn-out or death."

Sani held his gaze with chilling calm. "And if Tahl is incapacitated or dies?"

"Then the decision for or against colonization of this star system falls to you, Mediator."

Her eyes lifeless, her expression unreadable, Sani noted, "This mission must not fail because of unsubstantiated data and *venja-ahn* assumption, Bier."

The psychologist frowned. His reputation, his tenuous position in *bey* society, depended upon the successful conclusion of his experiment. If the mission failed, the colony ship would never be sent and Bier would not be afforded the opportunity to present his findings in person. The council had, of course, set up a contingency plan for Bier to transmit his findings if the *Dan tahlni* could not report the system inhabitable, but the psychologist's desire to prove himself worthy to the *du-ahn* majority demanded he do everything in his power to make that back-up plan unnecessary.

"I'll make certain that we don't fail," Bier said at last.

CHAPTER TEN

Tahl applied thrusters integrated into the backpack of his pressure suit and moved to a position above the shuttle docking bay. He watched in awe as Hane and Stocha secured the derelict spacecraft the *Dan tahlni*'s scans had been tracking for the past few hours. It began to move toward the ship on Hane's signal to a technician inside the cargo control room. Tahl shifted toward the forward section of the *bey* ship, then down again.

Hane's voice came over Tahl's helmet receiver. "It's old."

"How old?"

A heavy sigh punctuated the engineer's hushed words. "That's hard to say. A thousand years. A million . . . We'll know soon."

Or a hundred million? Tahl studied the battered alien machine as it passed by him. Too small for a ship, it appeared to be some sort of satellite or probe. The main body was pocked and scarred from years of micro-meteoroid bombardment. Broken parts hung at twisted angles, and loose wires and holes indicated that pieces were missing. Yet, there was a delicacy of design, obvious even in the craft's deteriorated condition.

As the aft section moved through the direct beam of the hatch floodlights, Tahl saw the markings. He committed the lines to memory, imprinting the signature forever on his mind.

The curving lines etched deep into the hull were the only visible symbols, the mark of an alien hand. If there had been others, they had been erased long ago by space debris.

Very old, Tahl thought as the machine started to disappear into the dock.

The decision to break orbit to pick up the artifact had been fuel expensive. More time table adjustments would have to be made to compensate. A computer check had projected that the *Dan tahlni* would have enough fuel left to make it back to Chai-te Five on time, with barely enough in reserve to put the small, emergency hydrogen-separation apparatus into operation in the planet's atmosphere. If the mission had not been so pressed for time, they could have set up and used the small fuel plant before heading into the inner planets, allowing themselves ample fuel for their explorations. But time is the one commodity the mission doesn't have in excess, Tahl thought as he silently cursed the transmission schedule. There was no longer any margin for error. The remainder of the mission had to progress with perfect precision.

Suddenly aware that his breathing had become uneven and shallow, Tahl took a moment to establish a safer, steady rhythm. He was exhausted and, he had to admit, more than a little unnerved by the tightness of the new schedule. Still, he had had no choice but to recover the alien machine. Although it was ancient and a derelict, the small spacecraft had been built and launched by someone. He had to know when, why, and by whom before he could make a decision that satisfied the edicts of the Law.

Tahl closed his eyes, trying to absorb the impact of the *bey's* first contact with another intelligence. They were no longer unique in the universe. There were others in space who were builders of machines and ships. Were they also masters of worlds and suns? Opening his eyes, Tahl watched the alien artifact disappear into the cargo bay and wondered.

With the alien spacecraft secured, Hane and Stocha moved toward the ship. Stocha followed the machine through the hatch without even a glance in Tahl's direction. Hane braked and hovered beside the *shtahn jii.*

Tahl did not acknowledge the engineer immediately. His gaze traveled the length of the ship that had become his world. The curves and angles of the superstructure stretched before him, a stunning, steel monument that marked the *bey's* first, bold attempt to reach the stars. Yet, though he felt dwarfed by the magnificence of the great ship, Tahl realized that the *Dan tahlni*, too, was but a micro-speck in the vastness of the alien dark it had breached, a ship whose ultimate fate might be no different than that of the ancient, alien probe. He shuddered, resisting the mental picture of a broken and lifeless *Dan tahlni* forever adrift and lost.

"Tahl?" Hane said softly.

The *shtahn* glanced at the engineer, who was also staring at the ship. Through Hane's faceplate, Tahl could see that the engineer's eyes were oddly glazed. "What is it?"

"What will become of us if the colony doesn't launch?"

Looking past Hane, Tahl studied the stars and wondered. If the colony was summoned, the main body of the *Dan tahlni* and the huge fuel tanks would be converted into a permanent spin-station in the asteroid belt. Mining and processing operations would begin in the atmosphere of Chai-te Five. Preparations for the colony's arrival would diminish the terrors of their lengthy isolation.

If he decided against colonization, death would rule.

Tahl winced, unwilling to accept death as the only alternative. "If we must transmit an abort signal . . ." His next thought popped into his head from out of nowhere. A subtle excitement seized him as he turned back to Hane. "We have everything we need to build the hydrogen-separation plant. So—we'll build it."

The engineer frowned. "Why?"

"We'll need fuel to get back to Hasu-din."

"Get back? But . . . the council made no provisions for a return trip. The ship—" Hane's eyes narrowed in thought. "The ship wasn't designed to withstand another interstellar acceleration. The high g-force needed to achieve fifty-percent light speed—"

Tahl interrupted. "We can take our time getting up to speed going back. We won't be on the council's schedule. You're the engineer. What do you think? Can the *Dan tahlni* make it back?"

Hane nodded slowly. "Maybe."

"Then we'll try. If it becomes necessary." Tahl was aware of the engineer's gaze following his as he looked toward the open cargo bay.

"We'd be old by the time we got there," Hane said absently.

Those that survived, Tahl added silently. A sadness washed over the *shtahn* as he thought that he had never been imprinted or known the pleasure of being oblivious to a female's pain during mating. He had never been chosen by Riitha . . .

"But," Hane said, "I guess that would be better than waiting around here to die."

"Much better," Tahl agreed, casting a curious glance at the engineer. A sharp pain shot through the top of his head without warning and passed almost as quickly. Stunned and breathless, Tahl applied thrust and headed into the ship.

* * * * *

On his way back to quarters after the alien craft had been secured, Tahl stumbled. Surprised, he swayed at an awkward angle in the narrow corridor, the claws of one foot tangled in the floor. Securing a hold on one wall, he pushed himself upright. It was a simple maneuver, requiring a minimum of effort, but it took all his strength.

He glanced down. The worn foam had begun to shred, and his claws seemed to be hopelessly snagged. He couldn't release himself. Clinging to the wall for support, the *shtahn* suddenly realized how tired he was. The weariness crept through him, and his head began to throb.

"Tahl?" Bier called from the end of the passageway.

A sickening sensation washed over the helpless *shtahn*. Tahl raked the wall, knowing he was going to black out.

Bier hurried to Tahl's side and put a hand out to steady him. The *shtahn*'s claws locked onto the wall.

"Easy. I've got you." Supporting Tahl with one hand, the psychologist pried his tangled claws free.

Tahl stared at Bier through a blinding fog, only mildly aware of the pain as his hand was pulled from the foam. He did not protest as Bier guided him down the corridor and through a field-barrier into a cube compartment. Failing to regain control of his body, the *shtahn* struggled to maintain his mental faculties. "Where?"

"My quarters." Bier pulled him to the sleeping net and fastened him in securely.

Tahl tried to move his arms, but he was too weak. Through blurred vision, he saw Bier drift to a terminal and initiate a sequence, locking the entrance.

"I stumbled . . . can't think—" Tahl muttered. He had to concentrate to prevent being dragged into unconsciousness.

"Take it easy, Tahl. Relax."

Tahl closed his eyes and flexed the muscles in his arms and legs, testing the tone. He was only forty-seven, still young, but he had abused his body on the long voyage. He had not hibernated as often as he should have for the same reason he had not allowed himself to be bonded. His responsibilities as *shtahn jii* required constant awareness. Winter-sleep and total union with a female were luxuries he could not afford. Now he was paying for that self-discipline.

"Tahl!"

Bier's sharp command brought the *shtahn* to. He fought back the blur that threatened to obscure his thoughts. "What happened?"

"You're exhausted and on the verge of collapse. I'm going to call Hahr."

"No." Tahl tried to raise his head. A dull ache stopped him. As he surrendered to the pain and fell back, the dizziness passed. "I don't need a doctor, Bier. I just need some sleep."

"I really think—"

"I'm all right." The headache ebbed, and Tahl sighed with relief. "I just came in from outside. Not used to it after all these years . . ."

"Outside?" Bier propelled himself to the web net and grabbed an anchor cable. "Outside the ship?"

"Yes." A subtle scent of uneasiness invaded Tahl's nostrils.

"What were you doing outside the ship?"

Tahl hesitated, then decided that there was no reason not to tell Bier about the alien machine. The crew would know soon, and he might need advice to avert their predictable descent into death-wish despair.

"Hane found an alien spacecraft, a probe of some kind. I went out—" Tahl heard Bier's startled exhalation. The tang of fear wafted strongly. He opened his eyes and found his vision had cleared enough for him to see that fear darkened the psychologist's face. "It's ancient. A derelict."

"An alien derelict." Bier threw his head back and stared at the ceiling. Minutes passed while he composed himself. Tension strained his voice when he finally spoke. "How ancient?"

"Don't know. Thousands of years—millions . . ." Talking had become difficult. Tahl frowned, sensing the strange calm that seemed to settle around him. A potent odor of wariness filtered through the room. "It has to be tested."

"Why must it be tested?"

Bier's close scrutiny made Tahl flinch. He tried to shift positions, but the webs held him fast. "There are things I need to know—facts. I have to find out—"

"What? If it's ancient and derelict, what more do you need to know?"

"Somebody built it and put it into orbit around Chai-te Two. I have to find out who and—"

"No, you don't. There's no one there now." Bier spoke in a low, perfectly modulated tone. "There's no other evidence of technology in this system."

"We can't be sure of that," Tahl said haltingly. The dull ache began again in the back of his head. "We didn't close-scan all the inner planets."

"A space technology would not have escaped our sensors. Whoever built the probe is not here now. If they are not here now, you do not have to concern yourself with them."

Tahl shook his head as the pain began to intensify. "But they were here. They might be back."

"Might? You are the *shtahn jii*, Tahl. You have to consider the facts. The facts! The aliens are not here!"

"I don't know that, Bier. I—" Tahl cried aloud as an even sharper pain exploded in his skull.

"Tahl—" Bier hung his head. Then, the deep sorrow surrounding the psychologist was suddenly absorbed by the putrid sting of menace. His voice struck like an icy barb. "You must not consider things that *might be*!"

An overwhelming odor of danger flooded the room.

Alarmed, Tahl fumbled with the straps confining him.

"Might!" Snarling contemptuously, Bier grabbed the webs stretched across Tahl's chest and yanked the *shtahn* toward him. The psychologist's eyes blazed with lethal intent. "What manner of *shtahn* are you, Tahl? What kind of *shtahn* considers assumption and speculation?"

Tahl cringed. His eyes widened with fear and confusion as Bier released his hold and drew back on the anchor cable with a growl. Then, ignoring the mounting pain, Tahl renewed his struggle against the binding webs.

"You're tired and weak, Tahl. You've pushed yourself beyond the limits of your endurance. You're helpless, too weak to loosen those webs. But you fight them. Why? Why do you fight them?"

Tahl glared at Bier, his upper lip curled back savagely. Increased blood pressure in his brain released an enzyme that dissolved blockages on back-brain receptors. A second enzyme made immediate contact with the opened receptors. Triggered impulses stormed along the back-to-front brain connection and surged into the *shtahn*'s consciousness.

Tahl shook violently as his mind flung itself completely free of analytic restraints. The blood drained from his face as he ripped one arm out of the web. He lashed out at Bier, his claws extended.

With a grunt, the psychologist pushed off the cable and out of reach.

Tahl fought the straps, oblivious to the pain throbbing in his ears and shooting through his neck. The straps held.

"Give it up, Tahl!" Bier taunted, although there was a hint of fear in his voice. The primal blood-lust gleaming in the *shtahn*'s emerald eyes and the raging viciousness of bared fang and claw were more than the psychologist bargained for. Still, he had to push on with his test. "You're beaten. You can't get free!"

Tahl tore at the bonds, thrashing and clawing in mindless fury.

"You can't give up, can you, Tahl? You won't give up. You'll fight—just like *venja-ahn*. You are *venja-ahn*!"

Tahl's agonized roar filled the room before it was absorbed by the cushioned walls. In shock, he blacked out before the last mournful note was silenced.

CHAPTER ELEVEN

For a full standard day Tahl's mind maintained a precarious balance between hibernation and the conscious paths of the trance. His brain fought a desperate battle to sift through the deluge of stored information. Fact, assumption, and emotion twined as the bio-analytic trance mechanism wove a matrix of substance from the scattered bits of data.

Only a single dream managed to penetrate the curtain of blackness shielding Tahl's awareness of his emerging *venja-ahn* creative processes. In that dream, the *Dan tahlni*, an ever-present light speeding through the darkness, was unrelenting in its bold challenge of the alien probe. The *bey* ship rushed toward the derelict, unable to stop or to avoid being consumed by the flames that suddenly burst from the ancient, alien craft.

Not until Tahl's mind had established firm control of his emotional trauma did the protective barriers begin to disintegrate. The *shtahn* withdrew from the chasm of hibernation to a sub-trance level and sought a stabilizing reference.

His mind filled with a vision of great *bey* ships under construction in orbit around the planet Chol's largest moon, ships that would be fueled for their interstellar journeys from the gas giant's hydrogen-helium atmosphere. He remembered pre-mission conferences, the faces of the five other *shtahn jii*. An identity link.

Scan . . . locate . . . focus. . . .

The serene features of Zar f'sta's face became clear. Zar's was the only other mission to have already reached its objective, which was less than ten light years from the *bey*'s home star, Chai-din. If the planetary system of Zar's target star contained but a fraction of Chai-te's wealth, the laser signal summoning a colony ship was now two years in transit.

But if the system was poor in resources or inhabited by an intelligence, Zar and his crew were now dead of their own will.

Tahl felt a slight flutter of instability, but it passed quickly. Rising slowly from unconsciousness into full trance, he began to examine the images of the fire dream.

In his youth, while he was training for the mission, Tahl had heard older, experienced *shtahn jii* describe a sense of identity they had with the ships they commanded, an identity that was so strong, *bey* and machine seemed to be melded together as a single entity. Tahl had not understood that feeling then, but he did now. His destiny was irrevocably linked with the *Dan tahlni*, and in the dream he and the ship were one and the same. The fire, he felt certain, represented the dangerous unknowns that haunted the alien darkness the ship and he had dared to enter.

As the images began to make sense, Tahl recalled the dream he had experienced, and had forgotten, on the surface of Chai-te Two. There, he had felt desperation, and death-wish had touched him. Now, he was beyond the sanctuary of death—he was *venja-ahn*.

Tahl's subconscious accepted and incorporated the new

mode. In an unemotional state of trance he was able to calmly explore the effects of the transition. All superfluous data had been removed from the range of his analytic consideration. His *shtahn* integrity was intact, and he began the structured process of sleep-analysis.

* * * * *

When he opened his eyes, Tahl was surprised to see Riitha bending over him, an uncertain smile pulling at the corners of her mouth.

"Riitha." Tahl's voice was a rasp in his dry throat.

"Don't talk yet." Placing a hand under his head, Riitha raised Tahl and put a water tube to his lips.

He sipped slowly. "What are you doing here?"

"Someone had to watch you."

The slight smile did not quite erase the depressions of fatigue and worry about her eyes. Riitha leaned over as she lowered the *shtahn*'s head. The long, silver-black hairs of her muzzle mustache brushed his face.

Tahl shivered. "How long was I asleep?"

"Just over sixty hours."

"Three days!" Tahl reached for the strap fastenings. "The alien—"

"The probe is in the shuttle bay, and we're on course to Chai-te Five—on schedule." Riitha put her hands on the *shtahn*'s shoulders and firmly coaxed him to relax.

Tahl frowned, but gave in to her silent urging. "Who ordered the ship to break orbit?"

"Sani did. It was the logical thing to do."

"Yes, it was." Feeling dizzy, Tahl closed his eyes. "The probe—it must be studied."

"The probe is being studied," Riitha said. "When the investigation team has something to report, you'll be the first to know."

"Who's on the team?"

"Stocha, Hane, Tena, Vuthe, and Siva. Asking Siva to take my place as team biologist may have been a mistake, though." The worry lines around Riitha's eyes deepened thoughtfully. "Siva was reluctant to work on the alien probe. The others volunteered."

"Tena's okay?" After the ordeal on the flight deck when they were first tracking the artifact, Tahl was surprised to hear that news.

"She's fine. She slept soundly after we knocked her out, and she woke up ready to go back to work."

Tahl nodded. Given the *venja-ahn* tendencies displayed by Hane and Stocha recently, he would have expected them to volunteer for such an assignment. However, neither Tena or Vuthe f'stiida, the linguist, had shown any signs of deviation from their *du-ahn* modes. He made a mental note to watch both of them more closely in case they, too, were undiscovered *venja-ahn*. The existence of inactive *venja-ahn* modes was no longer a mystery to Tahl, but he did not know which members of the crew were subject to the shift. Having only his own personal observations and his new, unfamiliar sense of intuition to rely on for information made him uneasy.

Needing any information he could get, Tahl asked, "Why was Siva reluctant?"

"She didn't say. I suspect she just didn't want to have anything to do with an alien machine."

Tahl watched Riitha curiously, wondering why she had taken on the responsibility of a trauma-sleep vigil. It was a duty of loyalty prompted by scent-bond or allegiance to a higher authority. They were certainly not bonded, and the biologist had seemingly never respected Tahl's authority.

"I'm rather surprised you asked Siva to replace you, Riitha. I would have thought you'd be anxious to study an alien artifact."

"I was, but—" She turned away from him.

Tahl caught her by the wrist. "Why? What could be more

important than the scientific find of a lifetime—in all of *bey* history?"

Riitha tensed, watching him warily, but refused to answer.

"Surely you had no personal regard for me." Tahl paused, captured by the sweet, undefined fragrance drawing him toward her. "You never chose me, Riitha. Why not?"

"Because all I could arouse in you was sexual desire, and when I rejected you, all you suffered was physical pain. Your response to me was no different than your response to every other female who wanted you."

A surge of nervous anticipation made Tahl's heart race, and the hot flush of desire usually associated with the act of mating flooded his veins. Bewildered by his physical responses and Riitha's perverse reasoning, he stared at her. The bonding ritual was for the purpose of producing children and insuring a stable environment until the *jehni* were grown. Sexual arousal was only the first step in that process, and yet Riitha seemed to expect something else from him.

Confused, but acutely aware of his mounting hunger to know Riitha intimately, Tahl asked cautiously, "Did you arouse something more than sexual desire in the males you did choose, Riitha?"

"Of course not. I needed them to satisfy the bonding drive, Tahl."

A touch of anger infused itself in the deepening confusion and desperation that rose like a sudden and violent storm within the *shtahn*. Tahl's eyes narrowed, and his hold on Riitha's wrist tightened. "And you don't think I'm capable of satisfying your bonding drive?"

Hissing, Riitha pulled out of his grasp. "Quite the contrary, but I want more from you than primal mating!" Her eyes flashed with an anger that matched Tahl's. Then, her tense body relaxed. "*Shrudan du-ahn.* You are a hopeless analytic, Tahl. You will never understand."

As Riitha started to turn away, Tahl gently touched her

arm. "But I want to understand."

Riitha glanced back at him uncertainly.

"Choose me next time," Tahl said softly. "You must choose me."

Riitha held his gaze for a long moment, then turned toward the wall terminal and changed the subject. "I have to call Norii and Hahr. They're quite concerned for your health, especially with a trance decision impending."

Watching her, Tahl's puzzlement was compounded even more. The intense, emotionally charged qualities that had animated her voice and body just a minute before were gone, replaced by a detached, *du-ahn*-like flatness.

"I promised to let them know as soon as you awoke," Riitha went on. "And Bier. He's been very depressed since you collapsed."

Tahl shook his head. Although he was greatly disturbed by the intensity of his desire for Riitha and her stubborn refusal to choose him, he sensed the futility of trying to discuss it further. Setting the problem aside, he gave his attention to more immediate matters.

"Don't call Bier. I'll contact him later myself."

Tahl knew that he could not openly accuse the psychologist of trying to kill him. Attempted murder was not a crime that could be absolved by admitting guilt and repaying the victim through service within society. A public indictment of Bier's possibly lethal intent toward the *shtahn jii* would force a ruling of exile. Tahl could not afford to lose the only person aboard who had a clear understanding of *bey* brain functions. He needed Bier to solve the riddle of latent *venja-ahn*, and that made it necessary to forego his own right to bring the psychologist to trial for his crime. Bier would not go unpunished, but Tahl would have to deal with him in his own way.

"How are things otherwise?" Tahl asked casually as Riitha scanned for the doctor. "With the ship, I mean?"

"Well enough under the circumstances. Finding that

alien craft was quite a shock. Some of the crew are beginning to show signs of lethargy, but others . . . There are some who are acting unusually alert for *du-ahn*. If I didn't know better—" Riitha glanced at the *shtahn* curiously. "You don't seem too upset by all this, either, Tahl."

Playfully, Tahl widened his eyes. "All what?"

Riitha could not resist the opportunity to try to unsettle him. "The beings that built that probe could still be around. It might even be an exploratory probe from another star system."

"Yes, I know."

"You do?"

Tahl hesitated, taking no satisfaction in having succeeded in surprising Riitha. *Shrudan du-ahn*, he thought. He was not a hopeless *du-ahn* any more. Though he was aware of what he had become, Tahl was not ready to admit it openly. Not even to Riitha. His acceptance was intellectual, not emotional. Society still punished the *venja-ahn* for their ancient crimes of disruption and aggression, even though history had proven the value of abstract thinking. Every major innovative advance the *bey* had known was rooted in the creative process. This had become apparent during the trauma-induced trance from which Tahl had just awakened. Even so, the *shtahn* was having difficulty adjusting to the idea that he was now *venja-ahn*.

There was a more critical reason for keeping his mode shift secret, however. Tahl knew that his power to analyze and make a just decision was functioning perfectly. No one else aboard the *Dan tahlni* was as capable of making the right choice concerning colonization. If he had to decide against it, Sani might choose to declare his decision null and void if she knew of his changed status. It would not be legal, but the crew might back her up.

"Tahl—" Riitha lowered her eyes, and her breath caught in her throat as she whispered, "Why didn't you strand us on Chai-te Two?"

"I can't tell you, except that—"

Riitha looked up, her amber eyes glowing with an unfamiliar warmth.

"I would make the same decision again." Tahl shuddered as a peculiar tension filled him. He could not tell Riitha that he would reach the same decision, but for additional reasons. He did not know why, only that he would not be able to leave her.

CHAPTER TWELVE

Tahl stared at the image of the alien craft on the view-screen in the cargo control room. Hane and Stocha stood on either side of him.

"We've cleaned it up as much as possible," Stocha said, "but I'm afraid it's beyond complete restoration. We're building a computer simulation to present with the general report."

Tahl nodded and tightened his grip on the anchor cable. Even after an additional six days of rest under Riitha's and Norii's constant care, he was still not completely recovered. However, the steady decline of the *du-ahn* crew into extreme states of fatigue and apathy, the preliminary phases of death-wish, demanded that he arrive at a decision concerning the colony transmission soon.

"Do you know what it was used for?" Tahl asked. "How old is it? Where did it come from?"

"Yes, but . . ." Stocha paused. "Although we have facts we can support, certain unknown factors must be assumed."

Again Tahl nodded. Transition *venja-ahn* or not, Stocha and the others affected were still functioning as analytics.

The geologist turned to a mobile vacuum chamber and pointed to an alien artifact that rested inside. "This has become the focal point of our investigation."

Fascinated, Tahl stared. The gold surface of the rectangular object was etched with graceful scrawls.

"The aliens took great care to protect it," Stocha said. "It was covered with a thick, transparent plastic material. There's not a scratch on the plaque itself. Vuthe has formulated an interpretation of the writings."

"The craft was a biological probe," Hane noted. "It was launched from the third planet about one hundred million years ago."

Stunned, Tahl stared at the geologist and the engineer in silence.

"It's all written here," Stocha added hastily. He placed his finger on the window of the chamber housing the alien plaque. "This series of small circles is a depiction of this star system."

"How can you be sure?"

"All the planets and their satellites are accounted for." Stocha moved his finger to a diagram resembling a rayed sun. "This was the star's pulsar position one hundred million years ago. We ran a computer check to verify it."

"And this?" Tahl indicated another diagram.

"The triangle is the probe. This line—" Stocha traced the S-curve "—is the trajectory from Chai-te Three to Chai-te Two."

"Why mark that?"

"The probe once carried a single-celled organism for dispersal into the second planet's atmosphere," the geologist replied.

Tahl scowled. "For what purpose?"

Stocha's eyes were bright with excitement as he explained. "To convert the carbon dioxide atmosphere to oxygen. These symbols illustrate the atomic structure of the basic elements. That fact, added to what we've learned about the life forms on Chai-te Two, give us some very interesting data. The probe clears up a lot of questions we've had about the second planet."

"All but one," Tahl said. "The third planet has a carbon dioxide atmosphere. Why would the aliens want to convert Chaite Two to oxygen?"

"Chai-te Three has a carbon dioxide atmosphere now. It didn't then." Pointing to yet another set of diagrams, Stocha continued with unabashed enthusiasm. "These circles represent the second planet, and these scrawls depict the changes the aliens hoped to achieve in the atmosphere. These other circles symbolize the third planet. An oxygen atmosphere is clearly indicated. Some undetermined process changed it to carbon dioxide after the probe was launched."

"Is that possible?"

"Theoretically. I don't have it worked out in detail yet."

Tahl paused as he tried to absorb all the input and sort through the endless questions that came to mind. He looked at Hane. "How'd it stay in orbit for so long?"

The engineer's subdued countenance brightened perceptibly. "Electro-magnetism. A field charging and discharging on the solar wind."

"And the aliens?" Tahl's gaze flicked between the two of them. "What became of them?"

Hane shrugged.

A look resembling sorrow shadowed Stocha's face as he turned to look at the view-screen image of the probe. "I don't know, Tahl. Not for sure. But—"

"But?" Tahl prodded gently.

"This probe was left out here on purpose. The plaque, a maneuvering system designed to maintain an orbit indefinitely— They meant it to be found."

"By whom?" The tightness in Tahl's throat forced the words out in a whisper.

"By anyone who might happen along. As it turns out—us."

"Why?"

Now Stocha shrugged. "I don't know that, either."

Tahl left the geologist and the engineer to their work and entered the shuttle bay, staying within the gray field boundaries that formed a life-support envelope around the probe. The alien craft stood off to one side of the large bay, diminutive between two shuttles at launch-ready on parallel tracks. There was no sign of activity.

Tahl stared at the probe while he secured wrist thrusters. As his gaze came to rest on the symbols etched into the aft section, he wondered at their meaning. The machine gave no clues as to the aliens themselves, and he wanted to know more about them. He wanted to know the sight, scent, and sound of a species that had transformed an entire planet. The *bey* had built contained environments on worlds that would not support life. They had never thought to alter the very nature of one.

Circling the craft, Tahl drifted toward the scarred surface and reached out to touch the hull. He traced the inscription with his finger and shivered. Part of him feared the *Dan tahlni* mission would find the descendants of the alien builders somewhere in the system. Another part feared it wouldn't.

*   *   *   *   *

Bier t'ahi was seated at a terminal in the conference room. Tahl, still wearing thrusters, hovered before him, his scent strong but without anger. The *shtahn* spoke with calm authority.

"Explain why certain members of this expedition, including myself, suddenly find themselves thinking in abstract modes."

Bier hesitated, and an essence of uncertainty diluted the harsh stench of his anxiety. "The back-to-front brain connection in some *bey* is dormant, not vestigial."

Tahl noted Bier's uneasy reaction with grim satisfaction. He had not wanted to acknowledge his *venja-ahn* status, but Bier had to know he was aware and unharmed by the abruptness of the final, completing shift.

"And what prompts activation of this connection?"

"Extreme stress releases an enzyme that clears blocked receptors," Bier answered in a monotone.

"Is the transition always instantaneous and total?"

Bier shook his head. "No. It seems to be gradual unless sudden, excessive pressure is applied. The shift doesn't seem to be complete in anyone—but you."

"Does anyone else aboard know this change is possible?"

"Only Sani s'oha."

Tahl tensed. He could control Bier, but he had no power to enforce silence upon Sani. He could only hope the mediator was aware of the possible ramifications if the information was disclosed.

"How many of these potential *venja-ahn* are there?"

"Thirty percent of Hasu-din's population—"

"I mean on the *Dan tahlni.*"

"Bier flexed his claws nervously. "Fifteen."

Tahl started. "Half the crew? Why would the council send latent *venja-ahn* on a mission of such vital importance?"

"Because *du-ahn* cannot make sound decisions and proper evaluations when faced with variables outside their experience and frame of reference."

"Be more specific."

"A *du-ahn* mind is limited because it can't perceive beyond what it knows. *Venja-ahn* can, and will perceive and question that which is unknown but may still exist."

This was something Tahl now knew to be true, but he could not believe the *du-ahn* mediators had agreed to a *venja-ahn* crew on those grounds. "Was a *shtahn* consulted about this decision?"

The psychologist nodded.

Accepting that, Tahl continued. "Why latents? Why not just send *venja-ahn*?"

"In addition to its stated purpose, the mission was also an experiment," Bier said evenly. "If the facts uncovered in the system were absolute and the situation obvious, latents would not emerge. They would continue to function as normal analytics. But if the facts were obscure and the situation uncertain, the pressure would cause emergence, and—" Bier shifted uneasily.

"And what?" Tahl asked impatiently.

"Emerging latent processes would be controlled by years of analytic training and patterns. Or . . . that was my hypothesis. I thought they'd perceive the unknown, but then consider those perceptions as a *du-ahn* would. It didn't work that way."

Applying thrust, Tahl drew closer to Bier. He hovered above the psychologist slightly, in a dominant position. "Why didn't it?"

Bier cowered. "If there were no latents aboard, analytics would have studied the planet, found no evidence of intelligence, nothing unusual, and that would have ended it. Instead, Stocha and Verda saw the obscure. They formulated theories that didn't clarify the situation, but added to the confusion."

"That's only how it seemed, Bier."

"What do you mean?"

"Yes, they saw the obscure, and their new aptitudes made them unpredictable. They couldn't escape the influence of their new modes, nor could they deviate from *du-ahn* conditioning. Instead, they took the only course they could to protect their integrity and the Law. They explored every fact and theory to be certain nothing of significance was overlooked."

"And they burdened you, the *shtahn jii*, with unnecessary and unsupported information!" Bier's voice rose defensively. "They triggered your inclination to speculate, and speculation might have led to—"

"A deviant decision because of my latent *venja-ahn* mode?"

"Yes."

"So you took it upon yourself to eliminate the danger by forcing me into burn-out or death."

"Yes," Bier confessed without flinching. "I thought the shock of confronting your changed mode would result in mental or physical death. I was wrong, but I had to try."

"Why?"

"I couldn't let you go into the decision trance knowing you might be influenced by meaningless assumptions and theories."

"You take great risks for the *bey*." Tahl backed away. "They weren't necessary, though. The bio-com processes of the *shtahn* make consideration of assumed data impossible."

A glimmer of doubt crossed Bier's face. "You can't be certain of that, Tahl."

"Oh, but I am. I went into trance while I was in trauma-sleep. The functions of the *shtahn* brain under trance deny all irrelevant or unsupported data."

Closing his eyes, the psychologist sighed. "I had hoped—" He looked up, resignation softening the tension lines about his mouth and eyes. "Will you choose death or exile as restitution for my attempt to take your life?"

After a long pause, Tahl said, "Neither. I don't understand the complexities of the *venja-ahn*, Bier. If we summon the colony ship, we face another fifty-seven years in this system before it arrives. Another high-pressure crisis might occur. That would cause another surge of emergences, and I'll need sound advice. You're the only one qualified to give it."

Bier's ears twitched nervously. "Under the Law, you must exact restitution."

"I intend to, but since no public indictment has been made, payment is at my discretion. I want your word that you will never again question my motives, abilities, or judgment as *shtahn jii*. I reserve the right to question yours."

"Done."

"And no one else is to know of the experiment or my changed status. The crew has enough to worry about without destroying their faith in their *shtahn*. You might advise Sani accordingly."

"I will."

"Also, you are to consult me about anything concerning the status of the other latents."

Without hesitation Bier nodded.

"Then the matter is closed. Now, I'd like to be alone."

When Bier had gone, Tahl seated himself at his terminal and keyed the holo-view. The open center of the oval screen filled with a holographic image of space and the stars as seen from Hasu-din. He located Chai-te, target system of the *Dan tahlni*.

Once, Tahl had watched the alien star's light from the soil of his homeworld and wondered what he would find in that system. He still did not know all of Chai-te's secrets, but for the moment, it didn't matter. Regardless of the outcome of the trance, the *Dan tahlni* had crossed eleven light years of interstellar space and touched a new system. The boldness of the attempt suddenly filled Tahl with a strange excitement and a profound sense of pride.

CHAPTER THIRTEEN

Tahl surveyed the group gathered around him, testing scent. The few *bey* in physical attendance at Stocha's final report on the alien craft reflected a mood of grim uneasiness. Most of the crew was absent, preferring to watch the proceedings on terminal screens. It was as though they believed that distancing themselves from the evidence about to be presented might somehow lessen the ultimate effect on their lives. Tahl understood how they felt. He, too, was filled with restless anticipation and a subtle sense of dread. The decision to colonize now hinged almost entirely on Stocha's findings.

Lights flickered across terminals, then blinked out as each person finished reviewing the preliminary report the geologist had given to Tahl several days before. When all terminals indicated completion, a reconstruction of the ancient probe appeared on the central holo-view. The gold plaque was mounted on a thruster platform and moved about the room from terminal to terminal. Those viewing the proceedings from other parts of the ship saw an image of the plaque on the screens instead.

Tahl watched as everyone studied both objects. Some viewed the holographic image and artifact with reluctant dismay, others with open curiosity. Only Sani seemed to lack interest in the alien objects. She was watching Tahl.

Knowing that the mediator was aware of his *venja-ahn* awakening disconcerted Tahl. Still, he returned Sani's stare and held it until she looked away. When everyone else's gazes began to drift toward him, Tahl signaled Stocha to begin.

The geologist hovered before the line of terminals, aided by wrist thrusters. "I am confident that life on Chai-te Two is descended from organisms that originated on Chai-te Three; that these organisms were placed in the atmosphere for the purpose of converting it to oxygen; and that some kind of chain reaction has altered the oxygen atmosphere of Chai-te Three to carbon dioxide."

A quiet tension filled the air as Tahl posed his questions. "How could such a shift happen?"

"A number of things could account for it." The geologist paused and scanned the room. "A major loss of vegetation would eliminate the carbon dioxide sink. A rise in the mean temperature of the planet would warm the oceans, releasing CO_2 that had previously remained dissolved in the cold waters. Also, carbon dioxide is a by-product of burning hydrocarbons—like coal. Whatever the reason, it resulted in an irreversible runaway reaction."

"Runaway reaction?" Tahl asked.

A hint of pain and regret crept into Stocha's voice as he explained the ecological disaster that had befallen the third planet. "A substantial increase of carbon dioxide in the atmosphere would retain heat in the ecosystem because it insulates. The hotter the planet became, the more carbon dioxide would be freed from the oceans to collect in the atmosphere. In time, no heat would escape."

The *shtahn* was appalled. "Surely there would have been some kind of warning—some way to stop the process."

With a heavy sigh, Stocha shook his head. "If the process had been recognized in its initial stages, before the mean temperature of the planet began to rise, the ultimate effects could have been reverted. But once runaway levels were reached, there was no way to stop it."

"No way at all?"

The geologist shrugged. "I suppose small organisms could have been released in the atmosphere of Chai-te Three as on Chai-te Two, but the complete conversion of the second planet's atmosphere took centuries. An accelerating rate of rising CO_2 levels on the third planet would have prevented conversion of its atmosphere back to oxygen until long after all surface life was extinct."

Traces of relief touched Tahl's receptors. "Extinction. There's no other possibility."

"Highly improbable." Stocha shook his head. "If the aliens were like us, rising surface temperatures would have caused sterility. If not, they might have tried to convert the second planet's atmosphere in the hope of migrating there. The length of time required for the conversion made success impossible."

"But they were capable of space flight!" Tahl's eyes widened with disbelief, and he snarled in agitation. He was having difficulty assimilating the scope of the catastrophe Stocha described. All life on an entire planet had been irrevocably destroyed. The very thought made Tahl's blood run cold. "Couldn't they have settled on their satellite until conversion was completed?"

"Of course. I don't think they did. Life on their moon would require advanced technology. They would have had to mine the asteroids to supply the light elements the moon lacks. Our scans of the asteroid belt have not uncovered any evidence of such past industry."

"Still—it's possible," Tahl insisted.

"Enough!" Sani's eyes glittered with loathing as she turned toward Tahl. "Traitor! *Maida shli, venja-ahn!*"

Tahl's pulse quickened, and the fur at the nape of his neck rose in warning as he met the mediator's venomous gaze. Fear and doubt were obviously clouding Sani's sense of judgment. Otherwise, she would never have dared accuse a *shtahn jii* of being a traitor or *venja-ahn*. The harsh odors of fright and confusion emanating from the other *bey* seated around the table filled the *shtahn's* nostrils as a stunned silence settled over the room. Tahl fought against the attack surge coursing through his veins. A *du-ahn* response was his only hope of restoring the crew's confidence and evading the questions he read in their stricken stares.

"You call a *shtahn* who is gathering information for a trance decision a traitor, Sani. Why?"

"Your questions beg for answers that will confirm the existence of an intelligence in this system, Tahl d'jehn."

Aware of Riitha's intense scrutiny, Tahl glanced at her and held her gaze for a long, poignant moment before turning back to calmly regard the mediator. "Why would I want to do that, Sani?"

"Because you are—" Sani tensed, bristling slightly as she looked at Bier. The psychologist's gaze shifted helplessly between Sani and Tahl.

The *shtahn* quickly seized the advantage. "My questions must be answered in order for my decision to meet the requirements of the Law." Before Sani could respond, he addressed Stocha. "Could the aliens have gone to their moon?"

"Uh—" The geologist blinked. "Perhaps. But where are they? If they had planned to move to the second planet, they would have done it long ago. They didn't."

"Well, Stocha," Tahl asked quietly, "is there an intelligent species living in this system now?"

"No. They are *jehda tohm,* a people lost—extinct."

Tahl nodded, relieved yet saddened by the devastation of

an entire world. The results of the trance seemed certain. The Chai-te system would become the territory of the *ahsin bey*. Still, the *shtahn* felt like an intruder into a time and space that were not his.

CHAPTER FOURTEEN

Clinging to the wall with Riitha pinned beneath him, Tahl pulled against the constricted folds of female flesh that enclosed his protruding sex. The musk of Riitha's frenzy, ineffectual on his drug-deadened receptors, thickened as her folds grew tighter around him.

Responding to the frantic demands of his body, Tahl drew in and pushed away violently. He felt Riitha tremble, then tense, her hormonal compulsion to mate waning as his intensified. She screamed as he swelled and throbbed against her sensitive membrane, her clawed fingers tearing at the tangled mat of his chest mane. Immune to the blinding and deafening effects of her scent, Tahl winced, but his urgency was beyond control. The force of his desire was stronger than compassion. She screamed again, slashing at him with her teeth and drawing blood as his burning seed exploded from rough, swollen pores.

* * * * *

They drifted together in Riitha's quarters, fingers twined in each other's manes to keep from separating as they dozed. Tahl awakened first, disturbed by a low moan Riitha had murmured in her sleep. Memory or dream? Tahl wondered as he brushed stray wisps of silver hair from her eyes. He shivered, his skin tingling where her body touched him. Sated and rested, he was also content. Finally, Riitha had chosen him.

She had offered no explanation, and it was not his place to question, only to refuse or accept. He had accepted and was pleased. The mating ritual was subtly different with her— better somehow, even with the distraction of female pain.

Riitha sighed, stretched, and drew closer. Her face was untroubled in sleep. The sight almost erased the memory of her features contorted by pain. Tahl wondered at the mysterious course of evolution, and whether the female's immutable right of choice truly compensated for the agony they endured.

Holding Riitha with one arm, Tahl pulled the anchor cable tethered to his ankle toward him, then made his way to the wall terminal. He keyed the controls, and an image of the third planet appeared on the small screen. He drifted again, staring as he had for so many hours after making his decision.

The transmission approving launch for the colony ship had been dispatched within the established time frame, though only barely. It had been close, and the success of the *Dan tahlni* mission was not an absolute certainty yet. There was much left to be done and twenty-two years to wait before they received the transmission from Hasu-din confirming the departure of the colony mission.

Riitha stirred beside him, sighing wistfully as she hooked a leg around Tahl's hips and rested her chin on his shoulder. "Do you think the aliens' planet looked like Hasu-din before its atmosphere changed?" she asked sleepily.

Tahl glanced at her, then back at the screen. "Perhaps."

They watched the image in silence together for a moment, then Riitha asked quietly, "Would it be possible to change it back with biological probes—like Chai-te Two?"

"I hope so." Tahl breathed deeply, thoughtfully, then added, "It would be a logical undertaking after the base is established and the colony is settled in."

Purring with amusement, Riitha pressed closer. "Stocha wants to investigate Chai-te Three's moon. Must we wait until the colony arrives?"

"No, but we have to get our industrial base set up first. I must admit, I'm a bit curious myself."

"You are?"

Tahl grinned. "Are you surprised?" They had not spoken of it, but he knew Riitha was aware of his *venja-ahn* shift. The biologist did not seem to care how or why he had changed, only that he had.

"Surprised? Not really . . . even though you declared Chai-te Two off-limits. Why did you do that? You know the colony ship's council is going to contest it. They're not going to let a whole planet go to waste."

Tahl's mouth set with determined resolve. "I'll deal with that problem when the time comes. Some things must be allowed to maintain their integrity."

The *shtahn* had decided that he would never agree to disturb the processes set in motion on Chai-te Two so many thousands of years before. The aliens, knowing death was inevitable, had sought to preserve something of themselves. The analytics aboard the *Dan tahlni* were certain the aliens had succumbed to death-wish because of their world's hopeless situation. Tahl knew better.

Only *venja-ahn* would build a foundation for a tomorrow they would never share. A living world marked the passing of the *jehda tohm*, the lost people of Chai-te Three, and their evolving legacy would continue unmolested. The *ahsin bey* had no right to Chai-te Two. It belonged to the past and a far distant future.

"If they had gone into space, Tahl—"

"They didn't," he said sharply.

Even Bier's theory concerning the movement into space by a

future intelligent species on Chai-te Two had proven sound. The absence of a moon made that possibility highly unlikely, and the fate of aliens native to the third planet supported that hypothesis. The people of Chai-te Three had had access to a moon suitable for mining, and they had possessed a satellite-probe technology. Yet, they had chosen not to exercise the options that might have saved them from annihilation. Tahl had always assumed any species capable of migrating into space and utilizing their system's resources would do so. Now he knew that was not always the case.

"We don't know they didn't try to use their moon, Tahl. Not for sure, anyway," Riitha noted absently.

"No—not for sure." Tahl smiled. His *shtahn* mind had processed the evidence and concluded that the *jehda tohm* were gone, lost forever from the universe, but deep in the recesses of his newly awakened back-brain he could not help but wonder.

His reflection was interrupted by sirens and flashing blue lights on the terminal. It was not a ship alert, but one confined to Riitha's cabin.

Startled, Riitha pushed to the terminal and pressed her thumbs against the control panel for identification. There was no response until Tahl placed an audio module over his head and keyed his own ID.

Hane's voice was thick and stressed. "Tahl—"

"What? What is it?"

"I'm picking up a signal—weak, but . . ."

The *shtahn*'s heart quickened, and his throat went dry. "Another probe from Chai-te Two?"

"No . . ." The engineer paused and swallowed hard. "It's coming from something in orbit around the third planet's moon."

PART TWO

EMBERS OF AN AGE
LONG PAST

CHAPTER FIFTEEN

The field-barrier sealed behind Tahl, closing him in darkness as he entered the *Dan tahlni* docking bay. He hesitated, then spoke into the remote scan-and-locate module around his neck.

"Nian. Bring the lights up."

Waiting with mounting impatience, Tahl reminded himself that Nian, like the other mission *du-ahn*, was subject to occasional moments of lethargy and sluggishness. It was a *du-ahn* condition that had persisted since the transmission summoning the colony ship had been sent twenty-one years before, and an inconvenience that Tahl usually tolerated with a measure of gracious understanding. Lately, however, as the arrival of Hasu-din's message confirming the launch of the colony approached, the *du-ahn* crew's lapses in concentration were becoming more frequent and intense.

Anxious to be on his way, Tahl snapped, "Lights, Nian!" He immediately regretted the sharp edge in his voice. The *du-ahn* were not to blame for the normal, psychological functions of their brains.

Forty-eight years had passed since the *Dan tahlni* had left Hasu-din. The crew had traversed eleven light years of deep space, had found a star system that was ideal for *bey* expansion, had survived the discovery of an extinct alien species, and since then had devoted their time and energies to the preparation of an industrial base to facilitate the colony's ultimate success. If the colony ship had not been launched for some unforeseen reason, all their efforts and sacrifices had been for nothing. The *du-ahn* were now buckling under the pressure.

The lights flickered but did not stay on.

"Is there a problem?" the *shtahn* asked calmly. The technician was handling the shuttle launch from the old flight deck, which was now the control room. Since the *Dan tahlni* had been converted into a permanent space station in the asteroid belt, more and more of its systems were being automated and diverted to a central bank of consoles. This had been necessary to accommodate the diminishing number of *bey* available to run operations as different personnel were relocated to the separation plant at Chai-te Five and the asteroid mining facility. Every once in a while they experienced a technical difficulty, and Tahl hoped that was the situation now. He did not want to risk a launch with an inattentive technician at the controls, but he had no choice. Speed was imperative.

As the *shtahn* reached for the emergency control that would switch the docking bay systems back to its original control booth, the lights suddenly flared on.

"Thanks, Nian."

"Sorry about the delay," Nian replied evenly through the audio module slung over Tahl's ear. "The relay was stuck. Everything checks out now, though."

"Good. Now I need a corridor to the shuttle."

"Right away."

Breathing easier, Tahl waited while the life-support field linking the docking bay hatch area with the shuttle unfolded before him. When it was in place, he applied a minimum of power to his wrist thrusters and started for the transport. Although most of the station now enjoyed the luxury of light gravity due to the installation's spin, the docking bay was located at the center of the rotation and was still a zero-gravity environment.

As Tahl glided across the open space of the huge hangar, his eye, as always, was drawn to the alien biological probe in the far corner. Surrounded by a protective maintenance field to preserve it from further deterioration, it stood as a constant reminder to the *shtahn* that the *bey* still might not be alone in their vicinity of the universe. The *jehda tohm* were gone, but Tahl now knew that two intelligent species had evolved independently on neighboring stars. It was foolish and arrogant to think that the life formation process was not an ongoing occurrence on other, similar planets.

The thought excited Tahl, but that was because he was *venja-ahn*. Although he had not yet fully adapted to the diversity of abstract speculation and seemingly irrelevant ideas that relentlessly assaulted him, he had coped with the emotional impact inherent in the change. Acceptance and stability had come easily once he had recognized the mental depth and enhanced perceptions of the *venja-ahn* mode. This also seemed to be true of Stocha, Vuthe, and Chiun.

Keying the hatch barrier, Tahl entered the shuttle and settled into the pilot's web. He powered up the systems and switched communications to the transport's console with the automatic certainty that accompanies years of experience. His mind, however, remained fixed on the latent *venja-ahn* and the various stages of change they had undergone since arriving at Chai-te Two so long ago.

Of the six latents who had demonstrated some degree of *venja-ahn* awakening, only Stocha, Vuthe, and Chiun seemed to have completed the transformation. The mineralogist, Verda, had reverted back to *du-ahn*. Norii, a physician aboard the *Dan tahlni*, and Hane, the engineer now in charge of the hydrogen separation plant at Chai-te Five, both showed occasional signs of active *venja-ahn* tendencies, but for the most part remained outwardly *du-ahn* in thought and action. The differences in *venja-ahn* development seemed to have a direct correlation with the amount of contact each one had with the aliens and their artifacts.

Verda had not had any actual contact with the alien probe. Although the mineralogist had walked on the surface of Chaite Two, she had gone into a trauma-induced state of hibernation as a result of Sani's accusations during the debriefing. She had not been aware of the existence of the aliens or their derelict machine until she had recovered. By then, it had already been determined that the *jehda tohm* were extinct, and the colony transmission had already been dispatched. The stimulus that had partially opened the pathway connecting Verda's front and back brain had not been potent enough to sustain and complete the transition.

Norii and Hane had both been subjected to situations involving direct contact with the probe, or in Norii's case, having to deal with medical problems arising from its discovery. Since then, the arenas of their interest and function had been confined solely to *bey* operations. Bier seemed certain that both were indeed *venja-ahn*, but neither one of them was even vaguely aware of the subtle alterations in their thought and behavior patterns. The psychologist attributed this to the routine nature of their current surroundings and circumstances.

Stocha, Vuthe, and Chiun were another matter altogether.

"Ready when you are, Tahl." Nian's voice boomed loudly from the shuttle console speakers.

"Beginning launch sequence," Tahl informed her as he adjusted the volume control and fired the shuttle's lift thrusters.

The *shtahn* turned his full attention to the shuttle console as the dark gray field-barrier shielding the docking bay launch window from open space became transparent. With a deft flick of his wrist, Tahl transferred power to the aft thrusters and slowly guided the craft through the hatch and away from the rotating station. Once the shuttle was clear, he checked his course settings, keyed for maximum-g, and activated the auto-matic pilot. With the small ship secure, he unstrapped and moved into the aft compartment where he fastened himself into a safety web.

As Tahl closed his eyes and prepared to hibernate for the du-ration of the long journey, his thoughts once again centered on the three *bey* beside himself who had become fully functional *venja-ahn*. He and Bier only suspected that Stocha, Vuthe, and Chiun were very much aware of their altered thought modes. On Bier's advice Tahl had never openly confronted them in order to confirm those suspicions. The psychologist feared for the three's emotional stability in the event he had misinterpreted the evidence and they were not cognizant of the shift. Tahl realized that their awareness was less vital overall than the one factor that had set them apart from the other la-tents. Unlike the others, Stocha, Vuthe, and Chiun had been in continuous contact with the aliens. Their work over the last twenty years demanded such contact.

Tahl shuddered as he recalled the urgency evident in the message Riitha had sent imploring him to travel in-system as quickly as possible. Something important had happened in the underground alien installation on the moon of Chai-te Three.

CHAPTER SIXTEEN

The summons from Riitha had been urgent. For the first time in the twenty-one years since the satellite beacon had been discovered, Tahl was afraid. He thought back to those anxious weeks after Hane had picked up the alien signal coming from something in orbit around Chai-te Three's moon.

A robot probe had been dispatched to the source immediately, while preliminary industrial operations proceeded according to schedule. Wisely, Tahl had maintained general secrecy, taking only Riitha and Stocha into his confidence along with Hane. Together, they had monitored the probe and evaluated the findings. Eventually, the *shtahn* had determined that this satellite, too, was a derelict and apparently malfunctioning as well. A buoy or surveillance satellite of some kind, it was beaming its simple signal into the empty vastness of interstellar space. Since the device might have been triggered by the passing of the *Dan tahlni* on its outward journey back to Chai-te Five, the beacon had been silenced. As an additional precaution, Tahl had also authorized the continued study and surveillance of the third planet's moon by the robot probe.

The alien installation had been discovered six years later.

Tahl put aside his recollections as his ability to focus returned. He glanced about the interior of the small room. A pile of *bey* utility belts was neatly stacked in a cubicle imbedded in the wall. The *shtahn*'s eyes began to water in the brilliant light as he took the top one, flipped the underbelt between his legs, and secured it to a wider belt around his waist. As Tahl tightened the broad waist panel, he swayed slightly, almost losing his balance in the low gravity. His muscles had not yet regained full mobility after the long journey in from the asteroid belt where the *Dan tahlni* now remained as a permanent space station. Anxious to reach the alien base, Tahl had pushed himself to the limits of his g-force endurance on the in-bound shuttle flight.

Worry weighed heavily on Tahl as he slipped coverings made of soft, alien materials over his feet. They were an uncomfortable but necessary concession to the installation. A *bey*'s claws automatically unsheathed and sought a hold during a fall, a reflex that had no effect on the hard-surfaced floors and walls of the underground structure. He decided to forgo the hand coverings. They were just too awkward. Tahl also ignored the eye shades Riitha and Norii had designed since the lights in the installation had been shielded and dimmed in areas beyond the docking station.

He turned to the intricate, mechanical airlock door and pressed a button for entry-ready. A green light flashed on the alien console. Tahl checked the corresponding red light on the *bey* terminal that had been modified to monitor the mechanism's status. The alien use of red to indicate danger was confusing and a hazard. In an emergency, *bey* conditioned to red-light safe could make fatal errors. The light code would have to be changed, and probably should have been changed long ago.

The security sequence clicked, and the ponderous door swung wide. The mechanism was sluggish compared to the

nearly instantaneous status shifts of the *bey* barrier-fields. Another danger, Tahl thought as he slipped through the opening,
one that could not easily be changed. He hoped he never had
to get in or out of any of the alien installation's sections in a
hurry.

The *shtahn* walked carefully on the hard floor down a short
passageway to a sliding, elevator door. He entered the lift,
keyed the down code, and braced his back against the wall for
the descent into the complex.

Riitha and Stocha were waiting for Tahl in the main access
corridor. When the *shtahn* stepped out of the elevator, Stocha
walked forward and placed a hand on his shoulder.

"It's good to see you again."

Tahl gripped the geologist's raised arm and smiled into his
solemn eyes. "It's been a long time."

"Almost two years since your last inspection tour."

"That long?" Tahl's nostrils flared in surprise. Time had become equated with the construction schedule. Days and
months went unnoticed, and the years were marked in relation
to the arrival of the colony ship, still thirty-six years distant.

"We didn't expect to see you so soon," Stocha said, the surprise evident in his voice.

Tahl frowned and glanced at Riitha. "Your message led me
to believe that something important required my attention—
as soon as possible. I came as quickly as I could."

"Too quickly, perhaps." Riitha stepped forward. "Maximum g?"

"Not quite." Tahl noted a faint musk fragrance drifting
lightly across his receptors. He held Riitha's gaze for a moment, then turned to Stocha, ignoring the sudden warmth in
his groin. "Why did you send for me?"

"I think—" Stocha looked questioningly at Riitha "—it can
wait until after you've had time to eat and rest."

"Not necessary." Senses alert, Tahl scanned their faces and
tested scent. Both were excited and tense with an urgency that
rode an undercurrent of apprehension.

"You're certain?" Riitha asked.

"I'm certain." Tahl's curiosity would not concede to the minor discomforts of high g-force hibernation. His muzzle fur bristled impatiently. "What's happening here?"

"The installation has another section," Stocha answered.

"A new section? Where?" Tahl's ears flicked forward. "I thought all sections had been breached after you got the life support systems working. When did you find it?" He glanced at Riitha.

"Seven months ago," Stocha said.

"I see." Tahl's frown deepened. Riitha had left the *Dan tahlni* for the alien base six months before. Such was her right, and Tahl had accepted the temporary loss of her as his mate. However, since Siva s'hur was already stationed on the moon base site, he had wondered why Stocha needed another biologist. His own apprehension intensified.

"Would you like to see it?" Riitha moved closer. "We can answer your questions on the way."

"Yes, I would." The unfamiliar musk scent grew stronger, then waned as Riitha turned and started away. Tahl swayed and shook his head, dismissing the sudden giddiness as nothing more than space fatigue.

"This way." Riitha sprang nimbly across the wide corridor and activated the airlock leading into the main complex.

The area beyond was already pressurized, and the airlock cycled quickly. Stocha went through first, leading the way into an equipment-packed room Tahl recognized as Base Control. While the two scientists consulted computer terminals, Tahl waited just inside the entrance and stared.

All the foreign devices seemed to be activated. The clatter of clicks and whirs almost drowned out the muted sounds of various *bey* terminals that had been incorporated into the system. The alien machines operated on the same basic technological principles as their own. It had taken time to unravel the aliens' applications of electronics and to interpret the mathematics, but Stocha's team had perservered and succeeded.

If Vuthe f'stiida had made as much progress trying to decipher the language, they might even begin to understand the extinct alien mind, as well. So far, they had learned nothing of how or why the lost people of Chai-te Three had become victims of rising CO_2 levels in their planet's atmosphere.

Tahl had been shocked when their scans had uncovered the entrance to the installation. Analysis of the evidence surrounding the destruction of life on the third planet supported the assumption that the aliens themselves had never left it. He had been wrong. The *jehda tohm* had not only ventured into planetary orbit, they had built an extensive, flawless base on their moon. Yet, the base was empty. It didn't make sense.

Neither does my decision to commit valuable time, equipment, and personnel to an unnecessary investigation, Tahl thought grimly. The excavation of the base was an extravagance without justification, non-essential to the mission's primary function: industrial preparation for the main colony. But nothing could persuade him to change his mind; not Sani s'oha, whose arguments were sound and whose silent accusations of *venja-ahn* were true; not his own desire to preserve his analytic status unblemished. Tahl had to know why the *jehda tohm* were gone.

Restless, Tahl moved into the room. He paused before a bank of terminals and watched small, white symbols march across a dull black screen. The lines meant nothing to him. He glanced at Riitha, who was intent on a *bey* console on the far wall, then at Stocha. The geologist stood before another curved screen, studying a display of linear, alien data. As though he understands what he's watching, Tahl thought. A chill swept across his shoulders.

"All systems secure." Stocha pressed a series of buttons and checked a *bey* read-out before joining Tahl.

"Is there a problem with the systems?" the *shtahn* asked.

"There hasn't been, but we check constantly. This installation is a hundred million years old."

"And working perfectly," Riitha said. "Ready?"

Tahl nodded and followed them from the room, across a wide central corridor, and into a connecting passageway.

The installation was not spacious, but it would house one hundred comfortably. Large, subdivided areas were connected by cylindrical corridors fitted with airlocks at both ends. The airlocks remained open. Constant cycling was unnecessary now that life-support sensors monitored conditions. Alarms would report a leak or contamination trace within a fraction of a second, allowing the inhabitants ample time to isolate, secure, and repair the damage. Tahl was not worried. The base had been built to last. Secured against the forces of space and time, it had survived.

Why had a dying species taken such care to preserve such a place? The question taunted Tahl and forced consideration of possible answers. Was it a monument like Chai-te Two? Or had the *jehda tohm* prepared it for their return?

The *shtahn* shook his head, making a conscious effort to stop the sudden barrage of *venja-ahn* questions that ripped through his mind. Taking a deep breath, Tahl focused his attention on the realities of the structure around him.

Quarters, a corridor, labs, a corridor angling to the right, agricultural units, a corridor, the spinning room. The rooms and cubicles, immaculate and orderly, instilled a sense of newness. Vacant for countless millennia, they were the only absolute evidence the *bey* had that proved the *jehda tohm* had once been a living, breathing, industrious species like themselves. Infirmary, refrigeration, another corridor veering to the right. . . .

Tahl bounded cautiously through the curved wall connections. Hard, white walls. The aliens had been obsessed with white—not the golden-pink whites of Hasu-din, but whites that were harsh, sterile, and cold. The tundra uniformity was broken only by the brass and silver sheens of metals and the translucence of glass.

Keeping his thoughts and observations to himself, Tahl followed Riitha and Stocha. They stopped before another elevator to the surface and filed in as the doors slid open. Ignoring the control panel, Stocha stepped on a riser newly bolted to the floor. He ran his hands lightly over the bare, metal wall, then paused to arrange the four digits of one hand and a finger of his other hand in a splayed pattern. He pressed against the wall, and a section of the surface recessed and slid aside to reveal another control system. Stocha punched in a code, activating the mechanism. A low tone chimed, and the elevator began to move downward.

"The other section is below us?" Tahl asked.

Stocha nodded.

The *shtahn* regarded the hidden controls thoughtfully. There could be no doubt that the system had been designed to deny access to a deeper level of the base. "Why did they try to hide this?"

Grinning, Stocha glanced at Riitha. His expression sobered as he looked back at the *shtahn jii*. "We have a theory. There's no way to prove it, but it's the only one that even comes close to explaining what we've found."

The lift stopped, and they stepped through the doors into a dimly lit foyer.

"All right," Tahl said as he strode after the geologist to an airlock on the opposite wall. "What is it?"

Stocha keyed the airlock to cycle. "What we've learned about base operations supports the assumption that the installation itself was built and used by the aliens for scientific study prior to the disaster that made their planet uninhabitable. We can only guess at their reasons for including a lower level with such extreme security."

"Why did they?"

Hesitating, Stocha stole another glance at Riitha before answering. "Fear of invasion."

Startled, Tahl gasped. "From whom?"

Riitha sighed. "From each other, Tahl."

The *shtahn* stared at the biologist. She merely shrugged in response.

The lock door swung open, and Stocha quickly tried to explain as they passed through the massive mechanism. "It's the only explanation that makes any sense. This section wasn't added after the main complex was completed. It was built first."

"And it was designed for secrecy and security." Riitha waited until Tahl was clear of the door, then closed and secured it.

The *shtahn's* chest mane bristled as his gaze swept the cave-like interior of the room.

"Nothing to worry about," Stocha said as he walked to one of the three doors set in the jagged, hewn rock walls. The geologist thumped the surface with his fist. "These rocks were brought inside the main structure for camouflage. The area is solidly sealed."

Tahl nodded, but remained tense as Stocha uncovered another hidden panel. "What's in there, Riitha?"

"The other level."

"And behind the other doors?"

"Nothing."

Nostrils and ears twitching, Tahl walked warily to the wall and touched it. "How did you ever manage to find this place?"

Riitha smiled. "Stocha's team has been systematically activating the base computers for years. They thought they were almost finished. Then, a program indicating the location of the elevator control panel showed up."

"A program," Stocha broke in, "that would have been impossible to initiate without sound knowledge of the base and its systems. We could never have found this level by accident. The *jehda tohm* went to great lengths to protect it from alien vandalism."

"Alien vandalism? I thought they needed protection from each other."

"When this base was constructed, apparently they did," Riitha said. "They would not have stored data indicating the entrance for others of their kind to find. The program was constructed and filed to prevent indiscreet alien penetration."

"Are you saying that they feared an alien invasion?"

Again Riitha smiled. "No, Tahl. They were depending on it."

"That doesn't make sense, either."

"It will."

Stocha keyed the massive door open and led the others into a narrow passageway. Trailing the scientists in the diffuse gray light, Tahl felt cold and strangely uneasy. A phantom essence enveloped and eluded him, infusing him with a feeling that the *bey* did not walk the ancient corridor alone. The *jehda tohm* remained there, too, a powerful presence.

CHAPTER
SEVENTEEN

Tahl noticed the cameras that were placed at strategic points along the ceiling and walls of the dim corridor. Similar devices had been found throughout the alien installation, components of an elaborate monitoring system that was operated from Base Control. As Tahl watched the overhead cameras track his movements through the passageway, he wondered who was controlling the lower level system and asked Stocha.

"No one controls it," the geologist said as he stopped by a large security door at the end of the corridor and punched a series of buttons that chimed in different tones. "This system is automatic. Some of the cameras are activated by heat, some by sound, and others by movement. Nothing passes through here without being detected."

Tahl frowned. "What did the aliens hide down here that was so valuable to warrant such precautions?"

Riitha looked at Tahl with dark, solemn eyes. "The future."

Before Tahl could respond, the large door slid into recesses in the walls. As he followed Riitha and Stocha through the opening, the *shtahn* noted that the door was extremely thick, and his throat constricted with apprehension. He could not shake the intense feeling that the straightforward course the *bey* had set for themselves when they had decided to expand their domain to the regions of other stars was about to take a radical turn.

Tahl caught Riitha by the arm as the door slid closed behind them. "Whose future?"

Placing her hand gently over Tahl's, Riitha smiled. "Be patient, Tahl. Stocha will explain everything in due course."

Nodding, the *shtahn* released his hold on her and surveyed the room they had entered. It resembled a smaller version of Base Control. Vuthe f'stiida sat before a bank of computer screens, engrossed in his work. Edii l'hai, a medical and power-com technician, was assembling a piece of alien equipment. Both acknowledged the *shtahn jii* with a nod.

Tahl waited, taking in every detail of the room, while Riitha and Stocha conferred a few steps away. Three walls were covered with alien terminals, screens, and related devices. Narrow walkways between the banks of complex equipment were filled with *bey* monitors. A shorter, wider aisle led from the entrance to the far wall, which was covered with overlapping metal strips.

"Tahl," Stocha called. "Over here."

Riitha and the geologist moved to a row of consoles facing the corrugated wall. Tahl joined them, his uneasiness mounting as Stocha activated a terminal.

"We had to rely on trial and error when we first tried to understand how the alien machines work," Stocha said. "Once we knew a machine's function, we could associate a meaning with a specific writing pattern, but we didn't understand the language itself. We do now."

Intrigued, Tahl glanced at Vuthe. The linguist remained hunched over his work on the other side of the room.

"The humans left comprehensive audio and video tapes. The programmed computer was running when we first entered this room. It was connected to an activation switch in the rock wall control panel." Stocha's eyes sparkled proudly as he spoke.

"Vuthe had the basic language keys unlocked within a month," Riitha noted. "Since Stocha already had some knowledge of the written language as a result of figuring out the systems in Base Control, he's been concentrating on learning to read."

"And Riitha has developed a sound understanding of the spoken words," Stocha interjected. "She can read, too, however."

"Only a little, Stocha." The biologist smiled impishly at Tahl. "Some of the sounds are hard to say, but others aren't too difficult. This is *Luna Base*."

" 'Luna Base' . . ." A long silence followed as Tahl absorbed the impact of the discovery. The *jehda tohm* had a name, "human," and with a working knowledge of the language, perhaps the answers to his questions were within grasp. "Have you found out why Chai-te Three's atmosphere changed to carbon dioxide?"

"*Earth*" Riitha said softly. "The home world of the *jehda tohm* was called *Earth*. And, no, we haven't learned anything about the disaster. The translation process is tedious and slow, and everything was systematically filed. We're bound to a data sequence locked in by the human programmers. However, if they left information about Earth's atmospheric shift, we'll find it eventually. We think a large portion of these databanks contain the aliens' accumulated scientific knowledge."

Tahl's gaze swept the room again. "A gift?"

"Not exactly," the biologist corrected. "More like a legacy."

Riitha paused, and Tahl met her amber eyes with a frown. "A legacy?" he asked.

"For the human race." Riitha quickly nodded at Stocha.

The geologist punched a series of lighted cubes on a console. Alien writings flowed across the screen. Then, an image of the metal wall appeared.

Tahl watched, fear a throbbing pain at the base of his skull.

On the screen, the metal strips folded into the ceiling as the wall began to rise. Behind it was a bank of consoles situated before another wall of partitioned glass and metal. The view enlarged, moved slowly through the airlock connecting the hidden control room and the room beyond, and began to pan the interior. The room looked like a scientific laboratory and was packed with computer terminals and other strange machines. There seemed to be no order in the room. Tanks, valves, piping, screens, terminals, intricate structures, and tangles of gear were strewn everywhere. The image moved again, advancing toward another airlock on the far side.

A human appeared.

Startled by his first glimpse of the creature, Tahl exhaled sharply. He took in every detail of the alien form that was not obscured by the white cover-all it wore. Black and smooth, the human was taller, leaner, and longer of limb than the *bey*. The face was flat and naked, the fleshy ears grotesque. The creature had two arms and was bipedal, but it stood perfectly erect rather than being slightly angled over a center of gravity.

As the creature moved toward the console by the inner airlock, Tahl held his breath, waiting for the awkward-looking being to fall. The human maintained his balance and walked with a long, sure stride. Fascinated, the *shtahn* watched intently as the human stopped before a console and began to make some adjustments. Another of the creatures joined him. The contrast was so unexpected, Tahl snarled in surprise.

Riitha laughed. "The black one is male. The white one is female. 'Man' and 'woman.' "

"And the colors . . . They're so stark." Tahl shook his head.

"There are a variety of shades. These are extremes."

The black man stepped to the airlock door, opened it, and stood aside. Two figures dressed in bulky pressure suits came into view, pushing a large metal box on wheels. Walking briskly in spite of their cumbersome attire, they moved the box into the small chamber visible behind the door. The black man secured the door when the humans with the box were inside the room, then returned to the console. Several minutes passed. When the airlock was opened again, the suited figures emerged without the box. The small chamber was empty.

Tahl narrowed his eyes and studied the screen. "What happened to the box?"

Stocha answered. "The area we're viewing is divided into two sections. The innermost section, where the box is stored, is a freezer. After the suited humans entered, the temperature in the outer chamber was lowered to minus two hundred degrees standard to match the temperature in the freezer."

"They had to shut down the mobile freezing unit without changing the temperature constant." Riitha spoke quickly in response to Tahl's questioning glance. "We think that box is still in there. We haven't tried to penetrate beyond the metal wall yet because we don't want to risk damaging what may very well be the most important scientific find in *bey* history. We're assuming an instruction tape is included in the data stores here."

"They went to a lot of trouble to prevent damage to that box," Stocha noted. "This installation is reinforced against the possibility of earthquakes, and the freezing chamber is lead-shielded to guard against radiation leakage from the naturally decaying elements in the moon's interior."

"What's in the box?" Tahl stared at the screen, his calm expression disguising the turmoil he felt inside.

Riitha sighed. "Several thousand human zygotes frozen in liquid nitrogen at the fourth cell division stage of embryonic development. The temperature at this level without functioning life-support systems is an exact constant. The design of the chamber, the shielding, the location—everything was calculated and constructed to maintain the zygotes."

"You mean preserve." Tahl's eyes narrowed.

"No, I mean maintain. Those zygotes may still be viable."

*   *   *   *   *

Riitha stayed behind when everyone else left for the upper level. Tahl, weakened by his journey and shaken by the shock of their disclosure, had decided that he needed rest. Edii had gone with him to make sure he was not in need of medical care, in spite of Tahl's protests. Stocha and Vuthe, having worked themselves into a state of exhaustion in anticipation of the *shtahn*'s arrival, had also left to eat and sleep.

Riitha wandered along the rows of silent, alien machines, reflecting on Tahl's reaction to their startling news. His only outward response had been a slight tensing of the muscles before he calmly announced he was ready to sleep. Riitha was not certain what she had expected—anger, fear, excitement—but something more than what appeared to be a casual shrug. That was what she would have expected from the old Tahl, not the Tahl she had come to know over the past twenty-one years. She had not been prepared, and her disappointment was acute and painful.

Very tired herself, Riitha climbed onto an alien chair and rested her head on her hands. She had not realized until now that she had been pushing herself along with everyone else on the base, trying to find as many answers as possible for Tahl. The problem was that the answers were few, and each one only added to the mounting number of unanswered questions.

Like Tahl, the biologist had a driving desire to know what had happened to the *jehda tohm*. She did not understand how a species that had constructed an installation that was still perfectly functional after a hundred million years and had conceived an ingenious, although risky, plan to save their unborn children, could not have saved themselves. And stranger still, even after Vuthe had unlocked the keys to their language and Stocha's team had unraveled the riddles of their machinery, no data concerning the aliens themselves, their history, or the world they had lost, was found. Frustrated, Riitha turned on the terminal before her and keyed for a replay of the tape they had just shown Tahl.

Nothing happened. Riitha noted the terminal's numerical

designation and sighed. "The broken one," she said aloud, her voice a hushed intruder in the stillness of the room. She rose to move, then paused with a puzzled glance at the blank screen. Sitting again, she continued to stare as several unconnected facts began to weave themselves together in her mind.

Knowing that machine failure could be expected, the aliens had been redundant fourfold with most of their equipment. There were other terminals in the room that did not work, but causes for the malfunctions had been found in all of them. Except this one. Edii had gone through it completely and could find nothing wrong. Yet, none of the normal activation procedures worked. They had finally given up, leaving it to sit in silent, electronic obstinacy while they utilized its more cooperative counterparts.

None of the *bey* had given the terminal another thought. Now, however, the machine's quirks seemed too odd and inexplicable within the framework of precision that had made the survival of Luna Base possible.

Curious and unable to quell a growing excitement, Riitha began to type different alien words on the keyboard.

—ACTIVATE—

—BEGIN—

She attacked the task with relentless determination, oblivious to the passing of time or the tremendous odds against finding the right word or phrase to unlock the mysterious and stubborn databank. The entire installation had been programmed for a methodical infiltration of scientifically motivated aliens, the only option left to the last members of the human race when their own survival proved impossible. A hundred million years later, the *ahsin bey* had found the base and penetrated its main systems. During the *bey*'s reactivation of the installation—a process that had taken several years and meticulous study—something had triggered the program that had eventually led them to the lower level and the cache of alien zygotes—humankind's sole hope of continuance in the face of imminent eradication from the universe. It fol-

lowed that this particular machine might have been programmed to respond to a future, unknown being with an even
more specific and questioning curiosity. A being like Riitha
herself.

The biologist stopped typing suddenly to stare at the keyboard. Questioning. Holding her breath, she carefully typed
the question that was uppermost in her mind at the moment.

—WHAT HAPPENED?—

The screen flickered, but remained blank.

Her pulse quickened. Riitha tried again.

—WHO ARE YOU?—

A white line fluttered across the screen, then cleared. Riitha
gasped as the image of an alien man appeared in the phosphor
light.

Golden brown hair shagged around his ears and over his
forehead, and a thick brush of hair grew over his upper lip.
Brilliant blue eyes gazed solemnly at Riitha from a face covered
with milky white skin that was lined around the eyes and
mouth. Not with age, she thought intuitively, but with worry
and fatigue.

"I'm Michael Jamieson, reporting—"

Riitha's hand went to her throat in thrilled shock as his melodious voice, a voice from an ancient, alien past, drifted
through the small terminal speaker. The human paused to
wipe his hands across his eyes. There was a tremor in his voice
when he began again.

"—reporting to you from the moon on, uh—let's call it
Luna Base plus nineteen months." He made a coughing sound
into his hand. The skin around his startling blue eyes was
moist. "I've, uh—just been told that all data not related to
running the base or to the care and feeding of humankind will
be erased from the databanks. I think that's a mistake . . . a big
mistake, but—" He stopped talking and hung his head.

Riitha sat mesmerized, too stunned to do anything but
watch and listen.

The man raised his head to stare from the screen. "The biggest story in the history of the world, and no one to tell it to . . ." He shook his head, sadly it seemed, then turned to look directly out of the screen at her. "Except you. Whoever you are."

Riitha inhaled sharply as the wondrous significance of the moment impressed upon her consciousness. This being, a human male who called himself Michael Jamieson, a man who had died millions of years before the *ahsin bey* had evolved into an arboreal species with a primitive social structure, was talking to her. Separated from each other by a hundred million years of time, they were in contact—face-to-face, one-on-one, human and *bey*. That there could be no exchange between them did not detract from the experience. A message, a desperate attempt to communicate with the future, had been left, and Riitha f'ath, an ordinary biologist from Hasu-din, was receiving it. She shuddered as a chill coursed up her spine.

"Whoever you are," Michael said again. The corners of his mouth turned upward slightly in what looked to be a smile. "So—you're either descendants of some friends of mine who hoped to launch a starship or . . . you're Andy's aliens." A droplet of water trickled from the edge of one of the man's eyes. Michael ignored it. "If you're human, then you already know this story. The thing is—I was a damn good reporter. Worked for a top-rated national television mag."

Riitha hardly dared breathe. She was familiar enough with the language to understand the man's general meaning, but she had to concentrate in order to piece together his more obscure references. Some of them eluded her entirely.

"Anyway," Michael went on. "Time has a way of distorting the facts, and an objective re-cap might help you understand your history and ancestors a little better. If Andy was right . . . if you're some sort of extraterrestrials, then you deserve to know what happened here."

Michael's expression changed suddenly. Riitha could not be sure, but she sensed that he had just experienced the same sense of wonder and awe that she had felt a brief moment ago.

Her heart skipped a beat as she listened to the whispered words that followed.

"My God . . . aliens." Michael leaned forward, as though he could peer into the camera and see who looked back at him from the far side of time. "Who are you? Where did you come from? Why are you here?" He paused, perhaps believing for an instant that the answers to his questions would somehow find their way back to him through the millennia. Then he sighed and sat back. "I guess it doesn't matter who you are. The important thing is that you're here.

"You've managed to activate this terminal, which means that the base is operational; you've found out about the zygotes; and you've learned our language. Do you realize what an accomplishment that is? Personally, I never gave you a chance in hell of succeeding or, for that matter, of even showing up. But you did, and I think you've got a right to know the truth."

Riitha gasped and tried to still the frantic beating of her heart. Michael Jamieson was about to reveal the answer to the one question that had been the basis of so much speculation among the Luna Base *bey* for so many years. What had caused the atmospheric change on the third planet? Very soon now, she would know. She leaned forward expectantly.

"This record may seem a bit disjointed," Michael continued. "I apologize for that, but in order to provide you with the most chronologically complete journal possible, it was necessary to use tape from a variety of sources. The audio and video tapes I've spliced together here best depict events as they happened."

Michael paused, lowering his gaze for a moment before looking back into the camera. "I kept copies of all my own tapes from the time I first started working on this story a little over a year and a half ago. Most of them were taken with a microcam, which I managed to smuggle up here. At least I think I smuggled it in. They might have just let it through because they knew I wouldn't be able to broadcast anything Earthside.

Whatever. I've done my best to record everything of significance that's gone on up here.

"I've also hooked into the base surveillance system and made copies of anything pertinent. This has been especially helpful since there were many times, critical times, when my other duties on the base made it impossible for me to utilize my own camera effectively. If the tape record seems confusing, please, just bear with it. The facts, regardless of the presentation, are what're important here. I mean, that's what I do—report the facts. And that's what you're going to see here."

Michael hesitated, his brow wrinkling. "This wasn't an easy decision to make. Ross has a valid point. We don't know what small facet of normal human behavior might make you decide not to revive our species. But I can't believe anyone with the patience to put this base back on line and to learn a dead, alien language won't have an open mind." Emitting a soft, rumbling sound, he fell backward against his chair and rubbed his eyes and forehead. "I really must be losing my mind . . ."

The words trailed off, and fear of missing something important snapped Riitha out of her transfixed gaze. Her immediate inclination now was to notify Tahl of her discovery. Then, she thought better of it. The "Ross" Michael Jamieson referred to did have a valid point. Like the humans, Riitha did not know what the *bey* might learn about the aliens that might seriously affect a decision to try and revive them.

From the moment Riitha had known that the alien zygotes might still be viable, she had eagerly anticipated setting the incubation process in motion. The idea of bringing life back to a strange alien species that by all rights should be extinct was too fascinating and awe-inspiring to resist. But she was *venja-ahn*, and the compulsion within her to venture into such a bizarre, alien-initiated project was strong. She felt certain the *du-ahn* contingent still left from the *Dan tahlni* would not view the enterprise as wondrous, but as dangerous.

Smothering a twinge of guilt, Riitha quickly decided to keep the existence of Michael Jamieson's tape to herself for a while.

She was duty-bound to report facts to the *shtahn jii*, but until she had viewed the tape in its entirety, she did not have all the facts. No one, not even Tahl, would dispute this reasoning.

Returning from his own long moment of reflection, Michael Jamieson began speaking again in a controlled, evenly modulated voice. "In the interest of objectivity, I'm not going to change anything I've logged to date. The hard disk in this terminal should last as long as this base. I've pieced together my tapes in what I hope is a cohesive account of the events leading up to our demise. It runs for hours, so if you need to take a break or anything, just turn the terminal off and turn it back on with your original key-phrase." He massaged his neck with one hand while he loaded a small rectangular cartridge into the terminal with the other.

Tense and excited, Riitha drew her legs up under her and settled back to watch. The man also relaxed in his chair, this same chair, Riitha realized with a shiver.

"I'm Michael Jamieson, and this is the way the world ended. . . ."

CHAPTER EIGHTEEN

The screen blanked, and Riitha tensed. She suffered through a long moment of dread, wondering whether or not the rest of the program had survived intact, then exhaled in relief as another image of Michael Jamieson appeared. It took Riitha another moment to adjust her mind to the sudden shift in perspective and scene on the monitor. The program running now had obviously been spliced in, and she assumed she was watching the beginning of the sequence of events that had eventually led to the destruction of the planet.

Michael Jamieson was definitely not on Luna Base. He was standing in a clearing, surrounded by large trees. Behind him, a number of other humans were moving around massive machines on wheels and handling intricate equipment. A smoky haze filled the air, and the activity seemed frantic.

A hot flush of excitement swept through Riitha as she realized she was seeing the third planet as it had been before increasing levels of carbon dioxide in its atmosphere had smothered and destroyed it. The trees bore a remarkable resemblance to those in the forests of Hasu-din. They were so similar in appearance that Riitha felt a deep and painful longing for the homeworld she had left so long ago, a world she would never see again. The intensity of that feeling drew her even closer to the once-living being called Michael. He, too, had left his world knowing he would never see it again. But, whereas Riitha had the comfort of knowing Hasu-din flourished a mere eleven light years away, Michael had watched his world die.

As Michael's image began to speak, Riitha leaned forward and strained to hear. His voice was almost lost in the din of background shouting and mechanical noise.

". . . fire has been raging out of control for three days in this northern California forest, and all reports indicate it may be days before it can be contained. Several hundred square miles of timberland have already been destroyed—" Michael stopped speaking suddenly and looked off to the side. He frowned, then glanced back at the camera and motioned with his hand. "There's something going on over there, Rob. Keep it rolling, and let's feed and copy into the microcams."

"Right," said a voice from off-screen as Michael opened his jacket and keyed what looked to be a small console fixed inside the garment.

The difference between this image of Michael and that on the previous section of tape, Riitha noted, was startling. There was no trace of the sadness in this Michael's eyes, no deep lines of worry and exhaustion on his face. He exuded a sense of excitement and enthusiasm for what he was doing, feelings that Riitha recognized. She had felt the same way when she had touched the alien soil of Chai-te Two for the first time, and again when she had discovered the similarities between the alien planet's life forms and those from Hasu-din, and still again when she had found out that viable human zygotes might exist. Michael Jamieson was a gatherer of facts and totally dedicated to the task. The bond Riitha felt toward him grew.

"We might run into a little trouble," Michael said.

The off-screen voice laughed. "A little trouble never bothered me before. It won't now."

Michael smiled. "Okay. Let's move in for a closer look."

The camera followed Michael as he made his way through the crowd to the far edge of the clearing, then panned over some cloth buildings with crossed red lines on them. Finally it lingered on a series of fence-type structures with the words "RESTRICTED AREA" marked on each one. Michael did not seem to notice as he walked between two of the barriers and moved toward a machine with a slowly whirling propeller blade on top.

A man in a white coverall was helping a woman step out of the machine. As she touched the ground, she yanked her arm free of the man's grasp and shouted at him. He began to argue. Then, his attention was diverted to another human being carried out of the hatch on a flat conveyance by two other men. The woman walked away briskly, but Michael intercepted her.

"Pardon me," Michael said, "but could I have a word with you?"

The woman's eyes narrowed, and Riitha read the expression to be one of anger or suspicion, as it was with the *bey*. Riitha was also shocked to see an ugly red gash and black smudges on the woman's face. Red blotches on her neck looked as if they were just beginning to blister. The woman, Riitha decided, had just been brought out of close contact with the fire.

When the woman addressed Michael, there was a hint of wariness in her tone. "Who are you?"

"Michael Jamieson. World and National News Network."

"Oh, yeah. Thought you looked familiar." The woman relaxed a little, although she kept glancing back over her shoulder. "What can I do for you?"

"You seem a little upset with the rescue team. Why?"

"I'm not mad at them. At least they're doing what they're supposed to do."

Michael didn't hesitate. "And someone else isn't? Who?"

"The jerks that are supposed to be putting out this fire." She pointed to the distant peaks. The camera followed, slowly scanning the mountains bathed in smoke and orange flames. "I've been sitting up there in a control tower watching them do everything but try to put it out."

"What?" Michael seemed genuinely surprised.

"You heard me. They're controlling it, making sure it burns where they want it to burn."

"Why?"

The same question entered Riitha's mind. She wrapped her arms across her chest and leaned slightly closer to the screen in anticipation of the answer.

The woman threw her arms up in an obvious gesture of confusion. "That's a good question, and I'll be damned if I know—"

Three other men seemed to appear out of nowhere. One took the woman firmly by the arm, while another walked toward the camera, blocking the image with his body. Picture and sound ceased simultaneously.

Riitha held her breath, then exhaled as the image returned. This time, though, the point of view had changed. Michael could not be seen, and Riitha deduced that the reporter was now recording the event with the tiny microcam attached to his jacket.

The man blocking the first camera grabbed the device away from a smaller man. As the smaller man lunged to wrestle the camera back, Michael shouted a warning.

"Rob! Look out!"

Rob stopped, glanced at Michael and then at a third man who was pointing a small, metal rod with a hand grip at him. Raising his hands, Rob looked back toward Michael's camera and shrugged.

Riitha frowned. She did not know what the metal rod was, but it was obviously an instrument of power, perhaps even danger. Michael and Rob seemed to respect it, and it was apparent that whoever held one of the devices controlled the situation. She tensed slightly as the first man led the angry woman away and the man holding Rob's camera drew a similar rod from a holder at his side and pointed it at the screen. Riitha sat back in alarm before it registered that he was actually pointing the rod at Michael.

"You don't need those guns, soldier," Michael said.

"Who said I'm a soldier?" The man's face creased with a look of suspicion as he walked toward Michael.

"A joke. Just a—hey!"

The picture on the screen darkened as the man passed in front of Michael, then canted at an angle as the reporter was grabbed and spun back around to face the barriers. Off to the side and just ahead of Michael, Rob was being pushed toward the barriers by the third man. The line of fences came closer, then disappeared as Michael was shoved through. He turned to face the man holding the metal rod.

"What about the camera?" the reporter asked.

The other man sneered as he took a step forward. "Sorry. It's been confiscated." A hand loomed large on the screen, and the image darkened again as Michael's microcam was blocked.

Michael's voice was indignant. "That's my press pass, buddy. You can't—"

"I already have. You lost your press privileges when you crossed those barriers. We're trying to save lives here."

The image focused on the man's face a moment, then turned back toward the larger clearing, scanning the crowd as it moved forward. Across the clearing, another group of people were being shoved about by other men with rods.

"Now what?" Rob asked.

"Let's find out."

Watching the unfolding drama from Michael's point of view, through his microcam, enhanced Riitha's sense of being on the scene, a part of these past events rather than merely an interested observer from the future. Her own feeling of urgency and curiosity heightened as Michael hurried toward the chaotic melee on the edge of the forest. As he drew closer, snatches of shouted words and phrases could be heard.

"We have a right . . . nothing but another government cover-up . . ."

"You guys don't even know what you're dealing with!" The microcam focused on an older man who was yelling at a soldier who was, in turn, pushing him toward a bunch of box-shaped transports on wheels. "You can't go on playing God and not pay—"

As Michael followed the older man with the camera, he saw another man hiding behind a large outcropping of rock. As Michael moved toward him, the man looked up, startled and obviously frightened.

"It's all right," Michael said softly. "Mike Jamieson. WNNN TV. What's the problem here?"

"A reporter, huh?" The man's tongue flicked over his lips as he glanced between Rob and Michael. Rob placed his hand on the man's shoulder and smiled. The man hesitated. "Did you, uh, hear about the kid who fell out of a tree up here last week?"

Rob frowned and looked at Michael with raised eyebrows.

"I don't get much chance to follow the local news," Michael said. "What about it?"

"The branch—it just separated from the tree, a perfectly healthy tree except . . ." The man leaned forward intently, his eyes wide and his voice hushed. "The inside of the branch was mush. Mush! And two people were killed in their sleep when their roof caved in on them. The beams had turned to sawdust."

"What's that got to do with this fire?"

The man's gaze shifted fearfully to the side. "Chem-Gen. The fire was started at Chem-Gen." He quickly ducked around the other side of the large rocks and hurried away.

Suddenly the image on the screen jumped up and down as Michael moved swiftly toward another wheeled vehicle. A hand reached out and opened a hatch in the side. Then, Mike and Rob were inside the vehicle. A split second after engine ignition, the picture that displayed the control panel of the vehicle began to jiggle, and Riitha realized that the transport was moving.

Michael's voice was difficult to hear over the sound of the primitive engine. "As soon as we get back to town, we'll make another copy of the microcam tape. Then, I want you to take it back to New York. I've got a hunch we can't risk an electronic transfer. Thank goodness I decided to feed from your camera to mine or half the stuff we shot would be lost."

"What are we going to do?" Rob asked.

"Look into this Chem-Gen business."

The screen darkened and stayed dark. Riitha slumped, feeling breathless and worn out, yet also relieved. She had made the right decision about viewing the tape first before telling Tahl of its existence. Although the *shtahn jii* would not form an opinion about the nature of humans based on the first segment of tape alone, he was irrevocably locked into a mind-set that put consideration of the *bey's* interests ahead of everything else. Even with the amazing alterations in his willingness to listen to theory and speculation, the bio-computer processes of his *shtahn* brain could not be circumvented, nor could the primary functions of the mission. Unlike Stocha, Vuthe, and Norii, who had somehow shifted modes during the crisis surrounding Chai-te Two and the alien probe, and who had thrown themselves completely into their studies of the aliens for the sake of the study itself, Tahl could not disregard how everything affected the *ahsin bey*. There was no doubt in Riitha's mind that Tahl would find humans frightening and dangerous given what Riitha had just witnessed on Michael's recorded account.

The range of emotions displayed by the humans in the burning forest was wide: anger, fear, outrage, defiance, dedication, and a disturbing inclination to control through violence. No *du-ahn* would be able to accept the existence of such a species, and Tahl could not escape his responsibilities toward the *du-ahn*.

But what, Riitha asked herself, if Tahl, like Stocha, Norii, and Vuthe, had experienced a total shift to *venja-ahn*? She had never questioned her three companions about the obvious changes in their thought processes. Although she had often wondered how a mode-shift might be possible, her curiosity was not as strong as her desire to maintain the solid relationship she shared with all of them. Since the subject of their shifts was never discussed, Riitha had no way of knowing if they were even consciously aware of what had happened to them.

On Luna Base the newly born *venja-ahn* were isolated from the *du-ahn* majority and so were never faced with having to defend their actions to mystified analytics. The one or two *du-ahn* techs they had been forced to cope with since the base was opened were constantly changing, since none of them wanted to stay long in the alien installation. While they were on Luna Base, the *du-ahn* techs tended to avoid the permanent staff. Riitha was all too aware of how tiring, frustrating, and discouraging it was to be *venja-ahn* in the midst of a *du-ahn* controlled society and was glad her friends had been spared that anguish. For herself, it was enough to have other *venja-ahn* to talk to, to be able to exchange ideas and fantastic extrapolations with people who had some concept of what she was talking about.

Defining the extent of Tahl's mode shift was complicated by his *shtahn* abilities. Even if his shift to *venja-ahn* was complete, he was still subject to the meticulous, immutable processes of the trance and his responsibilities as *shtahn jii*. And because he was *shtahn jii*, Tahl could never disregard the welfare of the *bey* that depended on him.

Riitha smiled at the irony, realizing that she and Tahl were in similar positions—on opposite sides. He was the guardian of the *bey*. She was keeper of the aliens' unborn children and the trust they had put in her—an unknown entity—a hundred million years ago. She was the champion of all humankind.

When the screen before her flickered, Riitha turned back to view Michael's tape with renewed vigor.

The screen remained blank, but a muted, modulated tone sounded through the terminal speaker. A woman's voice interrupted the tone.

"WNNN. May I help you?"

"Richard Burns, please. This is Michael."

Another tone sounded.

"Jamieson! What the hell's going on out there?" The speaker's voice was loud and gravelly. "Rob's in the hospital and babbling about chemical warfare or some such nonsense. You're supposed to be covering a fire."

"The hospital? What happened? Is he all right?"

"Yeah. Bumps, bruises, and a broken arm. He was mugged outside his apartment. They took his watch and wallet and a tape. He says they were after the tape. What's the story?"

"It's big, I think." Michael paused as though he were trying to catch his breath.

Riitha found the dialogue more difficult to follow without the picture for reference. She closed her eyes and discovered that it helped her concentrate to imagine Michael speaking into a *bey*-type remote audio module.

"Something weird is going on, Rick, and I'm not sure a copy of this tape would reach you if I sent it. I'm being tailed, so just listen, okay?"

The other man grunted.

"I did some checking on Chem-Gen Incorporated at the local newspaper office." Michael spoke hurriedly with an edge of fear, as though someone might stop him before he finished. "Seems they've been in a legal dispute with Crane Enterprises over some micro-organism they developed for commercial use. Chem-Gen won the case because they filed for ownership ahead of Crane, but no one at Chem-Gen is available for comment."

"Why not? Locked doors and reticent sources never stopped you before."

Michael laughed. "There aren't any doors. The fire took out Chem-Gen's entire laboratory and production facility, which included the executive offices."

The other man sighed. "Great."

"Hey!" Michael said with a tone of mock indignation. "I've never let you down before, and I don't plan to start now. I went to see the president of Crane Enterprises, Howard Crane. This is where it starts to get really interesting, and if you want to know the truth, a little frightening."

"Frightening?" Rick said in disbelief. "Either you're starting to get old, or you've stumbled onto a catastrophe of major proportions. Which is it?"

Michael paused. "I'm only thirty-three," he said quietly. "Unless you consider that old . . ."

The sound of Rick's heavy breathing filled the silence for a long moment. "Okay. Give it to me straight."

"Crane told me the dispute was over some micro-bug that pulps dead wood. It was developed to be sold to the lumber and paper industries along with a lot of advertising hype about it being a new revolutionary process that was ecologically safe. Apparently, the whole project got started because of all the flak the paper industry was taking from Greenpeace over the poisonous emissions and waste created by the old wood-pulping methods."

"No wonder they were fighting over it. Something that can revolutionize a whole industry is worth a fortune."

"It was worthless." Michael sighed. "Crane insists that his company actually developed the thing, and he suspects there was some industrial espionage going on, although he can't prove it. Anyway, Crane was going to scratch the program and destroy the critter."

"Why?"

"Seems they couldn't keep it from mutating into a strain that would pulp any kind of wood—dead or alive. He wouldn't say anything more, but I think this microbe got loose."

"Damn!" Rick whistled. "Got any idea what this means overall?"

"Not in any detail. Dr. Andrea Knight of the Genetic Research Foundation has agreed to see me. She's been pretty outspoken against biological engineering for profit. Apparently, some of these commercial companies don't use triple-redundancy safety procedures, and they're not subjected to the strict experimental regulations imposed on organizations operating on government funds and grants."

"So what else is new?" Rick asked with disgust.

"I'll let you know after I've had a chat with Dr. Knight." Michael paused, then spoke quickly. "Look, I gotta go. They've spotted me again."

There was a clicking sound, and then nothing. Riitha stared at the silent screen. The scenes were unfolding so fast and Michael was using so many words she did not understand that Riitha questioned whether she was truly comprehending what had happened. Was it possible that humans had learned to alter life on a genetic level, or perhaps even create it? The immediate implications of such an audacious scientific endeavor were thrilling and unsettling, and if one of the humans' creations had caused the destruction of their world, terrifying as well.

The biologist's reflections ceased as another picture appeared on the screen and she was again caught up in Michael Jamieson's story.

Riitha could instantly see that Michael was using his microcam to record. Even with the limited point of view, the biologist could see that he was walking toward a structure with transparent inserts across the front. Stopping before one of the inserts, Michael reached out to clutch a bar. When he pulled, the insert did not move. He hit the door with his fist, turned, and then pushed a round button with his finger. While he waited he figeted impatiently. Finally, a woman with brown eyes and dark hair that fell in fluffy curls around her head and shoulders appeared on the far side of the transparent material

Riitha now identified as glass. There was not much of the delicate substance on Luna Base, but judging from the amount evident in the building, it had been widely used on Earth.

The woman spoke into a device. "Mr. Jamieson?"

"Yes." Michael showed her a small card carried in a leather folder. "Dr. Knight?"

Nodding, the woman studied Michael through the glass, her mouth set in a firm line. "What do you know about Chem-Gen, Mr. Jamieson?"

"Not enough. I was hoping you could fill in some of the gaps." The hard edge Riitha already associated with Michael's speaking voice was absent, replaced by a soothing gentleness. "May I come in?"

Dr. Knight hesitated, studying the reporter intently for a moment. Then, with another, resigned nod, she unlocked the door and stepped aside to let him enter. "We can talk in my office. This way." Locking the door behind Michael, she turned and led him through a series of long, brightly lit corridors.

"What exactly do you do here in the Genetic Research Foundation?" Michael asked casually as he followed. Whenever he came to an open doorway, he paused to look inside, taping the interiors of the various rooms as a result.

Ignoring the question, Dr. Knight unlocked another door and led Michael through a small room into a larger one. As she walked behind a rectangular table, Dr. Knight indicated a chair in front of it. "Have a seat, Mr. Jamieson."

Michael turned, scanning the room before seating himself. The walls were covered in panels of rich woods and shelves lined with various colored rectangles. Leather-covered chairs, bigger and more comfortable looking than those on Luna Base, were placed before a long, wooden table. A container of brilliant red flowers stood on one corner of the table. A still picture of graceful four-legged animals standing in a meadow before a mountain range hung on the wall behind the desk. The camera lingered on the picture, and Riitha stared, awed by the majestic scene. The biologist felt suddenly saddened as she realized that that beauty no longer existed on Earth—just as those two people and the rest of their kind no longer existed.

Before finding the tape, Riitha had mourned the loss of an entire world on an intellectual level, as a biologist and as a caring, sentient being. Now, however, having become personally familiar with Michael Jamieson and some of his associates, the pain underlying the loss bit deeper and with an acute emotional intensity. For a brief instant, Riitha wanted to shut down the terminal, to reject the pain and the impact the ancient tragedy was having on her. Then, the image centered on Dr. Knight's worried face, and Riitha could not turn away. She settled back to watch, a vital player in the bizarre scenario, sharing an irrevocable link with the past.

Michael spoke. "I'd like to thank you for taking the time to see me on such short notice, Doctor. It's late, and I know you're busy."

"What's your interest in Chem-Gen?" Dr. Knight asked bluntly, eyeing the reporter steadily.

"The same as yours. I think they developed an organism in their labs that was intended to increase wood pulp production and decrease costs, as well as minimize the industry's harmful impact on the environment."

Clasping her hands before her on the desk. Dr. Knight leaned forward slightly.

"I think," Michael went on, "that organism escaped and is eating a forest just north of here. I also think Chem-Gen's labs and the forest were deliberately burned to destroy the organism. What I want to know is what all this means to the world."

Dr. Knight's eyes widened as Michael talked, and the tendons in her arms and hands tightened. "You're quite astute, Mr. Jamieson. How did you come by your information?"

"I'm an investigative reporter, Doctor. I gather bits and pieces, then put the puzzle together. But I'm not a scientist. I don't know what the destructive potential of this microbe is, except that it must be serious. Very serious. Nobody burns out hundreds of square miles of prime timberland without a damn good reason."

"I see." Dr. Knight's hands flexed uncertainly, and she averted her gaze.

Michael changed the subject. "What kind of genetic research do you do here?"

"Everything from trying to correct genetic birth defects to *in vitro* fertilization and artificial incubation."

"Genetic engineering?"

Dr. Knight's eyes flashed. "No! We're trying to eliminate disease and physical disorders, to ensure the births of healthy children. Unlike Chem-Gen and other companies like them, our research is designed to improve the quality of life for all people, not to make us a monetary gain."

"You think biological engineering for profit is wrong?"

"If it means cutting corners on safety precautions—yes. When commercial companies prematurely distribute organisms that have not been adequately tested for the sole purpose of an increased profit margin—yes. It is not only wrong, it is exceedingly dangerous."

"How dangerous?"

The woman swallowed hard, obviously very nervous. "I'm not sure." Her eyes flickered, and she looked down at her hands. "I think you'd better go now. If . . . You'd better go."

"I'm being followed," Michael said casually. "They probably already know that I've been here, that you've talked to me."

Dr. Knight looked up instantly. "For your sake, I hope not. You may be too astute, Mr. Jamieson. Too good at what you do." Rising slowly, she began to pace, her hand cupped around her chin in thought.

The picture bounced as Michael shifted position to follow the woman's movements with the camera. Riitha noted a new edge of urgency and fear in his voice as he quickly hurled several questions at Dr. Knight.

"Who's trying to keep the lid on this story, Doctor? And what's your part in it? Why aren't you speaking out on this the way you did about the Crane—Chem-Gen dispute?"

"Because it wouldn't do anything to change this situation!" She whirled to face him, her expression a mixture of anger and fear. "Maybe nothing can stop—Look, why don't you just get out of here while you still can? I shouldn't have agreed to see you at all."

"But you did. Why?"

"An impulse. I was curious." Dr. Knight's shoulders sagged as she returned to her seat. "Besides, your reputation precedes you, and I guess I just wanted someone to know—"

A soft ringing sound interrupted the woman. She glanced at a black box on her desk, the source of the sound. The device sounded again, and Dr. Knight picked up a receiver from this box with a shaking hand. Her face paled visibly as she listened to the unheard speaker on the other end of the line.

Looking through the eyes of Michael's camera, Riitha knew his attention was hard on the woman. The picture did not waver.

Without having spoken a word into the device, Dr. Knight replaced the receiver. She paused, sighed, and then turned to another machine and keyed it. "I'm sorry, Mr. Jamieson," she said softly. "I really am."

The picture jumped as Michael quickly rose out of his chair and turned. Four men with rods—*guns* Michael had called them—stood in the open doorway to the office, pointing the weapons at the reporter. One of the men walked forward and pulled a pair of metal circles connected by a chain from his clothes. He snapped them around Michael's wrists.

"Okay, Jamieson. Let's go."

"Where are you taking him?" Dr. Knight asked.

The man glanced at her with concern. "I really don't think you want to know—"

"He's going with us!" Dr. Knight's sharp, commanding tone startled all of them.

The man shook his head. "With all due respect, Dr. Knight, he knows too much. He could panic the whole country with this story."

"What story?" Michael's voice was steady. "She didn't tell me anything."

No one seemed to hear him.

"That's why he's coming with us," Dr. Knight insisted. "You may not have a problem with murder, but I most certainly do. He's coming along. I mean it."

The man exchanged glances with his companions, then shrugged. "All right. Frisk him, Walker."

Another man stepped forward, blocking the picture. A moment later, the sound stopped.

Riitha blinked, then tensed as the screen fluttered, and sound and picture returned. Michael had been moved to another door, which opened outward onto a docking bay for wheeled transports. Michael's microcam was still running, recording the busy scene. Several men dressed in identical clothes were rushing about, carrying boxes and equipment into the storage compartments of the transports. Other men, also dressed in similar, but not quite identical clothes, talked and shouted, apparently controlling the frantic activity. As Michael approached the back of one of the transports, a man standing beside it spoke into a remote communication device. A moment later, the door sealing the back of the vehicle opened.

Riitha gasped as the interior of the transport became visible on the screen. The metal box containing the zygotes was inside. Dr. Knight and a small man with sparse hair and metal-rimmed eye coverings made of glass were also inside and seemed to be checking connections and monitors on consoles surrounding the zygote box. Dr. Knight glanced up as Michael came closer.

"No!" she said sharply, looking at someone who was out of range for Michael's microcam. "Not in here. Put him in one of the other trucks. I've got enough to think about right now without having to field any more of his questions." The transport door slid closed with a resounding thud.

"Okay, Jamieson." As Michael turned, the unseen speaker came into view. He was wearing the same clothing as most of the other men. He waved the gun he was holding. "Come on. We're going on a little trip."

Michael's voice was low and menacing as he moved to a position alongside the man. "Where are we going?"

"To Hell." The man pushed Michael into the back of a smaller, box-shaped vehicle and slammed the doors.

Michael sighed in the darkness.

The screen darkened for a moment, and the sound went off. Eventually a picture of a well-lighted room appeared. Riitha sat forward slightly, recognizing furnishings and equipment similar to those in the Luna Base infirmary and patient recovery rooms. The camera focused on the door as it opened. Dr. Knight walked in, a tight smile on her lips and her hands jammed into the pockets of her blue coveralls. The word "NASA" appeared prominently on the clothing.

"Hello, Michael. How are you this morning?"

"Oh, just dandy. I've been locked in a room for four days, and now I've just had the most thorough physical of my life, and no one will tell me why." He shouted in anger and frustration. "You people have messed with my body, messed with my mind, and messed up my life! About the only thing you haven't messed with are the clothes on my back!"

"Look, I know you're upset, but—"

"Upset?" The image of Dr. Knight being recorded by Michael's hidden camera jumped slightly as the reporter stood up and took a step forward. "Of course, I'm upset! You haul me off to God-knows-where without a word of explanation and leave me sitting in the dark, literally as well as figuratively, like some kind of enemy of the state—what the hell do you expect?"

Dr. Knight slumped into a chair and stared at the floor.

"I mean, the last time I checked, I was still a member of the free press in the United States of America—not a political dissident in a South American dictatorship." Michael paused. His manner softened slightly when he spoke again. "Don't you think it's time you told me what's going on here?"

Dr. Knight raised her eyes to look at him but did not reply.

"Dr. Knight," Michael said with a hint of exasperation, "I work for a national network. How long do you think you can keep me here before my editor starts making inquiries?"

"Your editor has been contacted."

"Good. When do I get out of here and back to New York?"

"You're getting out of here soon, but you're not going back to New York." Dr. Knight's gaze remained steady, but Riitha noticed that her body tensed. She hesitated before speaking again. "You're going with me—to the moon."

"The moon!" The picture shifted suddenly as Michael rushed toward the woman, stopped, and looked down on her tired and troubled face. "I'm not going to the moon."

Dr. Knight did not flinch. "Yes you are." The image of the scientist's face grew larger on Riitha's terminal screen as Michael leaned closer.

"No, I'm not!"

"You are!" Eyes flashing, Dr. Knight set her jaw and spoke through clenched teeth. "If you stay here they'll probably kill you. I won't be a part of that, even if everyone on Earth is doomed!"

Michael backed off. "Why would anyone want to kill me?" he asked tensely.

"Because you know too much, and they want to delay the inevitable panic for as long as possible."

Michael laughed. "I don't know anything!"

"You're a very good reporter," Dr. Knight said with a hint of a smile. "You'd put everything together sooner or later. Probably sooner."

"In that case," Michael said softly, "why not just put it together for me now, Dr. Knight?"

"You might as well call me Andy—short for Andrea. We're going to be together a long time."

Seating himself, Michael let Andy talk.

Riitha, too, listened in stunned horror as the doctor explained.

"The wood pulping organism created by Chem-Gen escaped, just as you suspected, but then it mutated into a form that destroys all kinds of wood—like trees. Usually, such mutations die out after a few generations, or they mutate again into harmless forms. This one hasn't, not yet anyway. The fire was started to try and keep it from spreading. We don't know if it's been successful."

"And if it hasn't?"

"Then all we can do is hope something in the environment will destroy it or that we can develop something to kill it before it's too late."

"Too late? What's the danger? I don't understand."

"Our calculations show that, if it goes unchecked, this organism can devastate the world's forests in six to twelve months. Without the forests, there's no natural depository for carbon. Carbon dioxide will saturate the atmosphere and literally cook the Earth."

"You're kidding."

"I wish I were."

A long silence followed. When Michael spoke again, his voice was hushed. "So what do you hope to accomplish on the moon? Without Earth-based support, we can't last up there forever."

"No, we can't." Andy looked at him solemnly. "But we can last long enough to make sure that the zygote bank is safely stored for the future."

"Zygote bank?"

Andy nodded. "It's a depository of frozen human embryos that can be retrieved and incubated through fetal development to birth. Maybe the world won't end. I hope not. If it does, however, the bank is humanity's only hope for a second chance."

The camera fixed on Andy's stressed and saddened eyes for a sustained moment, then the picture slowly faded.

Dazed and shaken, Riitha quickly turned the terminal off. She needed time to absorb all that she had just seen before she could continue viewing the tape. The alien woman, Andy, had had a strange effect on Riitha, touching her on some deep level she couldn't quite identify.

Riitha leaned back feeling exhausted and emotionally drained. Warm, seasonal fires, forgotten in the excitement of finding Michael Jamieson's ancient account, stirred in her mid-section. The physical demands of her sex suddenly over-powered all other considerations. Shutting down the lab, she headed for the lift and the comfort of Tahl's body.

CHAPTER NINETEEN

Tahl switched off the terminal and leaned back in the modified, but still uncomfortable, alien chair. After several hours of
viewing and reviewing translations, he had reached his absorp-
tion limits. The bulk of new information gathered by Stocha's
team was staggering, but one fact overpowered all else: The
jehda tohm had decided to give their children into unknown,
alien hands.

Sleep beckoned, an oasis in the desert of ancient desperation
surrounding Tahl and filling his soul. He rose and moved toward the platform where Riitha slept. Exhausted and preoccupied, she had not stirred since mating many hours earlier.

Carefully the *shtahn* stretched out, trying not to disturb her.
He listened to the gentle rhythm of her breathing, relaxed,
and closed his eyes. In his weariness, he was only slightly aware
of the faint musk odor teasing his receptors.

He dozed, but not peacefully. Tahl's mind could not dismiss
the fantastic revelations of the past several hours. A prisoner of
his own abilities, he tossed fitfully as his mind drifted through

the rivers of facts about the *jehda tohm*, sorting out the significant.

One truth dominated: While Earth suffocated, humans had sought to secure a future for their children.

Tahl turned onto his side. He dreamed of a world smoldering in the last stages of heat death. Yet, her people remained defiant, refusing to fade from the universe without a trace.

The image diffused and was replaced by another. A Hasudinian city shaded in fire scarlets and blood crimsons lay deserted. Tahl saw through transparent walls and looked upon the faces of ten billion *bey*, sleeping where they had fallen—safe in the darkening bliss of death-wish.

In any hopeless situation, fear triggered the death-wish mechanism in *du-ahn*. Unable or unwilling to suffer or fight in the face of futility, their minds shut down their bodies. *Du-ahn* fell into a catatonic state of deep hibernation where the normal awakening reflexes stimulated by seasonal change, hunger, or alarm were not operative. They slept and peacefully starved to death.

Faced with the ultimate futility, the loss of their entire world, the *jehda tohm* had not given up. They had left their frozen seed to an uncertain and improbable—but not impossible—future.

And that seed might still be viable.

Troubled, Tahl sank into a deeper sleep, a sleep plagued by furless children ringed in fire. Their dark eyes reflected the flames as they stared solemnly into a star-sequined night.

* * * * *

Stocha's claws kneaded the smoke-gray shag on his thighs. The silver-tipped long-fur gracing his muzzle and ears bristled. Nearby, Riitha sat unmoving beyond the glow cast by the spherical lamp on the low table. The stars were visible through the transparent dome high above them.

Tahl dug his toes into the fibrous floor covering and shifted position in a wide, padded chair. Stocha's impatience and Rii-tha's shadowed silence annoyed him.

"I can't authorize additional personnel for Luna Base." Tahl felt Riitha stiffen and saw Stocha's ears flatten.

A low rumble sounded in the geologist's throat. "Why not? Preparations for the colony ship are ahead of schedule. We must have another power-com tech and a systems engineer."

"And a doctor," Riitha added.

Tahl shook his head. "I can't risk upsetting operations at this critical time."

"What could be more critical than the discovery of intelligent, alien life forms?" Riitha's anger was hushed, but intense.

"You haven't discovered alien life, Riitha—only a box of frozen protoplasm." Tahl glared at the dim outline of the biologist's face. "Dead protoplasm."

"That is an assumption." Rising from a plush, modular chair, Riitha moved into the light. "We don't know that for certain. We won't know if the zygotes are viable unless we have more help."

Tahl winced. Riitha's anger affected him like a physical blow, inflicting pain. A slight ache began to pulse in the back of his neck. He wanted to consent, but his responsibilities to the expedition wouldn't allow it.

"Riitha, I must assume they are dead. A hundred million years is a long time, and I don't believe living, organic tissue can be frozen and revived."

"The seed lives, Tahl." Riitha took a step toward him, her scent glands inflamed and the aroma of musk strong about her. "I know it does."

Tahl's nostrils flared as the trace scent assaulted his olfactory passages. He leaned forward, compulsively drawn to her. Then suddenly, instinctively recognizing the odor as bonding scent, he recoiled. Shaken, he exhaled violently and cursed his negligence. He had forgotten to take a *muath* booster before leaving the *Dan tahlni*. Remembering that he had been vaguely aware of Riitha's pain during mating only a day before, the *shtahn* braced himself to ward off another advance and hoped his receptors were still sufficiently desensitized to reject her.

"No, Riitha," he said adamantly. "You don't know."

"They live," the biologist countered with equal vehemence.

The ache at the base of Tahl's skull throbbed, but he continued to resist her efforts to bond him. "Don't you understand? Nothing must interfere with our primary function. I can't do anything that might endanger the mission."

Snarling, Riitha turned and stalked across the room.

"You must reconsider, Tahl," Stocha said firmly.

Ignoring the intensified pain in his neck, Tahl turned to look at the geologist. "I can't. If I assign extra personnel to Luna Base, Sani and everyone else opposed to the excavation of this alien site will want to know why."

"Then tell them."

"Tell them what? That you've discovered human seed you believe to be viable? That you are willfully taking action against the *bey*?"

Stocha stirred, muscles tightening. "A study of the *jehda tohm* zygotes can't hurt the mission or the *bey*," he said slowly.

"Can't it?" Tahl drew back as Stocha crouched forward and glared at him. The *shtahn* felt the fur on his scalp rise defensively and forced himself to remain calm, knowing that the geologist would not give up the fight. Stocha had completed the full transition to *venja-ahn*. Keeping that in mind, Tahl exercised caution in making his point.

"Let's assume the zygotes are viable." Tahl noted the flicker of interest in Stocha's eyes and breathed a little easier. "By definition that would mean that intelligent beings indigenous to this star system are alive, and we would be in violation of the Law."

Stocha stared at him. His upper lip curled slightly, and he flexed his claws in agitation. Then, as Tahl's reasoning was assimilated, he slumped back against the cushioned chair.

Tahl's body relaxed, also, but his mind was not at ease.

Stocha's attack warnings had been subtle, and it was quite possible that the geologist had not even been aware of his strike stance. Nevertheless, the incident made the *shtahn* realize that the existence of the human zygotes presented more than one threat. Knowledge of their discovery would create another high-pressure crisis. Tahl could only begin to imagine the problems he would have to cope with then.

Other latent *venja-ahn* would emerge again, perhaps permanently this time, and Tahl could not predict how they would act. And *du-ahn*? He wasn't sure what to expect of them, either. Most likely, they would not consider frozen, alien cells to be alive. A process for freezing, storing, and reviving an organism to a metabolic state just wasn't possible.

"You don't believe they're viable, Tahl." Riitha's voice drifted slowly across the room. "Perhaps, you're right. However, a study of dead alien embryos can't hurt the mission or the *bey*. We might even benefit." She turned majestically. "Operations will not cease if you send a few more people."

"No, but we might fall behind schedule."

"We're already ahead of schedule."

"And slowing down." Tahl paused. "The confirmation signal from Hasu-din is due in less than a year. Tension is building. We've spent forty-six years finding a suitable star system for *bey* expansion and setting up the initial industrial base. If, for some reason, the colony ship was not launched, it's all been for nothing. Knowing that possibility exists, a certain amount of listlessness has set in among the crew. Once the signal is received and things are back to normal, I'll consider your request. Even Sani might be more disposed toward the project by then."

"No." Riitha glided forward, her eyes locked onto Tahl's. "Once we know the colony ship is on its way, there will be an escalation of industrial activities. All available resources will be diverted back into operations. Now is the most opportune time to complete this project without depriving the mission."

Lulled by the steady drone of Riitha's words, Tahl felt compelled to obey her. The empathic surge peaked and subsided within seconds. He frowned and ignored the subtle pressure in his neck.

"Perhaps," Riitha went on, "we can compromise."

"How?"

"Send us a doctor and one technician qualified in general systems theory and application. Edii l'hai is a med-tech. She's not qualified for our purposes here and has consented to return to the *Dan tahlni*. Norii will accept assignment on Luna Base."

Tahl held her gaze without wavering. Riitha's arguments were sound, but there was more to her personnel requests than she was saying. Edii was not only just a med-tech, she was *du-ahn*. Norii was still exhibiting signs of a transition to *venja-ahn* thinking. The lure of the bizarre and the unknown would likely attract her, as it had Riitha and Stocha.

"Siva has also agreed to return to the *Dan tahlni*," Stocha said stiffly. "We can dispense with one biologist if we have Norii, and Siva's been briefed on Riitha's work with the Chai-te Two life forms."

"Venusian life forms," Riitha corrected, preferring the alien name for the second planet.

Stocha nodded and pressed the issue. "Siva is quite capable of continuing the alien life form study in the *Dan tahlni*'s labs."

Tahl glanced between the two of them. Siva was also *du-ahn*. He wondered if Stocha and Riitha were simply anxious to remove any and all *du-ahn* from the alien base.

"You would not be assigning additional personnel, Tahl, but replacement personnel." Riitha pressed him. "No one will question Siva and Edii's requests for transfer."

"I'll think about it."

"That's all we ask," Riitha pulled the long cloak she wore snugly around her and paused alluringly close to Tahl on her way to the exit.

Stocha rose quickly. "I'll be in the lab on the lower level if you need me, Tahl."

The *shtahn* only nodded at the geologist. The attraction of Riitha's scent was irresistible. He hurried after her.

Later, feeling both troubled and elated by the exquisite pleasure of mating without pain-awareness, Tahl returned to the dome. He knew the bond would not last since Riitha was sterile, but his oversight concerning the *muath* booster bothered him. Now more than ever he had to remain in complete and flawless control of his thoughts.

Tired but too restless to sleep, he sat in a chair and leaned back. He was seized by a peculiar loneliness as he looked up and let his eyes feast on the universe. The stars were familiar, comforting in the midst of so much strangeness. His mind drifted free on the eternal night. Free, but not alone. For him, there was no escape from the timeless gaze of ancient and unborn alien eyes.

CHAPTER TWENTY

Riitha entered the lower lab cautiously and found it empty. Weeks had passed since Tahl's departure back to the *Dan tahlni*, and she had not had an opportunity to continue viewing Michael Jamieson's tape. Either Stocha or Vuthe was always near the terminals working relentlessly to unravel the mysteries of the *jehda tohm*.

Riitha realized that, whether the *shtahn* knew it or not, the information stored in the terminal was critical to any decision he might make concerning the humans. Quite possibly, Tahl might consider withholding the information a traitorous act. If so, she did not want to involve her associates on Luna Base. Riitha alone knew that the record existed, and she alone would bear the burden of responsibility and blame for the secrecy.

The biologist felt a slight pang of guilt as she eased into Michael's chair and keyed up his terminal. The answers to all Tahl's questions were in the databank before her. Yet, she kept silent. Tahl's reaction to an investigation of the zygotes' viability had only proven that her assessment of his probable reaction to the ancient account was correct. The success of the mission and the *bey*'s expansion into the alien star system were his sole priorities.

Rested and eager, Riitha punched in the key-phrase to recall the program.

Michael's smiling face appeared on the screen before her. She recognized the room behind him as one of the auxiliary computer rooms on the upper level. It seemed deserted.

"Well, I've been on the moon for a month now, and they've finally found something for me to do. Report—sort of. Not like this, of course. As the newly appointed historian on Luna Base, I've just finished typing everything we know about the disaster into the computer banks. Very dull work. So now, for your amusement and mine, I'm going to give you the lowdown my way."

Smoothing his hair back, Michael cleared his throat. His expression turned serious, but seemed oddly exaggerated. His voice had an unnaturally deeper quality.

"Michael Jamieson. Entry number one, Luna Base Historical Files." He paused, his brow furrowing as he suddenly leaned forward. "It's all over, folks! The end of the world is here!" He raised a clenched fist, then slowly lowered it. His whole body seemed to sag.

"It really is, I guess, and it's all so—so ludicrous. Everything from Andy's 'baby box' to the unalterable fact that a glutton of an organism too small to be seen with the naked eye is turning the world's forests into the ultimate last supper. I just can't believe it."

Pausing, Michael bit his lip and shook his head. "How could we have been so stupid?" His blue eyes seemed to plead with his unseen audience. "That's easy. We didn't understand the principles involved. Some people knew, though. They warned us, but nobody listened. Nobody who could do anything about it. So now, there's only us."

Michael hesitated, then grinned crookedly. "And here's the real kicker, folks. There's not enough of us left on the moon to form an adequate genepool." His eyes widened as he shrugged his broad shoulders. "According to Andy, the minimum requirement for an adequate genepool is one hundred unrelated individuals. There are only forty of us. Twenty-three were stationed here before the terrible truth about the crisis was known, and seventeen came up with Andy on the last shuttle launch."

The grin disappeared as Michael leaned closer to the camera lens. "And I do mean the last shuttle launch. NASA's under siege. A supply shuttle is on the pad and ready to go, and ground control assures us that they'll do everything they can to get it off the ground."

Michael glanced at a computer printout on the desk beside him, then back at the screen. "Based on information obtained from the Space Surveillance Network commonly known as Hawk-eye, we know that there are forty-eight other people from various nations up here somewhere, too, floating around in low-earth orbits. There's not much chance we can get to them, though, and even if we did, we'd all be on borrowed time anyway. We don't have enough of whatever elements we need for sustained life-support. Andy has done her best to explain all this to me, but I never did have much of a head for science."

After another long pause, Michael sat back and smiled. "And now for the good news. Yes, folks. Believe it or not, amid all this doom and gloom there is good news."

Riitha held her breath in anticipation.

Cupping his hands around his mouth, Michael spoke in a low voice. "Bulletin! Bulletin! Bulletin!" He let his hands drop and peered solemnly into the camera again. "Just in from NASA. Creation I, II, and III have been launched. Each of these biological probes is carrying millions and millions of blue-green algae critters that just love to feast on carbon dioxide laced with sulfuric acid."

Cocking his head slightly, Michael nodded. "Yes, I said sulfuric acid. But wait! There's more. Each probe is carrying a gold plaque with just oodles of information about the disaster on Earth and who knows what else. And—" He looked from side to side, then leaned closer and spoke in a whisper. "This is the really important part, so listen up, folks." Sitting back, he raised his voice again. "And each probe is—I repeat—is a self-correcting orbital buoy that will circle Venus forever or until it's picked up by some E.T. who just happens to be passing by. So what does all this mean? It means Venus is saved! Isn't that great?"

Michael's cheerful countenance faded, and his shoulders sagged as he ran his hand through his sandy-colored hair. "No, I don't think so, either. I mean, I think it's wonderful that we developed a sulfuric-acid resistant strain of algae that will single-handedly—" He waved one finger in the air, his voice growing louder "—change Venus into a virtual paradise in five hundred years. I can even appreciate that it took years to put the whole project together. So why can't we use the same process to save Earth? Why?"

Sighing, the reporter paused. "We don't have time," he said at last. "Carbon dioxide is accumulating in Earth's atmosphere faster than our little green algae friends can convert it back. We could try, but in vain. Earth is doomed. Plain and simple."

A buzzer sounded on an adjacent panel. Michael listened to an incoming message, then turned back to his terminal. He moved to switch the computer console off, then muttered to himself. "Better take the tape with me."

Riitha saw his hand move toward the cartridge chamber. The screen blanked. Exhaling, she slumped back in the chair. She had been sitting on the edge of the seat, her body gripped with tension, totally enthralled by Michael's commentary even though she did not entirely understand the range of emotions he had displayed. Nor was there time for her to think about it now. Another image appeared on the terminal almost instantly.

A large number of humans were gathered in the lounge un-

der the observation dome, the largest single room on Luna
Base. Michael could not be seen, and Riitha assumed he was recording with his microcam. The camera turned to show Andy,
who was seated in the next chair, her legs drawn up under her.
The black man from the zygote chamber tape was seated in the
chair beside Andy, talking softly to a small woman with brown
skin and black hair sitting beside him. They all looked up as
another man standing in the center of the room began to
speak.

"We've just heard from ground control," the man said with
a tight smile. "One supply shuttle was launched this
morning—just before a tidal surge wiped out the launch pad."

Shocked silence filled the room.

"It's not as bad as it sounds. NASA was very selective with
the payload. We've bought ourselves a couple of years.

Michael's whispered voice hissed through Riitha's terminal
speaker. "Bob Crandall. Base Commander."

"Secondly," Crandall went on, loosening the cloth tie knotted around his neck, then adjusting the glass coverings over his
eyes. "After the supply shuttle arrives, we'll go ahead with rescue and salvage operations of all stranded orbiting installations. There are some good men and women out there. We can
use their knowledge, and there's no telling how valuable their
equipment might be. We have two shuttles now, and Ross assures me that we can extract oxygen from the local rocks for
fuel. Any questions?"

Voices in the background began to talk at a murmur as Michael spoke to Andy. "I could use a cup of coffee. Wanna
come?"

Andy nodded and glanced at the couple beside her. "Ross?
Sherry?"

The black man, Ross, turned and grimaced. "Yeah, but I
wouldn't go so far as to call that muck coffee." He grinned
then, his white teeth gleaming against the ebony tones of his
skin. Even seated, Riitha could tell that he was much larger in
stature than Michael and the other human males around him.

His black, curly hair was cropped short, accenting the high cheekbones and broad forehead.

Ross turned to the woman. "Want a cup of muck, Sherry?"

Riitha was fascinated by the distinct differences in human physical types. Sherry was smaller, finer boned than Andy, and both females, like *bey* females, were smaller overall than the males. Although Sherry's hair was as black as Ross's, it was straight and cut just above her shoulders. All the men, Riitha noted, tended to trim their hair short, a practice that would appall *bey* males who took pride in the fullness of their long, luxurious manes. Sherry's face was also remarkably flat compared to those of her companions, and her eyes were shaped and canted slightly differently.

The picture wavered, interrupting Riitha's study of human physical attributes, then cleared to show a different location. Andy, Ross, Sherry, and presumably Michael, were seated around a table in a room Stocha had identified as the mess hall in his initial studies of the Luna Base layout. All of them were sipping black liquid from transparent, capped cups. Riitha smiled, knowing from experience that liquids easily sloshed over the sides of containers in the moon's low gravity. Her smile widened as she realized that it was Michael's arm that blocked the camera's view every time he raised his cup to drink.

"At least we're still alive," Michael said.

"For a while." Ross took a tentative sip and wrinkled his nose.

"But why just for a while?" Michael asked. "We've got ag pods, oxygen—"

"But we don't have a ready supply of nitrogen, carbon, or hydrogen," Ross countered. "And without them, we don't have water or the nutrients to make plants grow. We can only recycle for so long."

"Why didn't somebody think of that?"

Ross shrugged. "I suppose because no one thought it was necessary. When I was contracted to build this base, I was told to build it to last forever. Nothing was said about making it

self-supporting, too. After Challenger and the loss of that Soviet space platform, all anybody could think about was
quadruple-redundancy safety measures and the 'forever factor.' Who knew the world was going to come to an end?" Ross
angrily hit the table with his fist, making everyone jump.

The camera angle changed to include Andy as she placed her
hand over Ross's. "It's the 'forever factor' that makes my plan
even remotely feasible, Ross. If this base doesn't last for eons,
there's no hope at all."

Ross patted her hand with his free one. "Well, maybe it
won't have to come to that. There's one other chance. It's a
slim one, but we don't have anything to lose."

"What chance?" Michael asked.

"All we need to survive is an asteroid. They're just loaded
with the light elements."

Michael laughed shortly. "And just how do we manage
that? Hop on over to Jupiter and pick one up at the local mar-
ket?"

"Something like that." Ross tapped the side of his head with
his finger. "I'm working on it." Michael and Andy laughed,
but the small, dark-haired woman at his side did not. Ross
glanced at Sherry with a worried frown. "You've been awfully
quiet. What's wrong?"

The oriental woman shrugged. "I was just thinking about
my sister back in Chicago. Her baby is due right about now—"
Her lower lip quivered, and Riitha saw the stoic strength in
Sherry as she took a deep breath and raised her head to smile at
Ross.

"Maybe you aren't taking enough vitamins." Ross touched
Sherry's cheek with his hand, then turned and blinked one eye
at Michael. "That's what she's always telling me."

"That's what you get for fooling around with a nutritionist,
Mr. Collins." Sherry poked Ross playfully, then stood up. "I
could do with some sleep."

Ross gulped down his coffee. "Me, too. Let's go."

Andy turned her head to watch them leave before turning

to look at Michael. "They seem to be really fond of each other."

"A lot of people up here seem to be getting fond of each other lately," Michael said.

Andy only nodded, lowering her eyes as she drank. "I guess that's to be expected . . . under the circumstances."

"Yes, well—" Michael coughed quietly. "Uh, when are you going to tell me about this plan of yours?"

"You don't know yet? It's certainly no secret." Andy's eyes twinkled. "You're slipping, ace."

"I've heard references, but they're so—so—"

"Preposterous?"

Michael hesitated, coughing again. "I thought I'd get the whole scoop from you."

"Fair enough." Setting down her cup, Andy crossed her arms in front of her on the table. "In a nutshell, I'm proposing that in the event the existing population can't survive and procreate, which seems likely, that the zygotes and all the data necessary for their incubation and care be secured for the future."

"What future?"

"An alien future. Maybe a space-faring species will come to this system. If their orientation is scientific exploration and study, they'll find this base and the zygotes."

"You can't be serious. What the hell are the odds on that happening?"

"About two hundred fifty billion to one. And I'm quite serious." Her expression turned cold as she rose to leave. "Excuse me."

"Andy—" Michael called after her, but she kept walking.

"You're spending a lot of time with the crazy-lady these days, aren't you, Mike?"

The camera moved to show a large man with abnormally well-muscled arms and chest, and long brown hair on his lower face. His eyes narrowed with antagonism as he scrutinized Michael.

"I happen to like her, Wilson, even if I don't understand her. And it's Michael—not Mike." There was a bite to the reporter's tone that made Wilson tense. "How's the maintenance game?"

"I'm security now."

"Oh, yeah. I forgot."

Wilson placed his hands on the back of a chair and leaned forward. "That's not smart, Mike. I'm on top of things. I don't know if you've noticed, but Crandall isn't holding up very well under pressure."

"I hadn't noticed," Michael said casually, apparently deciding to ignore Wilson's use of the diminutive form of his name.

"Well, plenty of other people have, and they don't like some of the decisions he's making. Nobody wants any Russkies or Chinks on this base. We gotta take care of ourselves, ya know?"

"Right."

Michael's responses to Wilson's comments seemed strange to Riitha, as though he were preoccupied and not really listening. She wondered why, then realized that the camera had turned back in the direction Andy had taken. Grinning, she sat back. Michael wanted Andy to choose him.

Suddenly the picture changed again. This segment, Riitha noticed, had been recorded by the surveillance cameras high on the walls of the main control room. Stocha had tried to figure out how the Base Control video system worked, recording and reviewing many tapes until he had tired of watching the Luna Base *bey* going about their routine business. It was a pastime humans apparently had not found boring. There were cameras everywhere, and since Michael's introduction on the permanent program suggested surveillance tapes of incidents he could not record himself were readily available, Riitha had to assume the base's cameras had been operating at the time when the humans still controlled Luna Base.

Ross, Michael, two men, and a woman were clustered around the main view-screen, looking at an image of a shuttle

lunar lander at rest on the perimeter pad. Several men in white
pressure suits were standing around the auxiliary ship, facing
outward and holding guns. A blue-suited NASA shuttle crew
emerged from the hatch with hands raised. Two other men
with guns followed.

Riitha's delight about Michael and Andy and her curious
conjecture about the surveillance system quickly waned.
Scowling, she drew her legs under her and watched anxiously.
From the screen, loud thumping sounds could be heard
against the control room's closed door.

"What do we do now?" Michael asked Ross.

"Not much we can do. Wilson's taken over both shuttles
and every pertinent section of the base except this room."

Rubbing his forehead, Michael cursed softly. "I should have
known this was coming. The other day in the mess—"

"Collins!" Wilson's voice boomed through the speakers in
Base Control.

Ross keyed a control panel under the view-screen. "This is
Collins."

"You might as well open the door. There's eighteen of us,
and we've got the weapons. We don't want anyone to get hurt,
but we'll blow that door open if we have to."

"Now just hold on, Wilson. We—"

"Blast it!" Wilson ordered.

Ross reacted swiftly, keying the console with deft fingers.
The doors opened a split second before a barrage of sharp reports thundered in the corridor. Two women and a man
charged into the room, firing before them.

A startled cry escaped Riitha as she watched one of Ross's
men fall to the floor. The man grabbed his upper leg and
writhed in pain as red blood stained and spread across the
white fabric of his coveralls. The woman with Ross rushed to
the fallen man's side. Everyone else raised their hands.

"You ready to cooperate, Collins?"

Ross's jaw tightened. "Yeah, Wilson. Whatever you say."

"I want everyone in the dome in an hour. Everyone."

Nodding, Ross moved back to the console.

Riitha shivered as the screen darkened. All humans seemed
to be *venja-ahn*, but some of them had no respect for the Law.
If there was a Law. She pondered that thought for a moment.
There had been no mention of one during the portions of the
account she had watched so far. Perhaps the guns were the gov-
erning force. Certainly they were a symbol of power. Yet, most
of the humans she was coming to know—Michael, Andy, and
Ross—all seemed to function by reason instead.

Was humankind plagued by a deviant strain of *venja-ahn*? If
so, then how could they have risen to such a high technological
level? The *bey*'s opposing thought modes had created conflict,
but *du-ahn* and *venja-ahn* had learned to adjust and live together as time passed, even though the situation was not yet
balanced. Perhaps the more advanced mode of human *venja-
ahn* had developed ways to deal with their violent and irrational counterparts.

Bewildered, Riitha set her thoughts aside as the program
continued.

The large observation room was once again filled with people, only now Wilson was at the center, in command, and the
tape was from Michael's microcam. Riitha snorted in disgust
seeing how Wilson cradled the gun in his arms, like it was a
newborn *jehn*.

"Someone has to look out for the survival of everyone on this
base, and that's what we intend to do." Wilson's dark gaze
swept over the gathering. "I'm sorry about those foreigners
stranded in orbit between here and Earth, but we can't risk
lives or a shuttle to go get them. Most of them are probably
dead now anyway."

A murmur of protest was stopped as Wilson shifted the position of his gun.

"We all know that we only have enough supplies and recycling capacity to last two, maybe two and a half years. The
more people, the less time. Simple. And all the equipment
and expertise we get from the foreigners won't do us any good

if we're all starving." Wilson's eyes narrowed, daring anyone to argue.

"If we had an asteroid, we might be able to go on indefinitely." The image turned slightly to focus on Ross. "All the light elements we need are in the asteroids. If we could get one into lunar orbit, we could replenish our supplies."

The image shifted back to Wilson. "And just how do we do that?"

"Send a shuttle and a three-man team with radio-operated explosives. Properly placed and exploded, they can power one of those big rocks right back here."

Wilson turned to a man behind him and spoke quietly. The man nodded, and Wilson looked back to Ross. "I think you'd better get to work on that right away."

"There's just one problem, though."

Wilson frowned.

"We don't have the equipment to build a processing plant. Every nut and bolt on this base has a purpose. There's nothing here we can scrounge."

"Get to the point, Collins," Wilson snapped.

"We need every scrap of equipment and metal we can find if we're going to build such a plant. We need anything we can get our hands on, which includes the low-orbit stations and platforms. Without them, we haven't got a prayer of pulling off a successful asteroid mission."

"We'll also need the personnel." The camera swung sharply toward Andy, who sat on Michael's other side. She did not turn to look at the reporter, but kept her eyes firmly fastened on Wilson. "Without them, we won't be able to make heads or tails out of how to use their equipment."

Riitha frowned, confused by Andy's turn of phrase. She did not understand what heads or tails had to do with technological equipment and wished she could ask Stocha if he had run across the usage in his own studies. The geologist was now as interested in the alien language device he called "slang" as he had once been in the surveillance system, but Riitha could not think of a way to bring it to his attention without telling him where she had heard the phrase.

Michael adjusted the microcam for a wide-angle view, which included both Andy and Wilson.

Wilson was glaring at Andy. "What would be so hard to figure out? Their equipment can't be that much different than ours."

Ross spoke up. "Not in function, maybe, but definitely different in design. You can count on that."

Wilson was stubbornly adamant. "We'll find a way."

Andy folded her arms across her chest. "Do you read Chinese?"

Eyes narrowing with menace, Wilson growled, "Don't push me, doctor-lady. I don't have much use for that baby-box of yours."

Andy's face flushed, but she kept silent.

Wilson glowered at her for another moment, then paused thoughtfully. "Okay. We'll get in touch with them. Anyone who can make it here on their own with something to contribute to this project can stay. The others will have to wait until after we've got an asteroid. And that's final."

Andy visibly relaxed and turned to smile at Michael. Behind and around her, other people were rising and leaving the dome.

"I'm impressed," Michael said. "You just saved a lot of lives with that bit of thinking."

Andy's smile faded as her mouth set grimly. "We should try to save them all. I shouldn't have let Wilson intimidate me that way, but I can't risk letting anything happen to the zygote bank. I just can't." Droplets of water began to stream from her eyes. "Anyone who knows anything about guns and fighting is on Wilson's side. What choice do we have but to try and keep him appeased without losing anything? That bank is the future. If Ross pulls off a miracle and actually creates an expanding ecology here, we'll still need the genepool."

"And if not, there's always the aliens." Michael reached out and tenderly wiped the tears from Andy's cheek.

"Even at odds of two hundred and fifty billion to one?"

"Those aren't any worse than the odds I'd give Ross's generation ship," the reporter noted.

"What generation ship?"

"Just another one of his hair-brained ideas." Michael's hand slipped behind Andy's neck and slowly drew her head toward him. "Speaking of hair-brained ideas . . ."

The picture blanked as their bodies touched.

Riitha relaxed. Reason had won over force, and the relief she felt was intense.

The sound of voices in the passageway spurred her to quick action. Shutting down the terminal, the biologist moved to another and turned it on. She looked up as Stocha and Vuthe walked in.

Vuthe nodded as he passed on his way to the language terminal. Stocha paused beside Riitha, frowning. With a weary yawn, she turned off the terminal she had just switched on and sat back.

"You look troubled," Riitha said, hoping to divert the geologist before he could ask her what she had been working on.

"More than usual."

"I am." His scowl deepened. "About you. You're pushing yourself too hard."

Rising, Riitha clasped Stocha's arm. "Don't worry about me. I'm fine. Tired, but fine." She hesitated, then headed for the airlock exit.

As Riitha walked along the dim corridor toward the lift to the upper level, she was seized by a feeling of great remorse for the many sane *jehda tohm* who had been forced to struggle against the powerful few like Wilson. Michael's tapes had shown that most humans responded to adversity with compassion, reason, and a sense of responsibility. Wilson was an aberrant personality. Riitha was confident that Andy had chosen the genetic donors for her zygote bank with care, avoiding anyone with Wilson's violent tendencies, and the unerring determination of the long-dead human woman strengthened the biologist's own resolve. Somehow, she had to convince Tahl to help humankind live again. Only then would human reason truly have triumphed.

CHAPTER TWENTY-ONE

Tahl stood on the flight deck of the converted *Dan tahlni*, anxiously awaiting a status report on the distant interstellar receiver, the mission *bey*'s only communications link with their homeworld.

"Attitude corrected and stabilized." Tena stared at the readout on her console, then nodded.

Nian d'char confirmed the adjustment. "Check."

"What caused the deviation?" Tahl's words were clipped, his tone sharp.

"I'm not sure." Exchanging a quick, nervous glance with Nian, Tena turned to another terminal and punched for a system analysis of the receiver. "No malfunction has been recorded."

Tahl growled. The unaccountable shift in the position and attitude of the apparatus posed a serious problem. Its long, slow orbit around Chai-te Five had been precisely calculated. Receipt of Hasu-din's transmission confirming the launch of the colony ship depended on accuracy.

Tensing, the *shtahn* watched the information about the interstellar receiver flow across the view-screen. Once again, the
Dan tahlni was locked into an exact and unnecessary communications schedule with their home world, a schedule imposed
by the Council of Mediators almost fifty years before on a crew
that was too young and inexperienced to understand the implications. Now, however, with the intricacies and depth of *venja-
ahn* thinking and perception at his command, Tahl believed he
understood the council's intent only too clearly.

During the crisis surrounding the possible existence of an indigenous intelligence in the Chai-te star system more than
twenty-one years earlier, Tahl had resisted closer examination
of the council's reasons for instituting a precise communications time factor. At that time, his newly acquired *venja-ahn*
thought processes had been too confusing and too frightening
to trust, and the questions raised by the complex *venja-ahn*
mode too disturbing to contemplate. But as Tahl had integrated and learned to cope with his enhanced mental abilities,
he had also been forced to study the problem of the schedule
and the council's probable motivations for imposing it. The
conclusion the *shtahn* had reached was logical and inescapable, and so terrible that his blood ran hot with anger and re-
sentment whenever circumstances confronted him with the
truth. There could be only one reason for the schedule: the
council wanted the *Dan tahlni*'s mission to succeed, but they
did not want the crew to survive.

Tahl snarled softly as he turned from the view-screen to the
com-techs seated calmly before their terminals. They had no
reason to suspect the Council of Mediators' duplicity, and he
almost envied them their ignorance and unshakable trust. Almost. The weight of Tahl's responsibility grew heavier with the
knowledge that he was the crew's only hope of living to reap
the rewards of their labors and sacrifices. There was nothing he
could do about the schedule itself. The mission was locked into
it, but Tahl was determined to make sure that the *bey* in his
charge did not succumb to hopelessness and death-wish be-

cause of it.

Taking a deep breath, the *shtahn* consciously dampened the surge of anger his thoughts had unleashed. Assuming the worst would prepare him to deal with the situation, but that would only be necessary if the confirmation signal was not received. He was uncomfortably aware that his evaluations of the council's motivations, influenced by *venja-ahn* perception, might be wrong. It was not likely, but it was possible, which only complicated Tahl's position. For the sake of his own sanity, he would have to proceed as though the signal confirming the launch of the colony ship had been dispatched from Hasu-din as planned and that it would arrive at Chai-te as expected. This decision brought Tahl's thoughts back to the pressing problem at hand. In order to receive the signal—or even to allow the crew to believe that possible—the interstellar receiver had to be operating properly.

Tahl turned back to the view-screen with an uncontrollable sense of irritation. The receiver's deviation had been noticed and corrected this time, but the cause was unknown. It could happen again.

"There's got to be a reason for the deviation!" he snapped. Plagued by one minor disruption after another since returning to the *Dan tahlni* asteroid base from Earth's moon two months before, the *shtahn* was unnerved and ill-tempered. He attributed the emotional fluxes to the discovery of the zygotes and the impending receipt of the confirmation signal, but he could not seem to subdue them. Taking another deep breath, Tahl clasped his hands behind his thick neck and paced before the consoles. "Are you certain we haven't overlooked some small gravitational influence, Tena?"

"Yes," the com-tech replied firmly.

"Then there must be a malfunction in the maintenance surveillance systems as well as the receiver." Tahl struggled to keep his voice calm. The crew, with the exception of the Luna Base team, was totally preoccupied with the confirmation signal and on edge because of the waiting. The *du-ahn* around him were mentally maintaining a delicate balance between life and death. Tahl could not afford to tip the scales in favor of death with any display of worry or uncertainty.

Tena turned to look at the *shtahn* thoughtfully. "That's a possibility, Tahl. If the equipment monitoring systems have failed for some reason—" She did not finish the sentence. Her eyes clouded suddenly as she realized a maintenance surveillance failure meant that they had no way of knowing whether the interstellar receiver was accurately functional.

Tahl quickly spoke to alleviate her fears. "That is a problem that can be eliminated easily enough." As Tena blinked and nodded, Tahl turned to Nian. "Open communications to the separation plant."

"What are you going to do?" Tena asked breathlessly.

Tahl answered with a nonchalance he did not feel. "I'm going to send Bohn n'til to check it out and fix it, if necessary." The com-tech relaxed, and Tahl looked away. Sending the power-com trouble-shooter out for a hands-on examination of the interstellar receiver was the logical thing to do. The operation was too important to be entrusted to a robot probe. Success, however, was not a foregone conclusion, a possibility Tahl wished to hide from Tena. Given the distance to the receiver, the capabilities of the shuttle, and the limits of Bohn's endurance, there was a chance he would not make it to the receiver in time to thoroughly check it and effect any repairs before the confirmation signal was due.

* * * * *

The blood smell of fresh-kill filled Tahl's nostrils and made his stomach knot painfully. He threw the skinned and gutted *reikii* carcass into the bowl-shaped depression on the lounger. He paused, dizzy from the lack of sleep and an extended fast, then turned to the dry storage bins and grabbed a handful of *chutei* nuts and shriveled *bishi* fruit. Reclining on the lounger, he nibbled the sweet bits and prepared his system for the gorging. Ravenous, he picked at the raw *reikii* meat and tore off a leg. His non-hibernating metabolism required him to eat every other day, but three days had passed since his last feed.

Eating kept Tahl's mind off his problems for a while, but as his hunger-pain eased, his mental torment intensified. Although he had learned to appreciate the deeper understanding and more expansive insights the *venja-ahn* thought mode offered him, the mental broadening also brought with it a new set of difficulties. The thought mode was a powerful influence in the *shtahn*'s waking hours, and Tahl was worried that it was beginning to affect the trance in ways that demanded additional consideration and interpretation once he was awake.

Stomach full and body sluggish, Tahl lapped water from a clear, glass globe and stretched out. He fought the natural inclination to sleep after feeding, knowing that he could not rest easily until the mystifying logic underlying his last trance conclusion was uncovered.

Turning onto his side, Tahl picked at the bones strewn in the bowl. There was no practical reason to invest more time and resources in Luna Base and several reasons why he shouldn't. Yet, he had not been able to stop thinking about Stocha's and Riitha's request since leaving Earth's moon. He had finally resorted to sleep-analysis to dispense with the matter once and for all.

Tahl sighed as he reflected on the unusual trance. There had been no internal arguments during the analysis, no sorting, defining, dismissing, or filing of data. The conclusion had been reached without regard to normal analytic processes. His mind had been filled with one thought only: investigate the viability of the zygotes.

Tahl threw down the bone he was holding and pressed a button on the side of the lounger. The debris disappeared into the recycling system with a whoosh. The open bottom of the bowl closed, leaving the depression vacuumed and immaculate. Shifting onto his back, Tahl focused on the ceiling. His bio-com processes could not have failed to function properly. Expe-

rience over the years since he had incorporated the *venja-ahn*
mode had proven to him repeatedly that the integrity of the
trance was unharmed. Somehow, in this case, his brain must
have evaluated all relevant data on a subconscious level.

Tahl's eyes closed, and his pulse slowed. Muscles flexed, relaxed, then tensed as a new thought charged along his drowsy
synapses. With a jerk, the *shtahn* bolted into a sitting position,
alert and awake. If his subconscious mind had sifted and
judged information without his knowledge, then his subconscious was aware of causes and effects that his conscious mind
was not aware of.

Investigate the viability of the zygotes.

What was it that his intuitive self knew that his analytic consciousness resisted?

Catching the scent of fresh blood, Tahl turned as Sani
stepped through the field-barrier and paused. She held new
kill in one hand, green and yellow *ahsta* leaves in the other.
The mediator stared at Tahl, surprised by the unprecedented
encounter. The regulated feeding periods of the *Dan tahlni*
residents did not overlap.

"Sani." Tahl's upper lip curled back as he sucked air.

"I've disturbed your feeding sleep."

"No, Sani. I won't be sleeping here. If you'll just allow me a
few minutes to rest, I'll leave."

"No need to rush, Tahl." She placed her kill on a storage bin
and sat down on the room's only other lounge. *Bey* ate in solitude except when bonded.

A spicy odor smote the air as Sani tore a thick *ahsta* into
small pieces in her bowl. She inhaled deeply, testing scent,
then sniffed sharply. Her eyes grew wide, and her nostrils distended.

"I'd better go." Tahl heaved his protesting legs over the side
of the lounger.

"No, Tahl. It's all right. Actually, I'd like to talk to you
about Riitha's latest report." Absently, Sani selected a juicy
stem piece and popped it into her mouth.

"You've read it?" Tahl did the mediator the courtesy of not watching her chew.

"I'm not free to ignore distasteful matters. It's my duty as mediator to keep informed."

"What about the report, Sani?"

"I object to her assumptions that the *jehda tohm* were very much like the *ahsin bey*. I'll admit that there are structural similarities, but beyond that, they were nothing like us. It's presumptuous of Riitha to imply that they were."

"I think," Tahl said evenly, "she was referring to the physical parallels—nothing more. It is rather remarkable."

"What is?"

"That two species evolved eleven light years and a hundred million temporal years apart and evolved with so much in common."

Sani laughed. "Not so remarkable, Tahl. The suns are similar. That's why Chai-te was chosen as a target star. The early composition and atmosphere of the third planet was probably similar to primordial Hasu-din. It follows that similar life would evolve."

Tahl did not pursue the argument. Sani would not be swayed, but he knew the odds against such an occurrence were improbable to the point of being impossible. On Hasu-din, primitive organisms had emerged with the capacity to reproduce themselves, mutate, and diversify. Life changed, its branches failing or succeeding, victims or survivors of shifting environmental circumstances. Identical shifts producing similar results on two different worlds was incredible.

"Ugly creatures," Sani said. "And they were certainly not as intelligent as the *bey*."

"How can you say that?" Tahl asked.

"They're extinct. Why? Victims of their own stupidity or worse, I'm sure. They launched a bio-probe to alter the carbon dioxide atmosphere of Chai-te Two. They must have known how rising levels of CO_2 would affect their own atmosphere. And why were CO_2 levels rising? Maybe they caused the disaster themselves. Stocha's team hasn't found any references to that situation in the Luna Base databanks, have they?"

"No." Tahl sighed. None of the translated data had solved the mystery or even given a clue.

"I think that's very odd."

"Perhaps." Coaxing his weary body to cooperate, Tahl rose slowly. Sani reached for her kill, and the *shtahn* left the galley unnoticed. The mediator now had no interest in anything but feeding.

Tired and aching, Tahl went to his quarters and sank into a webbed hammock. Sleep beckoned, but the *shtahn's* mind refused to rest and fought the needs of his exhausted body. Closing his eyes, he let his thoughts wander, and, as his mind was prone to do of late, it focused on the *jehda tohm.*

Sani's rigid judgment of humankind bothered him. Tahl did not agree with her assessment, but then he had access to facts he had denied the mediator. The *jehda tohm* had left their unborn children to an unknown fate at the hands of strange and possibly hostile aliens. The means was unique, if not entirely feasible. The overwhelming element in the situation, Tahl realized, was that the attempt, no matter how futile, had required a will to survive that was barely within the limits of his understanding.

A strong *venja-ahn* will.

Tahl stirred fitfully. The *bey* would never consider entrusting their children to such an uncertain and potentially dangerous existence. The restrictive effects of sexual imprint and bonding was but one reason for the sterilization of the expedition's female members. The *bey* valued their offspring too much to bring them into a life that offered only isolation and suffering.

Humans had deemed the risks of alien malevolence subordinate to the hope of species survival. They had bequeathed their children to a tenuous future—but a future all the same. The children of the *jehda tohm* had been given into his keeping by an accident of fate. Consequently, were they not also his responsibility?

Investigate the viability of the zygotes.

The thought stuck like a thorn in Tahl's mind and would not be shaken. But he could not authorize the transfer of valuable personnel without solid analytic support for the decision. An escalation of the Luna Base research effort could only be justified if it might contribute something beneficial to the *bey*. Beyond satisfying the scientific curiosity of a few *venja-ahn*, Tahl could think of nothing the *bey* stood to gain from an intensified study.

Worried and exhausted, the *shtahn* tried once again to sleep, hoping to hide in some dark, unconscious recess of his mind where the fire dreams could not reach him.

CHAPTER TWENTY-TWO

"Tahl?" Norii stared as the *shtahn jii* dragged himself into the medical section and fell into an examination recliner. "What's wrong? What happened to you?" She hurried to his side and placed her hand on his neck to check his pulse.

"I'm just tired, Norii," Tahl said, pushing her hand away impatiently. Two hours had passed since he had left Sani in the galley, two hours in which he had not been able to sleep more than a few minutes before the dreams forced him awake. He had finally given up trying to rest.

Frowning, the physician leaned over and looked into his eyes. She drew back with a sharp intake of breath, hesitated, then activated the strapping field.

"No!" Tahl protested. "You misunderstand. I didn't come here to be checked. I—"

"Be still, Tahl." Norii switched on the monitor-scan console and waited. The recliner shifted into a horizontal position. "You're not sleeping well."

Tahl did not comment. He hoped that Norii would not dis-

cover the extent of his fatigue. No one must suspect he was
facing collapse from lack of sleep. To sleep was to dream, and
his dreams were haunted by the sorrowing fire-eyes of a thousand alien children.

And Riitha's voice whispering over and over again. "*They
live . . . they live . . . they live. . . .*"

Tahl resisted her unrelenting call, though resistance was
draining his strength. He would not give in to the mysterious
and overwhelming impulse to escalate the Luna Base project
because Riitha pleaded with him in his dreams or because his
own mind demanded it in a trance that had ignored normal
analytic procedure. He would not give in without a sound
logical reason, even if he never slept dreamlessly and peacefully again. Tahl did not want Norii to know, but trapped in
the recliner, he could not keep her from learning that his
physical condition was seriously declining.

Helpless, the *shtahn* watched as the med-tech monitored
and recorded his vital signs. She worked in silence, extracting
and feeding trace specimens into the analysis module. Norii's
frown deepened as she studied the results of the tissue and
fluid scans. Tahl scowled when she activated the cerebral
probe, but the strapping field held him fast, and there was
no escape from the machine's prying, electronic eyes. When
the brain scan was completed, Norii shut down the console.
The recliner resumed an upright position, and the strapping
field dissipated.

"That really wasn't necessary, Norii." Tahl tried unsuccess-
fully to keep the irritation out of his voice.

"Yes, it was." The med-tech's eyes narrowed. "You're
bonded."

"That's impossible." Tahl's ears twitched uncertainly. "I
can't be bonded. I'd know . . . wouldn't I?"

Norii shrugged. "Not necessarily. The imprint is mild. I
suspect you delayed taking a scheduled dosage of *muath*. The
immunizing effect of the drug would decrease slowly until
you boosted. Someone got to you in the interim."

Tahl moaned. Suddenly, everything became clear. Riitha had succeeded.

"What I don't understand is why the bond would affect your sleep. Unless—" Norii's ears flattened against the sides of her head, and she growled softly. "Unless the female has rejected you."

"Not by choice," Tahl said dismally. "Riitha's on Luna Base, and I'm here."

"Riitha?"

Tahl nodded. "I was overdue for my dosage of *muath* when I arrived there, and I didn't remember to boost until a couple of days later. I've taken it on time since then."

"It can't be Riitha, Tahl," Norii said, shaking her head emphatically. "It can't be Riitha."

"But it is. I haven't been with anyone else since I got back to the *Dan tahlni*." Not surprising, he thought. Bonded male scent repelled all but the imprinting female.

"That was over two months ago. The bond should have lasted no more than twenty days—twenty-five at the most. When Riitha's mating cycle ended, the bonding imprint should have faded. It hasn't." Norii paused, fixing Tahl with a wide-eyed stare. "Riitha must be pregnant."

"How could that be, Norii?" Tahl's words were uttered in a hoarse whisper as his throat constricted. "All her eggs were removed before we left Hasu-din."

"Mistakes happen. Maybe the surgeon missed some of them." The med-tech's gaze shifted from the *shtahn* to the scan apparatus and back again as her own mind tried to absorb the startling news.

Desperately trying to assimilate the shock, Tahl closed his eyes and sought another explanation for what had happened. The *bey* surgeons were thorough. They would not have missed any of Riitha's eggs.

"You can't fight the effects of the bond much longer and stay healthy, Tahl." Concern and a hint of excitement made Norii's voice quiver as she spoke. "Either you'll have to go back to Luna Base, or Riitha will have to return to the *Dan tahlni.*"

"I can't go back to Earth-moon," Tahl said quietly. "And Riitha won't leave Luna Base."

Lines of confusion marred Norii's brow. "Why won't she leave? In fact, why did she let you leave without her in the first place? Your imprint is slight, and look what it's doing to you. Riitha must be going mad because of the separation."

Tahl leaned back, recalling the dreams and the presence of Riitha's voice in those dreams since he had left her. It all made a strange kind of sense now that he knew he was bonded.

"The bonded male is always driven to be with his mate, right, Norii? What's the one thing that will override the female's compulsion to be with him?"

Obviously puzzled, the med-tech hesitated. "Her children. But Riitha doesn't have any *jehni* yet."

"Maybe she does." He smiled at Norii's startled expression. "Can a chemical state of pregnancy be psychologically induced?"

Tahl rephrased the question calmly. Even though Norii had made the full transition to *venja-ahn* years before, he could not be sure how she would react to the speculative theory he was presenting, regardless of the evidence that supported it. "Is it remotely possible for the body to undergo the hormonal changes of pregnancy because the female's maternal instincts have been aroused?"

"No! Of course not." Norii spun about and stalked across the room.

Tahl rubbed the ache in his neck as he watched her. He felt sure that such a hormonal response was possible, especially in a *venja-ahn* female who had been forever denied the pleasure of motherhood. A critical mistake by the *bey* surgeons who had removed Riitha's eggs was also possible, but not likely. Riitha had been sexually active during the forty-six ship-time years they'd been gone from Hasu-din. The laws of probability favored the assumption that, if she had retained eggs, she would have conceived long before now.

Norii stood facing the wall for several minutes before turning and walking slowly back. She paused, staring at the floor as her mind opened up to embrace and consider the new concept Tahl had proposed. She did not look at the *shtahn* when she finally spoke.

"It's never happened before that I know of. If Riitha is experiencing a false state of pregnancy—" Norii sighed heavily as she weighed all the possibilities, then met Tahl's gaze. "If she is, I would assume she's following normal patterns. She'd do anything, take any risk—kill—to be with you. Only after birthing, when the *jehni* are hibernating and can't be disturbed, would that impulse be checked."

Dumbfounded, Tahl could only stare at the med-tech as her words supplied the missing piece in his own thoughts. "Yes, that's it." He blinked and inhaled sharply. "In a way, that's what's happening."

"I don't understand."

Tahl studied Norii for a long moment, wondering just how far he could trust her, and finally decided that he had no choice. He was in desperate need of a medical consultant, and Norii was the only member of the *Dan tahlni's* medical crew that had experienced a *venja-ahn* shift. Since the med-tech was *venja-ahn*, Tahl's experience with the Luna Base team suggested that Norii would ally herself with them. By sending her to Earth-moon, he would not only ensure Norii's silence and support, he would satisfy Riitha's demands. Then, perhaps, the effects of the bond would lessen and he could get some sleep. Taking Norii into his confidence was worth the risk.

The med-tech seated herself at Tahl's insistence and listened with rapt attention as he told her about the alien zygotes and Riitha's determination to study them for viability. When he was finished, Tahl sat quietly while Norii absorbed the information.

"I want to be sure I understand this." Norii's voice was hushed, but her eyes shone with a light of interest and excitement. "You think that the existence of human zygotes has aroused Riitha's maternal instincts to such a high degree that the hormonal sequence normally triggered by conception has been activated?"

"Yes, but since the zygotes are frozen and can't be moved, she's responding like a mother tending her hibernating *jehni* after birth. She won't leave them, and I can't stop thinking about them. She bonded me, the *shtahn jii*—the only one who can give her what she wants."

"What does she want?" Norii asked.

"You and a systems technician."

"Why?"

"To help her prove that the zygotes are viable."

"But why me?" Norii began to rock back and forth. "Hahr is certainly better qualified. He's an excellent physician with a secondary in medical hardware operation, construction, and theory. I'm really trained as an archaeologist."

"She asked for you, not Hahr." Tahl prudently did not mention that he suspected Riitha valued Norii's *venja-ahn* status above the *du-ahn* Hahr's equipment expertise. "The Luna Base site is an archaeological find, and you helped Riitha with her study of Chai-te Two's life forms. Would you consider a transfer to Earth-moon?"

"I don't know. This is all so unbelievable." A faint smile touched her mouth. "I must admit I am intrigued." The smile was replaced by a frown as Norii looked at Tahl. "You'll have to go back. If your theory is correct, the bond will last for ten years. You can't fight it."

"The bond seems to have manifested itself in the dream phase of my sleep cycle. I don't have any other symptoms except an occasional ache in my head. Your diagnosis about my not sleeping well is right, though. I haven't slept through a full cycle since I returned from Luna Base."

Norii's green eyes clouded with concern. "You just can't go

on this way. You must go back to Riitha."

Tahl shook his head. "No, I can't. My place is here at the control center of the mission. However, I think the sleeping problem will be solved once Riitha knows you and a technician are on your way to the moon. The dreams should stop when Riitha's demands are met. Even if they don't, now that I know a bond is the cause of the dreams, I may be able to adjust my mind to counter the effects. Besides, after you prove to her that the zygotes are nothing more than frozen, dead protoplasm, the hormonal sequence sustaining the imprint will end. I'll be free of her influence."

Her physical influence at least, Tahl thought ruefully.

Pulling thoughtfully on her long mustache, Norii glanced upward a moment, then back at Tahl. "What if they aren't dead? What if they are viable?"

"That's why I came to see you. I couldn't justify removing a physician and a tech from the main operation without a good reason—a logical reason. Bonded or not, my first duty is to the mission and the colony ship."

Norii's ears flicked forward expectantly.

"Let's say that the zygotes are essentially alive, that they are viable. If humans were able to freeze and maintain living cells, we could duplicate the process."

"What for?"

Tahl stared past her, absorbed in his thoughts as he spoke. "If a sixteen-celled embryo can be frozen and then revived to continue the growth process, maybe more complex organisms could be preserved."

"Such as?"

"Livestock."

Norii grimaced. "Preserved meat in any form can't provide the proper nutrition—"

"I'm not talking about freezing dead animals. I'm talking about freezing live ones—animals that can be revived. The crew would starve if some infection or accident wiped out the game pens. If we had a backup supply of frozen, living livestock, we'd never have to worry about being deprived of fresh-kill."

"What a fascinating idea." Norii paused thoughtfully. "There might be other applications, too."

"Then you think it might be worth an investigation?"

"Yes, I do, Tahl. Absolutely. Any process that will guarantee a constant supply of live game will be worth a great deal."

Tahl smiled. "So if the human zygotes prove to be viable, the *bey* will have a new science."

"And one less space-neurosis." Norii frowned suddenly. "What about the zygotes?"

"What about them?"

"What if they are viable? What then?"

Tahl was ready with an answer. "The responsibility of their disposition will be passed on to the Board of Mediators on the colony ship. They've waited a hundred million years. Another thirty-five won't matter."

Except to Riitha, he added silently.

After advising Norii to keep silent about the zygotes, Tahl left her to ponder her decision. He had new problems to worry about. He was bonded, and the imprint would remain until Riitha's hormonal status reverted to normal. Neither distance nor time could diminish the power of the mind-link between them. Nothing less than a miscarriage, the completion of the ten-year family cycle, or Riitha's death before birthing could sever the intangible chain.

But Riitha was mothering.

Tahl halted in the middle of the corridor and slumped against the wall, body and mind numbed by other implications of his bizarre circumstances. If the human zygotes were found to be viable and not just bits of ancient, alien tissue, how long would the bond and Riitha's power over him last? He had no way of knowing whether the bond would remain in force only until after the first human child knew life independent of the artificial womb or if it would endure, binding him to alien scent until the children reached maturity. How long was the human maturation process? Ten years? Twenty?

Tahl gasped and stumbled toward his quarters, stunned by the staggering realization that his destiny might be to assume the role of father to an entire alien race.

CHAPTER
TWENTY-THREE

Riitha completed the check of the ag-pod monitoring system, then joined Stocha at the drying table. He handed her a container of *ahsta* and gathered two more into his own arms. "I think we finally have all the *bugs* worked out of the system. This batch looks much better."

Riitha smiled as she started for the hatch. Stocha's fondness for human nonsense phrases, which he interjected into normal conversation whenever possible, amused her. Much to her dismay, however, he had not yet run across the phrase "heads or tails," and so the meaning still eluded her.

Halfway down the aisle, Riitha faltered and slumped to the floor, spilling the *ahsta*.

Stocha dropped his containers and leaned down to help her. "You're going to the infirmary, and no arguments this time."

Riitha snarled as his hand closed around her arm. "No. I'm not sick, just a little tired." She could not allow herself to be examined. Close scrutiny would reveal the inexplicable bond.

"*Very* tired." Stocha eased back with a frustrated sigh. "All right, but you *are* going to quarters, and you *are* going to sleep. You've been working much too hard the past couple of months, and I can't afford to let anything happen to you."

Riitha nodded as she pulled herself to her feet. Vuthe had almost completed the translations of the procedures for opening the metal wall into the inner lab. Soon, she could begin a real study of the human zygotes. Her knees buckled slightly as she reached for the scattered *ahsta.*

"I'll get that," Stocha said gently.

Riitha stepped back. "What are you going to do now?"

"Vuthe and I have to go outside for a while. We're days overdue for the RMC. You won't miss anything."

Riitha relaxed. The routine maintenance check would take hours, and she knew she hadn't been sleeping well or long enough.

Leaving Stocha to finish the weekly harvest, Riitha returned to her small white room and fell wearily into her bunk. She closed her eyes, but to no avail. Tahl's failure to send the personnel she needed was maddening, and as time passed, she was having more and more trouble controlling her temper. His disregard fed a mounting hormonal rage. The biologist did not know why the imprint had lasted so long, nor did she care. Bonded, she was as much a captive of her primitive instincts as was Tahl, and he was neglecting his duty toward her.

She lay, staring at the ceiling for several minutes, then finally gave up trying to rest. Dragging herself to her feet, she left the room and headed for the lower lab. It was empty. Riitha's restless anger ebbed as she sat before Michael's terminal and powered up.

Two figures in pressure suits appeared on the screen. They were outside and walking toward the entrance of the underground base, followed by the person who was shooting the pictures. Although the voices were distorted by the suit's audio systems, Riitha recognized the unseen cameraman's voice as Michael's.

"Slow down, Ross," he said breathlessly. "We're not running the lunar marathon."

One of the suited figures ahead turned and waved with a downward motion, then spoke to the third man. "Have you and Katya known each other long, Ivan?"

"*Nyet*. Only since going into space together. But of course, we would never have dared to become so—so close. *Nee kagdah!* It was thought that intimate relationships in such small quarters was, uh—inefficient. Such nonsense."

"Well, at least that's not a problem any more," Ross said.

"When did you last hear from your people?" Michael asked.

"Eight months ago. So we packed up and came here. We were most fortunate to have a platform with attitude jets we could modify."

"And we're most fortunate to have six such brilliant minds." Ross turned slightly toward Michael. "Too bad Wilson doesn't agree."

"Yeah, but he can't counter Andy's argument that we'll need them alive and well when we salvage the rest of their satellites and orbiting equipment."

The third man turned. "Your Andy. She is a genius, but a little, uh—unrealistic."

"I know." Michael laughed softly. "But I have to admit I admire her tenacity, especially now that Wilson's giving her such a hard time."

"I think everyone's being a bit rough on her," Ross said. "We don't have that asteroid yet."

"Such a wonderful plan! *Ochen khorasho!*" The pitch of Ivan's voice rose with enthusiasm. "And it seems to be working, *da?*"

"So far." Ross sighed. "It's so vital to our survival, I hate to think about it too much."

"Collins!" A frantic female voice intruded on the frequency. "Collins. Come in, please!"

"Collins here," Ross responded.

"Ross, get back to Base Control ASAP. There's a problem

with the rock."

As the party switched to thrust-packs and jetted toward the base, the image darkened and was abruptly replaced with a picture of Base Control as seen from the surveillance cameras.

Riitha felt the tension in the control room as she watched, and her stomach knotted as Ross, Mike, and Ivan ran through the door. Andy, Wilson, and four other humans were clustered around the main view-screen.

Wilson turned, his face contorting with anger. "Get that Russkie out of here!"

"Negative." Ross paused before the larger man, refusing to be intimidated. "They haven't heard from their government in eight months, either. That war's over. Ivan's a top-notch systems engineer and physicist. If the problem's as serious as you seem to think, I'll need all the help I can get."

"It's worse than serious." The woman monitoring the console shook her head. "It's a disaster."

Brushing past Wilson, Ross went to the console and sat in the empty chair beside the technician. Ivan took the next one. Michael walked over to Andy, who was standing apart from the rest, and slipped his arm around her shoulders.

"Okay," Ross said. "What happened?"

The technician spoke rapidly, but without panic. "There was a fight aboard the shuttle."

"A fight. What kind of fight? Words?" Ross's eyes widened as the technician averted her gaze. "Fists? What the hell were they fighting about?"

"They won't say anything except that one of Wilson's guys made a crack about—" The woman glanced at Andy.

"Don't worry about me, Jean. I know what they call me." Andy's tone was flat, her face ashen. "I just can't believe this has happened because someone thought they had to defend me. I just can't believe it." She rested her head on Michael's shoulder.

"What happened?" Ross asked impatiently.

Jean answered. "They accidentally triggered the

explosives—most of them anyway. The rock's out of control and speeding into the inner system. They—they lost it."

Ross whispered to Ivan, then turned to the console. Silence prevailed as the two men calculated and conferred.

The healthy pink glow on Ivan's cheeks paled to a dirty gray that almost matched the color of the lengthening beard adorning his jaw and chin. The wrinkles in his brow deepened as he leaned forward to punch a series of figures into the console, and his dark eyes were colored by the hard glint of determination. There was no hint of the excitement in Ivan's baritone voice as he asked Ross to plot the asteroid's altered trajectory.

Ross only nodded in reply, the ebony richness of his skin glistening with a fine film of perspiration as he concentrated on the computer console before him. The well developed muscles of the design engineer's arms and back bulged with tension under the white fabric of his shirt, and the flesh over his jaw flexed as he gritted his teeth.

Finally, Ross sat back. "It's too far off course, and it's going too fast. There's no way we can get it back."

Wilson cursed loudly and began to pace the room. Riitha was reminded of a caged *bita* preparing to attack, and she tensed unconsciously. The humans, too, watched Wilson nervously.

Ross stared at the security chief intently. "There's one other alternative."

"We can't risk the other shuttle to go out there again!" Wilson bellowed. He stopped, turning to glare at Ross with his fists clenched at his sides.

Remaining calm, Ross said, "I agree, but I have something else in mind. I've plotted the rock's present trajectory. It's on a direct course with Venus."

Ivan looked at the black human curiously. His ruddy face brightened suddenly, and he turned back to his companions.

"So what?" Wilson snapped.

"With the charges that are left, we have some steering capability. If we hit the planet at exactly the right spot, we can speed up its rotation period."

"We must not miss the opportunity," Ivan said. "Venus turns too slowly to generate a magnetic field, and the day-night cycle is longer than its year. We can change it. In fact, some scientists thought that an asteroid hit might be what slowed and altered the direction of its rotation in the first place, hundreds of millions of years ago."

"A magnetic field and a suitable day-night cycle will make it habitable," Ross added. "The algae are already taking care of the atmosphere."

"Is he right?" Wilson's gaze flicked over the faces watching him.

A fleeting frown tightened Andy's mouth. Michael noticed it but said nothing as she shook her head in warning.

Jean and another of Wilson's men exchanged a guarded glance. The technician spoke. "Yes, but the rock will have to be precisely on target."

Ross relaxed.

"That sounds better than trying to build artificial habitats here," Wilson said thoughtfully.

"Yes, but—" The technician cleared her throat. "The shuttle will have to follow the asteroid in order to set off the charges. They won't have enough fuel to make it back."

"I can't order them to do that." Wilson looked up, composed now and in control. "They'll have to decide."

Nodding, Jean opened a channel to the ship. Few words were exchanged. The crew unanimously opted to try for the Venus hit.

With the crisis diffused, the unnecessary spectators began to leave. Ross, Ivan, and Jean stayed at the console. Andy took Michael by the hand as they walked through the door.

Riitha stared as the screen blanked, her throat dry and her heart pounding. The asteroid hit on Chai-te Two had been engineered just as Stocha had hypothesized. The geologist deserved to know, but she couldn't tell him—not yet. He would want to see the source of her information, and she would not allow him to share the burden of responsibility for keeping Michael's record a secret from Tahl. One potential traitor among the Luna Base *venja-ahn* was enough.

Subduing a pang of guilt for having to hide a fact that would erase the blemish from Stocha's record, Riitha turned her attention back to the screen. This new scene was being recorded by Michael's microcam as he followed Andy into a small white room identical to Riitha's quarters on the base.

"You look tired," Michael said. "Maybe I should leave so you can get some rest."

"No, stay for a little while. I could use some company." Falling onto the bunk with a sigh, Andy closed her eyes and covered them with her arm. The image closed in as Michael sat on the bunk beside her. "Tell me something, will you?"

"Maybe," Michael chuckled. "Depends on what you want to know."

"How come it's Michael and not Mike?" Andy raised her arm slightly to peek at him.

"Because there were three other Mikes in my first grade class at good old P. S. 21 in Patterson, New Jersey, and I decided three was enough. I insisted on being called Michael. Even had to battle it out on the playground a couple of times to make it stick."

Andy grinned. "The rugged individualist even then, huh?"

"Yeah, maybe." Michael paused. "Now you tell me something."

"What?" Andy asked, feigning a scowl of suspicion.

"Seriously. I'm confused about why everyone was acting so secretive about the asteroid and Venus."

The coy playfulness left Andy's expression, and she lowered her arm over her eyes again. "They were bluffing Wilson, trying to buy time, to keep him stable by giving him hope. I think it's interesting that Jean decided to go along with it. Makes me wonder how many of Wilson's other supporters are getting uncomfortable with the way he's handling things."

"I've heard some rumblings, but I don't think anyone's going to challenge him, not at the moment anyway. He's just arrogant and crazy enough to shoot somebody if he's provoked."

"Unfortunately, I think you're right."

"Apparently so does Jean." Michael paused. "Which brings me back to my question about Venus. If we can make the planet habitable, why not try it?"

Andy lowered her arm and looked at him. "Venus won't be a fit place to live for centuries, perhaps millennia. Wilson's just a construction engineer who got stuck up here. He's not up on his planetary sciences."

Raising herself on one arm, Andy hesitated. "It's going to take hundreds of years for the algae to convert the atmosphere . . . if they survive. When that asteroid hits, it's going to throw millions of tons of dust and debris into the sky. Who knows how long it will take to settle or whether the little critters can adapt."

"Wilson's going to figure that out eventually. Then what?"

Andy shrugged absently. "We'll think of something when the time comes. Everything may be lost now anyway."

"Hey! What happened to the eternal optimist? You've still got your zygotes."

"What good are they if they're going to starve after they're born?"

"Come again?"

Andy sat up. "They'll have to eat. You think the odds on aliens finding them are high? Well, the odds against those aliens being made of the same amino acids as us are so high, I can't even begin to calculate them. Venusian life forms that are descended from Earth life forms will have the same amino acids. Something should evolve that will be nutritionally sound enough to sustain human life. If it doesn't, there really is no hope."

Michael leaned over and drew her closer to him. "Maybe it's time to let go, Andy. Sometimes there's just nothing more anyone can do to change the inevitable."

Andy drew back, her eyes narrowing as she studied Michael.

"No," she said softly, then shook her head emphatically as she pushed herself farther away. "No! I won't quit. I can't."

"Andy, the odds—"

"Damn the odds!" Andy's chest rose and fell in a quick, heavy rhythm. "I don't care how improbable or how hopeless it seems to you or Wilson or anyone else. That asteroid was the only chance any of us on this base had to survive. We lost it. We're on borrowed time. Now, more than ever, my 'baby box' is more important than anything. I don't want to die knowing the human race is just going to fizzle out of existence."

Michael didn't comment, and Andy curled up on the bunk, dismissing him with a wave of her hand. "Maybe you should go now."

"Riitha!" Edii l'hai called from the lock opening into the lab. "Stocha said I'd probably find you here."

Quickly shutting down the terminal, Riitha turned to glower at the approaching med-tech. "What do you want?"

Edii stopped short, startled by the biologist's abrupt sharpness. "Stocha's worried about you. He wants me to examine you."

Tense and wary, Riitha rose from her seat and moved slowly toward the tech. "I do not need an examination, and I do not appreciate being disturbed when I'm working." A hostile, guttural sound came unbidden from her throat, surprising her and increasing Edii's alarm. "Get out!"

Frightened, the med-tech began to tremble. She backed off as Riitha crept closer. "But, Stocha—"

"*Damn* Stocha! I'll deal with him. Now, go away!" Riitha hissed, then snarled in annoyance as the tech fled back through the lock. Knowing her odd behavior would be reported, but unconcerned, she returned to the terminal. She still had plenty of time before Stocha returned from the outside to confront her.

All senses alert, Riitha keyed for the program. The account resumed where it had left off, with Michael turning away from Andy and leaving the room. The next scene had been shot by the surveillance cameras in Base Control, the ones located on opposite sides of the large view-screen above the main computer console. Ross was seated at the terminals. He nodded as Michael took the seat beside him.

"How's it going?" Michael asked. His manner was casual, but his eyes betrayed the troubled weariness he was feeling.

Ross shrugged, his expression grim. "Fine, all things considered. They're on course, and the first correction went off without a hitch. Unfortunately, it's not going to help us get out of this mess."

"So Andy tells me," Michael muttered glumly. "It didn't take Wilson long to figure it out, either. I hear he tried to recall the shuttle."

"Too late. Besides, the crew says they wouldn't have come back anyway. They knew what the situation was when they chose to go in. Apparently, they want to make sure they leave the best world possible for the little green critters, just in case they eventually do turn into little green men. Gotta give them credit."

"At least they're doing something to help," Michael said softly, the muscles in his jaw flexing as he clenched his teeth.

"What's that supposed to mean?"

"I don't have any business being here, Ross. I just happened to be snooping around on the wrong story."

"Or the right one. You're alive."

"But for what? I'm not contributing anything. Andy intervened because she didn't want a murder on her conscience."

Ross sat back and rubbed his chin. "There's got to be more to it than that. She must have convinced someone that your particular talents were valuable. Otherwise, you wouldn't be here."

Michael gave him a long, hard look. "If that's true, then I've really let her down. Wilson so much as told me he was going to take over the base. I should have picked up on it, but I was so, uh—preoccupied with Andy, I didn't. Now, everyone's suffering because of it."

"How many times have you been in love—really in love?"

Michael smiled slightly. "Just once."

"And that's an acceptable excuse—once. So what else is happening?"

"Nothing. Like I said, I don't have much to do. Any word on the Europeans? If they'd land or something, at least I could make an entry in the historical files."

"No such luck, Michael. They're still orbiting."

"Wilson won't budge, huh?"

"Nope. They say they can hold out for another few weeks, but we've got to figure out a way to either persuade Wilson to let them land or get them down ourselves."

"Why don't they just come down? They could land anywhere and get to the base in suits."

Ross looked at him askance. "Would you want to bet your life on Wilson's good nature? There's no reason to think he'd let them into the base just because they got to the ground. No, they're better off waiting it out up there."

"I guess. We're all going to buy it soon anyway."

"Soon?"

"Relatively speaking. On Earth we'd all have anywhere from forty to sixty years ahead of us. Now we've got what? A year? A year and a half on the outside?"

Ross just nodded.

Rubbing his eyes, Michael said, "Too bad our technology isn't just a little more advanced."

Ross gave the reporter a sidelong glance. "If it were, we probably would have destroyed the world sooner."

"Maybe, but if we knew how to do that suspended animation stuff they used in the old science-fiction movies, we would be able to move to Venus in five hundred years."

Amazed, Ross stared at him, then laughed aloud. "You know, you might just have something there."

"What?"

"The edge we need to control Wilson. We can build cryonic preservation units."

"We can?" A perplexed frown exaggerated the worry lines around Michael's eyes and mouth.

"Sure, but we'll need that orbiting space station for parts and supplies."

Mike blinked uncertainly, then grinned. "Oh, yeah. Right. And don't they have an expert on this kind of thing up there with them?"

Ross's grin was broader. "They do now." They patted each other on the back, then Ross's expression turned serious. "Before we can put this plan into effect—" He stopped speaking suddenly as Michael put a finger up to his mouth and glanced at the cameras. Ross tilted his head back and lowered it slowly in a gesture of understanding. When Michael rose and walked across the room to the machine that dispensed coffee, Ross followed.

The picture cut out suddenly and was almost instantly replaced by a view of Ross grimacing as he took a sip of black liquid. He shrugged and looked directly into the camera, indicating that Michael was now recording with his microcam.

"Some sugar would sure help this a lot," Ross said.

"We don't have any sugar," Michael said quietly. "And we don't have any time to waste. I don't know if Wilson or his people actually watch every minute of these surveillance tapes, but we can't be too careful. Add some fake creamer and tell me what you were going to say back there."

Turning, Ross carefully and slowly spooned a white powder into his cup. He talked rapidly. "Before we can go ahead with the cryonic unit plan, we'll have to consult Andy. We can keep Wilson at bay for a long time with this one, but we'll have to be convincing, which means actually building the units. Andy's people are the only ones who can do that."

"I don't think that's a problem," Michael replied. "She'll agree to anything that will keep Wilson happy and lessen the threat on the zygote bank. I'll talk to her about it."

"And I'll start putting together a list of hardware and personnel still trapped in low earth orbit, and why they're essential to the success of the project for Wilson." Taking another

THE ALIEN DARK

sip, Ross rolled his eyes and set the capped cup down to add
more creamer.

"Why won't this plan work?" Michael asked.

"No reason why it shouldn't. Wilson's desperate—"

"No," the reporter interjected. "Why won't the preservation units work?"

"They will. It's just that the base won't run by itself. It
would have to be shut down, and people coming out of cryonic
freeze are incapacitated for a long time. So who's gonna be
around to turn on the power and play nursemaid?"

Michael paused. "Andy's aliens?"

"There's a thought." Picking up his cup, Ross walked back
to the monitoring console.

Michael continued to record as he left Base Control and hurried through the empty corridors toward the observation
dome. He stopped as he entered the large lounge to chat with a
group of people sitting at a table just inside the door.

"Hi, Ivan." Michael greeted the robust, heavy-set man.
"The beard's coming along nicely."

Stroking the gray growth, Ivan chuckled. "Yes. It is but another demonstration of rebellion against too many years of capitulation to Soviet conservatism. As is the conversation. Such
a joy." His dark eyes sparkled brightly.

"What are you talking about?"

"Anything we want to." Laughing, Ivan stretched out his
arms. The others at the table raised their cups, touched them,
then drank. When they were finished, Ivan's demeanor shifted
from joviality to intense seriousness. "Specifically, we were discussing the possibility of building a generation ship."

"You're kidding."

"Not at all. It would be possible if we had access to all the
known space stations and platforms orbiting Earth. Quite
possible."

"And if we had all the people that we know are still alive," a
small woman added. "We'd have a marginally adequate genepool."

"What about fuel?" Michael asked.

Ivan cocked his head, welcoming the questions. "The moon is composed of forty percent oxygen."

"Okay, then what about the elements the moon doesn't have?" the reporter countered. "The ones we sent a shuttle out to get because we can't maintain an ecological balance here on Luna Base without them, the ones we're not going to get because the mission failed. What about that?"

Ivan grinned, obviously enjoying the inherent challenge in the exchange. "A slowly moving ship could pick up an asteroid on its way out of the system. No problem. The equipment and people are the problem. And it's so—so—" He shrugged, turning his hands palm up.

"Frustrating?" Michael offered.

"Ah, *da*. Frustrating. It is so frustrating knowing that all we need is out there, but we cannot go get it. Worse than the Soviets, this Wilson who does not see the logic of collecting all available resources. But we make our plans anyway. It helps pass the time."

"Yes, I suppose it does." Michael turned away, then walked to the far side of the dome and sat down.

Riitha was disappointed when Michael moved on. Her interest in Ivan's plan had been aroused when she realized that, by definition, a generation ship was designed to promote the raising of children. There was no time to dwell on the fascinating concept, however, as Michael began to speak his thoughts aloud, in a hushed whisper that did not mask his depression and fatigue.

"Michael Jamieson. Personal diary. I don't understand them—Andy, Ross, and the others. No matter how bad things get, they can always come up with some preposterous idea to keep their hopes alive.

"Like this generation ship business Ivan's got all those people stirred up about. I mean, it stands to reason that if the scheme had a snowflake's chance in hell of working, we'd already be doing something about it. At least Ross's hair-brained ideas have been put to good use." Michael paused, then added, "Come to think of it, a generation ship was his idea, too.

"Guess I've been a reporter too long. I've had to deal with reality too often, and I've learned that all the hoping in the world can't change the way things are. And the truth of the matter is—we're all gonna die here soon. The end . . . except for Andy's 'baby box.' "

The image panned upward to scan the endless darkness visible through the dome. "Andy says there are hundreds of billions of stars in this galaxy. That's a lot of stars. Perhaps it's not too outrageous to think that some of them are inhabited by intelligent species. But why would they come here?

"Seems to me," Michael went on, "that it's more likely for intelligent life to evolve on Venus, provided the algae survive the bomb we're about to drop on them. Maybe they'll come here and discover the base." He laughed shortly. "Now that would be something to see. I can just imagine the religious shock waves when they find out they were planted and weren't created by some divine being."

He sighed. "Makes one wonder how we got started, or how anyone else out there got started, if there's anyone else out there. Are you out there?"

"Not yet," Riitha whispered. "Not then."

Before it faded, the image lingered, then panned again as though searching for some sign of life in the black expanse.

Too tired to watch any more, Riitha powered down the terminal and leaned back. The silence was soothing, but the peace and quiet did not last long. Stocha bellowed out her name as he strode through the airlock.

"Riitha! What *in tarnation* do you think you're doing?" the geologist demanded loudly as he came up beside her and looked down with fierce, angry eyes. "Edii's a *nervous wreck*. She's locked herself in her quarters, and she won't come out."

"She surprised me, that's all," Riitha said calmly. "I'm sorry I frightened her, but she should know better than to *sneak up* on me like that."

Stocha smiled at Riitha's use of the alien phrase, and his manner softened. "What were you doing that was so engrossing you didn't hear her?"

"Nothing, I'm just over-tired. My senses are duller than usual because of it." Riitha met his gaze evenly, then yawned and rubbed the back of her neck. "If it's all right with you, I think I'll go back to my quarters and rest now."

Stocha nodded. "A good idea. We're almost ready to raise the metal wall. You'll need to be rested."

Exhaustion dampened Riitha's outward enthusiasm, but her pulse quickened at the thought of being one step closer to coming into direct contact with Andy's precious zygote bank. "When?"

"Another day or so."

Smiling, the biologist rose out of the chair and turned to leave, then glanced back over her shoulder. "I'm really sorry about Edii. I hope she'll come out before too long."

Stocha grinned slyly, and his nose twitched with amusement. "Oh, she'll be out soon. I guarantee it."

"How can you be so sure?"

"Because Edii's going back to the *Dan tahlni*. Tahl has agreed to transfer Norii and a tech."

Finding it difficult to contain her relief and happiness, Riitha nodded curtly and hurried through the airlock. Stocha's news had filled her with an immediate sense of peace and tranquility. For the first time in two months, she could momentarily forget the driving need to work and enjoy the luxurious sleep of the untroubled. The zygotes would soon be within reach, and Tahl had not forsaken her.

CHAPTER
TWENTY-FOUR

"Bier!"

Filtered by tiers of dense foliage, the sound of his name reached the psychologist as no more than a mumble. Standing up, Bier parted lush leaves and spied Sani slowly moving through the tight rows of vegetation.

"Are you there?" Sani called.

Ducking out of sight, Bier cursed under his breath. The expanded hydroponic farm surrounded the small space he reserved for his hybrid experiments, and he resented any intrusion into his private domain. No one on the *Dan tahlni* station shared his appreciation for the beauty of plants, especially the mediator. He glanced at the measure of fertilizer clutched in his hand and sighed. It was too precious to waste, but Sani could not be ignored.

"Over here, Sani! Section six, third level."

While Bier waited for the mediator, he spread the nutrient evenly around the thick trunk of a potted plant. He smiled with satisfaction as he worked the mix into the soil, taking care not to bruise the exposed root knots. There was no other plant quite like *venja ahsta shan* in the universe.

Bier's feeling of peace was shattered by the rustle of leaves and Sani's complaints as she struggled through the narrow passage. He turned to a water valve and set it for a fine mist.

"Looks like a high crop yield, Bier. The ag-techs have done well." Breathless and slightly bedraggled, Sani stepped into the ornamental garden. As she adjusted her burnt orange robe and brushed her mane out of her face, the mediator's curious gaze swept the area. She frowned as she approached the plant nearest her and reached out to touch a long, slender leaf. "What are these?"

Bier grabbed Sani's wrist before her fingers brushed the plant. "The leaves are delicate. They'll turn brown if handled too roughly."

"What is it?" Pulling free of the psychologist's grasp, Sani cocked her head to peer at the plant more closely. Then, she turned and stared at the large plant Bier had been tending just before her arrival. "And that?"

"It's a variation of *ahsta*," he said softly.

"But it's so big." Clasping her hands in front of her, Sani leaned in to study the plant. "The leaf stems are much too fine. There aren't enough calories in this to satisfy a small scavenger."

"It's not a crop plant," Bier said defensively.

"Then what good is it?"

"I like to look at it." Bier turned away from the mediator's mocking eyes and flicked the water valve. Brushing dirt from his hands, he asked, "What's happened that's so important you've come all the way up here to see me?"

"I just wanted to talk to you without being overheard."

"No one will hear us here, I'm sure." Bier smiled, stopped, and pulled a couple of fur-covered cushions out from under a tier. "These are all I have to offer in the way of comfort."

Sani took one of the pillows, wrinkled her nose, then gave it a cursory dusting and tossed it on the floor. They sat.

"Something's wrong on Luna Base, Bier. I've just heard that Norii f'ach and Tena s'uch are being transferred to Earth-moon because Edii and Siva asked to return to the *Dan tahlni*."

"That doesn't strike me as unusual." Bier scratched behind his ear. "They've both been away a long time."

"I know. It actually makes sense. Edii's asked for permission to begin advanced medical training under Hahr. We could use a third doctor, now that we're spread out in four different locations. Although, we could do without Luna Base."

Bier simply shrugged.

"I can't help but wonder why Tahl is sending a power-com tech to replace a biologist, though. Tena's secondary isn't even remotely related to the organic sciences."

"Tahl must have good reasons."

Sani studied him evenly. "According to Tahl's report, Stocha's team has found something he believes to be of vital importance to the *bey*. He didn't say what specifically, but I don't like it."

"I've heard that the *jehda tohm* computer banks contain all their accumulated scientific knowledge. Since they seem to want a power-com tech more than a second biologist, Tena may be needed to help extract that knowledge from the data system."

"But there's so much to be done here and on the separation plant, I must question the wisdom of sending replacements at all."

"That's something to consider, I suppose."

Sani curled into a prone position and smoothed her robe. "Because we're ahead of schedule, Tahl feels that this is the best time to pursue the Luna Base project. Once the signal from Hasu-din is received and the departure of the colony ship is confirmed, industrial production will escalate as a matter of course."

"He may be right about that, Sani. That signal will be our first contact with home in almost forty-six years."

The mediator quickly shook her head. "But why Tena? She's

the best technician we have. When Bohn reaches the receiver, we'll need her on the *Dan tahlni* to coordinate and counter-check his findings. Making sure the interstellar receiver is oper-ating flawlessly is too critical to the success of our mission to let anyone but Tena handle the final equipment evaluation. What has Stocha found that could possibly be more impor-tant? Don't you think it's odd?"

Bier's nose twitched in thought. Tahl's decision to send Tena, knowing the receiver had malfunctioned, did seem suspicious.

A tinge of pain at the base of the psychologist's skull be-came a throb, and Bier started, realizing it was a manifesta-tion of guilt. His attempt to push Tahl into fatal burn-out had happened so long ago, he had almost forgotten the pledge of restitution he had made to the *shtahn jii*. He must not question Tahl's actions or decisions. Yet, if any of those decisions were potentially harmful to the *bey*, Bier could not ignore his responsibility as the mission's psychologist and re-main silent. Maintaining the delicate balance between the two was not easy, but unless Tahl deliberately committed an overt act of treason against the *bey*, Bier was honor-bound by his pledge.

Sani, unaware of Bier's oath to the *shtahn* or the mental and physical discomfort her suspicions evoked in the psychologist, continued. "There's something else, too. Tahl is bonded."

Bier inhaled sharply, startled by this news, then exhaled slowly to ease the tension. He knew that Tahl was adamant about taking *muath*. As the *shtahn jii*, Tahl recognized that he could not afford to have a bond influence his decisions. Still, Bier responded cautiously. "I don't see the significance."

"I've studied him closely all these years," Sani said, "look-ing for indications of deviant behavior. I know his patterns, and he's changed since returning from Luna Base. He's edgy, irritable, and he isn't sleeping. I'm absolutely certain that Tahl was imprinted on Earth-moon."

"He may have been bonded on Earth-moon, Sani, but that

bond couldn't possibly be in effect now. Too much time has passed."

Sani looked at him steadily. "The bond would hold if the female were pregnant."

Bier laughed. "That's not possible, either."

"Not necessarily. I have to admit it isn't probable, but it's not impossible. There's no other explanation for Tahl's sustained bond."

"Are you certain it's the same imprint? Couldn't Tahl have been bonded on Earth-moon, been released from that imprint, and then bonded again here?"

"No," Sani said emphatically. "It's the same imprint. I've been around him often enough to tell."

Being male and unaffected by bonded-male scent, Bier had to accept Sani's female judgment. "That might explain why Edii and Siva requested transfer back to the *Dan tahlni*. One of them—"

"It's not one of them," Sani scoffed. "It's Riitha."

"How can you be so sure?"

Snorting her impatience, Sani explained. "I'm aware of the *venja-ahn* inclination to mate for life. It's an illogical tendency caused by back-brain interference with emotional stability. No wonder there are so few of you left. This restrictive trait denies genetic diversification, and . . ." Sani's voice trailed off. "Neither Tahl nor Riitha has taken another mate in the past twenty-one years. I know her cycle. She was in heat while Tahl was on Luna Base. He's been bonded by Riitha."

Bier nodded, realizing Sani's deductions were correct. "Then why hasn't Riitha returned here?"

"I don't know. Why did she go to Earth-moon to begin with?" Sani's claws dug into the cushion. "It took her years to convince Tahl that a robot probe to visit Chai-te Two and collect specimens wouldn't violate the integrity of the planet or his edict to exempt Chai-te Two from *bey* exploitation. Luna Base is more important to her than her study of those alien life forms—more important than even her need to be with Tahl.

There's something on Earth-moon that might explain why the bond has been sustained. I must know what."

Thin leather shredded under Sani's hand. Bier flinched.

"I need an agent, Bier, a *du-ahn* technician to go to Luna Base in Tena's place. Someone I can trust." Sani glanced at the mutilated cushion, sheathed her claws, and pulled herself into a sitting posture. "Which technician can I safely engage as an aid?"

Bier hesitated.

"Surely there must be someone."

"Lish t'wan," Bier said quickly. Advising Sani did not violate his promise to Tahl, and he could not afford to antagonize the mediator. Besides, her suspicions about the Luna Base project were worth investigating. He had to ascertain the activities on Earth-moon were not endangering the mission, and subsequently the foundation for *venja-ahn* emergence.

Sani frowned. "Lish?"

"She's perfect for your purposes. Her dedication to the mission and the species is unquestionable. She's *du-ahn*, and her personal problem could work to your advantage."

"Ah, yes. Vuthe f'stiida."

"Lish blames Tahl for sending him with the Earth-moon expedition," Bier noted.

"He did not have to accept the assignment."

Bier shrugged. Mission males, with few exceptions, did not take *muath*. Since conceptions were impossible, they did not have to suffer the distractions of pain-awareness in order to retain their freedom from intent females. Lish t'wan was of weak-scent, however. Her musk was ineffectual, and everyone rejected her except Vuthe. Whether from pity or a perverted pleasure-sense, he had mated with her regularly until his transfer to Luna Base seven years before. Since then, although a few males had submitted to her, Lish had been forced to pass repeated mating cycles without sexual relief. Drugs helped, but the mental and physical trauma was still acute. Lish would do anything for the mediator if Sani could secure her a transfer to

Earth-moon and Vuthe.

"Lish t'wan." Sani smiled. "Strange. I was very upset when I learned of her scent deficiency. I was afraid it might cause problems."

"There was no way of knowing before we launched from Hasu-din. She wasn't mature."

"I would not have thought her affliction would become so useful." Sani paused, then nodded. "We'll send Lish."

"If Tahl agrees. He has the final word."

"He'll agree." The mediator spoke confidently. "There will be no logical reason not to. Tena's presence on the *Dan tahlni* is vital to mission safety, and Lish will have a medical recommendation from you and Hahr. He will have to approve Lish's transfer."

Bier turned to gaze at the hybrid *ahsta*. If the situation were not so serious, the ironic complexities would be amusing. Every effort Sani made to secure the mission's position in the Chai-te system reinforced the matrix from which *venja-ahn* would emerge in force. Once established, the intuitive mode would eventually gain supremacy over the limited *du-ahn*. All they needed was time.

CHAPTER
TWENTY-FIVE

"Initiate the sequence, Vuthe." Stocha turned to Riitha and smiled tightly. "Well, *here goes nothing*."

Riitha glanced at the geologist, puzzled by the meaningless phrase but too excited to ask for an explanation. A low-pitched whirring sound teased the stillness of anticipation as the metal wall began to fold upward, revealing a glass wall with an air-lock rather than an ordinary door. The three *bey* scientists gaped at the orderly laboratory on the far side.

Most of the alien equipment was covered with white cloth. Stacks of boxes, clearly labeled and numbered, were neatly arranged on the floor between tables and in the corners. Riitha took it all in with one swift glance before her attention fastened on another airlock set into the wall across the room. The zygote bank rested in the chamber behind it.

Unless, Riitha thought with a shudder, the human Wilson had destroyed it millennia ago. Considering the care that had been taken with the lab equipment, that did not seem likely. Chilled and anxious, Riitha wrapped her arms around herself.

Stocha let out a long, slow breath. "Everything seems to be in good condition. I suggest we wait until we've all rested before we attempt to open the next airlock."

"I agree," Vuthe said. "I want to review the procedure before we start."

Riitha nodded.

"At least we'll have more help in a few days." Stocha rubbed his eyes and yawned. "Tahl said Norii was quite positive about the prospects of the zygote study. Lish, of course, is another matter. Tahl's warning was explicit. She does not know why she is being sent or what we're doing."

Vuthe frowned. "And she must not know—ever. Lish is *duahn* and fanatically dedicated to *bey* expansion. I know her well, and she would consider the zygote study an act against the *bey*."

"Then why did Tahl send her?" Riitha asked.

Stocha shrugged. "Because Sani insisted, and she had logical reasons. He had to comply."

"But she's useless to us." Riitha looked helplessly at Stocha.

"Not entirely," the geologist said. "We'll transfer Chiun down here and use Lish in Base Control. It's a routine job and familiar to her. It's the only solution."

Riitha hesitated as Vuthe and Stocha turned to leave. Stocha glanced back. "Are you coming?"

"In a few minutes. I just have to finish filing some notes." Riitha had been taking better care of herself lately, so Stocha didn't argue. When they were gone, she wandered over to Michael's terminal and sat down.

During the past several weeks, Riitha's time and attention had been exclusively devoted to the task of raising the metal wall and gaining access to the zygote lab. She had actually resisted several opportunities to continue her review of the ancient account. It was not improbable to suppose that Wilson had ended everything a hundred million years ago, and Riitha's desire to know had been constantly overpowered by the fear that Andy's efforts and those of the *bey* Luna Base team had all been in vain. She remembered all too well that first image of Michael Jamieson. His extreme stress and fatigue might have been caused by the ever-present threat to the zygotes.

The orderly appearance of the exposed inner lab bolstered her courage. Riitha placed trembling fingers on the keyboard and called up the program.

The picture showed a terminal exactly like the one she was viewing, then shifted to focus on an unfamiliar man at the console beside it. Riitha glanced to the side, certain that the picture was of the same terminal at which she was now sitting.

On the screen, the man beside Michael turned his head to look at the reporter expectantly. Fair-haired with blue eyes, he looked even more exhausted then Michael. The dark circles under his eyes were accented against the pale smoothness of his skin, and the fine lines of stress and fatigue around his mouth and across his brow seemed out of place on his boyish face. He swayed slightly, his eyelids drooping closed, but when Michael spoke to him, he snapped awake with a start.

"Have you got that, Greg?" Michael's voice asked.

Greg nodded. "Got it. How much more?"

"Reams. We've been feeding cryonic control data into this system for weeks, and judging by what's left, we'll be at it for a few more." Michael paused. "I don't know about you, but I'd find it a lot easier to keep going if I wasn't hungry all the time."

Greg nodded. "When we got all those extra people to feed, Wilson didn't have any choice but to start rationing."

The image panned to the long gun at the man's side, then returned to a study of the man's face.

"I suppose," Michael said. "But there were only five Europeans and three Japanese, and they had six months worth of stores with them."

"Yeah." Greg frowned. "Still, the new projections give us an extra year, maybe more."

"If we live that long."

The man laughed, then the image jumped sharply. Andy emerged from the passageway airlock and looked directly at the camera. She motioned to Michael.

"Take a break, Greg," Michael said. "I'll be right back."

Michael met Andy in a corner of the outer lab by the language terminal.

"You look terrible, Andy. What happened?"

Riitha viewed the woman with alarm. The skin beneath her brown eyes was dark and puffy, and looked especially bad in contrast to the pallor of the skin drawn tautly over her sunken cheeks. Andy had lost a lot of weight, too, and a faded red shirt that had once fit the round curves of her figure now hung loosely on her bony frame. Her brown hair no longer gleamed with a rich luster, but fell in limp, straight strands to her sagging shoulders, and the fullness of her lips was lost in the grim set of her mouth. In all, Andy looked as though she'd just come out of trauma-induced hibernation.

"I just had another fight with Wilson."

Michael swore. "What's his problem now?"

"Same old thing." Andy rubbed her hands together nervously. "He's not pleased with our rate of progress on the cryonic plan."

"That ignorant son-of-a-bitch! It's only been six months. We've got four of them done and two almost finished, and the control program is being entered. Everyone working on this damn pipe-dream is headed for imminent physical collapse. What the hell does he want?"

Andy sighed again. "He wants us to suspend work on the zygote programming and setup until we've finished twenty units . . . which will take us roughly five or six years."

"Oh, well—that's only three or four years more than we've got. No problem." Michael inhaled deeply, and his hand became visible as he reached out to brush a stray lock of hair off Andy's forehead. "Look, I'll try to think of something, okay? I've been nosing around a bit and some of his own people are grumbling about him, too. In the meantime, let's just try and keep him happy."

Andy nodded. "All right. Guess I might as well start by checking out your program. Greg told Wilson you've still got a long way to go before you're finished, and he thinks you're stalling."

"I am—sort of. Contrary to what I've been telling Greg, we're quite close to being done."

"Why *aren't* you telling Greg?" There was a note of exasperation in Andy's tone. "I really don't need the additional stress of having to make unnecessary excuses for you to Wilson."

"I have a good reason. The longer the project takes, the more disgruntled Greg becomes. I'm sure I can turn him around to our way of thinking eventually."

Shaking her head, Andy brushed past Michael. The reporter turned to follow her to his seat at the terminal. Andy nodded to Greg as Michael slid into position behind the console and waited quietly as she quickly ran through the program.

"What you've got here is good," Andy said when she was finished, "but you'll have to step up the pace." With another nod at Greg, she left to examine another bank of terminals on the far side of the outer lab.

"Step up the pace?" Greg's eyes flashed with indignation.

"Don't blame Andy," Michael said. "Wilson just threatened the zygote program again. Seems he thinks we're not working hard or fast enough."

Greg scowled. "He's got a nerve."

"Yeah, he certainly does. I noticed he doesn't seem to have dropped any weight, either."

Greg only nodded, but his eyes narrowed thoughtfully.

The image stayed focused on the terminal as the data feed continued. Then, the tense silence was shattered by a loud disturbance at the entrance airlock. Michael shifted position to capture the scene with the microcam.

Wilson and three men burst into the lab with guns leveled. Each one took aim on a member of Andy's team, ignoring the men and women Wilson had assigned to work on the cryonic project.

Riitha's breath caught in her throat as she realized Wilson's objective could be nothing other than the destruction of the zygote bank.

"Jamieson! Dr. Knight!" Wilson barked. "Over by the wall and keep your hands in sight."

As Michael rose and walked toward the wall as directed, he kept his body angled to record the event as completely as possible.

Wilson turned to the other two members of Andy's team and waved his gun at them. "Gunther! You and your friend— the same." His finger flexed on the trigger as the two men slowly started to move.

"This isn't going to get your units built any quicker," Michael said, diverting Wilson's attention from the two frightened zygote technicians.

Wilson glanced toward the reporter and smiled smugly. "When you folks aren't preoccupied with that damn 'baby box,' they'll get built quick enough. Those units are soon to be your only hope of survival. Kiss your zygotes goodbye, Dr. Knight." He looked at one of his men and nodded toward the inner lab. "Do it."

The camera jerked as Michael turned suddenly to intercept Andy, who had lunged toward Wilson with a fierce cry. Michael wasn't fast enough. Andy eluded his grasp, and Riitha watched in breathless horror as Wilson swung his gun at the charging woman, catching her full force on the arm and throwing her against the wall. She slid to the floor, conscious but dazed.

The image closed in on Wilson slightly as Michael took a step forward, then stopped as the angry security chief trained his gun on the reporter.

"Don't tempt me, Jamieson. I don't need much of an excuse to get rid of you."

"Be reasonable," Michael said with strained calm. "You're

gonna need that zygote bank to perpetuate the human race one of these centuries."

"Give me a break, Jamieson. The good doctor has been feeding you all that garbage just so you'll help her. She used that preposterous plan to get herself a ride off Earth. Bought herself a few more years of life, just like the rest of us." Wilson waved his gun toward the inner lab again, ordering his man to move. "Help him, Harper," he said to a second man.

As the two armed men walked toward the airlock into the inner lab, the picture jumped crazily. Michael had sprung sideways to a nearby console. His hand appeared and hit the board. Then the image panned upward to catch a view of the metal wall as it began a quick descent. The sound of gunfire followed almost simultaneously, and the picture became a kaleidoscopic mixture of color and movement as Michael fell to the floor with a startled cry of pain. Another, more agonized scream reverberated through the room before the chaos ceased.

The camera now focused on the base of the console, moving slowly as Michael eased himself into a position to see what had happened. Wilson's frantic curses could be heard in the background, and as the microcam cleared the console, Riitha saw why. The metal security wall had crushed one of his men. The second man dropped his gun and stared in open-mouthed shock at the visible half of the body.

Michael groaned as he eased himself into a sitting posture, affording the microcam an oddly angled view of the immediate vicinity. Still cursing, Wilson lowered his gun slightly and angrily hit the wall behind him with a backward swing.

As though on cue, Greg, who was still seated at the cryonic terminals just in front of Michael, jumped up and threw himself at Wilson. The man standing right beside the security chief took a step backward, bringing his leg within Michael's grasp. As Greg's momentum pushed Wilson over the side of the console, Michael clamped his hands around the other man's ankle and pulled, throwing him off balance and toppling him to the floor. In the background, Wilson's head struck the corner of the console, and he slumped to the floor unmoving.

Ivan and a woman, another of Andy's people, appeared from the side of the screen. The man Michael had felled tried to raise his gun, but Ivan kicked it from his grasp. The woman quickly retrieved it, then she and Ivan collected the weapons from the rest of Wilson's people. All of them, still sitting at terminals, watched the scene in silence and did not react.

The sound of Michael's labored breathing hissed through the terminal speakers as he crawled past the fallen man in front of him. Just ahead, Andy sat on the floor, holding her arm. When she saw the reporter, her smile was wide and full of relief. As Michael drew closer, she reached out to touch him.

"You're all right." Her voice quivered. "I thought—"

"It'll take more than a little bullet to stop him," Greg said from off-camera.

Michael turned his body slightly. Greg was kneeling beside Wilson's body, holding the man's limp wrist. "How is he?" the reporter asked weakly.

Greg looked toward Michael. "He's dead. Must have broken his neck when he hit the console. Glad it was Wilson and not you, and that's a fact."

"Does that mean you've changed sides?" Michael asked softly.

"Guess so." Holding the gun he had taken from Wilson, Greg stood up and glanced around the lab at the others who had followed Wilson. "What about the rest of you? Anybody feel like carrying on Wilson's fight?"

The tension in the lab dissipated in a collective sigh of relief and the shaking of heads.

Greg smiled down at Michael. "Looks like the lab is secure."

"But there are others," Andy said. "They're still armed and stationed all over the base."

"Let's get Ross on line," Michael suggested. "Maybe he can figure out a way to handle this without anyone else getting hurt."

Greg squatted down beside Michael. "For what it's worth, Wilson's been bearing down pretty hard on everyone lately. I don't think anyone's gonna be very sorry that his reign is over. There are a couple who might argue the point, but I can deal with them."

"Sounds good to me. Let's get on with it." The picture shook as Michael coughed repeatedly.

"I'll take care of it," Greg said as he stood up. "You take care of him, Andy."

"I will."

Two others from Wilson's entourage joined Greg as he went through the airlock.

Andy's arm blocked the camera lens for a second as she brushed Michael's hair back over his ear. "You could have been killed. Why did you do it?"

Michael coughed again. "Guess I don't want to see us fizzle out of existence, either. If Wilson had destroyed the zygote bank . . ." His voice trailed off uncertainly.

Tears trickled from Andy's eyes, and a shudder rippled across her shoulders. She paused to catch her breath, then said quietly, "I think we'd better get you to the infirmary."

A shortness of breath gripped Riitha, also, as the screen darkened. As she reached out to turn off the program, she cried out softly, noticing the blood on her palm. She had been so involved with the intense events playing on the screen, she had stabbed herself with her own claws.

Turning off the terminal, the biologist sat back to collect her thoughts. Her heart was pounding erratically, and her temples throbbed with fear for the safety of the zygotes.

But the bank was intact, and the man who had threatened it had died.

Riitha breathed deeply, feeling a greater respect for the humans who, driven by something like blood-lust, had risked their lives to save the zygotes. The primal urge to defend their young was something even the *du-ahn* would understand. Perhaps, Riitha thought as her mind and body calmed, this was the key to the *bey*'s acceptance of the *jehda tohm*.

She felt certain that Tahl would understand, but the story it-self was too controversial and complicated to reveal by long-distance communication. She would have to wait until his next visit. Until then, there was much to be done. The continued existence of a viable human zygote bank was her responsibility now.

CHAPTER
TWENTY-SIX

Lish shifted in the alien chair. The furnishing was too high to allow her feet to rest comfortably on the floor and too narrow for her broad frame. Alone in her cubicle on Luna Base and unable to sleep, she sat and stared at the door.

A white door set in white walls—the brilliance muted to a level of tolerance by dimmed light.

She closed her eyes a moment, shutting out the alien sterility, and pictured the soft russets and golds of Hasu-dinian mountain peaks in high winter, the snows washed in the warm orange glow of Chai-din. Lish wondered how the rest of the excavation team lived in such harsh surroundings without going mad. After nine months, her longing for the steel blues and earth browns of the *Dan tahlni* was stronger than ever. She loathed humans and their works.

Lish shivered. Everything about the creatures repulsed her: their installation, their machines, the taped sight and sound of them. She sniffed and twitched her nose, grateful that she didn't have to smell them, convinced that they had possessed a vile stench. Humans, for all their basic physical similarities to the *bey*, were alien.

And a danger, though dead a hundred million years.

Frowning, Lish rested her chin on the table, eyes still on the door. She had not yet discovered what that danger was, and Sani was growing impatient for the information. The personnel and equipment being consumed by the Earth-moon project were needed elsewhere, but the mediator could not force the *shtahn jii* to terminate the operation. She was depending on Lish to provide data that could be used to counter Tahl's decision. So far, Lish had found nothing about the base or Stocha's research that threatened the mission or the *bey*.

Perhaps there was something she had overlooked. Lish recounted all that she knew, but there was nothing suspicious. The team spent most of its time translating the endless data files and studying the strange equipment found on the lower level. There was a special room that apparently contained frozen specimens of alien matter, but it remained sealed. The only thing of any consequence that Lish had learned was that the team was investigating a process that might enable them to store live game for long periods of time. She did not believe such a process was possible. In any event, it certainly posed no danger to the *bey*.

Lish had found nothing, but there was a section on the lower level she had not investigated. Although she knew about the strange lab behind the metal wall, she had not been allowed on the premises since it had been opened.

Rising from her chair, Lish went to her console and checked the hour. She growled in response to a quick, pressing pain in her lower abdomen. Afflicted with the sudden and intense nervousness that accompanied the beginning stages of her mating cycle, Lish began to pace. After a few minutes, she collapsed on the bunk, stricken with a burning spasm in the folds of her sex.

Would Vuthe accept her this time?

Rolling onto her side, she inhaled and tensed until the sensation passed. During her first cycle on Earth-moon five months earlier, Vuthe had responded to her as he had before his banishment by Tahl d'jehn. Though her musk was weak, she could imprint Vuthe; he had extraordinarily sensitive receptors. However, two weeks ago she had heard him ask Norii for *muath*. Desensitization did not necessarily mean he planned on refusing her. Still, she was worried.

She checked the time. Vuthe had been due back from the labs long ago. He had promised to come to her. Had he forgotten or did he intend to reject her without doing her the courtesy of explaining?

Angered, Lish dug her claws into the soft fabric of the alien mattress. She would not accept such an insult calmly.

Spurned for years and denied the intensity of fragrance that removed male inhibitions, Lish cast the rituals of society aside. Stumbling from the bed, she slipped through the door and headed for Vuthe's quarters.

By the time she reached his door, Lish was calmer. She hesitated before the solid barrier and had a moment's appreciation for the alien device. A *bey* field-barrier would betray her mood and intentions. Vuthe would sense nothing through the hard panel. She pressed the communicator button.

"Who is it?"

"Lish t'wan."

The door slid open, and Lish strode boldly into the room. Vuthe, his eyes heavy with sleep, looked up from the control panel beside the bunk.

"I woke you," Lish said evenly as she halted by the bed and peered down at him.

"What do you want, Lish? I'm very tired."

She arched her back seductively, hoping he had not taken the *muath*, hoping her scent was strong enough to seduce him.

"Lish . . ." Vuthe's dark eyes narrowed, and he shook his head with genuine regret. "I'm sorry. I'm so exhausted I forgot you had asked to see me."

Purring, Lish placed a hand on his thigh and began to knead

the thick shag covering his skin.

"I'm sorry, Lish, but I have to refuse this time." Vuthe pulled her claws out of his fur and clasped her hand. "I've been working too many days without enough sleep, and there's so much left to do—" He sighed. "I'm sorry, but I just can't. Not now."

Lish winced as the throbbing pain intensified. The compulsion to satisfy the mounting passion within her had been denied. Soon she would reach the peak of the hormonal drive, and the unrequited desire would torment her for the twenty days of her fertilization cycle. Despondency overwhelmed her, and she fell into a defeated crouch.

Vuthe stroked her coarse brown mane.

She shuddered at his touch. "Chiun?" she asked hopefully. The pilot had not accepted her in all the years they'd been gone from Hasu-din. There was no reason to think he would take her now, but she had to ask. Vuthe crushed her feeble hopes.

"He's not in any better shape than I am. We've just spent several very tense days removing the experimental specimen box from the first section of the freezing chamber."

Lish frowned savagely.

"We had to be careful not to disturb any of the operations in the second section, and the strain was extremely tiring." Vuthe smiled. "Next time, Lish, when I'm not so tired . . . after we've confirmed the viability of the zygotes. Next time, I promise."

A welcome numbness set in, and Lish got to her feet. "I think I'd better find Norii."

"She was still in the lower lab when I left a little while ago."

Dazed, Lish muttered her apologies, then hurried out of the room in search of the med-tech. She paused outside the door, feeling disoriented.

Norii . . . in the lab. . . .

Without a male, Lish desperately needed medication. She walked toward the elevator. Before she had gone through the next connecting corridor, another surge struck, sending her reeling against the smooth, hard wall. Extracted claws screeched across the metallic surface as Lish slumped to the floor, adding more pain and a deeper humiliation.

It's worse this time, she thought. Worse than the last time she had not mated. Kneeling in the empty corridor, ashamed and confused and alone on an alien world, Lish gave in to the wave of frustration that was sweeping over her.

To die . . . to be forever free of torment. . . . The peaceful darkness called to Lish.

Then, Vuthe's words came back to her, piercing the death-wish shadows that beckoned. *Next time . . . after we confirm . . . I promise. . . .* She had to maintain for the next time.

Concentrating on her hands and feet, Lish finally managed to sheath her claws. It was difficult to counter eons of evolved reflex. To prevent her claws from unsheathing again, Lish had to focus all her energies as she struggled to rise. When she regained her footing, the spasm was over.

She had to get to Norii before she had another attack, while she still had the will to resist the sanctuary of a forever-sleep. There would be a next time. Her situation was not hopeless. Once Luna Base was sealed, Vuthe would return to her.

Locking onto that thought, Lish started off again toward the elevator, the lower level, and relief.

She passed Norii's quarters without stopping, her mind fastened on her destination. *Next time . . . confirm the viability . . . promise . . . Norii's in the lab. . . .* Vuthe's words flashed through her consciousness, but were ignored as they fled into the fog of mating frenzy. Lish had to find the med-tech.

The debilitating effects of the last surge were gone as Lish entered the elevator passageway. She loped forward and leaned into the exterior panel, pressing the buttons and rushing inside before the doors were completely open. She fumbled with the hidden control panel, punched more buttons, and breathed a sigh of relief as the elevator began its descent.

*　*　*　*　*

Riitha placed several delicate alien instruments in a sterilizer and closed the lid, then slipped a dust cover over a large electronic microscope. Although neither Norii nor Stocha was prone to carelessness, the biologist gave the interior lab a final check before leaving and securing the airlock in the glass wall.

They were on the verge of a breakthrough with the test specimens found in the forward section of the freezing chamber. It was only a matter of days before they would know for certain whether the ancient embryos were alive. Riitha was confident that the outcome would be positive. Then their real problems would begin. The chances of convincing Tahl that human children should be incubated and birthed were slim. Their existence would threaten the edicts of the Law, which had allowed the *ahsin bey* to begin colonization of the Chai-te star system.

Tired and tense after her long hours in the lab, Riitha headed toward the outer airlock and the passageway to the upper level. Norii, Stocha, and Vuthe had retired over an hour ago, and she was anxious to join them in some much needed sleep. As she reached for the master controls to shut down the outer lab, she scanned the room to make sure all was secure. Her gaze swept past Michael's terminal, abandoned since she had learned that the zygote bank was safe. Further viewing of the tape had seemed unnecessary, and there had been no time. Now, though, she was drawn to the console.

The biologist sat down with a vague sense of unease and stared at the screen. A heaviness clutched at her heart and constricted her throat as she slowly realized why she had avoided what must surely be the final scenes of the humans' tragic story. She had developed a strange bond to these people, especially Michael and Andy. Once she had run the last phase of the historical account, they would truly be gone.

Riitha's raised fingers hesitated over the control board, then with a sudden, decisive movement, she keyed the program. Ignoring the curious pain that lodged itself in her chest, she settled back to watch. She owed it to Michael to finish viewing the tape, out of respect and because she knew what he did not: Andy's plan had succeeded.

Her pulse raced as the image of Michael appeared. The program had come full circle. The haggard and distressed face that looked out at her was the same one she had seen at the beginning.

"Now you know how the world ended and how the last seeds of our race were almost destroyed. We saved them, but to be perfectly honest, I'm still not sure why. I guess maybe Andy has a point. Any chance, no matter how great the odds, is better than no chance at all. For her sake, I hope you take good care of them. I—I'm sorry, but I—"

The screen blanked.

Riitha's shoulders sagged with the weight of the man's pain and despair. She reached to turn off the terminal, then stopped. The screen flickered, and Michael's face returned. He still looked tired, but the subtle nuances of defeat were missing.

"Michael Jamieson. Luna Base historical files." The hushed rasp of his voice was difficult to understand. Riitha leaned forward intently, her heartbeat quickening with anticipation.

"It's been four months since my last entry. I thought that was it, but things have been happening pretty fast around here the past few days. I'm still in a state of shock." Michael paused, drawing a deep breath and shaking his head slowly. "Maybe the best thing to do here is to let you see it as it happened—as I saw it and recorded it."

The image shifted to show a large group of people in the lounge under the dome. Michael turned to pan the room with his microcam, still postured in his jacket, then focused on Andy and Ross, who stood together at the center.

Riitha smiled, knowing that Luna Base command had finally fallen into the right hands. Ross was speaking.

"The shuttle crew's final report reached us just over an hour ago." Ross coughed quietly. "The asteroid was successfully deployed. Ivan has calculated that Venus's new rate of spin will stabilize at about fifty hours."

Shrill whistles and the thunderous hitting of hands rose on the air, then ceased as Ross's expression remained unchanged.

"The crew wishes us well and bids us good-bye." The design engineer wiped his eyes. "They've decided to self-destruct."

Several moments of silence followed. Some bowed their heads, while others looked at the stars through the dome overhead. Riitha curled up and rocked back and forth in grief and respect.

Andy stepped forward. "I'm certain the crew would want us to—to press on. It's come to my attention that a few of us disagree with the decision to eliminate all historical and cultural data from the computer banks." She looked directly at the microcam. The image altered slightly as Michael changed position. "But," Andy went on, "I'm certain this is the most prudent thing to do. The majority vote on this matter stands."

A murmur ran through the assembly.

"However, another possibility has come to my attention that deserves consideration. It might also take the edge off this other decision for some of you." She smiled at Michael, then let her gaze drift back over the gathering.

"We have four functional cryonic units. Ross thinks we should use them." Ignoring the stunned gasps and startled exclamations that ensued, Andy continued. "If this plan is approved by a majority vote, four people will be chosen to be cryonically preserved. All pertinent professional and personal data on anyone interested in volunteering for this somewhat unusual assignment will be fed into the computers. The computers will make the final selection of the four who will provide the best combination of talents for the ultimate survival of the zygotes and our eventual dealings with an advanced alien culture and species. Anyone who does not want to be considered can have his file eliminated from the selection process."

"Before we put this up for a vote," Ross interjected, "I think there are some things you should know. The units will be placed in the old weapons bunker behind the wall next to the freezing chamber. It's already lead-lined for protection against any internal radiation because our extinct government feared x-ray detection of it's contents."

"And the weapons?" Ivan asked. "Where are they?"

"They never got here." Ross paused with a wry grin. "Anyway, the presence of the cryonic units and their contents will be concealed from the aliens until after they've breached the second chamber of the zygote bank. Entry into that chamber will trigger a program with all pertinent data concerning the operation of the units. We are assuming that any species who gets that far will be motivated by scientific curiosity of a non-malevolent nature. We can't be certain, of course, so there is a risk involved."

"Also," said Andy, "we will finish the two units that are near completion and make them available to the aliens so that they can familiarize themselves with the equipment and processes before trying to defrost anyone. Actually, by then, their command of the language and our machines should make everything relatively simple for them to figure out. If you approve the plan, it will be put into effect one month from now."

"So soon?" Michael's voice was shaky and higher in pitch than normal. "What's the rush?"

Andy shrugged. "The zygote bank is safely stored and all the security and scientific data programming has been completed. There's no reason to delay. After the cryonic units and their occupants have been secured, the lower level will be sealed."

"Then he rest of us can get on with building Ivan's starship." Ross motioned to the large Russian to join them.

Ivan lumbered across the floor and turned to face the crowd with a wide smile. "An interstellar ship is possible, yes, but we must concentrate all our resources on gathering the equipment. Our one big problem is time, but thanks to Sherry Wong's remarkable work with bacteria and molds, we now have a broadened food base. It won't last forever, but it might be enough. And—" He held out his hands palm up "—if we succeed, if we build a ship that makes it to another star and our descendants survive . . . could they not eventually send back an expedition to retrieve the zygote bank and the cryonic units?"

A lively discussion broke out as people waved hands in the air and began shouting questions. The image wavered, however, as Michael rose and quickly walked out of the room.

Riitha stared at the blank screen, dazed by the implications. In all the years they had been exploring the base, no one, not even herself, had wondered what had become of the remnants of the inhabitants. No bodies had been found . . . and no shuttle ships or debris. Had they built their interstellar ship? Did they make it to another star? The questions were staggering. If they had, they had not returned.

She snapped her head around suddenly to stare through the glass partition at the blank wall by the freezing chamber. Her attention was immediately drawn back to the screen by the sound of voices.

Andy sat on her bunk, watching the unseen Michael with troubled eyes. "What's bothering you now, Michael? I know you think I'm crazy for persisting with my ridiculous plan, but—"

His hand touched her lips to silence her. "It's not that. Besides, I don't think your plan is ridiculous, just far-fetched. It probably has a better chance of succeeding than Ivan's spaceship."

"His plan could work. It does—on paper."

"If nothing else, it'll give us something to do . . . until the end comes." His finger traced a gentle line across her cheek, then fell away. "I'll miss you, Andy. I've never loved anyone before, and I just don't know how I'll keep going without you."

Tears welled up in Andy's eyes. "Michael, maybe I won't—"

He silenced her again. "Won't be selected? Don't be silly. Who else is better qualified to ensure the survival of the zygote bank or the successful incubation of human babies?"

Andy lowered her eyes, but said nothing.

Michael lifted her chin, forcing her to look at him. "We've got a month. Let's not waste it."

The picture darkened as they embraced.

Riitha had never before experienced such empathy. She had been able to deal with the separation from Tahl because of her work with the zygotes and because she knew he would return to her eventually. The physical bond between them made it difficult. Her preoccupation with the zygotes made it tolerable. Michael and Andy would be separated forever.

The picture switched back to the observation dome and a view of the stars. The sound of Michael's breathing was distorted by muffled sobs. As the minutes passed, Riitha watched and waited, sharing his silent and lonely vigil.

Ross suddenly appeared beside him.

"Is it over?" Michael's voice trembled.

"A few minutes ago." Ross pulled up a chair and sat down.

"So . . . who are the lucky few?"

Ross looked down at his clasped hands. "Andy, of course, and Sherry. She's a nutritionist, and since she's been working with Andy since she got here, that was a logical choice."

"No question there. Who else?"

"Me."

"Another logical choice." Michael sighed heavily. "You know more about this base than anyone else. And the fourth?"

Ross smiled. "You."

The picture jumped as Michael gasped. "That's got to be a mistake, Ross. What can I possibly have to offer?"

"A suspicious, inquisitive mind. A talent for digging out the truth. A sharp, observant eye—just to name a few."

Michael stood up suddenly. "What the hell kind of qualifications are those?"

"Good ones. What if the species that finds us isn't friendly? What if they're malevolent, but devious and clever enough to hide it from us? They'll know plenty about us, but we won't know beans about them. It'll be up to you to figure them out, to pick up on all the little details the rest of us are likely to miss."

"Just like I picked up on Wilson, right. I'm sure good at that."

Ross frowned. "Look, if you don't want to do it, why didn't you eliminate yourself from the selection process?"

"I didn't say I didn't want to; it just never entered my mind that I had a chance in hell of being chosen. I've spent the last four weeks trying to deal with having to carry on here knowing that Andy was a frozen corpse buried one level down. This is a bit of a shock."

"Are you in or not?"

"I'm in." Michael hesitated. "When?"

"The rest of us don't want to put it off. Is the day after tomorrow all right with you?"

"Yeah, but—is it just me, or do you feel like you're volunteering to die?"

Ross shrugged. "We all gotta go sometime, but I'm figuring we'll all wake up eventually. Personally, I don't want to miss it . . . whatever 'it' turns out to be."

"You've got a point. Where's Andy?"

"Waiting for you in her quarters."

The screen darkened, then Michael's tired face appeared again.

"Right now, this all seems like some kind of weird dream, but if everything went well with the cryonic process, Ross and Andy and Sherry and I are in frozen stasis behind that wall over there. We're probably dead. If not, if by some miracle we've survived . . . perhaps we'll meet soon. I'm sure there's a key-code installed somewhere to trigger the cryonic data program, but in keeping with our established practice of redundancy, I'm going to give you the access code here, too. It'll work on the terminal beside you."

Michael paused, inhaling deeply. "Good-bye." He smiled

slightly. "For now."

Michael's image disappeared and was replaced by the access code.

Riitha quickly leaned over and keyed the adjacent terminal. Clear, concise technical information of the operation of the cryonic units began to flow across the screen. She sat back and stared at the two shining screens for a moment, then turned to stare at the blank wall.

Her throat went dry, and her pulse quickened. "Be alive," she whispered hoarsely.

CHAPTER
TWENTY-SEVEN

Lish moaned as she raised the upper part of her body off the floor just outside the lift doors on the lower level. She did not know how long she had lain there and only barely remembered blacking out as she had stumbled from the elevator. But the pain of the intense cramps that had stricken her as the lift had completed its descent was very clear in her mind.

Easing herself into a sitting position, Lish leaned against the rough surface of the wall and took several deep breaths. An incessant but tolerable throbbing had replaced the intense pain in her abdominal muscles, and after a few minutes, she felt steady enough to stand up. Once on her feet, with the strength returning to her limbs, Lish focused on the airlock across the foyer and suddenly remembered why she had come to the lower level. Norii was in the lab beyond the airlock, and Norii had the medications that would sooth the hormonal chaos ravaging her body.

Driven by that single purpose, Lish reached the airlock in two long strides and keyed the control panel. She tensed as she

waited for the airlock to cycle and braced herself for another
painful spasm. Whereas she had been grateful for the solid
door that had separated her from Vuthe, she now cursed the
time-consuming mechanism that kept her from the inner
chambers. As soon as the lock opened enough to let her pass,
Lish dashed into the cavelike chamber, through the open airlock, and hurried down the dim passageway, stopping only a
moment as a minor spasm rose and abated. When she finally
entered the lab, she was extremely agitated and edgy.

Lish hesitated in the airlock opening to scan the room. At
first glance, the computer complex seemed deserted. Then
she saw Riitha, who was sitting at a bank of terminals. The
venja-ahn biologist did not seem aware of Lish's presence.
She was totally engrossed in the program on the screen before
her.

Remembering Edii's warning to her as she had arrived on
Luna Base, Lish hung back in the shadows of the airlock. She
had enough problems without inadvertently doing something
that would send Riitha into an irrational rage against her.
Lish's desperate need for medication was tempered by caution
for the moment, and she watched the biologist warily, trying to
decide what to do next.

Riitha stood up suddenly and shut down the terminal on her
right. She glanced at the screen on her left, then turned and
hurried through the maze of *bey* and alien computers to the
airlock in the glass wall and keyed it to cycle.

Blinking, Lish stared at the glass partition for several seconds before she realized why it seemed out of place to her. It
had not been there on the two occasions when Vuthe had
brought her to the lab to study his language programs. Then,
a massive sheet of rippled metal had formed the wall. Vuthe's
attempt to make Lish feel more at ease in the alien surroundings had failed. She had found the confines of the small lab
too constraining and even more alien than the rest of the
base, much of which had been modified for *bey* convenience
and a semblance of comfort. Now, as Lish watched Riitha

dart through the open airlock in the glass to a blank wall on the far side of another lab, she was glad she had succumbed to Vuthe's wishes and stayed long enough to familiarize herself with the surroundings.

Another throb warning of imminent pain gripped Lish, and she clutched her abdomen and scanned the rows of computer terminals again. Norii was nowhere in sight. Frantic with fear and the anticipation of the mounting pain, Lish left the protective enclosure of the airlock and moved quietly into the lab. Hoping to find that Norii was hidden from her sight behind one of the high banks of equipment, Lish glanced down each narrow aisle. Fear of disturbing Riitha kept her from calling out, but as she searched each walkway, Lish realized that Norii would not have heard her anyway. The med-tech was not there.

Panic seized Lish as an excrutiating spasm tightened her muscles. Silently, she cursed the cruel quirk of nature that had denied her adequate sex scent, cursed Vuthe for rejecting her, and cursed Riitha, whose presence prevented her from crying out in agony. Where was Norii?

In the lab . . .

No, Lish thought as Vuthe's words replayed in her mind, she's not in the lab.

Confirm the viability of the zygotes . . .

Lish gasped and stood upright to stare at Riitha through the glass that separated the two labs, Norii and the pain forgotten as the horrifying implications of that casual statement struck her awareness. Zygotes. Viability. The frozen bits of alien matter being studied in the lower lab were not dead and were not being examined for the purpose of duplicating the process for food storage. They were human embryos, frozen in antiquity by the alien race and possibly living.

Appalled and dazed, Lish walked slowly down the aisle to stand before the glass wall looking into the lab beyond, a silent and deadly witness. Zygotes. Why? To what end had humans sought to preserve their seed? She surveyed the scene in front of her with new understanding. The chamber, the equipment, the records; everything had been arranged for a similar species to put it all into operation. The aliens had left Luna Base prepared for the revival of their children.

And Vuthe, Chiun, Stocha, and Riitha seemed to believe the alien plan was plausible.

At first it was outside the capacity of Lish's *du-ahn* mind to grasp the idea fully. She watched unmoving as the unimaginable scope of the scheme found a clawhold in the fabric of her reality. One by one the known pieces of data fell into place until acceptance of the monstrous concept was possible.

Humans had left viable seed.

As the shock of the revelation began to subside, Lish glanced at the lighted screen Riitha had been viewing, then back into the complex lab beyond the glass wall. The biologist was systematically moving her hands across the blank surface of the far wall. Then, suddenly, a small part of the wall recessed and slid aside to reveal a control panel, a panel hidden just like the one in the lift to the lower level.

Lish's hatred of all things alien feasted on her fanatic dedication to the destiny of the *ahsin bey*. Here was the danger Sani suspected—not the base or the information contained in its data banks, but the aliens themselves. Viable zygotes could not be tolerated, nor could anyone with knowledge of their existence. All must be destroyed.

Without regard for her own life, Lish went to the computer console that controlled the life-support system in the interior lab. During the long, boring hours on Base Control duty, she had occupied herself with a study of installation operations. She knew exactly what to do to rid the *bey* of this alien threat. Riitha would be eliminated first. The base and the rest of its inhabitants could be eradicated by methodically overloading the power stations.

Lish turned and watched the biologist for a moment to make certain she had not been noticed. Riitha seemed totally absorbed in her manipulations of the control panel in the wall.

Assured and resigned to the necessity of her actions, Lish calmly turned back to the life-support console. She hesitated as Riitha suddenly took a quick step backward. The blank wall began to move outward into the lab.

Sensing she had no time to waste, Lish quickly initiated the lab airlock sealing sequence.

Riitha, as if warned by some intuitive alarm, turned to stare into the outer room.

Immediately Lish stepped to an adjacent console and triggered the sequence that would drain the life-sustaining elements from the interior lab.

The lights in the control room blazed suddenly, blinding Lish with their high-yellow harshness. A shrill, wavering siren assaulted her tender, low-register attuned ears. Clamping her hands to the sides of her head, Lish stared as the screen above the terminal flashed "INSTRUCTION ABORT" in alien, emergency red. Closing her eyes against the maddening glare, she stood in panicked helplessness and screamed in rage.

Then she was being slapped repeatedly across the face.

Lish stopped screaming. Her mind faltered under the weight of emotional chaos. She looked at Riitha without seeing her. All she knew was that she had failed.

Riitha had a vicelike grip on Lish's arm. Lish sniffed and shook her head, unable to identify the unfamiliar but somehow known scent coming from the biologist. Exhaling violently, she glared at Riitha, saw the fires of defiance and lethal intent smoldering in her eyes, and gasped with fear. The tech recognized the primitive and pungent odor of a female prepared to defend her territory against any threat. She drew back.

Riitha's grip tightened. Her words rumbled ominously in her throat. "What do you think you're doing?"

Cowed by the scent, Lish strained against the hold. Her nostrils flared as the stench grew stronger and ancient racial memory brightened in the dark of civilized ignorance.

Lish growled. "Traitor! *Maida shli*!"

"What do you mean?" Riitha frowned, and her hand relaxed slightly.

"Whom do you protect, Riitha f'ath?" Lish glanced toward the lab and focused on the airlock beside the wall that had moved. She remembered more of Vuthe's words. The zygotes were still in the chamber. Only an experimental specimen box had been removed. Rage welled up inside her. As Lish turned back to Riitha, her broad chest rose and fell rapidly, and her upper lip curled back to expose sand-colored teeth. "*Maida shli*! It is not the *bey* you are so eager to fight for!"

Lish was larger than Riitha, and her strength was augmented by her belief that the future of her species was in danger. She wrenched her arm free, flinging the biologist across the aisle and against a console. Her eyes widened with pain, Riitha slid to the floor.

"What on Earth?" Stocha's voice boomed from the entrance airlock.

"The chamber—" Riitha said breathlessly. "Guard the chamber!"

Lish paused, glancing between the two. As Riitha started to rise, Stocha ran past the tech into the interior lab. He cast a puzzled look at the wall the biologist had opened, but when he reached the chamber, his whole attention was on its defense. Claws unsheathed, he whirled to face Lish.

The angered *du-ahn* pursued Stocha through the airlock, then stopped in the middle of the room and roared with frustration. Stocha made no move to attack, and Lish, knowing she could not overpower the male in a direct assault, sprang sideways in an attempt to sweep a counter clean of precious, alien instruments. Her claws slipped on the hard floor, and she lost her balance. Grabbing for the edge of the table, Lish swung her free arm across the top of it, sending several pieces of glass and metal equipment crashing to the floor. Her hand closed around a glass beaker, and she threw it against the hard surface, smashing it. As she reached for another fragile piece, Lish screeched. Her knees buckled as Riitha hit her from behind. Blood-lust drummed in the base of Lish's skull. She brought her fist down hard on Riitha's face.

The biologist released the snarling brown female, and Stocha charged. Lish was quicker. She dodged him and broke for the freezing chamber. As the geologist spun and grabbed her, Lish raked his face and chest with her hands and tore the flesh on his legs with her pedi-claws. His howls of anguish fed her frenzy. Her teeth sank into the soft hollow of his shoulder. Stocha kicked her square in the chest, and she was thrown across the lab. With a grunt, Lish crashed into a supply cabinet and slid to the floor amidst a shower of broken glass and metal stripping.

Cut and bleeding profusely, Lish crouched and shook her head to clear the warm trickle of her own blood out of her eyes. Panting, she scanned the room.

Stocha had again taken up a defensive position before the zygote chamber. Riitha was on her feet, swaying uncertainly and glaring at her.

Compelled to defend her species by a bestial instinct, Lish kept her eyes on the enemy and felt about the floor. She found and palmed a length of metal stripping with an edge of jagged glass. She lunged at Riitha.

Metal and glass pierced the soft muscles below and inside Riitha's breasts and slid brutally between her ribs. The crude blade impaled the protective tissue around the biologist's heart, disrupting a valve. Riitha crumpled under Lish's weight.

Straddling her victim, Lish pulled the blade from the body with a cruel twist. A guttural cry of victory rang out as she raised the weapon to strike again.

Then she was choking. A massive arm was around her neck. Lish fought the restraint, and the hold tightened.

"Give it up,"

Lish recognized Vuthe's voice, but only as the voice of a traitor. He had been her only mate but she could choose him no more. The linguist was part of the Luna Base conspiracy against the *bey.*

Maddened, Lish shrieked and plunged the blade into Vuthe's side.

CHAPTER TWENTY-EIGHT

"You're making excellent progress, Hane." Tahl glanced at the projected fuel production figures for the next ten years. In spite of the *du-ahn* slowdown, the separation plant was still operating ahead of schedule.

Hane hovered mutely beside Tahl, then turned slowly and pushed himself away from the console to the large window screen set into the adjacent wall.

Tahl watched him uneasily.

Lazily the engineer held onto an anchor line stretching from ceiling to floor. He stared through the window, transfixed by the image of the large, colorful planet beyond. "Jupiter."

The alien word was spoken so faintly, Tahl barely heard it. Digging into the floor, the *shtahn jii* went to Hane.

The window screen covered a third of the wall and gave Tahl the impression that he was looking directly into space rather than at a projection. His gaze was drawn and held by the swirling, storm-clouded sphere of the gas giant, Chai-te Five, known as Jupiter to the ancient aliens.

The only indication that a *bey* installation was floating in the planet's thick, hydrogen-rich atmosphere was the electronic pulses being monitored in the control center of the command station orbiting Jupiter's fifth moon. The automated hydrogen-helium separation plant had drained only a trickle of Jupiter's atmosphere since it had been deployed twenty years before, and although the amount was negligible in terms of the planet's potential supply, it was enough to keep several robot transports constantly shuttling the fuel material to holding tanks.

Verda's team had almost completed its mineral-metal studies of several large asteroids in the vicinity of the *Dan tahlni*. Soon, they would be ready to construct the primary mining facility, and subsequently the plants where the ores would be processed and the refined metals used to manufacture additional holding tanks and barges. Large scale industrial operations would begin when the main colony arrived, and within another seventy-five years, Hasu-din would be preparing to receive its first interstellar freighters.

If the colony ship arrives, Tahl thought grimly. He cast a sidelong glance at Hane and frowned. The engineer was despondent, his body and mind sluggish, his eyes vacant. *Du-ahn*. Tahl had watched Hane closely since arriving at the separation plant, and he had not seen any sign of emergence in the latent *venja-ahn*.

Turning slowly, Hane propelled himself back to the array of consoles. Pausing before one terminal, he scanned the data on the screen, hesitated, then moved on to the next. When he finished his cursory check, the engineer looked at the *shtahn jii* with a blank expression and spoke in a flat monotone.

"Everything is in order, Tahl."

The *shtahn* pushed himself across the intervening space between the window screen and the consoles. Hane turned away, refusing to look at Tahl when he came close. Recognizing the depression that signaled the first phase of death-wish, Tahl honored the engineer's desire to withdraw and did not intrude on Hane's troubled silence. He had enough troubles of his own.

They were eleven days into the forty day window set for the receipt of the transmission from Hasu-din. No signal had yet been detected.

Respectfully ignoring Hane, Tahl glided to the hatch-field, his mind already sorting and filing the main facts of the problem. Hane d'eta, a proven latent *venja-ahn*, was succumbing to the death-wish syndrome. All the mission *du-ahn* were beginning to exhibit similar symptoms, some experiencing more advanced phases of the syndrome than others. The decline was happening much faster than Tahl had expected, since only twenty-five percent of the transmission time frame had elapsed. In view of the emergency, a conference with Bier was unavoidable.

Besides, Tahl thought, with everyone else on the Jupiter station withdrawing from personal contact and involvement, Bier was the only *bey* available to talk to.

The hatch-field glowed in stressed yellow as Tahl passed through.

*   *   *   *   *

Silent, deserted passageways. Eight *bey* were assigned to the separation plant control station, but none of them could be seen or heard.

As Tahl drifted through the narrow corridor toward Bier's temporary quarters on the station, the silence nagged at him. The death-wish quiet was a pall more absolute than the ancient stillness in the long-vacated passageways of Luna Base.

He paused, clinging to the wall, and listened.

Nothing. No sound. Not mere quiet, but total silence. Even the faint chiming hums of technology seemed more muted than usual, fading—the dying strains of a dying enterprise abandoned by a dying will.

Tahl closed his eyes and tried to recall the essence of existence that permeated the alien installation on Earth-moon. Not once had he walked the halls of Luna Base without knowing the touch of humankind or sensing their lingering presence. It was as if some intangible remnant of the species' life-force remained. Even now, as Tahl tried to remember, the presence demanded attention.

Odd, the *shtahn* thought. That powerful essence had not plagued him in months—not since he had appeased Riitha's bond-will by sending Norii and Lish to Luna Base. Odd that he should think about the aliens' tenacious will to survive now as the *bey* were calmly willing themselves to die.

The *jehda tohm* were dead—extinct a hundred million years—yet not dead. The spirit of the creatures refused to pass on, to relinquish its existence. Theirs was a formidable will that wafted through the white walls of Luna Base, a force that roamed a virgin planet, remaking that world in the image of its womb—Earth. It was a stubborn essence that touched Tahl, an alien essence that would not accept death.

He shivered, sensing the gentle tug of the bond that linked him to the aliens, Luna Base . . . and Riitha.

Suddenly, the *shtahn's* mind was jolted from the quiet depths of reflection. His eyes snapped open in chilling surprise, and he gripped the wall in panic. His body was trembling, then shaking violently. Dizzy and weak, Tahl shut his eyes again and dug into the spongy surface of the station walls. He convulsed, then the spasms slowly began to subside.

Stunned, Tahl carefully pulled his claws from the wall. His head ached, and his muscles hurt from the strain of the convulsion and the rigid, clinging stance. He hung suspended in the passageway, confused and terrified. The pain had struck without warning, a direct assault that had rampaged through the labyrinth of his mind. He felt as if he had been brutally, physically attacked . . .

Tahl suddenly realized that he *had* been attacked—through Riitha. He was aware of her pain, her anger, and a fear so intense it sent a ripple of cold terror coursing up Tahl's spine. The

strength of the bond's telepathic power left him feeling dazed
and disoriented for several minutes. Then, as his body began
to recover from the physical effects, Tahl shuddered and began
to move slowly along the corridor. His mind was filled with a
single purpose. Riitha was hurt and calling him. He had to go
to her.

* * * * *

Bier stared at the *shtahn*.

Impatient, Tahl repeated his announcement. "We're leaving for Earth-moon as soon as the shuttle is checked out and re-
fueled. Maximum-g."

"We won't survive a maximum-g on a flight that long!
That's more than a month—"

"You don't have to go with me."

Bier's shoulder muscles flexed. The long-fur on his ears and
muzzle bristled nervously. "Why are you going, Tahl? And
why the hurry?"

The *shtahn* blinked, hesitating. He could not tell Bier that
he was driven by the urgent demands of bond-will. He could
not explain an imprint of more than a year's duration without
telling the psychologist about the zygotes. The time was not
yet right for that.

Turning to the auxiliary console behind him, Tahl strapped
himself into the webbing and tried to relax. There had to be
another justification for a suicidal journey to the moon of
Chai-te Three. He closed his eyes and searched his thoughts for
the analytic reason he knew was there, but was obscured by the
bond.

Tahl had decided to make an inspection tour after death-
wish had begun infecting the crew on the *Dan tahlni*. None of
the other five latent *venja-ahn* stationed there had emerged,
nor had Verda on the asteroid survey team or those at the separation plant. The pressure brought to bear because the confirmation signal had not yet been received should have triggered

activation of the dormant *venja-ahn* mode, just as the delay had triggered death-wish symptoms in the *du-ahn*. It hadn't. Death-wish was overriding survival-will at all locations.

Tahl opened his eyes. Bier had moved toward him and was watching him intently. "Hane is slipping into death-wish, too, Bier."

"I know, but what does that have to do with Luna Base? The situation there is probably no different."

"But we don't know that. Everyone on Earth-moon is *venja-ahn* or latent—except Lish t'wan. I know Stocha and Norii made a permanent transition to the *venja-ahn* mode twenty-two years ago, but what about Chiun and Vuthe? If exposure to the aliens and their works causes emergence, I have to know about it."

Sighing, Bier rubbed the base of his neck. "How would simple exposure to the alien artifacts cause them to emerge? I mean, there wouldn't be any pressure in the study of a dead alien civilization's remains—not like there was when we didn't know the aliens' life-status. We know that the aliens are extinct now. There's no threat. No threat—no pressure. No pressure—no emergence."

Tahl nodded, but mentally he cursed the psychologist's logic. Although he strongly suspected that Vuthe and Chiun had also become permanent *venja-ahn*, Tahl did not have any solid evidence to support his suspicions, not unless he revealed the secret of the alien zygotes. He could think of no other argument to justify a high-speed journey to Earth-moon and cursed aloud in frustration.

"The aliens can't help us this time," Bier said, misreading Tahl's reaction. "*Du-ahn* death-wish is part of the *bey's* life-cycle. We off-set the effects once, but the circumstances are much different now."

"Be more specific." Tahl encouraged Bier to continue, stalling for time to consider other options.

"The problem now is not whether there is or isn't a strange indigenous intelligence to prevent us from colonizing this star system. The present situation is much more defined. Is the colony ship on its way, or isn't it? If it isn't, there's no hope for us at all."

Tahl stiffened, his whole attention returning to the psychologist. "If the signal from Hasu-din isn't received, that does not necessarily mean that the colony ship has not been launched."

Shaken by Tahl's sudden agitation, Bier rocked back slightly. "I don't understand."

"Any number of things could have happened to the beam between Hasu-din and the receiver here. It might have been deflected or diffused. There might have been a miscalculation in the trajectory or the schedule." Tahl's upper lip curled into a subtle snarl as his irritation mounted. The pressure of the bond that insisted he return to Luna Base and the damaging effects of the transmission time frame spurred him to anger. He growled low in his throat as he spoke. "I still haven't figured out why the council decided to enforce such a rigid schedule in the first place!"

Bier shrugged. "The cost—"

Tahl's eyes flashed. "Considering what's at stake here, the cost of transmitting for a longer period of time shouldn't have been an issue."

"I—I hadn't thought of that." Cautiously meeting Tahl's infuriated gaze, Bier cleared his throat. "In any case, the council's reasons are irrelevant in our situation. They did institute a schedule, and if the signal isn't received, we have to assume the colony ship isn't coming and prepare for the consequences."

"*Du-ahn* death-wish?" Tahl asked.

The psychologist nodded.

"No. I cannot accept that." Tahl's claws extended and retracted with outrage. "I just can't sit back and allow my people to wish themselves to death while there's still a chance. I can't."

"There's nothing you can do, Tahl. Nothing." Bier sighed wearily. "Believe me, I wish there were, but we've endured forty-seven years of isolation. *Du-ahn* will not continue to live and function for another thirty-five without some assurance that the effort won't be in vain. The colony ship is the only thing that gives their lives meaning. No amount of speculative reasoning, no matter how plausible it seems, can change their intrinsic nature. Without hope, they die."

Tahl exhaled in exasperation. "How did the *bey* ever survive with such a self-destructive instinct? It doesn't make sense."

"Quite the contrary, Tahl. Death-wish is simply an extreme manifestation of the submission trait, and according to the long-established principles of evolution formulated by the *shtahn* Laoh t'ar, the submission trait favored *du-ahn* survival. A *bey* who submits to a victorious invader is not killed. He survives to pass on his genes."

"All *venja-ahn* were not defeated, killed, or exiled in the past," Tahl stated emphatically. "Why is only five percent of the population *venja-ahn*?"

"Because," Bier explained patiently, "the gene for back-brain dominance has always been recessive in a mating between a *venja-ahn* and a *du-ahn*. Over the millenia, as our *venja-ahn* ancestors were killed or exiled and their numbers diminished, the gene had become rare as well."

Tahl sat back, frowning thoughtfully. "Then eventually, *venja-ahn* will fall out of existence."

"No. With the advent of *bey* expansion and the availability of unlimited resources, war has become obsolete. The *du-ahn-venja-ahn* population ratio has been stable for a long time. Eventually, the percentage of *venja-ahn* being born will increase. In fact, that's quite likely given that thirty percent of the present population may be latent. When latents mate, they have an even chance of producing *venja-ahn* offspring. The latents are the key to a *venja-ahn* future."

Tahl turned to look at Bier, his gaze hard and determined. "The latents are the key to this mission's future. They carry the *venja-ahn* gene and the survival drive it generates. We've got to force them to emerge."

"That may not be possible, Tahl."

"There has to be a way. The colony ship is depending on this mission to establish an industrial base. We haven't finished yet."

"You don't understand." Bier slid into the webbing beside Tahl and sighed. "If we all died tomorrow, our deaths would have little effect on the *bey*'s expansion into this system." He hesitated, suddenly lost in thought.

Tahl pretended ignorance. If Bier also realized that the council might have decided to sabotage the mission by not sending the transmission, it would lend credibility to the suspicion aroused in Tahl twenty-two years before. He gently prodded Bier. "We haven't set up the mining and manufacturing operations in the asteroids, and we haven't begun to stockpile the fuel necessary for unlimited travel. That would certainly effect the *bey*."

Bier shook his head, then sighed. "But we have completed our primary mission. We came to Chai-te, confirmed its industrial suitability and the absence of an intelligence. We've completed our secondary mission, too. The separation plant is constructed and operational. From this point on, whether we live or die won't make any difference to Hasu-din or the colony ship."

Tahl stared at the psychologist narrowly.

"There will be sixteen hundred *bey* on that colony ship, Tahl. They're educated and well-equipped. If we don't finish, their industrial schedule will only be delayed by two or three years. They don't need us anymore."

Cold rage brewed in Tahl's soul. "Do you think it's possible the colony ship was launched but the confirmation signal wasn't dispatched . . . deliberately?"

"I don't know. Perhaps they were afraid of the results of the experiment." The psychologist paused. "Is there any chance the receiver malfunctioned again?"

"None. Bohn is there, and everything checks out. Tena has even located the glitch in the remote automatic sensor program that failed to tell us about the first deviation. It's been corrected."

The transparent amulet on the thong about Tahl's neck began to glow, then flashed to blue and chimed. The *shtahn* stared at the remote scan-and-locate unit. Robot relays switched into action as he punched the receive sequence and placed his hand on the identification plate on the wall terminal. When the panel signaled "READY," Tahl spoke his name. There was a time delay, and he and Bier waited in silence.

The message was from Luna Base. The *shtahn* tensed as he read the light-coded transmission. Stocha d'vi pleaded with Tahl to come to Earth-moon. Riitha was injured, and Lish t'wan was dead.

"Death-wish?" Bier asked.

Tahl transmitted the question to Stocha. When the reply flashed onto the screen, the *shtahn*'s blood began to race with an urgency that matched the insistent command of the bond. Lish had not died of her own will.

"An accident, perhaps?"

"I don't know, Bier, but it wasn't death-wish." Tahl punched in a message confirming his immediate departure from the separation plant. "It wasn't death-wish."

Bier looked at him blankly.

"Lish t'wan was *du-ahn*, Bier! Every other analytic on this mission has begun the decline into forever-sleep. Lish didn't. Why not? I've got to find out. Whatever negated Lish's will to die might bring some of the others back." Freeing himself from the webbing, Tahl pushed off the console toward the field-barrier. "I'm going to Luna Base. Now."

Bier fumbled with the straps of his webbing and followed Tahl into the corridor. "You won't be much help if you're dead when you get there. A few extra days won't matter. A slower g-rate—"

"Maximum-g." Tahl began to repel down the corridor. "A few days might make all the difference. How many *du-ahn* will be beyond reach once we've exceeded the time frame for receipt of the signal?"

Bier struggled to keep up. "It'll already be too late when you get there. The time frame elapses in twenty-nine days."

Tahl stopped and wheeled to face Bier. "For the *du-ahn*, perhaps. Maybe there's nothing we can do to save them. But we might save some of the latents—enough of them to keep this mission alive."

Bier grabbed Tahl's arm, then smiled. "Yes, of course—the latents—"

Savagely the *shtahn* pulled his arm away. "I don't care if you come with me or not. If you are, be in the launching bay in one hour."

The *shtahn jii* turned and hurried away to prepare for the shuttle flight.

*   *   *   *   *

Riitha stirred slightly, moaning in pain, and Norii turned from the medical monitor to place a trembling hand on the injured *bey*'s fevered cheek. Pale eyelids parted in response to the touch, revealing glazed eyes that could not hide the agony Riitha was enduring. Smiling weakly, the biologist said Norii's name in a low, forced whisper, then gasped.

"Quiet now. Don't try to talk." Reaching for Riitha's hand, Norii held it and sat on the round stool beside the infirmary bed. "Save your strength." A shiver shot down Norii's spine as she watched Riitha's listless face, and she choked back the cry of anguish that welled up in her throat.

Riitha was dying, and she was helpless to do anything but wait for death to free her from her misery.

Fragile fingers closed on Norii's hand as Riitha drew a rasping breath. "Stocha. Is he—" The biologist's words were cut off by a soft whimper.

"Yes," Norii replied quickly to calm her. "Stocha took Vuthe and Chiun with him to the lower lab to look at the program." With an almost imperceptible nod of understanding,

Riitha seemed to relax, and Norii sighed.

When Riitha had first regained consciousness after Lish's attack an hour before, she had babbled frantically about an alien machine that could save her and would not rest until Stocha promised to go immediately to the lower level to find it. Since then, the biologist had drifted in and out of consciousness without speaking, until now. Norii glanced at the door, wondering why Stocha was taking so long. Riitha's belief in the mysterious machine was all that was keeping her alive, and although Norii desperately wanted such a machine to exist, she did not think it did. During the year she had been on Earthmoon, the med-tech had scanned most of the humans' medical databanks. Their knowledge had been expansive, covering disciplines and procedures that went far beyond the *bey*'s medical expertise.

The aliens had been more prone to illness and physical breakdown than the *bey*, which accounted for the detailed information and what seemed to be an ongoing effort to discover cures for their maladies and develop methods of repair for their afflicted or broken bodies. Norii did not doubt that somewhere in the databanks there was a documented operation that would enable her to correct the damage to Riitha's heart—if she had the time to find, study, and modify the procedure for a *bey*.

But there is no time, Norii thought, stricken with anger, frustration, and regret. And there had been no mention in the databanks of a machine that could wondrously fix the cardiac injury.

"Norii . . ." Riitha whispered.

Leaning closer, the med-tech brushed the biologist's tangled mane with her free hand. "I'm right here, Riitha. I'm here."

Another nod, and Riitha exhaled raggedly.

"Let me give you something for the pain." Torn by Riitha's torment, Norii pleaded, but the biologist was adamant in her refusal.

"No . . . can't risk it—" Riitha turned her head slightly to look at Norii and managed another weak smile that was filled with hope and meant to reassure her friend.

Norii smiled back, but inside she seethed. Riitha's attachment to the zygote bank greatly exceeded mere scientific curiosity. Convinced the frozen embryos were viable, she had appointed herself guardian and protector. She had given her life to save Luna Base and the zygote bank from destruction by Lish, and now, clinging to a hopeless belief in the *jehda tohm*'s technology, she was suffering needlessly. Afraid that *bey* medication would interfere with the effective function of the imaginary alien machine, Riitha would not allow Norii to ease her pain, a pain that was almost more than Norii herself could bear to witness. But she had no choice. Norii was honor-bound to respect the desires of a dying comrade.

"Tell Tahl—" Riitha paused to draw breath, her gaze begging Norii to listen.

Knowing that every word Riitha uttered was an exertion that taxed her waning strength, Norii tried to coax her into silence. Again Riitha stubbornly refused to take the med-tech's advice.

"Tell Tahl—the aliens are here." Riitha's facial muscles contorted as another agonizing spasm racked her body, but she would not desist. "They are—here and—alive . . ."

"Yes." Norii's sense of helplessness and frustration mounted as Riitha, with death so near, still fought for the zygotes. "Tahl knows, Riitha. He knows."

"No . . . the terminal—" Anxiety and desperation deepened the furrows pain had etched in the biologist's brow. She cried aloud, closing her eyes and tightening her grip on Norii's hand as she struggled to withstand another spasm. When she spoke again, Norii had to move even closer to hear the breathless words. "I want . . . to meet them. I don't want to die—not now. . . ."

"I know." Norii whispered softly into Riitha's ear, unable to quell the quiver in her voice. "I know."

"Yes, of course you do . . . my friend." Inhaling with short, labored gasps and exhaling slowly, Riitha drifted back into the painless depths of unconsciousness with a whisper. "My *venja-ahn* friend."

Dropping Riitha's hand, Norii sat back suddenly and froze. On a subconscious level, she noted that the biologist was still breathing, but consciously, she had gone into shock. The med-tech sat unmoving, staring at the ashen stillness of Riitha's face without seeing it, her mind paralyzed.

When Stocha ran back into the infirmary several minutes later and called her name, Norii heard it, but ignored it. It was just a sound, distant and removed, without relevance in the sanctuary of mental numbness that engulfed her.

"Norii?" Stocha said quietly.

"What's wrong with her?" Vuthe and Chiun asked with hushed concern.

"I don't know." Stocha touched her shoulder. "Norii."

The sound and the touch remained meaningless to the med-tech, and it stayed outside the protective fog shielding her from a conscious recognition of the truth in Riitha's last words. For a long time, the alteration in Norii's thought mode status to *venja-ahn* had been known to her in the deeper recesses of her mind where a subconscious sense of self-preservation had kept the truth submerged, allowing it to slowly weave itself into the matrix of her intellectual and emotional being. Now, as she was suddenly seized by the shoulders and vigorously shaken, then slapped hard across the face, the protective shields weakened, and the knowledge broke through to flood the conscious pathways of her awareness. She screamed.

"Norii!" Stocha slapped her again, then grabbed her hands to keep her from ripping open her face with her own claws. "Stop it, Norii! Stop it!"

The shrieks of distress ceased instantly. Breathing heavily, the med-tech blinked and looked at Stocha through dazed eyes. Behind him, she was vaguely aware of Vuthe and Chiun and their tense, worried faces. Then, without warning, she began to hyperventilate.

Placing his hand over the med-tech's nose and mouth,

Stocha waited until her breathing calmed, then released her and asked anxiously, "What happened? What's wrong?"

"Riitha—" Norii's throat was constricted, making it difficult to talk.

Panic flared in Vuthe's eyes as he quickly moved to the head of Riitha's bed. "She's still alive," he said.

"It's all right, Norii," Stocha said. "Riitha is still alive."

Focusing on Stocha, Norii said the dreaded truth aloud. "*Venja-ahn.*"

Stocha leaned back slightly, hesitated, then smiled as he drew Norii into his arms and held her close. "It's about time."

Still dazed and feeling dizzy, Norii welcomed the comfort of Stocha's embrace for a moment before pulling back and pushing him away. "I mean me, Stocha. I'm *venja-ahn!*" Her voice rose in angry confusion. Then, realizing she had confessed the terrible truth, that she would forever be branded and outcast from the comfort and acceptance of *du-ahn* society, Norii jumped to her feet and lunged for the door.

Chiun sprang in front of her, wrapping his powerful arms around the med-tech to keep her from escaping. Norii fought against his hold, struggling as he dragged her to a chair. Stocha rushed to help the pilot force Norii down, and together they restrained her until she gave in to their superior strength and stopped fighting.

While Chiun and Vuthe took positions on either side of the stricken med-tech, Stocha knelt down in front of her and tried to calm her.

"We already know about it, Norii," the geologist said in a quiet, steady voice. "We know."

Norii stared at him blankly for several seconds, then looked warily at the two technicians. Vuthe and Chiun exchanged knowing glances, then nodded at her with somber but sympathetic expressions. Shaking her head with rigorous denial, the med-tech screeched and began to pound on Stocha's chest with her fists. "No! No!"

The geologist grabbed her wrists again and forced her to

look at him. "Norii! Stop! It's okay."

Devastated, her energies spent, Norii stopped struggling, and Stocha let go. Clamping her hands to the sides of her head, she began to rock back and forth with a keening sound laced through her words. "This can't be. *Venja-ahn*. How could such a thing happen?"

Running his hand through his mane in a gesture of helplessness, Stocha sighed and waited patiently until Norii grew quiet. He kept his voice even and low in an attempt to comfort her. "I don't know how it happens, Norii, but becoming *venja-ahn* is not the horrible fate you imagine it to be. You've been *venja-ahn* for years. You just didn't know it—not consciously. But I can tell you this for certain. Being *venja-ahn* has made you so much more than you ever could have been as *du-ahn*. So much more."

Norii stopped rocking and snapped her head up with a menacing snarl. "How would you know, Stocha d'vi?"

"I know." The geologist grinned sheepishly. "We all know. We've been through what you're going through now. Chiun, Vuthe, and I—we're *venja-ahn*, too."

Inhaling sharply, Norii stared at him in stunned surprise.

"So is Tahl," Chiun added.

Norii sat silently, shifting her gaze from one to the other as she tried to assimilate the staggering information and their casual acceptance of a thought mode shift that would deny them the *du-ahn* respect and credibility they had known all their lives.

Taking her hand in his, Stocha held it firmly, as though he could transfer his strength and serenity to her through the simple contact. "I'm sorry you have to deal with this now, but believe me, once you've accepted it, you'll realize how very fortunate you are."

"How can you say that when you know that *venja-ahn* thinking cannot be trusted? When you know that the *du-ahn* will reject and ridicule you for the rest of your life?" Norii sobbed deep in her throat, and she began to tremble.

"I know how you feel," Stocha said. "It's been years since I found out, but I remember it clearly. A short time after we opened up Luna Base, I awoke from a dream and just knew that for some mysterious reason I had become *venja-ahn*, that I had been *venja-ahn* since I walked on Chai-te Two twenty-two years ago. I went crazy, Norii. None of the furnishings in my cubicle escaped my rage unscathed."

Norii smiled slightly, reassured in spite of the fear and confusion still clouding her thoughts.

"It took me two days to come to terms with what had happened to me," Stocha went on. "But once I realized what the shift had given me, I've never regretted the change."

"What did it give you, Stocha?" Norii asked.

"Freedom and power," the geologist said simply. "It gave me a free mind and the power to wonder, to imagine, to dream, to think beyond the boundaries of a limited reality."

Shaking her head, the med-tech slumped in the chair and began to retreat back into a daze.

Stocha grabbed her by the shoulders and shook her again. "Norii! You've got to accept it now! We all had time to get over the shock, to ease into the realization, but you don't. You don't have time."

Raising her head slowly, Norii just stared at the other *bey* in the room.

Fixing her with a piercing gaze, Stocha spoke sharply. "You're Riitha's only hope."

"No." The med-tech shuddered, knowing that the biologist was beyond help. "There's nothing I can do for her."

"Yes, there is," Stocha insisted. "There is a machine, Norii, but we need you to make sure we use it correctly. You're the doctor. We need you!"

Her ears twitching, the med-tech blinked as a spark of interest cleared some of the fog that dampened her mind and glazed her eyes. "There really is an alien machine that can save her?"

"Yes. At least there's a chance."

Vuthe and Chiun nodded, confirming Stocha's affirmation.

Rising, Norii looked down on Riitha's comatose form. She had a chance to save her friend, to defeat death. The last shreds of the med-tech's resistance to the final phase of the *venja-ahn* shift, conscious acceptance, dissipated as her mind latched onto the primal motivating force that drove all *venja-ahn*: survival at all costs.

Taking charge suddenly, Norii turned to Vuthe and Chiun and ordered them to carefully move Riitha back to the lower lab. Then she sprinted toward the door, calling to Stocha as she ran. "You'd better show me this machine. We don't have much time."

As Norii sped through the Luna Base corridors, an odd, almost alien resolve grew within her. She would not surrender Riitha to the finality of death without a fight.

CHAPTER TWENTY-NINE

"Tahl?"

The sound of Norii's voice was remote and muted. The *shtahn* tried to open his eyes and could not; nor could he speak. He hurt everywhere. Behind lowered eyelids, on the verge of awakening, Tahl listened. He heard the forced rasp of his own shallow breathing, the whisper of voices.

"Is he coming out of it?"

"Not yet, Stocha," Norii said. "Soon."

"How's Bier?"

"He's not as young or as strong as Tahl, but I think he'll be all right."

"How long, Norii?"

That was another, different voice. Tahl concentrated and identified the speaker as Vuthe f'stiida.

"I don't know, Vuthe."

Then Chiun. "Will he recover?"

"Yes," Norii sighed.

"We will wait—patiently," Stocha admonished the techs.

"Just *hold your horses*, okay?"

Then silence.

Hold your—what? Tahl's head spun, and clear thought eluded him in the haze. He was aware of anxiety and a driving sense of urgency, but he did not remember why. He tried to focus his mental energies and, failing, slipped into a deeper fog.

* * * * *

Tahl's eyes fluttered open. He saw Norii peering down at him, and behind her, Stocha, Vuthe, and Chiun. He groaned and turned his aching head. Bier lay on an alien sleeping pad next to him. The psychologist's eyes were glazed with pain and staring blankly. Tahl closed his eyes again and struggled to orient himself.

He was on Luna Base with Bier. Stocha, Norii, Chiun, and Vuthe were keeping watch over them. Lish t'wan was dead and Riitha—

The *shtahn* frowned and flinched in pain. Riitha was not in his mind. Her bond-will was gone.

"Riitha!"

"Easy, Tahl." Norii put her hand on his chest.

Tahl clasped her hand and squeezed it. "Where's Riitha?" No one answered.

Tahl's gaze darted from one saddened face to another as he tried to raise his head. A shooting pain ran the length of his body. "No bond, Norii. Riitha—"

"She's in the lower lab, Tahl." Stocha spoke quickly with a glance at Norii. "Just stay calm."

Tahl relaxed, concentrating his diminished strength on his thoughts. The bond had been broken. The possibility that Riitha might have been pregnant had been ruled out months before. No imprint. She was no longer mothering. The team, Tahl decided, must have discovered that the human zygotes were not viable.

Slowly Tahl recalled the powerful flux that had attacked him in the corridor of the separation plant control station. Given the absence of the bond, there was only one conclusion Tahl could draw. When Riitha had learned that the alien seed was beyond life, she had lashed out in her grief. Strangely, he shared her pain even now, even though they were no longer linked.

Clenching his jaw, Tahl released Norii's hand and raised himself up on one elbow. Breathing deeply in spite of the discomfort in his chest, he forced himself to move in order to counter the lingering effects of space-stress.

Sharp, needlelike twinges coursed through the muscles of Tahl's arms and shoulders as he stretched. He frowned suddenly, looking at the anxious faces surrounding him and remembering the other reason he had risked his life to get to Earth-moon without delay.

"How long have we been here, Stocha?"

"Three days."

Tahl nodded, pushing away the feeling of despair that was crowding the edges of his mind. They were now fourteen days outside the confirmation signal's time frame. He fell back onto the sleeping pad.

"Tahl? Is something wrong?" Stocha stepped closer to peer down at him.

Sighing, Tahl turned to the geologist, then gasped. His questioning gaze quickly scanned the worried expressions of the others. Worried, he thought with a racing pulse, but none of them showed any traces of death-wish syndrome or stress beyond a concern for his health.

Violently the *shtahn* grabbed Stocha's wrist. "The confirmation signal. . . . When was it received?"

Stocha's brow furrowed as he looked at Norii. She shook her head and shrugged. Vuthe and Chiun exchanged perplexed looks.

Puzzled, Tahl asked again. "When did the *Dan tahlni* contact you?"

"We've had no communication with the *Dan tahlni* since

before you and Bier left the separation plant." Stocha's ears
flicked back and forth in puzzlement.

"None?" Ignoring the searing spasms in his protesting muscles, Tahl gripped the frame of the alien bed and pulled himself into a sitting position. "We've got to reach them. The time
frame for the signal from Hasu-din expired fourteen days ago."

Norii snorted and held onto Stocha's arm for support. "The
signal—" She whispered, shaking her head slowly. "I forgot
about the signal."

"Forgot?" Tahl stared at her. "You forgot?"

"No, I didn't forget exactly," Norii stammered. "I just lost
track of time. I had no idea—"

"None of us did," Stocha said.

Stunned, Tahl slumped and tried to sort out his thoughts. If
the transmission had been received, Nian or Tena would not
have failed to notify every installation. He had to assume the
signal had not arrived since no word had been sent to Luna
Base.

Although he did not expect a response, Tahl had to try to get
through to the *Dan tahlni*. The slow process of death-wish hibernation and starvation would have already begun in the *du-
ahn*, but there was a chance one or more of the latents might
have emerged. If so, he had to let them know they were not
alone. Tahl could not sit by and let the rest of the mission *bey*
die without trying to save them, no matter how futile the effort
might be. Until the last breath left their sleeping bodies, there
was hope—for the *du-ahn* as well as the latents. The stubborn
refusal to calmly surrender hope and life that had been the
curse of the ancient *venja-ahn* was the mission's only chance for
salvation, and Tahl was determined to use every means at his
disposal to bring life back to his people in spite of themselves.

He knew the answer was somewhere on Luna Base. The entire Luna Base team was unaffected by Hasu-din's lack of response concerning the launch of the colony ship. If nothing
else, Tahl thought, the alien base would provide the key for
saving the latents.

"How could you forget something as vital as the transmission confirming the departure of the colony ship, Norii?"

The med-tech looked at Tahl helplessly. "I don't know. I guess I was just so involved in our work with the zygotes everything else was just pushed to the back of my mind."

Tahl glanced at the others. "Is that true for the rest of you, too?"

They nodded.

"And Lish? Are you absolutely certain she showed no signs of death-wish before she died?"

"No," Stocha answered, "but she didn't know about the human embryos, either. We took your advice and didn't tell her. She was assigned to Base Control. She hated the aliens and the base so completely, she wouldn't have been any use to us in any other capacity."

"But she was *du-ahn!*" Tahl searched their faces for some recognition of the significance, but found none. "Why didn't she begin the decline into forever-sleep? If she hated the *jehda tohm* and exile on Luna Base, receipt of the signal should have been uppermost in her mind. Obviously, it wasn't. Something overrode the isolation factor. What?"

Stocha shook his head. "I don't know, Tahl."

"You've got to know!" Tahl glared at the geologist, then turned to Norii. "There's a reason Lish didn't succumb to death-wish, and I've got to know what it is! It's important. She was *du-ahn.* You're all *venja-ahn*—" He stopped speaking, stricken.

"It's all right, Tahl," Norii said softly. "We know. Although I admit the initial shock of finding out is difficult, the adjustment is relatively easy after you've accepted it." She cast a grateful glance at Stocha, then smiled at the *shtahn jii.* "Actually, I've never felt more alive. There's an energy to this existence I never knew as *du-ahn.* It's hard to explain."

"I understand," Tahl said, finding a strange sense of peace in finally being able to openly admit that he, too, was *venja-ahn.* "I've been through that trauma myself—thanks to Bier."

Tahl glanced at the psychologist, who was still sleeping, and pondered the irony of the situation.

He controlled Bier through a pledge of restitution because the psychologist had tried to use the shock of the mode shift to kill him. Oddly, Tahl had gained a tenacious hold on life instead, as well as the mental ability to guide the course of the mission more effectively. That did not absolve Bier from the crime, but the *shtahn* was grateful nonetheless. He was free, no longer just an extension of the *du-ahn* Council of Mediators' will, a mindless puppet who would carry out their decrees without question, blindly submitting to their distant rule, or ignoring their malicious, murderous intent. He, Tahl d'jehn, was in control of his own destiny now.

And he was not alone. With the vitality of hope flowing through his veins and a renewed strength in his determination to fight the death-wish syndrome, Tahl turned to the other *venja-ahn* gathered around him for help.

"We are only seven, Stocha."

"Seven?" Stocha cocked his head and frowned at Tahl.

Tahl nodded. "The four of you, Bier, Riitha, and myself. Seven *venja-ahn* are not enough to finish the final phase of the mission. There are other latents, but they have not emerged or else you would have heard from them. Death-wish is taking them as well as the *du-ahn*, but I think there's a chance we can reach them. Getting through to even one would make the attempt worthwhile."

"I agree," said Norii. "But if they've fallen into a forever-sleep, they may be beyond reaching."

"But we don't know that. As far as I know, no one's ever tried to shock anyone—latent or *du-ahn*—out of death-wish."

A slow smile spread across Norii's face as she listened to Tahl. "You might have something there. There are recorded instances of *du-ahn* coming out of deathlike hibernations when the conditions that forced them into death-wish were reversed."

"Such as?" Tahl leaned forward expectantly.

"The case that comes immediately to mind," Norii went on with mounting excitement, "involved a mine cave-in. By the time the rescue team reached the trapped *bey*, the miners had all fallen into death-wish sleep. Voice contact and oxygen brought four of the ten victims out of their trauma-induced hibernations."

Stocha scowled. "But that was a rare occurrence, right?"

"Yes, it was."

"But," Tahl interjected, "it proves that it's possible."

"Maybe," Stocha countered. "But at the risk of playing *devil's advocate*, I should point out that we can't invent a signal that hasn't come. Unless we can prove that the colony ship was launched, we don't have anything to shock them with."

Tahl found Stocha's use of alien terms in normal conversation disconcerting, but decided that the specific meanings were irrelevant as long as he got the point. "Not necessarily, Stocha. I must know what was so important to Lish t'wan that she either forgot about the confirmation signal or considered it secondary in importance. Whatever it was might have the same effect on the others."

"I'm sorry," Stocha said. "I just don't know."

"But I do."

All eyes turned to Bier. The psychologist had managed to shift onto his side. He glowered at them, his facial features twisted in anger. "I know."

"Then tell us." Tahl stiffened but kept his voice evenly modulated.

Scanning the expectant faces before him, his eyes dark and menacing, Bier growled deep in his throat. "Lish was Sani's aid. The mediator suspected that this project posed some danger to the *bey*, and apparently she was right. Lish did have a purpose more important than her innate fear of isolation, more important than her own life." Bier turned on Stocha with a snarl. "How did she die?"

Vuthe stepped forward. "I killed her."

"How?" Tahl asked, surprised. "Why?"

Stocha defended Vuthe before the *shtahn jii*. "Lish attacked Riitha and tried to destroy the zygote chamber."

"I thought you said Lish didn't know about the zygotes?"

Stocha sighed. "She didn't until just before the incident."

"I wasn't thinking," Vuthe said, hanging his head. "I told her."

"And she died!" Bier raved. "She died trying to protect the *ahsin bey* from your aliens!"

Confused, Tahl frowned. The aliens were extinct. The zygotes were not viable. They couldn't be. He sat up and clamped his hand around Stocha's arm. "The zygotes are dead, aren't they?"

"No, not at all. Our preliminary tests indicate the survival rate may be as high as seventy percent."

Heart pounding, Tahl tightened his grip. "Then Riitha must be dead."

"No," Stocha said emphatically. "She's not dead, Tahl."

Bewildered, the *shtahn* relaxed his hold and studied Stocha's troubled face. "I want to see her."

"Later." Norii moved beside Tahl and forced him onto his back. Her voice was firm. "After you've rested. We could all use some rest. None of us have slept much since your shuttle touched down. Riitha will wait."

"The mission won't. No time—"

"A few hours won't matter."

Tahl didn't agree, but the intense discussion had drained his energies, and he was suddenly too weak to argue. He closed his eyes and listened as Norii, Stocha, Vuthe, and Chiun shuffled out of the room. His mind was in turmoil. Riitha wasn't dead, but the bond was no longer in effect and the zygotes were viable. The facts didn't fit together properly.

With the sound of Bier's low, accusing growl echoing in his ears, Tahl willingly surrendered to the darkness of sleep. It was his only escape from the puzzling questions and Bier's mumbled insults.

"*Maida shli*, Tahl d'jehn. Traitor to the *bey.*"

* * * * *

Tahl hurried through the white halls and curved passageways, breaking into a lope when he rounded an angular corner and saw the elevator doors ahead. He glanced over his shoulder as he entered the lift to the lower level. No one had followed him. The Luna Base team, exhausted after three days of watching over Bier and Tahl, slept behind closed cubicle doors. And the *shtahn* had taken great care not to disturb Bier, who was also sleeping soundly, when he had finally given up trying to rest.

Unable to stop thinking about the fatal decline of the mission *bey*, Tahl had slept little. His muscles throbbed, and his mind was still foggy, but the crisis simply couldn't wait. A trance was needed to find a solution, but he was too physically and mentally depleted to risk it alone. He needed Riitha for strength and stability.

Ignoring the stabbing pains in his shoulders and back, Tahl reached up and moved the hidden control lever that operated the lift. A queasiness roiled in his stomach during the descent, but once he was on solid ground in the foyer outside the elevator, the uncomfortable affliction passed. Locating and activating the airlock in the rock wall without trouble, Tahl cautiously walked through the dimly lit passageway toward the lab. He was forced to pause as he stepped through the last airlock into the lab control room, momentarily blinded by the harsh glare of full alien light. Closing his eyes, the *shtahn* stood quietly and listened while he waited for his vision to recover from the light-shock.

The room was filled with sound: whirring, humming, chiming sound. It was the song of technology in full operation—too much sound. Too much loud, hard alien noise.

Opening his eyes carefully, Tahl surveyed the room. The place he remembered was small and filled with orderly rows of alien computers and screens. This room was larger and stuffed with alien devices and *bey* consoles. All of them were blinking, buzzing, and busy.

Too busy.

He stood still for several more minutes, disoriented by the conflict between the lab as he remembered it and the lab he saw now. The alien machines, idle for millions of years, were idle no longer. The small, crowded control room was still crowded, but not small. Tahl's mind finally made the connection. The corrugated metal wall was missing. In its place was a glass and metal partition, and beyond it, the interior of the extensive laboratory he had seen on the *jehda tohm* datafile during his previous visit a year past.

Intrigued, Tahl walked down the short pathway between consoles and stopped to peer through the window. A conglomeration of *bey* and alien machines littered the confines of the lab, and all appeared to be operational. Tahl frowned as he scanned the interior for Riitha. She wasn't there.

His gaze was then drawn to a door in the far wall that resembled an airlock, a door he also recognized from the alien video record Riitha and Stocha had shown him. It secured the chamber that housed the frozen human zygotes. A chill sprinted down his spine. They were still viable after a hundred million years. He had not believed it was possible.

The *shtahn* stared at the chamber and considered entering the lab, then changed his mind. Ignorant of the complex alien systems, he did not want to risk damaging anything. Besides, locating Riitha was more imperative at the moment. Anxious in her absence, Tahl turned and wandered aimlessly past rows of consoles, glancing at screens and wondering at the strange alien marks while he pondered where to look next. Riitha was not in her quarters, and he had seen no sign of her between the infirmary and the lower level.

His depressed disposition brightened slightly when it occurred to him that she might be feeding. Spinning about to head back to the main level, he hesitated as his gaze flicked across a screen displaying *bey* light symbols. The *bey* terminal had been integrated with an alien console.

TEMPERATURE: CONSTANT −200

Curious, Tahl moved in for a closer look.

VACUUM INSULATION: STABLE
MARK: 23: 4—27.10

Tahl searched the *bey* terminal for the data file switch and pressed. He cried aloud as the subject identification information flowed onto the screen.

EXPERIMENTAL CRYONIC PRESERVATION
SUBJECT: RIITHA F'ATH
ADULT AHSIN BEY
FEMALE
AGE: 59
CAUSE OF DEATH: DISRUPTED HEART VALVE

Sinking to his knees, Tahl raised his head and roared in grief-stricken anguish.

* * * * *

Tahl heard Stocha call his name, but he did not look up from the cryonic monitor until the geologist was standing by his side. When the *shtahn* turned, the his gaze was cold and accusing.

"Tahl—" Stocha reeked with nervous distress.

"Where is she?"

The geologist flinched under the bite of Tahl's menacing tone and shrank from the predatory glint in his eyes. He pointed toward the expanded lab and stammered. "In—in there. In one of those two long, metal containers behind that partition."

Tahl glanced at the viable end of the stasis unit. "You lied to me, Stocha d'vi. She's dead."

"She's not exactly dead." The geologist fell into the chair at the adjoining console.

"She's either dead or alive. There's no in-between."

"By definition, Riitha is actually . . . asleep. Her anterior primary cardiac valve was severely damaged when Lish stabbed her. However, we're certain now that the damage can be repaired."

Tahl's eyes narrowed.

"It's too complicated to explain in detail right now," Stocha continued hastily, "but there are some innovative medical procedures we can use, procedures perfected by the *jehda tohm*. According to their records, it's possible to replace an injured organ—such as a heart—with one from a donor who has died of other injuries that cannot be repaired."

Skeptical, Tahl grunted.

"Such a procedure is entirely possible, Tahl," Stocha insisted. "Since the accident, Norii's done nothing but search the aliens' medical files for a means to save Riitha. A heart transplant will work. It was routine with the humans."

"Then why didn't you use Lish's heart?" Tahl snapped viciously, lashing out at Stocha in his intense pain and inconsolable sense of loss.

"There were good reasons," Stocha said calmly. "For one thing, it's going to take some time and research before we can perform such operations. We've never done it, and even with the comprehensive data left by the *jehda tohm*, everything has to be modified before we apply it to the *bey*. Secondly, Lish was not a suitable tissue-match. Riitha's body would have rejected her heart."

Tahl listened, but only some distant part of him seemed to hear. He was caught in an explosive emotional vortex unlike anything he had experienced before. Gripping the sides of the console before him, he looked into the interior lab. The crowded tangle of complex equipment blurred through the fine mist covering his eyes. He closed his eyes, shutting out the unbearable sight of the alien machines, then opened them again, unable to tolerate the imagined horror that flooded his mind, rejecting the vision of Riitha's trapped and violated body.

Tahl's grip on the terminal tightened as his eyes focused on the gruesome alien coffin that held his mate. He wanted to rip the hideous cryonic control console off its base and heave it through the glass, to rescue Riitha from the experimental prison to which she had been condemned. But something Stocha had said, something obscured by the intensity of his outrage and grief that Tahl did not quite understand, prevented him.

Still, the *shtahn* raged, "How could you do this to her, Stocha?" Eyes flashing and teeth bared, Tahl shook his fist in the direction of the interior lab. "How could you? You had no right to deprive her of a dignified ending! No right!" As he vented his anger and despair on Stocha, the need to release his charged emotions through violence eased. "Is Lish frozen in one of those things, or was she allowed to return to the elements?"

"Lish was recycled, but—"

Tahl slammed his fist into the console. "Then why not Riitha? Why not?"

Stocha refused to be intimidated and met Tahl's furious accusing gaze steadily. "Because if I had done that, Riitha would be gone. There would be no hope for her."

"What hope, Stocha? You could not use Lish's heart to save her. She's dead!"

"She's not dead!" Stocha shouted, then paused to take a deep breath. He continued in a softer tone. "By preserving her body in nitrogen stasis at the moment of death, all tissue deterioration has been stopped."

"She died." His emotional energies spent, Tahl fell into the chair by the terminal.

"In a manner of speaking, yes—she died. But she doesn't have to stay dead. Once we finish our research on the operation and we have the proper medical facilities and a donor, Riitha will be revived and her heart repaired."

"Revived?" Doubt and a spark of hope flickered across Tahl's face.

"Yes, revived. That's what the cryonic unit is for—to maintain an injured or diseased body for the future when a cure or repair is not possible in the present."

Tahl stared at Stocha, but his mind reeled. Had he not come to know the *jehda tohm* over the past years and to understand their stubborn unwillingness to accept extinction, he would not have thought such a thing was possible. Hope welled up inside him suddenly, for he knew that if anyone in the universe could invent a machine to defeat death, it was the *jehda tohm*.

Mistaking Tahl's silence for disbelief, Stocha quickly added, "Riitha was certain the process would work, Tahl. It was her decision to use the machine. She knew we couldn't help her, and she knew about the aliens' medical achievements. She stumbled onto the cryonic units and the instruction programs just before Lish attacked. She willed herself into near-death hibernation for the express purpose of being frozen."

"Death-wish? Riitha?"

"More like life-wish. It was her only chance, and she took it."

"Do you really think it will work?" Tahl asked cautiously.

"Everything checks out. Norii is certain it will."

"Then why didn't the aliens use those machines themselves?"

The geologist shrugged. "*You got me.*" Unaware of Tahl's perplexed gaze, Stocha shook his head and continued. "The technology is sound and the systems are functional, so they must have had their reasons. They've done a lot of things we don't understand."

Tahl nodded, but the question disturbed him. All the humans' works revealed a tenacious will to survive. They had gloried in life. Venus was habitable because of them. The zygotes of their children lived, and perhaps, Riitha would live, too. So why hadn't they used their cryonic technology to save themselves?

However, knowing that there was hope for Riitha, Tahl's mind immediately dismissed the question and returned to the problem of trying to salvage the mission and the lives of the Chai-te *bey.* "Are you certain the zygotes are viable, Stocha?"

"Yes. *Absolutely.*"

"If necessary, you could revive and incubate them."

Stocha started with surprise, but answered smoothly. "Eventually. We were making preparations to enter the main freezing chamber when Lish—"

Rising suddenly, Tahl touched the geologist on the shoulder. "Come with me. I need you."

CHAPTER THIRTY

Tahl rose slowly from the trance and paused on a level just below waking. He sensed Stocha and another, more intense presence: Bier. The watchers tensed as he opened his eyes, but he looked past them. His breathing was too rapid, spurred by excitement and urgency. With effort, he slowed his respiration rate. Neither Stocha nor Bier spoke until he turned to look at them.

Stocha wore a worried frown as he leaned forward and peered anxiously into the *shtahn jii*'s eyes. "Are you all right?"

Tahl nodded and sat up. He swung his feet onto the floor and glanced at Bier. The psychologist was seated on a chair by the table and set into the wall. His fawn-colored face was flushed dark, and the thick brush of his brows was knitted into an angry **V**. His eyes burned with rage.

"Will you betray us again, Tahl d'jehn?" Bier asked insolently.

"I have never betrayed the *bey*, Bier."

"You knew there were human zygotes on this base, Tahl. Viable human zygotes! You allowed Stocha to continue the work here knowing that. *Maida shli!*" Bier sneered.

Tahl eyed the infuriated psychologist steadily. "I did not know the embryos were viable until a short time ago. Neither did Stocha. No one has betrayed the *bey.*"

"You are traitors. All of you!"

Without warning, Stocha sprang from his chair and moved toward the psychologist with a menacing snarl. "Beware whom you call traitor, Bier t'ahi!"

Tahl stopped Stocha's advance with a sharp word. "Enough! We have more important matters to concern ourselves with now."

Stocha paused, flexing his claws, then returned to his seat. He said nothing else, but his menacing gaze remained fixed on Bier.

The danger passed, the psychologist turned on Tahl again. "What could be more important than a threat to our claim on this star system? The existence of viable human seed negates our position here under the Law!" Bier's ears and muzzle twitched in agitation, and his gaze flicked back and forth between Tahl and Stocha. "They were extinct! Why couldn't you let them stay extinct!"

"The alien zygotes would not be any less viable if we hadn't found them," Tahl replied patiently. "They would still exist."

"But we are in violation of the Law!"

"No, I think not. When we summoned the colony ship, we had no idea an ancient species had left the seeds of their race behind. We cannot be held responsible for an alien act of which we had no knowledge."

"And what about the zygotes? What happens to them?"

"Unless they are incubated, they will stay as they are forever," Stocha said. "They pose no threat to us."

"I'm not so sure about that." Bier sniffed uncertainly. "Their very existence is a threat."

"Their existence may very well save this mission, Bier." Tahl stood. "Where's the remote scan-and-locate panel, Stocha?"

"Main control."

Bier stepped in front of Tahl. "How can they save the mission?"

"The same way they saved Lish t'wan."

"Lish is dead."

"But she wouldn't be if Vuthe could have pulled her away from Riitha without breaking her neck. She did not decline into death-wish. Her need to protect the *bey* from the aliens gave her a reason to survive. Others will choose to live for the same reason." Tahl brushed past the psychologist and triggered the door panel.

Bier and Stocha followed Tahl into the corridor. They walked carefully, three abreast toward Base Control.

A faint odor of uneasiness drifted across Tahl's receptors. He glanced at Stocha. "What's troubling you?"

"I was just thinking about Lish. She tried to destroy the zygote bank. If we actually manage to reach any of the others, they'll want it destroyed, too."

"And you don't, do you, Stocha?"

"No."

Tahl nodded. "Nor do I."

"Why not?" Bier grabbed the *shtahn jii*'s arm.

Tahl slipped on the hard floor and almost fell. Yanking his arm free of Bier's grasp, the *shtahn* growled.

Bier either did not hear the warning or chose to ignore it. "If the zygotes are destroyed," he rumbled, "there will be no threat to our rights in this system."

Clenching his jaw, Tahl forced himself to stay calm. To even briefly contemplate the destruction of a hope that had survived for a hundred million years made his blood run cold, but he knew that Bier would not understand. The psychologist had to be appeased with a reason that went beyond an unwillingness to commit a crime against the universe.

"If," Tahl said sternly, "the zygotes are destroyed, there will be no reason for the *du-ahn* on this mission to live. You and I know that non-receipt of the confirmation signal does not necessarily mean that the colony ship isn't on its way. They don't. I will not let them die, and we need the zygote bank to keep them alive until I can convince them there's a chance that the ship was launched whether Hasu-din let us know about it or not! And then we'll need the zygote bank to keep them going in the uncertainty of the situation. It will be protected."

"By whom?"

"By me, Bier." Stocha moved up beside Tahl. "Norii, Vuthe, and Chiun, too."

"And I will protect all of them." Tahl took a warning step toward Bier. "The zygotes will not be harmed, and I will not tolerate any more questions. There will be no more arguments. The decision is made."

Bier cringed under the *shtahn's* snarling gaze.

"We're wasting time." Tahl turned and continued down the passageway, quickening his pace. Stocha followed closely, Bier at a distance.

When they entered Base Control, Stocha immediately activated the remote scan-and-locate system that had been incorporated into the alien equipment. Tahl sat at the central array, motioning for Stocha and Bier to sit on either side of him.

"There aren't enough relays to connect with everyone simultaneously," Tahl said, "so we'll concentrate on the latents. If we can reach just one at each location, they'll have a good chance of reviving the others."

Stocha shook his head, his expression grim. "It's been two weeks since the time frame for the signal expired, Tahl. Do you really think it's possible to get through to anyone now?"

Tahl shrugged as he slipped an audio module over his head. "It takes a long time for a *bey* to starve to death with the slower metabolic state of a body in deep hibernation, so we know they're still alive. I think it's also possible that the stress of the situation might have stimulated the latents enough to open some of the back-brain pathways. Even without full emergence, their subconscious minds might be receptive to an outside influence."

"I don't know, Tahl," Bier said, his anger and fear apparently forgotten in the midst of the immediate task before him. "Even partial activation of the back-brain connections should erase the death-wish inclination. If they were awake, they would have tried to contact us. They didn't, so they must not be awake."

"Not awake," Tahl said as he keyed for the identification codes. "But not necessarily in death-wish sleep, either. They may be in normal hibernation."

"Why would they do that?" Stocha asked.

"Because they were surrounded by *du-ahn* falling into death-wish sleep with no other stimulation to counter the tendency."

Bier began to nod vigorously. "Yes. That might be possible, and if they're in normal hibernation the alarm reflex will be fully armed and not subdued as it is in death-wish hibernation."

Tahl punched Hane's code into the board and set the remote for continuous transmission and maximum shock. "The electrical charge induced by an emergency call should activate the alarm reflexes."

"It's a *long shot*," Stocha said, locking Verda's code into his panel.

"Meaning?" Tahl asked.

"The odds are not in favor of success."

Tahl paused thoughtfully. "I don't suppose the *jehda tohm* believed the odds were in favor of an alien species actually finding their zygotes, either."

Stocha looked at Tahl and grinned. "No, I suppose not." Turning back to the terminal, the geologist fitted an audio module against his ear. "*Well, here goes nothing.*"

Tahl did not ask Stocha to explain, but he made a vow to begin learning the alien's phraseology as soon as the crisis was over. Shifting into a more comfortable position, he instructed Bier and Stocha to lock in the other seven latents' identification codes.

The scan-and-locate panel glowed bright blue as nine distress pulses sped away from Earth-moon. Tahl kept track of the elapsed time as he waited for the emergency signals to reach their various locations in the vicinity of Jupiter. When the *shtahn* calculated that the first signal had reached the *Dan tahlni*, he began a mental countdown for the turn-around time, and waited some more.

"Stand by to receive," Tahl said finally. "If the initial transmission had any effect, we can expect an answer soon."

They waited silently, tense and alert, watching the panel and listening. Minutes passed, and then an hour without a response.

"Tahl—"

The *shtahn jii*'s head snapped around at the sound of Stocha's hesitant whisper. The geologist's nose wrinkled, and his ears flicked forward. Tahl held his breath, and Bier tensed beside him.

"What?" the psychologist demanded impatiently.

Stocha paused, then smiled. "Tena's on line."

Tahl quickly opened a channel and motioned for Stocha to switch Tena over to him. The faint, small sound of her voice indicated that she was not fully awake yet. Tahl opted to go for the full shock value of his news in order to expedite Tena's recovery process.

"This is Tahl d'jehn. Wake up! This is an emergency." He wished he could wait for a response but the time delay would not allow it. Too much time had already elapsed since she had first received the scan-and-locate signal. He had to get Tena's adrenaline surging through her system before she discovered that she alone was awake and functional on the *Dan tahlni* asteroid station, or risk losing her to the panic of isolation.

"The *bey* are in danger, Tena. Great danger. There are aliens on Earth-moon. Living aliens." Tahl saw Stocha frown out of the corner of his eye, but he had no other options. "Set off the ship alarms. Wake up everyone. Do whatever you have to, but wake them. Do you understand? You must answer me before you leave the com-panel. Answer me, Tena."

Tahl hesitated, then signed off, unable to think of anything else to say that could make the message more clear. Exhaling wearily, he sat back to wait for Tena's reply, feeling Stocha's gaze hard upon him. He turned to meet the geologist's fierce, gray eyes.

"What if they decide to invade Luna Base, Tahl?" Stocha asked. "What if they attack with the intent to destroy it all?"

"They won't," Tahl said confidently.

"Why not?"

"The *du-ahn* loathe everything alien. When we've explained that the living aliens we found are frozen zygotes, they may want to destroy the bank, but the threat it represents won't be dire enough to provoke an actual attack." Tahl rubbed his eyes, then checked the time. "Besides, the technology here has too much to offer to justify its destruction."

"What technology is that?" Bier asked caustically.

Tahl glanced at him evenly, too tired and anxious to challenge his tone. "There is a working cryonic preservation machine on this base, Bier. It proves that fresh-kill can be successfully stored. That technology may mean the difference between success and failure as the *bey* begin to move farther out through the stars. The potential value is incalculable."

As Bier was about to respond, he hesitated, then made an adjustment on his panel. "I think I've picked up Hane. I'm not sure."

"Keep trying." Tahl looked back at Stocha. "Anything?"

Stocha shook his head.

A moment later, Tena's voice came clearly through the open channel.

"Message received, Tahl. I'm on the flight deck, and the alarms are sounding. I think I can patch into the alarm systems at the separation plant control station and the asteroid mining facility. As soon as I do, I'll go see to waking everyone up personally. I'm leaving this channel open for a reply. Are you in any immediate danger there? Are the aliens contained? Please send further instructions. Tena out."

With a heavy sigh of relief, Tahl slumped in the chair. He had barely had a chance to catch his breath when Bier reached over and opened another channel.

"It's Hane," the psychologist said simply.

Nodding, Tahl straightened and prepared to repeat the process that had worked so effectively on Tena. The first part of the plan his mind had formulated during the trance was going to succeed if Tena's reaction was any indication of how the other latents could be expected to respond. He did not want to think about the second phase just now, even though the justification for implementing it was irrefutable.

Putting the unsettling second phase out of his mind for the moment, Tahl leaned forward and began to alert Hane to the alien threat on Earth-moon.

CHAPTER
THIRTY-ONE

Tahl strolled around the base of the large, vacuum-contained telescope, his hand caressing the polished metal, his fingers probing indentations and complex mechanisms. His mind searched for a diversion, and his gaze was irresistibly drawn to the night beyond the transparent wall.

The stars shone brilliantly in the absence of light. Dark and stars . . . forever.

The Luna Base team had not yet modified the telescope for *bey* convenience. Tahl glanced at the huge device and snorted. He would have liked to scan the universe, to bring its infinite wonders within reach for a moment. He wanted to escape the second conclusion of the trance. He could not.

Tahl had entered sleep-analysis expecting verification of his initial idea for saving the mission *bey* from death-wish. As expected, the bio-com processes had agreed with his conscious conclusions. The plan for reviving the *bey* located in the out-system installations had worked.

Tena, Hane, and Verda had all been awakened by the remote scan-and-locate emergency signals. Six others had also been revived, including Sani s'oha, and they were continuing their efforts to awaken others on their respective installations. At least half the mission's personnel would live to proceed with operations in preparation for the arrival of the colony ship.

Then, the insistent quality of the trance that demanded attention to all facts in any given situation had forced Tahl to examine his suspicions concerning the schedules for all the mission's communications to and from Hasu-din. The stinging questions evoked by the problem could no longer be relegated to casual consideration or ignored—no more than the *venja-ahn* lust to survive that burned in his soul.

What if the colony ship had not been launched?

There would be no litters of *jehni* to inherit the results of their labors.

Tahl walked softly across the carpeted floor and pressed his face against the transparent wall of the dome, seeking solace in the stars as he reviewed the basic facts. By the time of the colony's projected arrival, the crew of the *Dan tahlni* would have spent eighty years establishing a position in the new star system. Now, after almost fifty years had passed, they had to face the possibility that the ship might not be coming. The confirmation signal had not been received. Bohn's investigation of the interstellar receiver on the Chai-te frontier had negated any possibility that the equipment had malfunctioned, and Tahl had to admit that, although *bey* technology was precise, it was not perfect. The light-beam trajectory could have been miscalculated or deflected. It was possible, but not likely.

It was more likely, Tahl thought, that the ship had been launched and the signal never sent.

The Council of Mediators, guided by a loyal *shtahn* who would not withhold information from them, knew that non-receipt of the confirmation signal within the time frame of their unnecessary schedule would be a *du-ahn* death sentence. Tahl could only guess at the possible reasons the council would not want the mission *bey* to survive.

Perhaps the Hasu-dinian *shtahns* had considered that a scout ship might not encounter an alien species until after their transmission summoning a colony ship had been dispatched. Receipt of a message confirming the eventual arrival of the colony would give a hostile species plenty of warning and time to prepare for a confrontation. Considering the severe xenophobia displayed by the *Dan tahlni du-ahn* toward the human aliens they believed to be extinct, this was a distinct possibility.

Perhaps the council's reason was more specific, dealing only with the crew of the *Dan tahlni*, a crew that was potentially half *venja-ahn*.

Tahl frowned, knowing that the Hasu-dinian *shtahns* might have deduced in trance that emerged *venja-ahn*, unfettered by the repressing prejudices and restraints of normal, *du-ahn*-controlled society, would develop their abilities and gain a sense of security and freedom that could not be easily suppressed. The Council of Mediators, not knowing what the outcome of Bier's experiment would be, would not want to risk that such an emergence would occur before the colony ship arrived.

The thought of such treachery made Tahl's blood run cold. Still, the trance had proven to him that the council's reasons for not sending the signal were irrelevant to the fate of the mission *bey*. If time proved that the missing signal was a deliberate attempt to sabotage the *Dan tahlni*, the council would have to face the consequences of their duplicity when the colony ship arrived.

And if the colony ship never arrived, the decision not to send the signal had provided Tahl with the only possible means to ensure that his life and the lives of his people had not been wasted.

The second phase of the plan would be initiated: for Riitha who had shown him love, and for the *jehda tohm* whose science would give her back to him.

Closing his eyes, Tahl called an image of Riitha's sleeping face into his mind. Even frozen and on the very brink of death, her countenance retained the aura of determination and passion for life that had so closely linked her with the spirit of the alien race that had refused to die. Riitha would not die, either. She would return to share the future—a future far different than the life she had left. Riitha would re-emerge in a future she had risked her life to create.

Tahl placed his hands on the thick, clear glass of the curved wall, symbolically touching the stars that had beckoned him in his innocent youth. There had been a time when merely reaching Chai-te would have pacified Tahl's sense of destiny, a time before he became *venja-ahn*, the ultimate survivor. No longer. He could not leave the labors of his life to disintegrate in the emptiness. He would leave them to the aliens.

Turning slowly, Tahl faced the darkness under the dome and let the phantom essence wrap itself around him. It is a powerful essence that defied death, Tahl thought again. Humans had given their children into an unknown and tenuous future, had given them into the alien hands of Tahl d'jehn. He would give them tomorrow.

The *shtahn* cared not for the consequences he might suffer when the colony ship arrived, if it arrived. The thought of exile did not terrify him now. Isolated from the *bey*, he would never be alone in the vastness of the universe.

The *jehda tohm* would be there.

EPILOGUE

Michael Jamieson woke with an excrutiating headache. His eyes burned under swollen lids, and his throat felt hot and raw. When he tried to move, every muscle in his body spasmed with sharp, shooting pains.

He swore slightly, cursing the painful preparations and the computers that had chosen him. He didn't know what drug had been used to knock him out, but the after-effects were almost as debilitating as the medication itself. Assuming that he was regaining consciousness sooner than the medical staff expected, he wondered why they had not frozen him yet.

It was just as well, Michael thought. He was having second thoughts now that the prospect of being buried alive was imminent. He wasn't at all sure he wanted to become a cryonic stiff just because the base computer had a bizarre sense of what talents might be useful in some nebulous future.

Michael smiled at the joke, then groaned as a thousand pinpricks pierced the skin around his mouth and over his jaw. Then the rustle of hushed whispers caught his attention.

Bracing himself for more pain, Michael tried to open his eyes. Soft orange light filtered through the narrow slits as he finally managed to pry apart his eyelids. A filmy haze blurred his vision, but his hearing seemed to be fine. An excited murmur rose around him.

Closing his eyes again, Michael wondered if Ross, Sherry, and Andy had already been put under.

Andy.

A great sadness welled up inside Michael's chest as he thought about life without Andy. It would be intolerable. No, he thought, better to lie together in cryonic death than to go on alone. He would see the ordeal through to the end rather than desert Andy and the plan she herself was willing to perish for. Sighing, Michael once again resigned himself to his questionable destiny.

Wondering again why he was still awake, Michael blinked. When he opened his eyes this time, some of the haze had dispersed. A tense stillness seemed to surround him as he closed his eyes again, hoping to clear his vision further. An anxious thought intruded. Maybe the computer had made a mistake. Maybe they weren't going to freeze him after all. Relief and regret vied for priority in his mind.

Taking a deep breath that almost made him pass out with the pain, Michael steeled himself for the worst. He had always known that fate had a warped sense of humor and was often unkind, but now that he had again decided to join Andy in her folly, it would be just too cruel to revoke the dubious privilege at the last minute. Opening his eyes again, he was able to discern several faces looming over him.

Furry faces.

Startled, Michael shut his eyes quickly and winced as he inhaled sharply. Obviously he was still under the influence of the drug and hallucinating, or the entire medical staff needed to shave. Or—he paused mentally, hesitant to consider the other alternative. Perhaps, he had been frozen and was now being revived by Andy's aliens. The medical staff was mostly female, so hallucinating seemed like the more logical of the two remaining options.

Ignoring the pain in his chest, Michael breathed deeply and opened his eyes. He was not hallucinating.

Five feline creatures with long shaggy manes and large round eyes were staring at him. Curiously, he hoped. He could not be sure. Their features gave an illusion of ferocity, but the expressions in their eyes seemed intelligent and concerned. Michael looked from one to the other without moving anything but his eyes. Whoever or whatever they were, they came in a variety of colors. Gray, tan, silver, and black. His reporter's gaze took in every detail.

Something touched his hand.

Flinching, Michael gasped and turned his head. The movement set off a jackhammer in his skull. The pain passed quickly as the reporter focused on Andy's pale face. Her eyes fluttered open briefly, and a hint of a smile played across the roughened texture of her lips as her hand slipped off his.

One of the aliens tapped Michael on the other arm. He looked up, his breath catching in his parched throat. The creature's lips were parted to reveal yellow-brown teeth. The sharp teeth of a carnivore, Michael observed uneasily.

The huge, gray creature clasped the reporter's shoulder gently. Michael held the alien's intense gaze a moment, then swallowed nervously as it smiled—or snarled. Again, he could not be certain.

"Hello, man," it said in a rumbling baritone. "You are *A-OK*?"

Stunned, Michael could only nod.

A larger, black and silver creature stepped up beside the gray and peered down at Michael with questioning, emerald-green eyes. The gray moved aside, apparently in deference to the silver-black's authority. The gray had spoken English remarkably well, in spite of the unusual accent, as though it had been using the language a long time. The other, larger creature uttered the words haltingly.

"I am Tahl d'jehn."

"Michael Jamieson," Michael managed to mutter hoarsely.

A gentle rumble sounded in Tahl's throat as he nodded. "*Jehda tohm* no more. Now you live."

"Yes," Michael said, sensing a deep peace and joy in the being that hovered over him. "Now I live."

Michael had no idea what this one-in-a-hundred billion chance at a new life had to offer, but at the moment he didn't care. For now, it was enough just to be alive.

He reached for Andy's hand and smiled at Tahl. "Thank you."

B • O • O • K • S

Outbanker
Timothy A. Madden

Ian MacKenzie's job as a space policeman is a lonely vigil, until the powerful dreadnaughts of the Corporate Hegemony threaten the home colonies.

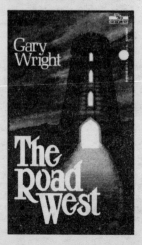

The Road West
Gary Wright

Orphaned by the brutal, senseless murder of his parents, Keven rises from the depths of despair to face the menacing danger that threatens Midvale. On sale in October.

B•O•O•K•S

DARK HORSE
Mary H. Herbert

After her clan is massacred, a young woman assumes her brother's identity and becomes a warrior—all to exact revenge upon the chieftain who ordered her family slain. With an intelligent, magical horse, the young warrior goes against law and tradition to learn sorcery to thwart Medb's plans of conquest.

WARSPRITE
Jefferson P. Swycaffer

On a quiet night, two robots from the future crash to Earth. One is a vicious killer, the other is unarmed, with an ability her warrior brother does not have: She can think. But she is programmed to face the murderous robot in a final confrontation in a radioactive chamber.

NIGHT WATCH
Robin Wayne Bailey

All the Seers of Greyhawk have been killed, each by his own instrument of divination. And the only unusual sign is the ominous number of black birds in the skies. The mystery is dumped on the commander of the City Watch's night shift, who discovers that a web of evil has been tightly drawn around the great city.

EMPIRES TRILOGY

HORSELORDS
David Cook

Between the western Realms and Kara-Tur lies a vast, unexplored domain. The "civilized" people of the Realms have given little notice to these nomadic barbarians. Now, a mighty leader has united these wild horsemen into an army powerful enough to challenge the world. First, they turn to Kara-Tur.

DRAGONWALL
Troy Denning

The barbarian horsemen have breached the Dragonwall and now threaten the oriental lands of Kara-Tur. Shou Lung's only hope lies with a general descended from the barbarians, and whose wife must fight the imperial court if her husband is to retain his command.

CRUSADE
James Lowder

The barbarian army has turned its sights on the western Realms. Only King Azoun has the strength to forge an army to challenge the horsemen. But Azoun had not reckoned that the price of winning might be the life of his beloved daughter. Available in January 1991.

DragonLance® Saga

H·E·R·O·E·S II
TRILOGY

KAZ, THE MINOTAUR
Richard A. Knaak

SEQUEL TO *THE LEGEND OF HUMA*. STALKED BY ENEMIES AFTER HUMA'S DEATH, KAZ HEARS RUMORS OF EVIL INCIDENTS. WHEN HE WARNS THE KNIGHTS OF SOLAMNIA, HE IS PLUNGED INTO A NIGHTMARE OF MAGIC, DANGER, AND *DEJA VU*.

THE GATES OF THORBARDIN
Dan Parkinson

BENEATH SKULLCAP IS A PATH TO THE GATES OF THORBARDIN, AND THE MAGICAL HELM OF GRALLEN. THE FINDER OF GRALLEN'S HELM WILL BE REWARDED BY A UNITED THORBARDIN, BUT HE WILL ALSO OPEN THE REALM TO NEW HORROR.

GALEN BEKNIGHTED
Michael Williams

SEQUEL TO *WEASEL'S LUCK*. GALEN PATHWARDEN IS STILL OUT TO SAVE HIS OWN SKIN. BUT WHEN HIS BROTHER VANISHES, GALEN FORSAKES HIS BETTER JUDGMENT AND EMBARKS ON A QUEST THAT LEADS INTO A CONSPIRACY OF DARKNESS, AND TO THE END OF HIS COURAGE. AVAILABLE IN DECEMBER 1990.